This book is brought to you by
Kol Sason Press
Kingston Beach, Tasmania, Australia

Title: Mountain of Secrets
Author: Demelza
Copyright © Demelza 2020

ISBN 978-0-6488699-0-0

Cover by Wayne Amos

Mountain of Secrets

Demelza

Chapter 16   183
Chapter 17   195
Chapter 18   207
Chapter 19   217
Chapter 20   229
Chapter 21   245
Chapter 22   255
Chapter 23   267
Chapter 24   279
Chapter 25   295
Chapter 26   307
Chapter 27   313
Chapter 28   325
Chapter 29   337
Chapter 30   353
Chapter 31   367

Chapter 1

Elma squinted her eyes and peered towards the next corner, 'Where the heck is he?' she said, letting her feet fall in heavy steps across the road hoping the next car might be her father's ute. The glare from the river was strong; waves of heat shimmered vertically, forming imaginary lagoons of water across the molten road.

Black mozzarella tar clung to the soles of her sandshoes. She stopped to scrape the grainy mass back and forth against the edge of the gutter. 'He said he'd pick me up!' she complained again and looked about to see if anyone was watching. The footpath was empty.

Of course it was – why would anyone be out in this damn heat?

It was true the temperature gauge at the café showed almost forty and Damien, her boss, had suggested she stay in the cool and wait for her father to pick her up. But Elma didn't want to wait.

No, he said he'd pick me up – and **he** *is late –if I die from heat exhaustion, it'll be his fault!*

She scanned each passing car – still no dad. She cursed her

gran – blaming her for the sun, for the heat and for the inconvenience of walking with her bag stuck like glue to her back.

Two more corners but it could have been a million. The rubber tip of her shoe snagged on a crack flinging her into a wild chicken pose – any amount of corners was too far.

Wish he cared about me as much as he does for her. I bet she's not sweltering outside in all this heat – they're probably drinking iced tea in the air conditioning.

She could think it, but that didn't make it real.

--

Truth was Martin wasn't finding the afternoon any more pleasant than she was.

'It's not fair, Martin,' Miriam jabbed her walking frame at the carpet – her hands clamped tight around the moulded grips. 'You've trapped me here against my will. You and Livinda, always siding against me. If you'd done your job properly and put ramps in the house when I told you to I wouldn't have tripped on the blasted step and broken my blasted hip. But you don't listen. You just do what you want and to hell with me!' the metal frame rattled with every new allegation.

'You call yourself a builder!'

Miriam cursed and tried to stamp her foot. Her slipper jerked up and down as if attached by chewing gum to the floor.

'Mum,' Martin sighed, glancing down at his watch. 'Another tantrum isn't going to help. We've been through this a dozen times already. You signed the papers and this is your new home.' He hoped Elma hadn't left work early.

'Well, I don't like it and if I'd known that sooner I'd never have given my consent. You don't want what's best for me at all. You and Livinda just don't care enough to look after me. You only think of yourselves. I'm a burden to the lot of you.'

'Oh Mum, you know that's not true.' Martin thought of Aunt Livie preparing to leave for the mainland and wondered how he would cope without her.

'Of course it's true!' Miriam interjected. 'No one cares about what I need. No one!'

'Mum,' Martin tried again, 'I can't work and look after you at the same time. Look around, this place is warm and clean.' He swept his open hand in an arc as if he was a real-estate agent selling the place. A male nurse walked past, a smiley face sticker attached to his paisley print uniform. 'You don't have to think about cooking or shopping or even making your own bed! What more could you want?'

'I want to go home! Livinda can look after me; I don't need your help.' Miriam clenched her hands, her knuckles white against the handles on her frame. 'You never helped anyway. Always leaving it up to Livinda.'

Martin shuddered, shifting his weight from one foot to the other, his work boots leaving an imprint in the woollen carpet. He didn't blame Aunt Livie for moving away – she'd served her time, cared for Miriam longer than anyone expected – she had her own family to think of. He looked at his mother; her dark hair pulled back off her face and tied "just so", a fancy clip holding her perfect bun in place. He looked down at his steel-capped boots and closed his eyes. His bag slipped from his shoulder and slumped to the floor – the leather strap falling against his leg like a shackle. Earlier he'd taken a brochure from the half round Queen Anne table in the foyer. He fiddled with it now, his fingers tracing the embossed lettering, "Nut Grove Nursing Home – your space at our place." He waited while Miriam continued her scathing tirade.

'Mum, are you finished?' he said placing the pamphlet back on the pile, 'I need to pick Elma up from work.'

11

'Oh Elma, well that's a pretty thought, another being more important to you than me. You've spoilt that girl, Martin, given her too much of everything and not enough responsibility. You've made her soft.' Miriam manoeuvred her frame, turned her back on her son, and shuffled off down the hall looking for her room. 'It's a rabbit warren in here. I can't tell one corner from the next.' She kicked at her frame leaving a trail of curses in her wake.

Well, thought Martin, at least that's one thing we agree on. He reached down and picked up his bag. It was better this way, he thought, to meet her in the foyer. No chance of getting lost and easier to escape if necessary. He made his way to the double glass doors of the main entrance, his mud streaked ute parked in plain view across the road.

Elma would be finished work by now – perhaps she's even started walking.

Martin sat in the ute and stared back across the hot asphalt to the nursing home, the glass façade of the entrance upmarket and contemporary but incongruous with the buildings joining either side of it. Unrendered red bricks strong and sturdy depicting the era of their construction, his mother inside, frail and confused, despite her use of language. Had he done the right thing by leaving her there? The thought niggled at him, repeating itself over and over. All he'd ever wanted was to make her happy.

But she is right, he thought, it **isn't** fair! It **isn't** fair being a single parent! It **isn't** fair being ripped off and abused or raising a teenage girl alone. It just **isn't** fair!

He ran his fingers through his thinning hair and slumped forward, the 3pm summer sun beating in through the dirty windscreen. How on earth am I going to cope without Aunt Livie?

12

His heart rate increased, he could feel it happening, the wound was opening.

'It's not real,' he said aloud. 'I **am** able. I **can** do this.'

But the chasm continued to widen, ripping bit by bit – drawing in fears of doubt and self-loathing – rising, like bread dough, in his chest.

"You never listen – call yourself a builder – you've never done a damned thing right!"

His mother's words repeated over and over in his mind. Her voice gnawing at his self-esteem.

Beads of moisture swelled and ran down from his brow, sticking to the vinyl where his head now rested, slumped against the steering wheel. The humid air of the cab expanded in his lungs, working like a one-way valve – his chest tight – muscles pushing up against his ribs.

He could see himself standing on the edge of the Tasman Bridge – its smooth arc spanning the Derwent River. Icy wind cutting through to his skin – whipping shreds in his clothes. Dark water churning below him, swirling in and out of focus.

It always seemed so real, the wind screaming past, the water barging at his chest, crushing him against the concrete pylons. Always pushing, always moving – always fighting against the weight. His heart raced. He was trapped, couldn't breathe – couldn't cope with the pain erupting through his body.

Elma pounded her fist on the windscreen, her voice high and loud.

'Dad! Wake up! Wake up!' She dropped her bag by her feet, lipstick and Impulse deodorant spilling out and rolling under the cab of the ute. Martin looked up; Elma was down on her hands and knees scrambling to retrieve the wayward contents. He exhaled hoping the pain would go before she stood back up.

'It's so hot in here!' Elma declared opening the door and climbing in. 'I thought you were going to pick me up!'

She dumped her bag on the seat between them.

'You said you'd pick me up!' She looked directly at her father. 'What's wrong, Dad? Were you asleep in here with the windows up? It's 38 degrees outside. No wonder you're sweating,' she continued, fastening her seat belt, 'I thought I was going to die just walking from the café.'-

She rummaged through her bag retrieving her travel pack of Spiced Coconut hand sanitiser and rubbed her hands together, not satisfied until all the road dust had been removed. 'I finished work twenty minutes ago, Dad. I really thought you'd be there.'

Martin gripped the steering wheel – one breath in – one breath out – deliberate – slow – forcing himself to take control of his body. 'Sorry Elma,' he said not hearing what she was saying. 'I should have been there to pick you up – should've gotten my act together –' he said, almost to himself, 'done what we'd arranged. Sorry,' he repeated, his heart rate slowing as he attempted to change his thoughts from the dark place to the here and now.

Elma put the hand sanitiser back in her bag and waited for her father to start the ute.

'What happened?' she asked sensing he was not yet quite ready to drive off. 'It's Gran isn't it?' She turned in her seat to look at him more closely. 'She said something to upset you didn't she? What's she done now? Silly old bat, I don't know why you care so much.' Elma refocussed to look at the building across the road; she narrowed her eyes and shook her head – staring at the glass façade as if it were a disobedient child.

'Elma!' Martin snapped.

Elma moved back against the seat and sighed.

Why is he so touchy about her?

She weighed it up.

Hmm, Gran the grump, Gran the grisly, Gran the ungrateful. Nope, there's nothing I can think of that would make me ever want to visit that woman. Why he cares about her so much is beyond me. Maybe it's a blood thing – like blood being thicker than water or maybe it's a fear thing. Like he lost his wife, is about to lose Aunt Livie and maybe he's worried about losing his mum as well? Still – ugh – why? Miriam is awful!

She looked at her dad and studied the drops of sweat on his receding hairline. A clear dull gap contrasted with glistening sparkles where he'd wiped his hand across his forehead. His mum, her gran, was Miriam. Mad Miriam, Elma called her behind his back. Aunt Livie? Yes, of course they would both miss Aunt Livie.

But Gran? Nah, never.

Martin turned the key and pressed the button to open the windows, his heart still pounding from the vision. It felt so real. 'Must have fallen asleep,' he mumbled, trying to appear calm.

The radio sprang to life: 'I'll-be-there-for-you'. Bon Jovi's passion filled the cab, the volume way too high. Martin groped with the knob, turning it the wrong way in his haste.

Words of undying commitment blasted out.

'Damn!' he exclaimed.

Elma glared at him but kept her mouth shut.

He pushed at the knob silencing the chorus and wiped the palms of his hands on his jeans before re-gripping the steering wheel. His calloused hands fitted into place among the grooves of the sun-cracked fabric covering it.

'Hey, Dad –' Elma sounded sweet. '– to make up for not picking me up and for making me walk all this way and in all this heat –' she paused for effect, '– you could let me drive home, you know, like, give me a driving lesson.' She looked at her father and tipped her head slightly on an angle – batting her eyelids at him.

'No,' he said flatly.

Elma didn't challenge him. 'What about an ice-cream then?'

He rubbed at the back of his neck and paused. 'Okay, we can pull into Macca's on the way home.'

'Aw, no Dad.' Elma screwed up her face. 'I was thinking more like Cold Rock or the Renown. The Renown, yes, why not?'

It had always been her favourite pick as a child. She remembered sitting on a bar stool at the front window after Aunt Livie had taken her for a treat to the State Cinema. She and Aunt Livie, her great aunt really, both squeezed into the narrow space on the right hand side of the door, her little legs dangling earthwards, as she perched up on the orange vinyl bar stool. They'd enjoyed watching the people pass, commenting playfully on what they wore and speculating about where they might be going or who they might be meeting. Aunt Livie was never far from her thoughts, although today was about a cold ice-cream as compensation for being let down, not a childhood treat.

Chapter 2

Martin watched from the footpath as a steady stream of cars flicked past the ice-cream shop.

'Come on Dad, it's too hot out here,' Elma called heading in through the door.

They'd compromised on destination, and ended up in Sandy Bay, 'I am not driving across town in peak hour traffic, and that is that.'

He stepped into the shade, his reflection staring at him from the glass door. Dishevelled hair and weathered creases stretched in waves across his forehead. His keys clinked in his hand.

'Come on Dad, the ice-cream's melting,' Elma called again, opening the door of the shop. 'It's rum'n'raisin. Here take it. I haven't paid yet,' she added, licking a runaway drip from the side of her cone.

Hope he comes right soon. He always lets Gran get the better of him. At least Aunt Livie won't have to put up with her bullying anymore – going to be hard for Dad, she thought, *and for me.*

'Hey Dad,' Elma said, sitting down at a window seat, 'I know we've talked about this already, but seriously, I really would like some driving time.' Pink ice-cream slipped down the side of her face, making her look like a small child. She dabbed at it with the serviette, thankful the shop was as good as empty. 'I'm not a kid, you know.' Elma slurped again at her ice-cream and Martin burst out laughing. 'Go on, laugh if you want.'

He rolled his eyes as she spoke and she stared back with mock indignation, relieved to see his mood was changing.

'No, Dad, I'm serious. I want to get a car, I have my L's and I want to get my licence.'

'And who is going to pay for that, may I ask?' He managed a smile. His anxiety was easing. The attack had been intense but recovery was in sight. He let out a sigh. Still, he was not letting Elma drive in peak hour traffic. At least not today.

'I'm working now, I can save.' She was serious.

She watched him out of the corner of her eye suspecting the subject was dangerous. Last week's decision to quit study and continue on at the café was a biggie, but, as she'd reasoned then, she wasn't quitting, just not returning from the summer holidays. She'd expected him to explode, but he hadn't. Somehow he just vagued out – like she hadn't said anything at all. They'd been sitting outside their South Hobart house – it was after dinner and everything seemed caught in time by the Tassie twilight. She'd stared back at him, calmly watching for some sign of emotion but there was nothing, just him – her dad sitting on the back step with one hand resting on a Cascade Light wedged between his knees, his other picking at the label. She'd looked to where he was looking, and watched the colour drain from the man ferns planted against the back paling fence. The sunlight took all the colours with it. That was a phrase she'd picked up from her mother: "The sun taking all the colours."

'Well, that's it then,' her father had said. And she wondered if that was what he'd said when her mother had left. There seemed to be so much they didn't talk about – there seemed to be so much that Elma was too unsure to ask about. Even Aunt Livie never gave her all the answers or maybe she never asked Aunt Livie all the right questions.

Either way I'm old enough to make my own decisions. I am old enough to drive, I have a job and I can save money.

She could see her reflection in the window of the ice-cream parlour. Bright fresh raspberry ice-cream smeared across her lips. She reached for the serviettes.

Martin turned to look at his daughter, her dark hair pulled back into a tight ponytail. 'My goodness,' he thought, 'She's the spitting image of her mother.' Apart from the undercut – he'd never liked that, but she'd had done it thanks to Chloe, her oldest friend and, in his opinion, not the best influence.

'Come on Dad,' Elma interrupted Martin's thoughts. 'I can do this. I can work, I can save. I can get a car.'

'Well, I hope that's not your life ambition,' he said, more to himself than to Elma. 'To own a car, to get to work, to save money, to buy fuel, to get to work ...'

His voice trailed off and Elma watched his face for signs of humour or anger but neither seemed to be present. She was just sitting in an ice-cream parlour with a slightly balding middle-aged man sitting next to her, gazing out the window, watching the stream of cars surge and stop as directed by the traffic lights in the late afternoon.

Elma took a deep breath in before wiping her hands with the serviette and tossing it in the bin by the counter.

'Come on Dad, it's time to go,' she said.

Martin lingered, still thinking about his mum. How was she going to cope without Aunt Livie? Who would visit her? Heck even he couldn't do that every day.

'Dad, did you hear me?' Elma repeated. 'Come on, it's time to go.'

'No, wait a bit,' Martin responded. 'About your driving lessons – I may have a plan that will suit both of us.'

Elma sat down again and took the hand sanitiser from her bag.

'Well, you know how I finish work early on Thursdays to catch up with you and Gran?' he said,

Oh no, he mentioned Gran. This is not going to be a solution that will suit me, I'm sure. Thursday is my "Dad and Me Day" not my "Dad, Me and Gran Day"!

She turned her face towards him, squinting her eyes and squishing her lips sideways, still rubbing the smell of coconut into her fingers. Waiting. Waiting for the disappointment she was sure she was about to receive.

Gran Steals Time

She could see it written in her notebook under the section 'News Headlines'. Her pen beckoned but she resisted.

'Well,' began Martin again. 'You visit Gran once a week and I'll take you driving when I pick you up.'

No way!

For as long as she could remember, her dad had finished work early on Thursdays. When she was younger, he would pick her up from school and they would spend an hour or so at a park before getting takeaway for tea.

Our once-a-week treat night – just me and Dad.

The other nights she would have dinner with Aunt Livie and Uncle Dave. Their own daughter, Cathy, Elma's second cousin, was grown up and living on the Mainland with her partner.

Weekends were always messy – Dad had work, Chloe and I had sports.

20

Later, in her high school years, they'd walk around Bellerive Beach or Alum Cliffs or even Salamanca. Sometimes the tradition was embarrassing – occasionally she got teased.

Chloe said they were jealous 'cause their dad didn't have time for them. What was the consolation in that, Elma thought? They had mothers. Mine left the day I started school – and without warning.

Well, no warning that Elma could recall anyway.

She just dropped me off at the door of my classroom the morning of my first day and never came back. Aunt Livie showed up that afternoon and took me back to her place on the Eastern Shore. We lived so close to the school, I couldn't work out why Mum wasn't there. I expected to walk home with her. But I never saw her again. Gone, just like that. My mother just left me and no one talked about it.

Elma had, in the beginning, asked Aunt Livie where her mother was, but the answers had never been satisfactory. Perhaps this was why she'd given up asking questions. She recalled feeling it had somehow been her fault that her mother hadn't returned. In later years she came to believe that her mother had left both her and her dad for someone she'd met on the internet and had travelled half way round the world to live a life of luxury on some romantic island.

Don't know where I got that info from. It's funny what we think when we're little.

But she'd thought it so long it had become concrete in her mind.

'What do you think?' her father's question brought her back to the ice-cream parlour and her desire to get home.

'I don't know Dad. You know how much Gran and I don't get on. What would be the point?' Elma's shoulders drooped; she looked down and began rubbing her hands together as if the hand-sanitiser had not been completely absorbed. 'I mean

I do want driving lessons an' all, but can't we find another way, you know, like one that doesn't involve Gran?'

'Oh come on Elma, don't take it so personally. Mum doesn't get on with anyone; it's not just you …' His words trailed off and neither of them spoke for a moment. 'I know. Think of her as a lonely old lady, someone who needs a friend,' said Martin.

'You want me to be her friend?' Elma laughed.

Martin looked up at the ceiling, inhaled and closed his eyes. He knew she was just being a teenager. He exhaled; pleased he'd held his tongue.

'You gotta be a friend to get one,' Elma quoted. 'And your mum obviously doesn't want friends.'

Martin stood, his chair screeched behind him, stopping just short of a potted plant. The shop assistant glared from behind the counter as he scooped up his satchel and keys. He strode across the room – shoved the door open, his bag swinging into the glass making a dull thud, before swinging into the back of his legs.

Elma followed – her head down.

'You're damned lucky you're not walking home. You and her are as bad as each other,' he said, throwing his bag on the floor of the cab.

'Sorry Dad, I was just joking.' She looked down at her feet wishing she could take the words back.

I need a backspace bar on my mouth. He tells me not to take it personally but he takes it personally. I can't say anything about her. How can I tell him what I'm thinking without him throwing a fit? She continued to study her shoes. *Friday, tomorrow is Friday. Tomorrow I wake up to a new day. I'll eat my breakfast. I'll catch a bus to work and I'll never mention driving again.*

But she knew as soon as she thought it that it wasn't the truth.

Chapter 3

'She was always up the mountain, your gran.'

Aunt Livie turned the teapot three turns to the left and three turns to the right, her wrinkled hands performing the well-rehearsed manoeuvre.

Elma wriggled her toes inside her sandshoes. It seemed normal these days to be sitting 'doing nothing' in Aunt Livie's sunporch. There wasn't much left to do now – maybe a bit more cleaning.

You can never do enough cleaning.

She looked at the bright unworn patches of green carpet, vacant spots that stood out between well-worn tracks where the lounge and Lazy Boy recliner no longer rested.

Carpet Unmown

She mentally wrote the headline into her notebook.

The clean blue–grey walls held invisible frames of unfaded wallpaper. The only things left, it seemed, were shapes and shadows, tell-tale memories of the past. Worn wooden steps, an out-of-order doorbell and moss growing under the slow drip of the outside tap. The moving people had taken the rest, packed it up and left her great aunt in the house with a borrowed bed, two chairs, a teapot and a sunporch full of memories.

'Mum couldn't stop her.' Aunt Livie fingered the paper serviette on the makeshift table, which was a cardboard box with Bells Removals printed on the side. 'From the moment she got out of bed in the morning she'd be out the door and into the bush. She had a game; we'd both play it to see if we could get out the back gate without alerting anyone. It wasn't always easy, mind you, and generally Miriam didn't wait for me to join her. No, she'd be up and off before I was even out of bed. The first challenge was the gate. It squeaked and had a tendency to bang shut. It wasn't loud to us but Mum always heard it.' Livie brushed a curly wisp of white hair away from her face.

Elma knew all the stories. She'd heard them many times, well, these ones anyway, the ones about Livinda and her sister's early days growing up on Inglewood Road under the shadow of kunanyi/Mount Wellington. She watched Aunt Livie tuck the wayward wisp of hair behind her ear and continue with the story.

It's funny how Aunt Livie and Gran are so different. Gran's hair is always just so and Aunt Livie always has bits hanging about her face.

Elma's notebook was in her hand and she quickly wrote down the thought before it scurried off, adding it to a headline she'd thought of earlier.

'If we made it through the gate we'd need to watch out for the rooster.' Aunt Livie laughed.

'My knees would be shaking just thinking of that mean old bird, but Miriam wouldn't care. She'd just walk past him like he wasn't even there and if he went for her leg, her boot would go up and she'd just push him away. But he always squawked and Mum always heard it. If he went for me the noise I'd make would have Mum out there faster than a jack rabbit.'

Aunt Livie paused for breath.

'The next step in the game was Dad's workshop. He was always working. Out there sharpening his saws no matter what time of day it was.' Aunt Livie's face changed briefly from a smile to a frown. 'He was a saw doctor you know. Miriam could smell him before I could. Her nose was tuned into anything out of the ordinary. She'd give me a signal.' Livie mimed Miriam turning back and signalling by holding two fingers to her mouth and taking a pretend drag on an invisible cigarette. 'I'd creep out of the shadow of the pump shed and head to the wood stack.

"Miriam, wait for me," I'd call. Sometimes she would but I reckon her mind was ticking over, knowing the game would be up sooner if I was with her. Some days Mum would get so exasperated when it came time to walk down to the school yard. She'd be calling out "Miriam, Miriam, get in here or I'll find your father's belt."'

'She never hit her though, did she, Aunt Livie?' Elma smiled at her aunt. She already knew the answer. Sometimes she wondered if Livie was losing her memory like Gran had. Aunt Livie was, after all, only one year younger than Miriam.

'Heavens no, girl, your gran would have only been five or six years old, but oh, she hated school. It made me think something terribly, horribly wrong was happening in there, in that building. The year I turned five I didn't want to go to school either! I was worried about the school yard, the buildings, even the teachers. Miriam never told me but I suspected monsters and roosters lurked in the shadows between the buildings, until I got there, of course and then I couldn't work out why Miriam had been making such a fuss.'

Livie laughed and turned her head towards the window, the river beckoning her gaze, its continuous movement begging to be watched. It was what Elma called a grey-on-grey day. A monotone of watercolour brushstrokes layered the sky. Silver grey, bleeding into ash, blending with steel and fading into sock grey as if greys were the only colours left in the paint box. The colour names were from Elma's notebook. Concrete grey, pale blue grey and pencil lead grey were at the top. They were the beginning of her **Grey List**. She could choose from a list of thirty 'grey words' now and added to it daily. Her latest grey was graveyard grey but even this needed to be broken down into categories of old, fresh, shiny or rough. It seemed there were never-ending possibilities.

The grey clouds hung in a heavy mood, sitting low with their undersides ready to release the rain.

Aunt Livie looked up for a moment and gazed out the window, thinking about the possibility of rain as she stared at the flat slate-grey river. She watched the red and white sides of the *Emmalisa* pass by, the old wooden ferry loaded with tourists, most likely listening to the history of the river as it made its way towards the pylons of the bridge where the Lake Illawarra had struck the bridge and sunk. She turned back to her tea making. Yes it was well past time to leave her Apple Isle but she would miss it dearly – the river, the mountain and all the in-betweens.

Elma stared at the upside down words on the side of their makeshift table. Destination – Ballan – Victoria stood out in red marking pen, some words bigger than the dotted lines provided.

Elma, too, would miss this warm room with its soothing views of the river. She could see most of the Tasman Bridge with its thick dinosaur legs moving slowly across from the Eastern Shore to the Botanical Gardens.

"One day it'll pop its head out of the ground and eat the flag right off the top of the pole on Government House." She could hear her Mum's words in her head. Funny the bits of her she remembered and the bits she didn't.

Perhaps I'm getting old too.

But she wasn't, she was only 18 – well nearly 18. Old enough to be called an adult but young enough not to want the responsibilities that come with the title.

Not just yet.

Perhaps that's why she'd miss Aunt Livie so much. Aunt Livie never seemed to expect more from anyone than they could offer and always seemed happy with what she got.

The brew smelled 'right'. Aunt Livie declared it so and began to pour. It sounded right too, thought Elma, as the Earl Grey liquid swirled into the china cups set out before them. She looked around the room for some wrapping paper to protect the cups after they finished their tea.

Aunt Livie had chosen two china teacups from Elma's favourite set and kept them out especially as a parting gift for her. Elma took a sip of the fragrant tea and stared at the perfect red flowers on the Royal Doulton cup.

'Are you sure you want to split up the set, Aunt Livie? I know they're very dear to you.' Elma thought of the fine china display cabinet that, only a few days earlier, had stood proudly in the corner of Aunt Livie's lounge room. Uncle Dave had made it not long after he and Livie were married. It was made from oak.

"The finest oak," he'd say, "Nothing but the best for my Livie."

And he should know, thought Elma, he was the best cabinet maker in the world, according to Aunt Livie. The front of the cabinet curved around so Elma could see into it from any angle of the room. When she was small she was fascinated by the highly polished Queen Anne feet and Aunt Livie would give her a special cloth to shine them with. On reaching the grand age of eight Aunt Livie let her use the little black key that was always kept in a hollow on the top of the cabinet.

I'd push it into the lock on the front, turn it precisely half a turn to the right and feel the little bump as the lock opened. Then she'd let me do the dusting. Only the bottom shelf, but I loved it, I'd carefully take the crockery out, one piece at a time. Wipe it with a soft cloth and arrange it just so, as I put it back in its place. If there was a flower pattern on the cup I'd line it up to match the flower pattern on the saucer.

Elma smiled to herself.

That cabinet must be half way to Victoria by now. Packed, sealed and sailing off into the sunset. Uncle Dave was so patient; I guess that's the difference between a cabinet maker and a builder. Not that Dad couldn't make a cabinet.

Elma thought of the jewellery box that her father had made for her mother. It was somehow hers now because her mother had left without taking it.

'And you, My Love, are even dearer. Now rub a bit of salt around the rim if they get stained but never put them in the dishwasher,' Livie said, breaking into Elma's thoughts. 'And whenever you have a cup of tea you'll think of me. And when I have a cup of tea I'll think of you.'

Only it won't be the same will it? You won't be here; you won't be here when I need you.

'Oh yeah,' Elma forced a laugh, 'and every time you pass the china cabinet you'll notice half the set missing.'

'All things change, my dear, all things change...'

Elma sat still for a moment listening to the hum of a motorboat in the distance.

Elma ran her finger over the top of the delicate floral cup, 'Sorry Aunt. I can't seem to focus on too much today. Dad wants me to visit Gran and if I do he'll give me driving lessons.'

'And,' said Aunt Livie, 'what do you think you'll do?'

'Oh Aunt Livie, I just don't know. I mean, I want the lessons – Chloe's nearly got her P's – but, well, you know how angry Gran is.'

'I guess I do, Darling. But just think for a moment how it must be for her knowing she's got family out here who don't care enough to visit.' Livie felt like a hypocrite, after all she was running off to Ballan. 'Elma,' she continued in a gentle tone, 'no one can make you visit her, but with me away off to the Mainland, Miriam will be getting a lot less visitors.'

'She doesn't remember your visits half the time though, does she? When I went with Dad last week, she said she hadn't seen you for months. She just tries to make everyone feel bad. I don't know why she has to be such a pain.'

The sky became darker; a few drops of rain hit the window. Elma looked out at the river – ruts were forming on the once smooth surface, changing this way and that as if the wind was making up its mind about which way to blow.

'Do you remember me teaching you how to play two handed patience?' Aunt Livie asked.

'Yes.' replied Elma, 'you taught me every card game I know.'

'Well it was Miriam, your gran who taught me.'

'No way, I've never seen Gran play a game of cards in my life.'

Elma lifted her eyebrows, squinting at her Aunt Livie and put on her best 'I don't believe you' face.

'It's true. She did – she's very good at cards, your gran, and it took her a fair amount of effort to teach me, I tell you. She was always so patient… oh I miss those days. But that's not why I'm telling you.'

Gran, patient? She's got that wrong. She's never anything but impatient and grumpy.

Elma watched a few raindrops change places as they raced from the top of the window to the bottom sill, pooling in the aluminium slider.

Those days – I've heard this before, how Gran was always happy, always fun to be with, the compulsive adventurer.

'Are you listening dear?'

'Yes Aunt Livie, of course I am.'

'Well I'm telling you this because she still enjoys a game of cards and I've left a couple of packs in the top drawer of her bedside table.'

'You what? Are you telling me you sit in the nursing home and play cards with Gran?' Elma shook her head in disbelief.

'Well yes, Elma, we do. And,' she added her eyebrows wrinkled in a serious expression, 'we enjoy it!'

Elma stretched her arms high into the air and placed her hands behind her head, successfully suppressing a yawn.

I'd be bored as hell if no one visited me. Still, we get what we deserve, don't we?

She looked at her aunt, an almost pleading look on the older lady's face. 'Alright, okay. I'll visit her once at least. But only because I don't believe you.' She laughed louder than intended, hoping she hadn't hurt Aunt Livie's feelings with her disbelief.

'Dad said I might be able to fly over and visit you, by myself, but only if Cathy picks me up from the airport. I'll be 18 this year; I think I could do the whole lot myself. I mean the train runs regularly to Ballarat and always stops at Ballan. It's not like I haven't done it, like, a million times already.'

Livie and Elma watched spits of rain land on the path in front of the sunporch. The concrete absorbed the first few drops completely, but the rain was setting in, the path morphing from a light mottled grey to a dark stony one.

'I bet Cathy's looking forward to having you live with her.'

Cathy was Aunt Livie's daughter. She had two adult children, Sarah and Josh, who both lived in Victoria. Cathy usually met them at the airport for the two-hour drive trip back to Ballan. Sometimes for a treat, they made their own way by taking the SkyBus into the city and catching a train the rest of the way out. Elma enjoyed the experience of passing through the CBD, perhaps staying the night in a cheap apartment and shopping for clothes in one of Melbourne's factory outlets or just wandering by the river watching all and sundry, as Dad liked to call it.

'Dad's going to miss you, Aunt Livie.'

'I know Darling, I know, but this has to be done. Your gran's settling into the nursing home now and it's time for me to be with my other grandchildren – before I get too old to enjoy them.'

'You're so funny Aunt Livie, they're more grown up than me. But thanks.'

Elma liked the way Livie referred to her as a grandchild. There wasn't too much she remembered of her own mother and Grandma Miriam had never warmed to her. *Not that I care whether Gran likes me or not. I'm going to miss you, Aunt Livie… we're all going to miss you.*

Elma sat with Aunt Livie for one last time listening to the sound of rain on the roof, the intensity of noise increasing as the bridge faded from view.

Chapter 4

I'm off now! See you tomorrow.'

Elma walked past the front counter of the café, her candy-striped duffle bag slung over her arm. Damien glanced up from wiping the cake cabinet and looked her way.

'Hey, good luck, girl. And stay off the footpath.'

A chair in the courtyard scraped, metal on concrete. A woman turned and looked at Elma, the creamy love heart on her latte stretched out of shape, a white streak of foam clinging to her top lip.

'Thanks, Damien.'

Elma smiled, adjusting her sunglasses on her head. She knew he was referring to her driving lesson.

But first I have to pass the 'Gran test'. Reckon I'll need more than luck with that one.

Another customer sat close to the door in the shade of the veranda, his black and white dog sprawled out with its legs crisscrossing the pathway in a bid to capture the small draught of air that seeped through the gap below the door.

Smart dog, thought Elma. *The 'tongue-out look' though … yuck.*

She stepped cautiously over the panting dog – its master apologising profusely for the inconvenience. The half-round shadow of the veranda extended part way across the road and beyond the shade Elma could see heat waves shimmering on the black tar. She lowered her sunglasses and stepped out into the 3pm heat, contemplating the advantage of walking for ten minutes to the nursing home or waiting fifteen for a bus.

It's too hot to wait – I'm melting already –so are my sandshoes.

She crossed the road and, with a quick glance back, viewed the Jet Service Station and Damien who now stood in the café doorway, framed by the redundant signs of Cut Price Petrol. Creamy-brown paint peeled from the metre-high façade of the pressed tin veranda and flaked away in the sun like blistered skin.

I don't remember it ever being a servo but the signage is still there – maybe for historic interest.

And why not? There are heaps of cyclists, locals and visitors who go past every day. Working there certainly keeps me busy. I love it.

And she did love it. More than she'd expected.

In the beginning Damien had teased her about being shy, but he'd also given her plenty of encouragement. He was like that – he could see the potential in people. Some of the customers were like that too. PJ Allen, for instance, a self- employed life coach who came in every morning at precisely 7.15, always with a cheery smile and always the same hot pink Keep Cup, with her initials PJ written loud and clear in black marker.

'No one's stolen any of my cups in the last forty years,' she'd say.

Elma would smile – she liked PJ. She always had time for a chat.

She'd convinced Elma to at least look at what the university had to offer, 'you could always study part-time you know,' she'd said.

*Maybe I could – I know Chloe wants me to – but the money –
I'd miss that. I'll just wait a bit maybe 'til the midyear intake and
decide then. Besides I am loving the smell of coffee…*

Elma Unfaithful to the Memory of Tea
Great Aunt in Shock

She thought of those headlines and waved a farewell to
Damien before heading south.

The footpath ran parallel to timtumili minanya/Derwent
River. Bright blue snippets of water flashed and sparkled between
the grand houses, most of which were surrounded by strong
stone walls or thick, high hedges that protected flourishing
gardens. *And obstructed the view for pedestrians like me.*

She was tempted to stop at the top of an opened driveway
to stare at the glistening river but the need to escape the heat
was stronger. Sweat trickled down the back of her neck.

*I wish I'd brought my hat; I'm so hot – can't be much further –
sweaty forehead– fingers – arm pits – I stink, I know it …*

She mentally whinged her way along Sandy Bay Road past
the Red Chapel with its faded bricks and heavy wooden doors,
the historic building marking the approximate halfway point
of her journey. At ten past three she stopped in the shade of a
hedge. Nutgrove Avenue swerved off to the left and downwards
into a small leafy suburb, hidden by trees below the main road.
The nursing home was well positioned in a sheltered cove only
a few corners from where she stood. Close enough for residents
to walk to the village shops and cafes but far enough away to
block out the noise from busy Sandy Bay road.

It looks peaceful down there, a harbour of homes.

She pulled out her notebook and added her newly coined
collective noun to a list of notes and odd sayings.

Maybe a pocket of properties.

Her sunglasses stuck to her face. She removed them and wiped away the sweat gathering around her eyes.

A place of old, heaps of old. Old Houses, old trees, old people – everything old.

Some of the houses were pretty cool, with large verandas and ornate gardens kept green by automatic sprinkler systems. One road in particular caught her eye.

'Elma Road!' Why would anyone name a road Elma?'

She stared at the street sign, black letters on a white background. She looked away and back again but the sign was still there – bright and shiny.

I wonder how I missed that. I guess I've never walked this way to visit Gran before.

Elma laughed at the thought. She'd only ever walked to the nursing home once before,

And I took the other road – but still – why would anyone name a road Elma? It's not such a great name. I'm yet to achieve greatness with this old name. I don't even know why I have it. Hmm.

She stopped again and made another note in her book.

I'll ask Aunt Livie later, she might know. Or maybe I can ask Dad. He's probably the one who named me. Weird that I don't know where my own name came from.

Elma thought about her gran's name, Miriam.

I know that means bitter. Well, I'm pretty sure it does. I remember someone telling me that, but Elma or Livinda, for that matter, I have no idea at all what they mean.

Some of the answers would be easy; Google would help her out with them. But she would have to wait until she got home to do the research as she had misplaced her phone again, and was giving it one more week to turn up before she looked into buying a new one. She didn't have quite enough money for an iPhone 6 and hadn't been successful in convincing her dad to provide her with an early birthday present. Her birthday was still a good nine months away. She cringed and shook her head feeling the muscles in the back of her neck tighten.

If Gran didn't always say what she does about Dad spoiling me I'm sure he would've caved in by now and bought me the phone.

'But Dad,' she remembered saying, 'they're on special and all my friends have one, and,' she added, 'their dads pay for them.'

She had groaned and flopped herself down on the couch in a bid to look desperate, checking his face for signs of anger in case she'd gone too far.

Again.

'Well, ask your friends' dads to buy you one then,' he'd replied, not turning from his accounts on the computer.

'Money doesn't grow on trees,' he continued, 'you have to work for it.'

Oh no, here we go again. Clichés, clichés, why must he always speak in clichés?

She'd rolled her eyes and replied with confidence, 'I am earning my own money now, Dad. I can easily pay you back.'

'Well' Martin said turning from the computer to face her, 'if it's that easy then just buy the phone now.'

'But I don't have enough money yet, do I,' Elma rose to her feet.

'What's the point? You never listen to me anyway!'

Martin's eyes grew wide and his mouth dropped open in disbelief. Did she really say "You never listen to me anyway!"?

He looked back at the accounts on the screen. It was hopeless. He hated doing the numbers but he didn't trust anyone else with his finances, so there was no choice. He might be a good builder but he wasn't good at accountancy or fatherhood, according to Elma.

36

"You never listen to me anyway!"

Was that the family catchcry? Did everyone think that? Or was Elma just pushing the teenage boundaries of their relationship? She certainly was growing up, wanting a car, wanting driving lessons, working over the summer holidays.

"You never listen to me anyway!"

Hadn't his own mother said that to him just recently? Wasn't that what Liz, his ex-wife, used to say? His heart began beating faster.

'Stay strong, Martin,' he said to himself. 'She's just a kid. She doesn't know what she's saying. She's just angry because she wants everything right now. Car, phone, everything. It will do her good to wait for it,' he thought.

He switched the computer screen off and closed his eyes, his head resting in his hands.

'It'll pass,' he told himself.

--

Elma reached the parkland near the nursing home and stopped to catch her breath beneath the shade of one of the large pine tree that formed a crooked row along the north side of the sports field. She was still annoyed with her father's decision, but resolved to save the next three weeks' pays and quell her craving with her own resources.

She rubbed her eyes in a bid to refocus, for although the tree offered shade, it was no protection from the hot, humid air. Beads of sweat dribbled down her forehead mirroring in an odd way, the amber sap oozing from the trunk of the tree.

She sighed and breathed in the heady smell of warm pine oil.

Hmm, Aunt Livie's laundry on wool wash day

A carpet of pine needles lay beneath her feet and she scuffed at them to create a small hollow in which to place her bag. A haze of fine dust stirred up and settled like powdered cinnamon on her white shoes. Her hands, also cinnamon, contrasted against her dark blue jeans. She examined them checking for particles of dirt or dust or some invisible germ that might be lingering beneath her sight. They were clean – sweaty, but clean. She'd washed them before leaving work. Of course she had. She always did. She remembered pushing the door open with her backside to avoid touching it. But now the tree beckoned her. It was silly – she knew trees didn't beckon, yet she felt compelled to reach out and touch the ancient ever-green.

This is so weird.

Hands poised, zombie-like, she stood just centimetres away from the trunk, willing herself to continue, battling the desire to clench her fists and drop her arms.

It's a dirty tree, Elma! Don't touch it. Dirt's poison. You'll regret it.

She stood firm, overriding her self-talk.

The bark of the trunk could have been made from giant pieces of Cadbury Flake stacked unevenly, layer upon layer in rough formations against the tree. Deep ruts formed valleys that ran between the mounds and flowed from the top downwards before vanishing with the roots into a hundred seasons of fallen pine needles.

Elma pressed her fingers into the grooves, her first and second knuckles disappeared from sight. The bark was stronger than a Flake and her attempt to remove a piece yielded nothing but sticky fingers and scratches to her nail polish.

Unaware of time, she gazed, enchanted by the knobs of rough, gnarled wood twisting this way and that until they formed the creviced skin of old men and women – here a wrinkled brow, there a crooked nose, a furrow of concern, a tired droop, lengths of stringy hair, a rough beard. Wrinkles, crinkles, scabs and scars. It was as if the tree was staring back at her. She stood in the heat, mesmerised by the comings and goings of the faces in the bark until suddenly, there in front of her, was the stern face of her grandmother. She stepped back, too quickly, and tripped over her bag landing with a dull thump, a pile of pine needles beneath her bottom. The muffled snap of her pencil inside her pocket, bought her back to her senses. She looked at her shaking hands. A gnarled piece of bark fell to the ground almost touching her foot as she scuttled backwards before rising to her feet. Amber gum and pine needles stuck to her fingers, transferring from one hand to the other as she tried to rid herself of them.

I don't know why I did that, I really don't!

She grabbed her bag, knowing exactly where to find her bottle of hand sanitiser.

That was crazy. How could Gran be in the tree?

She flipped open the little white lid and squeezed out a generous amount of liquid, rubbing it vigorously into the palms of her hands to remove the feel and the smell of the pine and exchange it for something more familiar, something more comfortable. Some of the resin stuck stubbornly to her skin and she prised it loose with her fingernail, creating more marks on the once-perfect surfaces. After replacing the cleaner and fastening her bag she looked sheepishly around, hoping no one had seen her fall over. But, apart from a few piles of pinecones, there was no one in sight.

They're all too smart to be out in this heat.

Her heart was still racing.

What was I thinking when I said yes to Dad? This is crazy. I hate this place. Why am I doing this? Is it for Dad or Gran? Or Aunt Livie?

Elma looked at her watch.

Heck no! I'm doing it for me, for driving lessons. Stay focussed Girl. You can do this. One hour with Gran equals a one hour driving lesson. I'll get my licence and I'll never have to come here again.

Elma bent down and picked at the pine needles lodged in the eyelets of her new running shoes. She blew hopelessly at the pine dust covering them, brushed at the back of her pants, re-sanitised her hands and slung her bag over her shoulder knowing there would only be fifteen minutes left to spend with Gran – if she hurried. For the smallest of seconds Elma entertained the idea of not visiting at all.

Dad won't know and Gran won't care – she won't even remember. If it wasn't so jolly hot I'd just stay here and wait for him.

But it was hot. Way too hot to be standing outside. So, with her head held high, Elma strode the remaining distance to the nursing home, grateful for the expected air-conditioning.

'Oh my goodness, I hate this place,' she sighed as her backside sank into the weakly sprung armchair beside Miriam's bed, the smell of stale urine accosting her nose. Her grandmother stirred a little in her nursing home bed, but not enough, thought Elma, to be awake. She looked around. Gran's sheets were awry, the blankets hung down one side more than the other and the curtains were closed. What remained of the lunch meal sat abandoned on the bed table next to a vase of brightly coloured dahlias, their array of reds and golds heralding the coming of autumn, the changing of seasons – perhaps the coming of something good! *Not likely! There's not much good happening around here. Look at you, Gran. You're 71 and condemned to a life in prison ... well, it may as well be prison. I would never want to live like this.*

But it wasn't Elma's choice or Miriam's even. It had been Martin's.

'I don't care if you're here or not,' Elma spoke aloud to herself. 'I just wish it didn't mean Aunt Livie had to leave.'

The decision to move Miriam into a nursing home had been made after Miriam's last operation. God knows Miriam was enough to cope with before her first hip replacement. But now, with the other hip causing her pain, coupled with arthritis and the early onset of dementia she wasn't much fun at all. Elma laughed to herself;

*Gran was never much fun.*She'd never been the cuddly gran depicted in the story books or the one that baked biscuits and cakes for the delight of small children or the gran that took you away for the weekend. In fact Elma's gran hadn't done anything for her at all – that she could think of. They'd never played eye spy, or cards, that Elma could remember. Never been shopping or even holidaying together. *She is my gran though. Whatever that means.*

The long hand on the clock moved closer to the twelve – it was almost 4pm. Martin would be waiting out the front by ten past.

Certainly been a waste of time today – you won't even know I've been here, will you Gran?

Elma tangled her fingers in the crocheted blanket folded across the chair in which she sat and stared down at the floral designs on the carpet beneath her Nikes, the first pair of shoes she'd ever paid for with her own money. The carpet wasn't old, it was new but it had a timeworn look about it. Elma groaned. Had they chosen an old-fashioned pattern to make the residents feel at home, or had old become new again like the decor of the café where she worked? 'YUCK!' Elma cried, leaping out of the chair as if bitten by a tiger snake – wetness seeping through the seat of her jeans. She turned, looking down at the crocheted blanket and lifted the corner just enough to reveal a pool of liquid on the vinyl surface of the chair.

'Oh no, oh no,' she repeated, quite sure the moisture had come from her grandmother's bladder. Gritting her teeth she brushed frantically at the back of her pants, reviving the smell of pine in a failed attempt to rid herself of the new substance.

'That's just what I wanted! Not!'

She shook her fist at the sleeping woman and mouthed something never to be repeated. With her hands held out in front of her, Elma pushed past the end of the bed, heading for the hand basin on the other side of the room.

'Damn,' she cried as her elbow caught on the bed table, sending the ceramic vase of flowers cascading to the floor. She swung around just in time to watch the vase spill out its floral contents in a spray of red and gold. The carpet absorbed most of the noise and water, but the sudden collision with the bed disturbed the old lady in it.

'Who's there?' came the voice from the bed.

'Is that you Charlie? You've been drinking again.'

The last sentence was a statement, not a question.

Elma stilled herself to listen to it. She turned the tap on just a bit at a time so it would run quietly while she washed her hands carefully. Yes, of course she needed to wash her hands frequently at work, but Elma frequently washed her hands anyway. Her dad had said it was her duty to wash her hands every time she passed a tap. OCD is what her school psychologist had called it. She couldn't help it. And in this case she felt justified, very justified!

Yep, call me a crazy clean freak if you want. But at least I'm only crazy about being clean.

Elma shot another glance at her grandmother and turned the tap off with her elbow.

'I hate this place' she said again, beneath her breath, and wiped her face with her hand as if removing the smell of urine caught in her nose. She needed to get home quickly to change her jeans. Charlie, she knew, was Gran's husband, her grandfather. Well, sort of – she'd never met him and he was dead now anyway. From all accounts he hadn't been much of a husband or a father. He'd left Miriam when Martin was only five years old.

History repeats. That's what my mum did to me.
At least we had Aunt Livie.

She smiled at the thought and then frowned again, knowing that Aunt Livie had moved interstate.

'Hello,' said a voice entering the room.

Elma turned to see a nurse with a bulky drug trolley in tow.

'You visiting your granny are you?'

'Gran, not granny,' Elma answered, before realising she probably sounded rude.

'I need to wake her for her medication. You might like to stay and talk to her,' the nurse continued, flicking over a page on her drug chart.

'I'm not staying,' Elma replied, wiping her hands on a paper towel, desperately aware of her need to change her pants. She bent down, scooping up the mess of amber flowers from the floor.

'I'll come back another day. She's awake now, I think,' said Elma giving another glance towards the bed.

Her gran's eyes were shut. Maybe she had gone back to sleep.

Elma wasn't hanging around to find out. It was time for her driving lesson and she'd need to stop home and have a shower first. There was no way in the world she would wear clothes soaked in Gran's pee even if it was 40 degrees outside and a high chance they'd be dry before she even crossed the road.'What's this, then?' the nurse said manoeuvring the heavy trolley out of the way as Elma slopped the flowers into the basin and strode out. She could feel colour rising in her cheeks and an urgent need for fresh air as she shook droplets of water from her hands. 'Don't sit in the chair,' she flung the words back behind her, more to herself than the nurse. *Now what did Gran say?*

"Is that you Charlie? You've been drinking again."

She felt for her notebook, the pencil broken but thankfully still long enough to write with, although when she tried to pull the notebook out, the cover stuck to the wet of her pants and she was left holding a broken pencil and a coverless notebook.

By the time she reached the main foyer she had thought of a new heading – **Gran's Ravings. S**he flicked through her notes, until she came to a blank page for her new section and wrote the words as she remembered them, being careful to put the date at the top. This could be something of interest.

I'll ring Aunt Livie when her phone is connected and see what she has to say.

Oh Aunt Livie, what am I going to do without you?

Chapter 5

'I can't do it Dad! It's not wide enough!'

Elma pulled hard on the steering wheel and the ute crunched onto the gravel beside the narrow mountain road, wheels skidding as it lurched forward and stalled to a halt.

Two trailing cars revved their engines on their way past, one honking its horn in angry jabs.

'What the hell, Elma!? There's plenty of room!'

Martin rubbed his neck.

'Buses and trucks can pass. Of course it's wide enough!'

But Elma didn't budge, her hands gripped the steering wheel, her knuckles, white knobs.

'And that's not how you stop a car!'

He glared at her from the passenger's seat.

'Pull the hand brake on, Elma, and get out.'

He sucked in a deep mouthful of mountain air and released it slowly from the side of his mouth.

'I'll drive!'

'Thanks Dad.'

Elma stepped out of the ute, grimacing as her feet sank a little into the muddy gravel. She moved quickly around the back of the car in case her father changed his mind.

'Just wait here, Elma, give me a minute.'

Martin, climbed out, leaving the door open for Elma, and strode up alongside the road, his work boots heavy on the loose stones.

Elma watched the label on the back of his Hard Yakka overalls become smaller and smaller until she could no longer distinguish the letters from the khaki coloured fabric on which they were sewn. Martin was a good way up the road when he turned into the bushes and disappeared from sight. Elma wasn't sure if he was angry at her or upset by the way she'd driven off the road.

Probably just needs to pee.

She climbed into the passenger seat of the Toyota Hilux. The view from where Elma had 'parked' was minimal, just heaps of trees casting dappled shadows across the road in the late afternoon sun.

This was driving lesson number five, which meant Elma had spent more time visiting Gran this month than she had in the entire previous year.

The first week Gran had been asleep. That was a bad week. Easy because I was only there for 15 minutes but bad because I sat in a chair full of wee. I'll never trust a crocheted blanket again. I swore I'd never visit again.

Elma smiled to herself.

Week two Gran accused me of being late and bringing a lemon tart instead of a jam one. She had such a snippy voice: 'You should know by now that I like jam, not lemon!'

I didn't tell her it was the only one left over from the café.

The driving that week was good though. Dad let me drive all the way down Sandy Bay Road and into Taroona to the unused shopping centre. I practised starting and stopping without being on the road.

The next week was a bit interesting because Gran was up and about and wanting to go outside. So I took her. It'd felt like we were escaping or something. I can see the headlines now: **Gen Z Flees Nut Groan with Granny!**

That's my name for the place: Nut Groan. It's not really a home, more like two old houses side by side, joined together by a giant see through brolly. We escaped via the games room door and I was so nervous I pressed the exit code wrong three times and had to wait for a staff member to let us out. They must have thought I was stupid.

It was true the adjoining houses that made up the nursing home were old, but they were a stylish old rather than a worn out one. And maybe, with a good imagination you could see the imposing glass façade as an umbrella. But really it was a cleverly designed atrium with a cathedral ceiling that joined the two early 19th century houses together – not unlike the architecture of the State Cinema. The exterior walls of the houses were now the internal walls of the atrium and the glass ceiling ran the entire length between the buildings.

Elma had been impressed by the grandeur of the atrium. It was spacious and contained the nursing home's offices, physio, hairdresser and an area where residents could sit in the café, play cards, board games or just enjoy the potted plants that surrounded an ornamental fountain. The 'Fountain of Youth' they called it at the home.

Elma laughed at the irony of it.

Why would anyone call it that in this place? Why not Peaceful Waters or Old Man's Pool.

She didn't say it aloud for fear of offending someone.

But really, 'Fountain of Youth'?

The café looked eastward towards *timtumili minanya* and glimpses of river could be seen between the native trees. Directly above the café was a mezzanine floor to receive the lifts. If there was one place Elma did like in the nursing home it was here, with the cane chairs, potted palms and slivers of light caught in the ripples of *timtumili minanya*.

Elma led Miriam through the café and out to the deck. Miriam's walking frame tapped out a dull thud as she placed it a step in front of her sensible shoes and shuffled into it. Thud, shuffle, shuffle. Thud, shuffle, shuffle.

I know that tune.

The constant sound of the waves lapped at the shore, beckoning them further from the nursing home and Miriam shuffle-thudded down the ramp until the noise of her frame disappeared into the pine bark. It was only a few minutes before Elma seated her gran on one of the wooden park benches that faced the river. She plonked her own bottom down on the other end of the seat, leaving a two-bum space between them and studied her gran as she swung her shoes in the knolls of sand built up under the wooden slats.

Funny but I don't think I've ever seen Gran barefooted.

Her gran looked much younger than most of the residents in the home. Her dark hair was tied back in a bun with a metal clip.

Weird – Aunt Livie's hair has been grey for as long as I can remember but Gran doesn't have a single grey hair at all. I wonder how it'll be for me. I'll dye mine anyway, unless grey is the new black.

She laughed out loud. Miriam stopped swinging her feet and turned her face towards Elma, their eyes catching each other's for what seemed like the first time ever. Elma saw something gentle in her companion's eyes, something that she longed for, a warmth, a desire, something strange yet familiar.

Probably my fat imagination.

She looked away, unsure of herself.

'Can I take your shoes off Gran?' she offered, turning back to the older woman.

Miriam looked at her with disgust.

'You silly girl – I don't want that filthy stuff tracked all through my house.'

It's only sand, Gran, it won't hurt you.

But I understand 'cause I don't like it in my shoes or clothes either.

'Scarlet?' Miriam said, looking straight at Elma. Her legs weren't moving now, 'You don't look well.' She stared intently into Elma's eyes.

A shiver crept up Elma's spine like a spider stalking an unsuspecting prey. She laughed nervously, not knowing what to say.

'Your laugh won't fool me. I can see you're not okay.'

'I'm not Scarlet, Gran, I'm Elma,' she said, looking sideways at her gran.

'And I'm fine, not sick at all.'

'Oohh,' Gran sighed, her shoulders sloping forward but her eyes bright.

'My Scarlet laughed just like you. She was about your size, too. I couldn't keep track of her. She would race all over that mountain, up the Saw Mill Track, down the Myrtle Gully … she knew it like the back of her hand.'

The old lady looked quickly from side to side checking to see if anyone was about. Her hand fidgeted and she leaned closer to Elma – almost teetering off the edge of the bench.

'You've got her perfect blue eyes you have. Forget-me-not blue, just like that river.'

She looked up and gazed out across the water.

Elma looked too. The water was as bright as ever. The sparkles so pretty she wanted to collect them and string them together for a necklace.

'I've got photos.'

Elma watched, confused, while Miriam reached under the park bench, fishing about for something.

'It's gone!' she said, straightening up, her face red with indignation. 'Someone's taken it! Someone's taken my album! They've got no right to take my things!'

Elma looked around.

What is she talking about? We didn't bring anything with us.

'Calm down, Gran, there's nothing there.'

Miriam furrowed her brow, pursed her lips and began muttering to herself.

'There was never anything under there,' Elma repeated, thinking Miriam hadn't heard her.

'Well what would you know, you dirty little thief! You filthy liar! Look at you!'

Miriam stood, gripping the handles of her walking frame to steady herself, and headed back up the lane to the nursing home. One of her stocking socks slipped down and Elma caught sight of a large patch of discoloured skin glaring out from beneath the hem of her skirt.

The scar. I remember that, or rather Aunt Livie telling me Gran had burnt her feet and legs and even the top of her head, in the fires of '67.

Later, when Martin picked Elma up for her driving lesson she'd tried to explain what had happened, but Martin just seemed to brush it off.

'Well she's lost it, hasn't she? You know she's lost it. What do you expect?'

Elma thought for a moment.

I expected you to be less off-hand. After all it's your mother and you are the one who usually tells me off for saying anything negative about her.

'I don't know Dad? What should I expect?'

The conversation finished with that question. Elma was less than satisfied.

No answers, no one ever gives me answers, no one talks about anything. I don't know who Scarlet is. Is she Dad's sister? Does he have a sister? Oh there's no sense in that. I only know she has "perfect" blue eyes and loves the mountain. Was she sick? And what photo album was Gran talking about? Nothing makes sense.

Elma made a new note about Scarlet in her book and put in under the list of things to ask Aunt Livie when she phoned her. Her growing list of questions.

There were only shadows on the road now the sun had dropped behind the mountain and the dappled patterns had disappeared. The sensor on the dash showed that the air temperature was 20 degrees. Elma scanned the road watching for her father to reappear. Despite being warm inside the cab she gave a shiver. Pale green and blue lichen grew in blotchy patches across the rocks that formed a bank beside the road. A vehicle sped towards her and flew past, buffeting the ute.

The road is still too narrow – I don't care what he says.

She slipped the side of her finger under the thick plastic and peeled the L-plate from the front of the windscreen.

Where are you Dad? You've been way longer than a minute!

Another car came past. And another. She removed the second L-plate before groping around in her bag for her hand sanitiser. 'Apricot Pearl' – it was a new one. She held the small bottle in her hand and flicked her thumb upwards to open the lid.

'Oh no!' she said as the lid came off the bottle and pinged against the windscreen, ricocheting past her shoulder before disappearing behind the passenger's seat. Placing the cap-less bottle on the dash and turning round to kneel on the seat, Elma squeezed her hand down between the chair and the back of the cab, but the lid had fallen from sight.

Probably underneath the seat.

She scrambled back around and, with her bum in the air she lowered her face towards the floor. Stray locks of hair escaped from her ponytail and fell forward over her face. A few strands caught in her mouth. The smell of dirty carpet released a queasy sensation in her gut.

It was useless. She pulled herself up and opened the door.

This is not going to get the better of me!

She "pffed" the hair from her mouth and wiped it away with the back of her hand. Climbing out she took a deep breath and held it in as she bent over to look under the seat.

Heck! I'm going to need more than hand sanitiser after this.

She ran her fingers gingerly under the seat. Carpet grime stuck to her fingers. The first thing to come out was an old Macca's bag, followed by some grocery receipts and a half full packet of spicy Doritos. A few escaped corn chips scrunched under her feet as they fell to the ground.

Disgusting, I can't even remember eating them.

Yes! There it is!

She stretched her arm a little further, the lid just out of reach.

'Got you!' she shouted, grabbing at the little white piece of plastic, the back of her hand disturbing a brown paper bag as she did so.

That's odd – the bag's not empty.

Placing the lid safely on the seat, she reached back in to grab the paper bag that had a few weeks earlier held a Florentine biscuit from her work place. It felt about the same weight as her missing phone – the phone she'd been intending to replace but never quite seemed to have enough money for.

How the heck did you get here?

But as with all phones with flat batteries, there was no answer.

For a brief moment Elma forgot about her dirty hands and messy hair and busied herself in the hope of finding a cable charger for her phone. The search began in the glove box, but no luck. There was one on the outlet but the plug at the end of the cable was too large.

'What have you got there?' Martin asked, as he climbed back into the ute.

'You'll never guess where I found it, Dad,' she said, holding the device up to the side of her face and beaming at her dad.

'Your truck is such a mess I'm surprised you can find anything in here.'

'Can't be worse than your backpack,' Martin retorted.

'How about a quick drive to the top of the mountain and a souvlaki from Mykonos for tea?'

'It's a deal,' Elma said, abandoning her search for a charger and dropping her phone into her bag with the sanitiser, before grabbing her hairbrush.

Okay, my bag might have lots in it, but it's not dirty like your ute.

Trees flashed by, dark in contrast to the city below. The Eastern Shore could be seen in the distance, bathed in sunlight, the Western Shore dull in the shadow of the mountain, a stretch of blue dividing the two.

Martin slowed the vehicle as they approached The Springs. The shiny roof of a new BBQ shelter flashed into sight and he slowed even more before turning left onto the side road that led past the ruins of the old Springs Hotel. Elma remembered playing here once or twice when Cathy's kids, Sarah and Josh, had visited from the Mainland. They were both a little older than her but that had been a good thing as they could go off exploring for the day and Cathy and Martin would let them take the younger Elma in tow.

'Just make sure you bring her back,' were usually the last words they heard as they scurried out the studio door before the grown-ups could change their minds.

Elma wound the window of the ute down. It seemed there was nothing much to see here, just the outlines of foundations of some old buildings on a grassy flat. They drove on, past the clearing and back onto the main road, snaking left and right as the road led them to the top of kunanyi. A flash of sunlight hit the front windscreen of the cab as they rounded the last corner and into the carpark at the summit.

'I used to bring your mum up here in the old days.'

Martin's voice was wistful. Elma wasn't sure if she should ask a question or wait for him to continue.

Wow! It's the first time he's ever mentioned her that I can think of.

She held her breath and waited.

Come on, Dad don't stop there.

'Could she drive?'

That's such a dumb question. Why did I say that!?

Elma stared out the window watching the sun dip in the hilly horizon hoping he hadn't heard her.

'Yes, of course she could – but not much better than you,' he added, and gave a laugh.

'She'd always make me drive up this road. "It's not wide enough," she'd say,' he said, in a mocking voice.

'Sounded just like you too …'

His voice trailed off but Elma thought she detected a hint of delight in what he'd said and she felt a little warmer. They were driving down now, sinking into the shadow.

54

'Just over there, the other side of that fire trail,' he pointed north-west as they rounded the corner labelled Big Bend, 'is a hut – a secret one. Your mum and I would come up here with a picnic dinner and sit on top of the roof to watch the sun set.'

I don't believe what I'm hearing. He never talks about her!

A sad look came over Martin's face.

He's still fond of her.

Elma's heart beat a little faster. She looked at her hands. They were shaking. Breathing in was okay, but breathing out wasn't really happening. She felt lightheaded.

'I think my ears are popping, Dad.'

'Hold your nose and blow,' Martin said.

'It's because we're driving down. Or yawn – that'll help.'

What am I doing? I always wanted him to talk about her and he never did and now he said something and I changed the subject! What's wrong with me? It shouldn't be this crazy.

Elma held her nose and blew hard, the sudden pop clearing the pressure in her ears. She breathed in and out deliberately for a few minutes before calming herself enough to breathe without thinking.

Dad used to come up here with Mum, I never knew that. All the walks we've been on and I never knew that. I'm going to come up here sometime and find that hut.

'Will you take me there sometime?' Elma said, finding her voice. 'Will you show me the hut? Dad...?' She wondered if he was listening. It wasn't an easy road to drive and she knew he needed to focus. The twilight made it even harder. Too light for the headlights to be of much use and too dark for them not to be on.

At least it makes the oncoming traffic easier to spot.

Elma closed her eyes each time a car approached, hoping it wouldn't be the last thing she ever saw.

Chapter 6

'Hey Aunt Livie, second time lucky. I have to be quick though, my bus leaves in a minute.' Elma flicked a glance at the wall clock; the phone line had dropped out earlier – maybe the bad weather in Ballan. 'I wanted to ring last night but Dad said it was too late. How are you?'

'Oh, I'm fine, Elma. Settling in just nicely, although I'm looking forward to getting a place of my own. This phone is hard to hear on, Elma dear, can you speak up?'

'Well maybe I can ring you back on Cathy's mobile. Is Cathy there?' Elma took another glance at the clock. She had fewer shifts at the café now that summer had ended.

'She's in the shower, Love. The real-estate gentleman found some units only a couple of blocks from here and we're taking a second look at one today. It would be nice to be in walking distance of Cathy. But enough about me, how about you, Elma? Did you get the little card I sent last week?'

'Yes, Aunt, thanks so much. I've put it on my bedside table.' She could see the card from where she was sitting – a superb blue wren standing on the frond of a man fern. She could see most of her bedroom through the doorway from where she sat at the kitchen table drinking her morning cup of tea. The tea was to wash away the taste of Weetbix. The Weetbix were because her dad had said she had to and the hurry was because her bus would leave in 15 minutes.

'Hey, Aunt Livie can I ask you a question?'

'Well, go ahead Elma. You know me. I don't always have the answers but I hope I can help anyway. What's your question, Love?'

The line gave a little crackle. Elma hesitated and held the phone close to her ear. 'Did Gran have another child?' There was a pause. She tapped her fingernail on the side of her tea cup, pink shellac made a 'tingy' sound against the red rose painted on the fine bone china, her 'Great Aunt Livie Cup'. The clock showed 8.05 am.

'Of course not,' Aunt Livie responded. 'What would make you say such a thing, Elma dear?'

The phone crackled again. Elma strained to listen. The reception had not improved by redialling.

'She told me she had a girl. I mean she was rambling at the time. She thought I was her girl.' Elma's voice was shaky. Her heart raced. She wasn't sure if she should tell Aunt Livie everything that Gran had said. She loved Aunt Livie and didn't want to cause her grief. 'Scarlet. She called me Scarlet.'

Elma had her notebook open on the table in front of her and a list of questions ready to ask Aunt Livie.

She'd transferred some of the writings from her old notebook into her new one after the **Urine Incident** when she'd ripped off the wee-soaked cover. She cringed involuntarily thinking about it. Her new book was divided into five sections, a habit she'd formed not long after starting high school. It was her way of keeping a journal. The psychologist had suggested it – 'it might help you become aware of hidden triggers,' she'd said.

Elma tried the journal thing, poured her heart out in angry words – but only briefly,

What if I lose it? What if someone reads it?... What if Dad reads it?

She'd promptly torn the pages out and burned them in the kitchen sink. And thus began her more cryptic notes and headlines. The first heading of the new notebook was **Thirteen Year Old Tests Fire Alarm While Father at Work**.

The notebooks were always the same size and thickness but Elma changed the headings to suit her needs. **Collective Nouns – Colours and Such – News Headlines – Notes to Self** and, her latest heading, **Gran's Ramblings**, which would replace **Puns Intended**. Each new book was covered with pictures from old calendars or birthday paper.

Aunt Livie provided the calendars.

'I think you know as well as I do that your dad is her only child.' The line crackled again. 'I don't think I'd worry too much about it, Elma, although I sometimes wondered if Miriam would have been happier if she'd had a girl. She had a soft spot for Cathy when she was younger.'

Gran had a soft spot for Cathy?

It was hard for Elma to believe Gran had ever had a soft spot for anyone.

Cathy and Martin were born the same year in the same hospital and Cathy was the eldest, but only by six weeks. They went to the same schools, shared the same friends, and most people thought they were brother and sister rather than cousins. Elma liked Cathy.

But I can't imagine Gran being kind to anyone.

The line crackled again. 'I can hardly hear you Aunt Livie. The phone is fading in and out. What did you say?'

'I said, poor Martin, your dad, he always did his best to please her. God knows, we all did, but she never did recover.'

Elma knew what Livie was referring to when she said the word 'recover'. Everyone knew the story. Elma felt she'd heard it more than a million times.

It was like the population of Hobart was divided over this one date in history – those who were there and lived through the devastating bushfires of 1967 and those who came after to live through the stories second hand. Not that Elma wanted to make the event any less horrific than it was. No, she thought it was, on all accounts, an horrendous time. Over 2000 people lost their houses, their schools, their workplaces and, worst of all, 64 people lost their lives. Elma couldn't think of anyone who lived in Hobart who didn't know someone who had lost something in that blaze.

Since the Dunalley bushfires in the summer of 2013 and the recent 50 year anniversary of the '67 fires a lot of feelings had been rekindled by the collective memories of the general public. Elma was particularly aware of it. She thought of her friends who'd lived down the peninsula at that time. Both families were evacuated by boat to Hobart. Both their families lost their houses, their belongings and their pets. Elma remembered sitting outside on the deck with her dad one afternoon watching little flakes of ash falling into their dinner from the fires which seemed so far away. She'd catch them one at a time on her fingertip but, try as she might, she couldn't transfer them from one hand to the other – they just dissolved instantly when touched. Everything smelt like a woodfired BBQ, even her clothes that she'd hung inside hoping to avoid the ash fall, smelt like ash in the grate of a wood fire. Looking from their place towards the east they could see clouds and lightning caused by the weather patterns created by the blaze.

I was so worried about my friends because we had no idea what was happening to them. We felt safe because the fire wasn't on our side of the river – but we also felt bad because we were safe. We spent a lot of time crying when we finally caught up. Chloe and I couldn't believe it when Kelly's family moved to the Mainland. We didn't even get to say goodbye. But that was only five years ago. It's been more than fifty years since Gran's fire – why doesn't she just get over it? She's alive and her mum and dad didn't die, their house didn't even burn down. So why is it that most everyone else recovered, or at least appeared to, but not Gran?

Elma hadn't been there in 1967, she wasn't even born but she still felt the fire had left its burden on her family.

The Curse of the Manning Family

Only that was Gran's married name, not the name she had at the time of the fire.

Part of the story, as Elma recalled, was Miriam's vow: "I'll never, as long as I live, set foot on that mountain again!"

Which seemed, to Elma, a crazy thing to say. But, from what Aunt Livie and her Dad had said, Miriam was quite sure about it and it forced her family to move across the river from their home on Inglewood Road in South Hobart to Lindisfarne on the Eastern Shore.

Elma had never cared too much for Gran. They didn't seem to get along ever.

'You just need to give her a chance Elma,' her dad would say with that serious look on his face, slight wrinkles forming waves across his forehead connecting the grey patches of hair at either side of his temples.

'Why don't you just give her a chance?'

Elma wouldn't answer but she thought to herself,

Because she's mean to me, she never plays with me or reads me stories and she tells me to brush my hair and tie it back. She tells me I look like a feral cat. She tells me I'm a magnet for mud and that I track dirt all over her house. She tells me I'm no good at this and no good at that and don't touch the curtains and don't touch the windows and dry the dishes properly and you missed a bit with the broom and you've stained your dress! Why can't you keep anything clean?

Clean! Clean! Clean!

Elma's thoughts weren't new thoughts. They were thoughts that she'd lugged around with her since she was little.

But I'm not little now, am I? I can think for myself. Those were all Gran's thoughts of me, not mine. I am clean. I am tidy. I can wash dishes and sweep floors – properly. I don't even know why Gran accuses me of something that is not true? Well not anymore...

She could hear the sound of Aunt Livie talking on the other end of the phone line, the crackling taking away a word here and there, but she wasn't listening to her aunt. 'Sorry, Aunt it's a bad line. I'll call you back later.'

But Elma knew it wasn't the phone line preventing her from hearing her Aunt. It was something else entirely. Something big that she had never thought of before. News headlines in the making!

She sat there with her phone in her hand, staring at it as if it were a lost puzzle piece.

Why have I never noticed this before? Gran, are you the reason why I am such a clean freak? Are you the reason I wash my hands constantly and stress like crazy if my hair is out of place?

She'd never put the two together before.

Gran's dislike for me and my compulsive cleaning? No, no way, there is no way. How could someone like her have such an effect on me? Why would I screw up my life with compulsive idiosyncrasies to try and please her? I don't even like her!

Elma stood up and pushed her phone into the pocket of her jeans. Livie would have to wait; right now she needed to get to work.

The words on the machine flashed red: "low credit" as Elma flicked her Green card over the scanner at the front of the bus. The money seemed like so much when she'd first started at the café. Three or four days of work were perfect during the summer school holidays. She'd had enough time to spend with her friends and enough money to do the things she'd wanted. Most of her days off had been spent with Chloe. They'd seen the new Star Wars movie, bought the latest denim overall shorts, swum to the pontoon at Long Beach and hung out with friends in the Mall, but, as planned, Chloe had started her nursing degree in the February intake and now their relationship was reduced to texting and the occasional phone call.

Still, she liked working at the café, even with fewer hours. She liked the routine of "make food, serve food – wash-up and repeat". It was comforting to be part of a machine. And she was forming relationships with people she'd never have met otherwise.

Houses and cars flashed past the bus that was too full to stop for passengers. Elma knew she was lucky to find a seat on the bus at all at this time of the morning on a school day. She looked down at her fingernails, the smooth polish shiny and new.

Maybe I should have spent the money on my bus card, not my nails. Dad's not going to be pleased with me if he finds out I'm broke again. It's still two days before I get paid. Lucky I found my phone.

She smiled to herself, remembering the headline she'd posted in her notebook that evening:

Thankful Female Finds Fugitive Phone in Florentine Bag

There is no way I'll ever be able to buy a new phone or a car at the rate I'm going. I haven't saved anything… I thought I'd be able to save in case I started nursing. I've only got two days of work on next week's roster.

Elma let out a sigh,

I'll just have to get up earlier and walk to work. Don't even know if I want to do nursing anymore, not now I've seen the inside of a nursing home … and Chloe will be way ahead of me. I guess that could be a good thing. Seems the less I work the more I have time to want.

Snippets of the morning's conversation with Aunt Livie popped into Elma's mind throughout the day and she was surprised to find her shift at the café finished and a growing urge to visit Gran.

It's only 2pm. A bit early I suppose, but the weather is warm and I could do with a walk. Why am I making excuses to visit her? Because I just need to know if there really is a link between Gran's dislike for me and my compulsive behaviour. Am I really trying to please her? I won't become obsessive about it. I just want to know.

Elma hadn't seen a therapist since leaving school at the end of last year. Her dad had suggested she continue but Elma was working part-time now and enjoying the change from the school routine and perhaps she didn't need that stuff anymore.

I'm aware of my obsessive behaviours and I can manage them myself. After all I'm a 'big girl' now, aren't I?

She had taken to finding Gran's room the long way round via the elevator, going up to the first floor just so she could see the river.

Dad's a builder. I wonder if it was the architecture that attracted him to this place?

Elma sat on one of the cane chairs on the mezzanine floor, contemplating what she might say to Gran about her morning's revelation. The tall fronds of a healthy parlour palm gave shade, creating lazy zig zag patterns on the low table beside her.

'Chamaedorea elegans,' how do you even say that?

She stared at the label on the palm, becoming distracted by her surroundings.

Don't think so – he said he did the research and showed Gran through a dozen places. This is the one she picked.

'Well, she didn't say that last time you visited, did she Dad?' Elma had said to Martin and he'd turned his face away from her. She thought he was going to explode, but when he turned back his lips were pressed tight together and he said nothing. 'Aw, come on, Dad. I'm just joking. I didn't mean to hurt your feelings.'

'She did choose that place!' Martin stood firm, his shoulders tense, his words slow, 'I don't want to argue with you, Elma,' he'd said, turning and walking out the back door of the studio.

Elma could see him sitting at the outside table with his head in his hands.

I wish I hadn't said that. He always tries his best. I know he'd never try to trick Gran into moving into a home. We all know that Aunt Livie was getting too old to look after her any more – she'd already looked after her way too long as it was. Besides, there's no going back. There isn't any room for her at our place and Aunt Livie lives in Victoria now.

She turned her gaze back to the window. timtumili minanya flashed her diamonds above a ribbon of blue silk. Most people knew her as the Derwent River but there was change coming – a welcome change, thought Elma, to recognise the island and its place names with dual naming – the Aboriginal name and the European name. Finally people were accepting that the place had been inhabited before the appearance of the white man with his egocentric claims to ownership.

Perhaps every house between the river and the road could be demolished so we could all enjoy the view.

Elma stared at the path below. A fresh mulch of pine bark rolled out like mottled carpet bordered by painted white rocks, winding a short way from the café through the trees to the river.

Ah, the river, banked by sand, always looks so inviting, so intriguing – always the same but always different.

She became mesmerised by the changing flow of the tide.

Blue if the sky is clear, grey if the clouds are thick, smooth or rough depending on the wind and the tide. Hmm, a bit like Gran, sometimes up and sometimes down. Sometimes with the programme and sometimes confined to bed. I never know if she's going to be nice and play a game of cards with me or in one of her moods where she pretends she doesn't even know who I am.

A lazy fly buzzed past her ear and Elma flipped her hand instinctively at the side of her face.

Oh my goodness, look at the time! Dad will be here soon and I haven't seen Gran yet.

She pulled herself from her thoughts of the river and headed back to the elevator and down to her grandmother's room.

Miriam sat in her chair beside the bed with a colourful crocheted blanket across her lap. Her head bent forward.

Is she awake or dozing?

Elma watched as Miriam's fingers moved, pinching together – pulling at a loose thread of wool on the blanket.

'Hi, Gran,' she spoke softly, undecided as to whether Miriam was fully awake. 'I hope they've washed that blanket since you um …ah …,' Elma paused. 'I mean, since I was here last,' she blustered, knowing the event had been weeks ago.

'How are you today?' she continued, not waiting for a reply, but bending down to kiss her grandmother superficially on the cheek.

'There's a worm in here,' Miriam stated in a flat voice. 'I hate worms,' she said without looking up. 'Martin put them there, disgusting child, got them straight from the garden. Look! Look at all that dirt and muck on the floor … didn't even take his boots off.' She flicked her head up. 'Take them. Take them outside. Get them out of here! Quick girl. Do as you are told.'

Miriam thrust the blanket toward the bewildered Elma.

'Gran, it's just a blanket. What are you on about?' She stepped backwards. The blanket fell between them. Elma stared at Gran and Gran stared back, her sharp eyes pinning Elma to the spot.

'Charlie! Charlie she's here again!' her voice became louder with each summons. 'That ratty girl with the burnt legs, she's here again, tracking blood all over the carpet! Do you hear me Charlie? Come here now! Come and get the wretched thing out of the house!'

'Gran! It's me! Elma,' Elma yelled back, her voice high pitched, each volley of words louder than the previous. 'There's no blood or mud here. It's just me!' She could feel the muscles in her neck tighten as she glared back at her grandmother, shaking her head.

'I said, get her out of here!' Miriam waved her arm towards the confused Elma. 'Get her out now!' she repeated. 'You filthy bitch! Look at you! You should be ashamed!'

'Come now, come now. What's all this noise then?' A staff member came into the room, his voice calm but direct. 'You been upsetting our Miriam, have you?'

If this was humour, Elma was unable to perceive it.

'Of course not!' she defended. 'She swore at me.'

Elma turned her gaze to the nurse, becoming aware that he didn't mean to accuse her. All at once she stopped talking and stood still like a giant fish, upended with its mouth wide open. So much was happening at once. Gran was still yelling, the nurse was trying to make himself heard and the realisation she had created a commotion loud enough for the entire nursing home to hear suddenly became too much.

'I'm so sorry,' she said, trying to make it right. 'I didn't mean to upset her; she just started yelling at me.' Elma's voice was shaking, just like her hands. 'I didn't do anything, really I didn't do anything.'

'It's okay, just be calm, it's okay, really it's all right,' the nurse repeated, continuing in a soothing tone, not needing to hear her defence.

Miriam's voice was calming; her hands were now on her lap, smoothing out the edge of her skirt. She was still muttering to herself, asking everyone to leave at once or she'd call the police.

The nurse touched Elma's elbow and gently led her out into the passage.

'I'm so sorry; I never meant to upset her.' Elma's cheeks felt hot and she knew she was blushing.

I'm so embarrassed.

Another staff member brushed past them and Elma could see out of the corner of her eye the nurse was tending to her grandmother, talking to her as if nothing in the world had happened. Just another sunny day in Nutgrove Nursing Home.

'You're okay now, Love,' the nurse said. 'Go get yourself a cup of tea – you'll be all right now,' he repeated and began walking her down the passage towards the atrium.

'Thanks, I'm okay. I'll be all right now,' Elma responded without feeling and took a step slower than the nurse, causing their walk to be out of sync.

'Your gran will be all right too,' the nurse reassured her, before walking off to attend to other things.

Heck, I don't even know what that was all about! One minute I'm kissing her on the cheek, the next she's screaming at me saying I'm covered in blood. I don't know what Dad will say. I won't tell him – she's nuts – I'm not coming back!

Chapter 7

'I may be late picking you up from Gran's today so don't wait outside. I'll ring when I arrive. I might even sneak in and find you,' Martin smiled down at Elma.

'You're happy, Dad. What's up?' Elma smiled back, stuffing the last corner of toast into her mouth, careful not to let any of the butter drip onto her fingers. Martin's clothes were his normal work overalls and his flannel shirt was nothing new …

But I don't think he usually wears aftershave to work …

'It's Thursday, Dad. You don't shave on a Thursday. Where are you going?'

Martin rubbed his chin, 'How would you know if I shave on a Thursday or not?' His brow furrowed and he gave a look of mock indignation. 'What on earth are you on about?' He didn't wait for an answer but grabbed his keys from the breakfast table and headed out the door, the smell of his aftershave lingering in the air.

Elma screwed up her nose.

'I hope she's worth it Dad. Seriously, I didn't like the last one.'

I would like to say don't waste your time with any of them but I know Aunt Livie would disapprove of me disapproving – "Leave your father alone, Love, you let him make his own decisions — it isn't up to you to decide who he goes out with unless you want him to choose for you ... "

Oh, Aunt Livie, I do miss you.

But I can't be sad today! Today is a day of celebration!

Elma and Chloe had the same day off.

Like first time ever!

And Chloe had progressed through the driving system, upgrading her learner's license to a provisional one.

Oh, what freedom to be able to drive whenever you want without having to beg or wait for lessons. The day was all planned.

First we make a picnic and then we drive up the mountain and see if we can find the hut Dad was talking about.

Elma began clearing the table and placing the dishes in the sink.

And back down in time for my own driving lesson.

She turned the tap on and squirted detergent into the warm water, letting the bubbles cover the plates and cups.

Hopefully Dad won't be late for that. It's not like him to go on a date on a Thursday afternoon. That's my day! And I'm already sharing it with Gran; I certainly don't need someone else getting in the way of me and my licence.

She rummaged through the fridge seeking supplies for the picnic when Chloe whooshed unannounced into the kitchen.

'Woo-hoo! This is it! No work, no study, no time limit and no ...'

'There is a time limit, Chloe. I need to be at the nursing home by 3pm,' Elma interrupted, pulling her head out of the fridge – boiled eggs in one hand and a pot of hummus in the other.

'Well of course I know that! But we're free until three.'

Chloe shrugged her shoulders, took the food from Elma and placed it on the table before grasping Elma's hands and swinging her around in a circle.

'Please, there's still carrots and celery to cut up,' Elma protested, escaping the impromptu dance. 'Cheese, that's a must. Do I leave the eggs whole or put them in a sandwich?'

'Wow, too many questions. This is my day off. All my assignments are up to date and ...' Chloe's voice became loud and sing-song, 'I have my Peeeees! So come on, let's go!'

Chloe, still singing, hustled Elma out the door and before long she'd driven up the winding mountain and was backing her mother's car into the carpark just below Big Bend on the north-east side of kunanyi.

Elma took a few deep breaths.

'I don't think I'll ever be able to do that,' she said, removing her sunglasses and rubbing her eyes. Chloe looked at her, a frown on her face.

'Oh, you know, drive up that road like you just did.'

Chloe laughed, 'Oh Elma, you just have to keep your eyes open when you drive. I find it hard to believe your Dad lets you drive with them shut.'

Elma pulled a face. Her eyes had been shut most of the trip.

It's just too scary; the cliff always feels so close, how am I ever going to do it?

She climbed out of the car feeling intimidated by **The Confident Chloe**. Today's headlines formed in her mind, **From Freedom to Fear**, **Pathetic Picnicker Paralysed by Panic**.

Probably too self-deprecating to put into my notebook but it is how I feel – Chloe makes everything seem so easy. School, nursing, driving she just does it all so effortlessly.

Elma wiggled into her backpack and retied her loose boot-lace.

'Wow, look at you, Miss Fancy Boots. Where'd you get them from?'

Elma squirmed and looked down at her feet – she wore a pair of leather Colorado boots, freshly polished with Kiwi Dark Tan. She scraped her foot on the dry gravel. Her feet were well protected. The boots felt firm and strong around her ankles.

'Um ...' she said, biting her lip, not wanting to tell Chloe, *just yet,* where they'd come from.

'Ahh ... Dad found them in the shed.'

Chloe raised her brow.

'Sure, Elma, you know friends are s'posed to share their secrets,' she laughed and shook her head. 'Come on, this is our day off, let's go find this mysterious hut.'

She flung her bag over her shoulder and headed across the road towards the fire trail.

'So, where to from here, boss? What were your dad's instructions?'

Chloe stood on a large boulder overlooking the rough gravel path. Elma looked to the west

'He said two things.'

She tried to conceal a smile.

'Firstly, never laugh at your own jokes and secondly, this is him not me –' she hesitated, '– if I tell you, I'll have to shoot you.'

'Wow,' Chloe stopped moving, one leg sticking out like a crane, 'that's not like him to make a joke,' she laughed and jumped pirate fashion, down from the rock.

'Got a new girlfriend has he?'

Elma's face changed. She glared at Chloe.

Chloe ignored her.

'Come on! We haven't got all day – show us ya map.'

'It's not really a map, well not a proper one.'

Elma pulled a scrap of neatly folded paper from her pocket and spread it out on the palm of her hand.

'This is Big Bend, this is the fire trail, and there is supposed to be a cairn about here.'

Elma looked up and pointed to a wobbly fence made from star pickets and rusted chicken wire. 'And then you head this way and downwards and around here, or up over this way,' she moved the map around as she pointed the features out.

'Apparently, we should find it hidden beside a cliff face.'

Elma looked at Chloe who nodded her head slowly as if understanding.

'I know I don't sound very convincing, I wouldn't go with me either but …'

'Come on, don't take all day, I'm ready. Is there a coffee machine at this love nest of yours?'

'Chloe, stop it. It's just a hut.'

Elma caught her foot on a rock and stumbled forward, momentarily losing her balance.

'Of course it's more than a hut, Elma.'

Elma caught Chloe's arm to steady herself.

'You may have been conceived up here …'

'Stop it, Chloe,' Elma frowned. She looked up and spoke directly to the back of Chloe's head, 'I don't like you saying things like that.'

'I'm sorry, it was just a joke.'

Chloe threw the comment back over her shoulder.

'You really are touchy about some things, aren't you? Hey look is this the cairn thingy you were talking about?'

Elma looked down at a small stack of flat rocks in a neat pile beside the fire trail. Each one slightly smaller than the one beneath it, creating a pyramid shape.

'That really wasn't very far at all. Hey there's another one just up there.'

Both girls turned their heads to the second pile of rocks.

'Oh that's confusing, which one do we pick?'

'They all just look like possum tracks,' Chloe said venturing off the main fire trail.

'Come on, let's go. We can't get lost just standing here.'

Elma followed this way and that, weaving though the labyrinth of rock and low vegetation, heading in a general northerly direction towards some larger boulders blocking the view of the north-west side of the mountain.

'I think we should be down there, not up here,' Chloe said, loosening the straps on her pack.

'Let's just stop and eat. I'm hot as – there are too many little tracks.'

Elma agreed, it was hard to know what to do. Sweat was beginning to make its way through her clothing, the straps of her pack rubbed against her bare neck and her shirt stuck to her like cling wrap. 'I think we've followed almost every path there is.'

It's certainly been longer than ten minutes.

'Okay, I'm up for food,' Chloe repeated, removing her hat to wipe the sweat and sunscreen from under her fringe. She scrambled up a ledge between two boulders and grabbed a branch, hoisting herself the remaining metre to the top of a rocky outcrop. Elma dragged her backpack along the ground to the base of the rock and called out.

'What's it like up there? I hope there's some shade.'

'It's amazing. Throw your bag to me and I'll help you up,' Chloe called down.

Within minutes both girls were sitting on the warm rock, gazing out over the Derwent Valley.

'We may have taken every wrong turn to get to this spot but it's perfect for a picnic.'

'Absolutely!' agreed Elma popping the sanitiser back in her bag and bringing out the picnic food.

Grazes on my knees and scratches on my legs but I'm all right ... hot, but all right.

Chloe took a selfie, the ominous 'Candle' on the summit of kunanyi stood, framed, in the distance behind them marking an easy reference point for their return to the car. She turned her face towards the tower, 'Crazy! We've climbed up and down boulders and around a million scrubby bushes and yet it really looks like we are still only ten minutes from the carpark.'

She touched the phone out of selfie mode and took a couple of photos of the view in front of them. 'I'll forward them in Messenger if you want. The valley looks gorgeous.'

'Thanks,' said Elma, 'you know me, I'm out of credit – again ...' she added with a tilt of her head and a set smile on her face.

'Why don't you just ask your dad for more money?'

Chloe lifted the lid on the hummus and stirred it with a piece of capsicum, 'This is great.'

'Because I can't. He doesn't have any,' Elma said.

'Well, we know that. The question I want to ask is why? Does he drink it?'

Chloe looked at Elma with a huge smile, 'Okay, I know he doesn't drink ... well, not that much anyway. What about gambling?'

'What about it?'

Elma thought her sharp response would be enough to end the conversation but Chloe continued.

'Well, does he gamble, you know like pokies or horses or the casino or something?'

She stuffed a piece of celery into her mouth. A small blob of hummus fell from it onto her bare leg. She swiped at it with her finger, picking it up and watching Elma's horrified expression as she licked the hummus and wiped her hand clean on the hem of her denim shorts. Elma breathed out slowly,

Don't do it, don't! I am not going to react, I am not going to react ...

She deliberately returned her focus to the view.

'I think I would know if he did, wouldn't I?'

Chloe shrugged her shoulders, 'I don't know. I thought all builders were well-off. What's your theory on where the money goes?'

'I don't know, I don't have one.'

Actually I think I do know now – but I just can't say ... yet.

Elma watched the hilly horizon, small clouds smudged onto a canvas of heat-haze blue,

It's so pleasant up here and quiet. I'm as high as the clouds – I'd like to come back here – there is something special about this place ... maybe it's the whole mountain.

'Maybe he's got a secret debt somewhere or he's one of those people who just love collecting money. I've heard about collectors like that.'

Elma ignored the speculation.

It's none of her business.

Chloe looked at her watch, tiny specks of sweat glistening on her arm.

'It's almost time to head back.'

A fly buzzed around Elma's mashed egg sandwich. She flicked at it with her hat.

'Thanks though for bringing me up here. Sorry we didn't find the hut,' Elma said.

'Do you think your dad was pulling your leg?' Chloe asked.

'No, he was serious and besides he showed me some pictures online. He just didn't give the right directions, I guess.'

Elma wasn't bothered.

Maybe I'd rather find the hut by myself anyway.

'Scout Hut he called it. He said there were other secret huts up here too, as well as the ruins, you know of the huts burnt down in the big fire of '67.'

She stared out over the valley watching cloud shadows change shape as they passed over the landscape.

'Aunt Livie said there was a heap of ruins on the eastern side, where the trees grew tall. She said, in the old days people would stay up here all the time and camp out in them like holiday shacks.'

Chloe listened contentedly, enjoying the view and her first day out with her P's.

'Sarah and Josh took me to some ruins a long time ago, when they were over here staying for the summer holidays. I think I was about ten. I wouldn't have a clue where to go now though. Their friend, I don't remember his name, knew a lot of things about the mountain. I think I'd remember that place because it looked like just an old chimney, but inside there was a spade or axe or something hanging there. And oddly, well I thought it was odd, there was a rhododendron bush growing next to it.'

'Why is that odd?' Chloe had become intrigued by the story.

'Because rhododendrons aren't even native to Australia, let alone Tasmania.'

'Oh,' said Chloe, 'I don't think I'd know what a ro-de-o-dren is.'

'Really?' Elma asked, a little surprised.

I thought you knew everything.

'Remember Aunt Livie's garden? Out the back by the man ferns there was, well still is, a tree that is covered in bright pink flowers, not all year but from springtime on 'til, I don't know.'

She gave a shrug.

'Well, it was like that, only bright red, like really bright red.'

She thought for a moment, 'It was flowering ... just seemed weird to have bright red flowers suddenly appearing in the middle of the bush.'

Elma repacked her bag as she talked.

I think I'd like to find that chimney and tree again. Only I remember the walk was really hot and really long – I was only ten ...

She took a last look westward at the hazy hills, soaking in the pleasant feeling of holidays.

'Come on, let's get going. "The Gran" will be waiting for me.

Although I bet she isn't – she doesn't even know what day of the week it is, let alone care if I turn up or not.

Chapter 8

I know for certain I couldn't drive up kunanyi, but I will be able to someday. I just need to get more driving time on the easy roads first. I'm getting better in traffic ... Dad hasn't shouted at me for weeks. And weirdly, I'm okay with Gran and her silly games, although I wish she'd think a bit before throwing a tantrum because it's ... well, it's just embarrassing.

By now Elma was used to Miriam calling her by other people's names,

I think she does it just to tick me off.

The most common name was the mysterious Scarlet, but not always. Sometimes Gran would lean over while they played cards and call her Livinda. She'd share what Elma believed were secrets.

I don't know why she does this. I'm obviously me! It's not a fun game at all.

Even so, after the event, Elma would sit in the mezzanine floor and write down what she could remember of their one-sided conversations, trying to work out what they meant.

Does she really think I'm Scarlet or Aunt Livie? And what about the girl who bleeds all over the carpet?

Elma placed a new unopened pack of cards on the low table by her knee.

We didn't get to play today – she was too confused … or was that me? I was only suggesting Snap – it's not that hard. Last week she played two-handed Patience with no problems at all. She's just so unpredictable.

Martin was probably going to be late. She looked at her watch – 3:35pm.

Hmm, I didn't spend much time with Gran at all. There's no point when she's in that mood.

Elma stared down through the glass wall of the mezzanine floor, watching the movement below. Residents were coming and going through the café. A couple of card games were in action. Soft bursts of laughter rose up to where she sat. On the other side of the landing she could see more people, paisley-clad staff and fashionless residents going about their business. The warm commotion of a hairdryer became louder and softer as the salon door opened and closed. An elderly man wearing a brushed cotton checked shirt and braces, waited in an armchair outside the physiotherapy rooms, chatting with a younger, animated carer, the light catching, now and then, on his glossy silver hearing aids. Bits of conversations from the main desk and various other places drifted up and around the atrium. Elma closed her eyes – a TV turned up too loud, the clinks of china cups – these had all become normal bits and pieces of Elma's Thursday afternoons.

Sounds like a shopping centre.

Elma opened her eyes.

Some of them shuffle, some of them walk hunched over like candy canes at Christmas and some even look normal, if normal is a word I can use, probably not politically correct but only my thoughts anyway, it's not like I'm going to speak with any of them. Well, apart from the ones who accost me if I'm not quick enough to dodge them.

Elma had counted the steps between the end of the hallway on the ground floor and her grandmother's room and avoided eye contact with staff and residents alike by looking down at the floral patterns on the carpet. One normal pace equated to three golden roses and an extra-large step to four. She wondered how far a running step would take her. Gran's room was thirty-three steps or ninety-nine roses. Either way, by looking down and concentrating, most of the nursing home occupants would disappear.

Elma stood, picking up the pack of cards as she did so and turned towards the lift, still deciding whether to put them in her bag or return them to the drawer in her grandmother's room. The plastic cover felt sticky in her hand.

If I take them away they'll be in my bag for a week, but I don't feel like going back to her just now.

'I can wait for you,' came a man's voice from inside the elevator. Elma looked up to see an arm protruding out of the lift doorway.

'Don't rush,' the voice continued, 'there's no need to hurry.'

She stopped walking and fixed her eyes on the wrinkled hand sticking out of a loose white coat. She followed the arm up to its owner, an elderly doctor.

I know him. He was here, in the café, on that first day when Dad dragged me here to show Gran around her new forever home.

Tour d'Nutgroan was the headline that day.

Elma didn't care to talk with him and certainly didn't want to share the lift but she also didn't want to appear rude.

'Thank you, but I was going to take the stairs.'

'Oh well, you can always change your mind. The stairs are definitely the healthy option. Do it while you can,' he said with a chuckle.

She paused for a moment and looked at the kindly old face, his bespectacled eyes and wrinkled nose, his white fluffy hair and beard. There was something intriguing about him, maybe the charming smile or the fact that he didn't insist. Whatever the attraction this elderly gentleman possessed, it disarmed Elma's habitual wariness.

'Okay, I will,' she replied changing her mind,

What could be the danger in sharing a glass elevator with Father Christmas?

'Visiting your nan, I guess?' he said. 'Is it Nan or Gran?'

'It's Gran,' replied Elma.

The doctor pressed the G on the control panel and the doors closed.

'Ah, and if I remember rightly, you are the fair Elma, only granddaughter of the aged one.'

He looks as old as half the people in here and yet he remembers my name just from one brief meeting. I don't even know his.

Elma looked at him quizzically.

'Doctor Gordon,' he said, as if reading her mind. He held out his hand and Elma obligingly shook it.

'I'm just about to stop for a cup of tea, young lady, and would be most delighted if you would care to join me.'

Elma wiped her hand on the back of her jeans. The lift stopped, its doors opening on both sides, with the eastern exit facing the river. Elma could just see it shimmering between the pine trees through the large window at the end of the day room, or the café as it was called. A dozen or so tables were covered with bright yellow gingham cloths and each possessed a posy of flowers, a stainless steel sugar bowl and a saltshaker. A bench seat ran the length of the low window and the internal wall, the one with the elevator, had a shelf full of books and games.

Despite her feelings about the nursing home Elma liked this room, its openness and natural light. She could get onto the outside deck by tapping a code into the security panel by the door, and sit outside to read or drink tea under the protection of the pine trees. Sometimes, if the tide was right, she would follow the shoreline from the café to the nursing home and enter via the back door.

I wonder why he eats here instead of the staff area on the other side of the kitchen?

She caught herself staring at the elderly doctor and anxiety rose in her. She could feel her cheeks getting hot. Her words tumbled out faster than she intended.

'I'm sorry, I don't think I have time. I have to go. I've got to meet someone,' she babbled.

'Oh well, I'll dine alone.'

Why am I such a sook? I can do this. Stop being such a wuss!

Dad's not picking me up 'til after four and it's only three thirty something now. I want to know why he knows who I am and Gran doesn't.

'Okay, no,' her voice wavered.

She made a show of checking the time on her phone.

'I have got a bit of time.'

'Well, what will it be young lady?' said the doctor, his face lighting up as if it were an honour to spend his time with her.

'Tea,' she replied, falling into step beside him as they walked into the café.

The doctor headed to the counter while Elma looked about for a place to sit.

God no, not there, not on a crocheted blanket, I'm never going to do that again ever. Looks like they've had a gambling event in here today.

She knew the home had activities spread out over the day. It was one of the reasons Livie had liked the place. Packs of cards and a few crib boards were still out on some of the tables and others were cluttered with food debris and crockery. The card game she could hear from upstairs was still going strong.

I'd get the sack if I let this amount of work build up at my café.

Elma pushed a few chairs tidily under their tables as she passed them.

She found a clean table near the window by the beach entrance and stared towards the path she and Gran had escaped down a few weeks earlier. It had been a magic day.

Gran was really happy and even called me Elma, not that I care. It was nice to be outside in the sand. I can't remember seeing Gran smile like she did – a real smile not her usual 'I'm trying to make you happy' smile that she saves for her moments of manipulation. The sweet smile she gives when you know she's going to say something you don't want to hear. Like you should have arrived earlier or bought a better brand or, well, it's okay – but barely. Hmm, that smile that makes me want to kick her in the shins but I can't 'cause she's old and it would be wrong and Dad would kill me ...

Elma's thoughts were broken by the doctor's chair scraping the floor as he pulled it out to sit down. Her gaze turned from the path to face him.

'It's a lovely place just here by the river. Tasmanians are very lucky to have everything so close,' he said.

Elma thought of the beach and kunanyi and how all the streets were squeezed between the two.

Hmm, another one of Mum's sayings "squeeze the houses between the mountains and rivers and both the rich and the poor get a view."

She thought the saying probably came from an old nursery story somewhere but she'd never discovered which one. The closest she felt she'd got was "The Five Hundred Hats of Bartholomew Cubbins," but somehow it didn't quite fit the saying.

I wonder if Mum is looking up at the palace or down at the village, or if she's even still alive?

She'd long since decided that her mother wasn't living her life in the lap of luxury on the proverbial exotic island depicted in her memory. She didn't know when her memory had moved on from that unrealistic, simplistic thought. She didn't know why she remembered her mother's sayings but why she couldn't remember her mother ever tucking her into bed or brushing her hair.

'I'm sorry, I've forgotten your name again,' she said, swapping the pack of cards from one hand to the other.

What am I meant to say? Oh, awkward.

She looked down at the table. The lid of the sugar bowl was open and she stared at the spoon sticking out like a spade in a sand-pit. Sugar crystals encased the shaft.

Gross! The spoon's been put back wet.

She screwed up her nose and looked back at the doctor;

No sugar for me, that's for sure.

'Dr Gordon. Dr Geoffrey Gordon. But you can call me Geoff or Dr G if you like. How is your gran today Elma? Do you think she's happy here?'

Gran wouldn't be happy anywhere, but I bet he already knows that.

What a dumb question to ask.

He's just making conversation.

Who could be happy in here?

'I don't know. I guess she is. But there's times when, like, she doesn't even know me. But I feel like she does and she's just having me on or something. I know, she's old and old people are supposed to be forgetful …

Oh no, what am I saying? I'm sitting in front of an old man telling him he's supposed to be stupid.

'I'm sorry, Dr G, I didn't mean to say that. My dad says I need a rewind button, you know like a backspace on a key board, where you just go tap, tap, tap and all the dumb things you say get deleted.'

Elma's pointer finger tap, tap, tapped on an invisible key-board in front of her.

The warm smile never left the doctor's face and Elma took a deep breath in. She could feel her shoulders relax a little as she began to exhale

Wow, I didn't even realise I was so uptight.

The tea arrived on a tray, two plain white cups, a small jug of milk and a stainless steel teapot. Dr Gordon remained quiet and began pouring the tea.

He doesn't seem offended. That's surprising – I would have been. Maybe he's deaf and didn't hear me … or he's seething underneath that never-ending smile …

She studied his expression as he placed a cup in front of her. Elma watched the thin wisps of steam rise from the cup. Dr Gordon turned the handle of the milk jug towards her, gesturing for her to use it first.

'Thanks Dr G, I just don't know why she sometimes thinks I'm Livie? It's just that Livie's really old and I'm not. I mean, Aunt Livie is old like Gran.'

She let out another sigh.

'Well, she wasn't always, was she?' Dr Gordon spoke at last.

'What do you mean she wasn't always?'

Of course she wasn't always. We all grow up, don't we?

'What did Livie look like at your age?'

Elma thought for a moment.

*What **did** Livie look like at my age?*

She thought of the assorted photos that had been on the mantelpiece at Livie's place before she moved to Ballan. The pictures stood in their wooden or silver frames, all dusted in case the "Queen dropped in" and, just like Livie, organised with love.

Elma's favourite was the one with herself and her dad embracing in a "squeeze the laughter out of a pig" hug.

I must have been about seven – I was so small he had to pick me up for a proper cuddle – I always flicked both my legs up behind me – I was lucky that day I didn't kick Gran's teeth out, although I thought I had, the way she carried on. Aunt Livie had taken that photo. Oh Aunt Livie, I miss you.

The photo next to it was of Aunt Livie and Great Uncle David on their wedding day. It was black and white and showed them cutting the cake. Hmm … that's the photo that took centre stage on the mantle for sure. The frame was made out of Huon pine and Great Uncle Dave had made it for his Livie before they were even married and had carved patterns of leaves into it. He was very clever with the carving. Aunt Livie told me the leaves were birch leaves, heart-shaped birch leaves – the symbol of love. He sounded so romantic; I think I would have liked him … if Aunt Livie liked him I'm sure I would have.

There were a couple of family photos with Livie's mum and dad.

That's my great grandparents. I never met them.

And some of herself and her Dad. Elma suspected Aunt Livie had removed the wedding ones of Liz and Martin. There were some of Aunt Livie's own child. Baby ones and a graduation one.

Cathy definitely looked like her mum. Fine features, curly hair and deep set eyes. Blue eyes. I guess maybe we all have blue eyes.

'I don't really know what Livie looked like at my age, I can't remember any photos. I know we both have blue eyes but that's about it really. My hair's dark brown, and I've never had any curls … ever. Aunt Livie has always had curls,' she added, just to be clear.

'Well, the blue eyes might be enough to remind Miriam of a younger Livie,' the doctor mused.

Elma placed the cards on the table and wiggled forward in her seat, placing both her hands around the cup of tea.

That wasn't so helpful.

And what about Scarlet? Should I mention her?

'So, why does she play games with me and call me Scarlet one minute and Livie the next? And, and,' Elma's voice became louder, 'and why is she sometimes normal and sometimes telling me my dad went to Hutchins when we all know he went to the public school in Rose Bay and thinking she still lives with Charlie, who left her years ago – probably because he couldn't cope with her tantrums?'

'Can I have these a minute?' Dr Gordon asked, reaching over to Elma's pack of cards.

'Yeah, sure you can.'

Why does he want my cards?

I only just bought them yesterday. I won't play with the ones they have here – they're too grubby that's for sure.

Elma watched as the doctor took the Red Slipper cards out of the packet, testing the weight of them in his hands. He slid the side of his thumbnail along the side of the inner plastic cover and cast it onto the table.

'I see they're all in order,' he said, flicking through them.

'Yes, they're new and Gran wasn't in the mood to play today.'

Of course they're in order – you just opened them!

It confused Elma that Miriam knew how to play so many card games. She'd never seen her do so in all the 17 years of her own life.

Life before me – aye Gran, what things did you and your sister get up to? And why remember how to play Patience and the like and not remember what you had for lunch or when I last visited?

She placed her empty cup on the table and straightened out the kink in the tablecloth. It's not a good place to play cards anyway. She looked around and noticed the tables with the cards and crib boards on them had their table clothes removed or pushed to the side.

'Well, let's say this pack of cards represents your Gran's memories,' he paused, waiting for Elma's full attention.

There's a lot of stuff in here, childhood memories, maybe her first day of school, her little friends, going shopping with her mother, meeting boys, marrying, babies, etc. etc.'

Can't imagine Gran meeting boys, but I know what he means.

She nodded her head.

'Lots and lots of memories,' he repeated before he began to shuffle the cards, his hands moving very slowly, letting the cards change position with exaggerated movements, allowing two or three to fall onto the table in front of him.

'Do you see here,' he said slowing his voice to keep Elma's attention.

'If these cards were your grans memories they are a little bit out of order now and,' he said looking at the loose ones on the table, 'there are a few missing all together. Elma I don't think your Gran is playing mind games with you. I think she's probably doing her best.'

'Well maybe, but …' Elma looked at the clock on the wall aware that Martin could ring at any time now.

'… that doesn't account for things she's saying that aren't true though, does it?'

The doctor turned to the table next to them, reached over and picked a dozen or so cards from the pack of blue cards sitting on it. Elma could feel the muscles in her neck tighten, her hands beginning to clench.

Don't do it, don't put those grubby things in my pack please, please don't. What's wrong with you!

The edges of the cards were split and the slipper finish had long since worn off. Elma cringed as the doctor peeled two cards apart and wiped the sticky substance from each of them with a serviette.

'Now, these cards,' he said, 'apart from the colour, are very similar to your own pack, would you agree?'

Elma nodded her head in agreement, but her thoughts were very different.

They are not anything like mine. They're dirty and damaged and probably covered in an incurable disease for all I know.

'Now,' he paused again. 'When you were younger did you ever imagine what life might be like as an adult? Did you ever think about being a nurse or a teacher, or an astronaut?'

Elma nodded her head.

'Did you play games and pretend you were shopping or cooking or even imagine your wedding day?'

'Well, I don't know about the wedding bit, but I guess my friends and I were always playing imaginary games. That's normal, isn't it?'

Elma looked at the doctor, hoping for a yes.

'Of course it is, of course. It's very normal.'

He started reshuffling the red cards and adding the blue ones to them. If he saw the look of horror on Elma's face he ignored it.

'The problem for your gran is that not only are the memories out of order, the real memories are mixed up with the pretend memories and she can't tell the difference. We can.'

He turned the cards over so the backs could be seen. Most of them were red but the dozen or so blue ones stood out.

'Well, we can if we know the person's history. But people like your gran can't always tell us.'

He let some more cards fall to the table.

'And I'm sorry to say it's not going to get any better. Your gran will have good days and not so good days but her condition won't improve. It is up to us here in the home and you, her family, to make life the best we can for her.'

'Thanks Dr G.'

Elma stood up. She could feel her phone vibrating in her pocket.

'My dad will be waiting.'

That's so much to process at once, I'll need time to think it through. He made it seem so simple, like she can't help herself. She's sick. Like, weird, 'cause I knew she was sick, I think, I just didn't think what that meant, I guess.

She looked at her phone. There was a missed call from her father.

'It's a pleasure talking to you, Elma. Please, get the staff to find me if you have any more questions. I'd love to help if I can.'

Dr Gordon stood to say his goodbyes and sat again as Elma left.

Elma glanced back.

I wonder if he ever stops smiling?

'Just a minute, Elma, you've forgotten your cards.'

The doctor began sorting them into their correct piles.

'Oh, no, no please, I don't need them anymore. You can have those ones.'

Elma reached into her bag, rummaging for the hand sanitiser as she hurried for the front door.

Chapter 9

'Dad, you just can't do that!'

Elma gripped her phone tightly. She could hear her father on the other end and she could also hear the muffled voice of a woman in the background.

He's not alone.

She stood beside the glass door of the nursing home entrance.

There's someone in the ute with him.

'You can't make an arrangement to take me driving and have someone else in the car!'

'Well, I can't see why not. We can drive up Mt Nelson and drop her home on the way.'

Elma thought about the narrow winding road up Mt Nelson. It wasn't much different than the road to kunanyi.

As if I'm going to drive up there, with or without some strange woman sitting beside me!

'I'm not coming out there while she's still in the car!'

'She has a name. Her name is Paula. You'll like her when you meet her.'

Martin's words became muffled; *he's discussing me with her, I just know it!*

Was there a touch of desperation in his voice?

No! We had an agreement and he can't change the rules without telling me.

'I'm not going to meet her, Dad! Not while we're meant to be driving! We have an agreement.'

'Oh, Elma that was ages ago. You're nearly 18 now. Surely you can't hold on to that anymore.'

What do you mean, anymore?

'An agreement can't change just because it suits you – we made a deal.'

Elma breathed in and bit her lip attempting to prevent the air escaping. Her arms dropped down by her sides.

I can't believe it – our "No Surprise Thursday" ruined again. He really doesn't get it. Things can't change without talking to me first.

She stepped back away from the 'escape door', looked at her phone, and swiped at the "end call" button.

I hope he doesn't wait long for me because I'm not going out while she's still there.

Her phone rang. She pressed Decline, then held the side switch down until the Turn Off screen appeared.

An agreement is an agreement.

I can't believe it.

Her hands began to shake – not much – just a little, but enough for her to notice.

I need more air.

She stuffed her phone in the back pocket of her jeans and rubbed her hands together. She took another glance through the window. Her father's ute was parked on the other side of the road.

What is wrong with him?

With her eyes down, she turned, headed for the side passage and counted the carpet roses, turning left and right until she stood at her grandmother's open door. She didn't enter the room straight away but leaned against the broad wooden door frame, steadying herself as she caught her breath,

At least if I faint I'll land on the carpet.

Her eyes were stinging, tears trying their hardest to break through the "no cry barrier". She rubbed at her forehead.

I just don't need a headache right now.

Gran was still there, still sitting in the same day chair where she'd left her earlier in the afternoon,

Still with that damned crocheted blanket on her lap.

'Hi Gran. How are you today?

Remember me? I was here about an hour ago.

Gran looked up but didn't speak.

'I said hello,' Elma repeated taking a step into the room.

'No, you didn't.'

'What? I did.'

'No, you did not. You said Hi.'

What the heck does it matter?

'Now shut the door, quickly,' the old woman added.

'Before they find you here!'

'What? Who?' Elma protested, but Miriam cut her short.

'Quick! I said quick.'

Not sure I can play your games, Gran. I've had enough crap for one day. I just want to sit somewhere in the sunshine and fall asleep for a week or so ... or more.

But she obeyed, retracing her steps to the door, quietly pushing it and feeling the click of the latch.

'What do you want, Gran?' she said turning back towards

Miriam, who was now standing by the window peeping through the curtain as if there were something to look at beneath the trees.

'Can you see them?' she paused, but not long enough for a response.

'Don't they look so happy? The little one, that's Livie, she's my sister.'

Elma could hear some pride in her gran's voice as she told her all about her shy little sister who was such a great playmate and the best keeper of secrets in the whole of Hobart.

Elma didn't look out the window. She watched the lace curtain quivering in Gran's hand, but she didn't look out. She knew there was no one there, just the wooden paling fence with some wattle bushes in front of it and a bit of a flower garden in front of them. But instead of challenging her, she thought about what Dr Gordon had said regarding Gran's memory being shuffled like a pack of cards –

– or something like that,

Gran's probably doing the best she can.

Dad's probably doing his best too, but it doesn't matter because the rules are the rules, and the rules were NO SURPRISES. If you are going to bring someone home you have to check with me first.

Elma tried hard not to remember why they'd made the agreement. But the problem with trying not to remember something is you can't stop thinking about it.

Penny was her name and I didn't like her from the first time I unfortunately set eyes on her stupid naked body. She could have at least put a towel on. Like I needed to see her unexpectedly first thing in the morning before school. Heck, I think I was only eleven.

I miss you Livie, where are you now? Not helping with the rules are you? I need you and I'm stuck here with Dad and Gran acting like idiots.

The tears spilled out – quick and copious. Elma slumped into the spare chair unaware of her red face, her hair tie slipping from its hold or her need to wash her hands after touching the doorknob.

It shouldn't be like this; I don't know what to do.

She hadn't wanted to shut the door for Miriam but now she was grateful. Gran had sat back down and pulled the blanket back over her knees,

When did she do that? Is she singing?

It was a strange noise that caught Elma's attention and distracted her from herself.

Elma held her sobs in and sat as still as she could trying hard to catch what her gran was saying. The dizziness had gone.

It isn't a tune I know. I'm not sure if it's a tune at all.

Elma had never heard any melodies or songs from her gran ever.

Maybe it's a nursery rhyme.

'Care-at-all … care-at-all-it's-not-enough-don't-care-at-all-can't-pick-yourself-up-to-care-at-all-dust-yourself-off … fall-at-all-they-don't-care-at-all.'

She's crying. Oh my goodness. She's crying! I've never seen her cry, never thought of her as having feelings before. Well, not soft feelings anyway, only angry ones.

Gran the Grump, Grieves

That wasn't a headline Elma had ever considered.

I had only thought about her harshly because that's the way she treats me – or I let her treat me.

For a spilt second Elma thought about comforting the old lady.

What am I doing here? I need to go.

There was a knock on the door and without an invitation it opened, drawing in the smell of hot food.

Oh, hello there. Elma, isn't it? Do you want to help me get your gran down to the dining room?' the paisley-clad aide asked in a kindly voice. They'd met before. Kari was written on her name tag. Elma had liked her simply because she didn't call her Love or Darling like some of the other staff did.

'I suppose so,' Elma responded, not knowing whether she should call the woman by her name.

Will I have to walk all the way home?

I guess I'll catch a bus.

I've never been here at tea time before.

'Well Miriam, what will it be today?' Kari asked.

'The walking frame or the wheelchair?'

She spoke clearly to Miriam who still seemed to be caught in her chant.

'I can walk! You know I can walk!' Miriam snapped at the woman and leaned forward to stand.

'Easy does it, Miriam,' Kari said encouragingly, reaching for the walking frame and placing it in front of the unsteady Miriam.

'Actually, no I won't,' said Elma, darting past the nurse and out into the passage.

'I've got a bus to catch.'

And I really don't feel like being around people and questions and mashed-up food.

The presumption that old people ate mashed food must have come from somewhere. True or not, Elma wasn't hanging around to find out.

It was twilight by the time Elma got off the bus and headed the short distance to their South Hobart studio. She fished around in her bag for her key.

I'm surprised Dad isn't home yet. It's nearly dark.

She entered the dining area and placed her bag on the table and took her phone from her pocket forgetting that she had turned it off earlier.

Heck, I hope he's not too angry at me – I didn't mean to upset him. It seems a bit silly now but he should have asked. He just should have!

Three missed calls and a couple of text messages. Martin knew not to leave a voice message on Elma's phone, as Elma never seemed to respond to them.

Be home late. Get your own tea. There are plenty of eggs and such in the fridge. Sorry about this afternoon. Talk about it tomorrow. Love Dad xx.

What the ... he never talks like that. He didn't write that – she must have made him stay out. Cow! I hate her, whoever she is, Paula Pus-head, for all I care.

Elma threw herself onto her bed.

What more could go wrong? Livie doesn't care about me. Dad doesn't care about me. No one cares about me. I may as well not exist!

The landline rang from just outside Elma's room. She looked at her phone. It was 9 pm.

I must have fallen asleep

She groaned a little and heaved herself up, grabbing the handset before its final ring.

Aunt Livie is the only one who ever rings on that line. Oh, and all the sales people. Should have checked the caller ID.

But it was Livie and it was obvious she'd been talking with Martin.

'I'm so sorry, Darling; to hear you two had a blue. You should think about your words before you say them, Elma. And,' Aunt Livie added, 'I don't think your dad was any too happy about you hanging up on him either.'

Elma was stunned.

'I thought of all people you'd be on my side.'

'Oh, I'm not taking sides, Elma Darling. I'm just saying the way you behaved towards your dad was rude. What do you think his new lady friend will think of that?'

I don't know. Why would I care what she thinks?

Just when I needed reassurance and love I get a blasted telling off.

'Sorry, Aunt. I, um, don't know what to say. I thought you would understand – but you don't.'

The tears were close again and Elma fought hard to keep them back.

Stop it! You are not going to let her know how upset you are.

'I do understand, Elma. Your dad did wrong too and I hope you work it out sooner than later. In the meantime I wondered if you might like to come visit me in my new flat.'

What? I can't! I've got a job to do.

Elma wanted to say yes but instead she said nothing – just looked at the calendar on the wall above the phone, aimlessly studying the dates.

'Did you hear me, Elma? Are you still there?'

'Yes I am here, Aunt Livie. I just don't know what to say.'

'Well, that's it then. I'll get your dad to book the tickets ASAP.'

'Do we have to talk to Dad about this? Can't you just book the tickets?'

'Oh, Elma you know I can't. Your dad can do it all on his computer. You just let me know the date and the price and we'll go from there.'

'Well, I s'pose so,'

But I really don't want to talk to him right now.

Elma stared at the calendar.

I've only got a couple of shifts a week at the moment so I guess it will be all right at work. I don't have much money in the bank, but I do have more than last week.

Chapter Ten

'One-week-to-go, one-week-to-go, hi, ho-the-derry-o, one-week-to-go.'

'Calm down Elma, let's have a bit of quiet. I think the whole neighbourhood knows by now you're off to Victoria,' Martin had told her that morning while she was singing around the house.

It was possibly true – I even told PJ at the café.

'That's great news Elma,' PJ had said. 'You deserve it – a chance to catch up with family.'

Elma had beamed and handed PJ her change.

'I'll be gone a whole week.'

'I hope we'll have time to chat before you leave.'

'Sure,' Elma said.

She probably wants to talk about me going back to Uni.

She knew Damien and PJ had her best interests at heart but it was her choice whether to study or not.

Not theirs.

Elma was thinking of her next list.

Elma's Acquiescent Approach to Avoiding Annoying Advice

Martin sat at the dining table, his laptop open in front of him, the website demanding details of the name and numbers on his debit card. While his voice sounded harsh when he spoke to her, the smile on his face showed his true intent.

He's been happy lately.

She'd expected a lot more of a mouthful from her dad over avoiding him the previous day. Instead he'd seemed rather chilled about it. Said it was her loss for not meeting Paula or having a driving lesson.

'Oh Dad, I just can't wait to see Aunt Livie and her new place and Cathy and Steve and Sarah and Josh of course.'

She wiped her hands on a tea towel and squinted over her father's shoulder, checking to see what time the flight left.

'Print it out, Dad. I need to see the hard copy. I'm so excited.'

'Right, that should do it. The printer is warming up as we speak.'

Martin turned in his chair to face his "office" desk and watch the action.

He smiled to himself.

Elma discarded the tea towel and stood in front of the printer waiting to whip the confirmation out of the machine as soon as it appeared in the tray. Her fingers grabbed the A4 paper and she sprang into a waltz around the kitchen table, holding it as if it were Aunt Livie herself. She looked at her dad and smiled.

'Thanks so much! You're the best dad in the world!'

Martin kept his smile but muttered under his breath, 'Well, that's not what you said last week.'

He turned the laptop off and closed the lid.

'And you'll miss out on your driving lesson.'

'No, I won't,' Elma quipped back.

'Josh says he'll take me. Oh, blast it! Dad, the spuds are burning!'

An acrid smell infused itself into the kitchen as Elma raced to the stove.

'It's okay, they're not burnt. Just browned,' she said, tipping the potatoes from one pot to another.

Oh dear, that's not going to scrub off easily.

'I'm thinking of going for a bushwalk tomorrow, Dad.'

Elma placed the plated food down on the table where her father sat. One pea rolled onto the floor.

'Where?'

'Maybe the top of the mountain.'

She hesitated.

Maybe Big Bend.

'Where would you start?'

Martin scraped the potato from one side of the plate to the other, not really sure whether he should inflict another mouthful on himself. It didn't look burnt but the taste was not exactly what he'd expected.

'Well, I kinda thought I'd just walk along the rivulet and up the Myrtle Gully Track and 'onwards and upwards', if you know what I mean.'

'Got a map?'

Elma nodded.

'Got credit on your phone?'

Elma nodded again.

'Raincoat, first aid ...'

'Oh come on Dad, I'm not five years old,' Elma interrupted.

'I'd prefer you didn't go wandering around up there all by yourself, but,' he paused, 'you are a big girl. It's your choice.'

Martin looked down at his plate and back up at Elma's beaming face.

'And there's plenty of leftover spud to take for your lunch.'

--

The sun pulled itself up over the eastern hills, levelling its rays above the horizon. Heatless beams of light greeted Elma as she stood, catching her breath, looking down over the grain silos behind the brewery. There were no clouds yet and if the weather forecast held to its predictions the day would continue to be bright and clear. A little cool, but that was normal now that autumn was languishing in its final days.

Elma figured she'd warm up as she walked. She adjusted the straps on her backpack, pulling the clip above her hip just a little tighter and wiggling her shoulders as she felt the weight lift from them. Her pack contained the usual assortment of bushwalking gear, including an extra notebook and spare bottle of hand sanitiser.

By 9am Elma had made it up to the top of Old Farm Road via the Rivulet Track and now stood at the start of the Myrtle Gully Track. She removed her backpack and let it plop to the ground, snapping a twig as it did so. The half dozen wallabies grazing on the grassy fire break bounded off on their well-worn paths.

Whoops, I didn't mean for that to happen.

She waited, holding her breath as long as she could, hoping they'd return.

I'm surprised they're out and about at this time of the day – they must be hungry.

One by one the wallabies crept back and resumed grazing, each one lifting its head now and then watchfully taking turns to protect its mob.

Wallabies on High Alert After Autumn Break

Elma replaced her pen, notebook and water bottle into the side pocket of her backpack and turned from the fire trail to face the narrower path leading up to the Myrtle Gully Falls. Native trees created a shadowy arch and she stepped out of the sunshine and into the folds of kunanyi. The earthy aroma of decomposing vegetation caught her nose and she paused briefly.

Is there someone there?

A breeze created by the warming earth followed her into the shadows. She shivered involuntarily, rubbing her arms with a self-hug. In some places the path sank a little beneath her feet, softened by recent rain, the leaves from the myrtle trees littered the path, preventing the mud from sticking to her walking boots.

They're so pretty – a million shades of brown and orange – an autumn carpet of confetti leaves. I must have missed the wedding.

Her eyes adjusted to the darker environment.

The smell, hmmm, a mixture of Aunt Livie gardening beneath her ferns and her old worm farm. I wonder if she has them growing at her new place. Six days and counting …

Myrtles, ferns and leaf litter lined the path, a couple of old tree stumps, interrupted in their growth by the '67 bush fires, carried the scars of 'mountain fire black' along their waist high remains. Their decaying wood supported a mass of new and old lichens, colourful funguses, including miniature and aged oyster mushrooms that had continually added to their balconies each growing season.

The tops of the sawn stumps were decorated in growth rings and moss.

Soap Boxes for Mountain Creatures

I remember when Sarah and Josh brought me up here all those years ago. We took turns dancing on that stump, like it was a stage. It seemed so much bigger then. And the one back there was still standing, and hollow. I remember creeping inside it – freaking out about spiders. I'll see them next week – Josh anyway. Those ruins must be up this way too, then. I wonder why Dad and I always walked the flats and beaches? It's so lovely up here. Maybe he didn't want the memories of Mum.

Elma thought about her mother and automatically looked down at her boots. Brown leather Colorados. She hadn't told Chloe where they'd come from because they were her mother's and she hadn't been up to talking about her on their walk together the previous week. She thought Chloe would ask too many questions – questions that she couldn't or wouldn't be able to answer.

Elma had claimed the boots after finding them in the shed when she and Martin were doing a clean out.

'Don't know where this came from,' Martin said, dragging a hessian sack out from behind the metal chest that Elma had used as a toy box in her younger days. They'd moved house twice since her mother's disappearance. Elma remembered crying the day her things were packed and moved from their spacious four-bedroom house into storage because there wasn't enough room for all their furniture and stuff in the tiny rental property that was their home for the next couple of years. Eventually they moved into the two-bedroom studio/flat that her father had built in his spare time, after work and between jobs. The excess 'stuff' was sold in a garage sale with the leftovers going up to the South Hobart tip shop.

'You can visit them up there if they don't sell,' her father had joked.

How this bag of stuff had been overlooked was a mystery.

'I swear I'd chucked this lot out when we moved in here.'

Martin stared at the sack, edging slowly backwards as he would from a disturbed snake.

Elma knew instinctively the sack held some sort of emotional baggage and the right thing to do to respect her father's pain would be to turn her head while he threw the bag out for the rubbish or Vinnies. But she was curious. What was in the bag?

'Can we just check it out Dad? There could be something useful in there.'

'Nothing I'd be interested in.' Martin snapped.

He turned and pushed past her, his footsteps shaking the wooden floor as he headed out of the shed and onto the street.

Elma stared at the bag.

Will I? Won't I? Will I? Won't I? Either way, he's already upset. I just want to know. I don't even know what I want to know.

Elma didn't have any photos or mementoes of her mother, apart from the jewellery box her dad had made.

Everyone's always been so secretive about Mum. Or maybe they're just protective of Dad – don't know which. Either way, no one talked about her or why she really left.

Elma had vague memories of her mum and internet dating but these days she wondered whether they were actual memories or just snippets of things she'd overheard as a small child.

Now she was older, more able to think for herself. Her world was changing from black and white to a mess of greys like the ones she tried to order in her notebook. Something kept pricking at a tender spot beneath her skin.

Curiosity got the better of her and she wiped the dust from her hands onto the back of her jeans and sat on the toy box staring at the hessian sack.

I hope Dad chills a bit before he comes back. I didn't mean to upset him. I don't know how I do that. Good at something, I guess. What's in the bag? Should I open it or wait for him to come back?

Dust covered her fingers as she struggled with the knot in the rope at the top of the sack. The harsh fabric scratched her hands.

'Blast!'

A piece of thread caught in a small split on the side of her fingernail, ripping the top part off as she pulled her hand back.

Oh no, not another nail!

She stood up and kicked the bag.

Dust puffed out from between the gaps of the loosely woven fabric and spread about the floor. The room filled with a musty odour and Elma's eyes filled with tears. She wiped at them with her dirty hands, leaving grime smudged across her face.

Oh damn, another dumb thing to do.

'I am not giving up,' she said aloud.

'You stupid thing. I won't let you get the better of me.'

She looked around for something she could use to prise the knot loose. The knives were kept in the kitchen only a door away as the shed was connected directly to the studio.

Her father's tools were kept in the lock-up or the back of his ute or at the site he was working on.

'Hedge clippers. They'll do.'

She spoke aloud, viewing the gardening equipment stacked against the wall. The smaller items rested neatly on a shelf within reach. Without letting the bag out of her sight she took two steps towards the bench and reached out far enough to wrap her fingers round one handle of the shears. They were sharp and heavy. Opening them, she slid one blade of the clippers down between the tight folds of the hessian bag and the old rope. Elma pushed down, feeling a small amount of resistance. She pushed harder. The blade slipped forward – the rope cut – sliced completely through – it was done.

No going back.

The neck of the bag flopped loosely in her hand, a pattern

of light, dark, light alternated round the top of the now open sack. Dust caught in her throat and she coughed. Martin hadn't returned.

I guess that's a good thing.

Elma gave a glance over her shoulder towards the open roller door.

I'll do this quickly and then have a shower; it'll all be gone before he even gets back … I hope.

She bent forward and picked up the bag from the corners of its unopened end, letting the contents drop onto the ground in front of her.

Dirty boots, snow gloves, a grubby blue cardigan and what looked like a bundle of documents, maybe letters, sat in a mound at her feet. A dark blue button rolled unnoticed beneath the toy chest. Elma sat back down to observe the findings.

Not much, really. What was I expecting?

Envelopes and papers were bound with a red rubber band that had long since lost its function and Elma could see grubby red/brown strips of the degraded band stuck to the discoloured paper beneath it. The letters clumped together because that's how they'd landed. She pushed them aside with her sneaker.

I'll get back to you.

The cardigan had seen better days and she watched as small moths flittered up from their recent lodgings. The colour was one of her favourites in her blue collection – Prussian blue. 'Black velvet mixed with indigo'. She thanked Werner's colour chart for that description.

Although it might be something completely different if I gave it a wash. But that's not going to happen.

She slipped her hand inside a gardening glove and looked around to see where the rubbish bin had been moved to while they cleared the shed. She saw it out near the road and carefully picked up the garment, letting the free-loading bugs and grubs fall to the floor. It looked about her size but it was hand knitted without a label.

If this was Mum's she must have been about my build.

Elma lifted the rubbish bin lid with one hand and lowered the decaying item onto the garbage inside.

Well, that's it, I guess.

She repeated the process with the snow gloves, careful not to touch the fabric with her own skin and finally did the same with the hessian sack.

All that was left from the bag was a pair of boots and the few old bits of mail. The boots, although dusty, looked in good condition.

Hardly worn, if ever, and they might be my size.

Elma put the other gardening glove on and picked them up.

They are my size.

She stood them upright and placed them against the wall next to the rake. The mail, or whatever it was, she wrapped in a clean tea towel and, after removing the gardening gloves and as many articles of clothing as she could, she headed for the shower, placing the tea towel and contents on the desk in her room as she did so.

That had been a few weeks ago. Plenty had happened since then.

She continued on up Myrtle Gully Track listening to the sounds of the bush and the endless tinkle of the creek that coursed not far from where she walked. She stopped on the curved wooden bridge, set like an art work, level with the base of falls and wondered again why she and her father never walked these tracks when they were so close to where they lived,

It's so beautiful.

Things at home had changed since the 'hessian sack' incident. Small things. Elma didn't know exactly what they were but she suspected it was her view on why things were the way they were.

Well, things really couldn't stay the same, not now. Not since **The Discovery**.

Puzzle pieces, small snap chats on Mother and why she left. Couldn't talk to Dad and didn't say anything to Chloe, even though I wanted to.

After her shower Elma had put on the rubber gloves from under the kitchen sink to take a better look at the boots. Martin was still out so she took them outside and placed them on the grass beside the deck. She turned the tap on and sprayed them with the hose, filling the insides up with water until it overflowed out of the tops of the boots.

Thirteen years of debris, seeds and cobwebs flowed out onto the grass, followed by a couple of spiders. She tipped each boot upside down to drain. The water poured out and so did what looked like a driver's licence.

Elma quickly dropped the hose and picked up the card, spraying water all over herself and the deck.

Blast, I didn't need a second shower.

She scrambled to turn the tap off.

She stared at the card.

It is a licence and it looks just like me. Seriously this looks just like me. Same shaped face– same nose – same mouth – no fringe, the hair is even tied back from the face like mine. If I didn't know it wasn't me I would really think it was. The eyes are the wrong colour though.

Elma knew she wasn't making sense, but the photo was such a likeness it really didn't seem to make sense. The quality of the photo wasn't quite as good as the one on her own licence but it had of course been taken more than thirteen years earlier. And there weren't any floating kangaroos printed on it either.

And it doesn't have my name on it – it has Mum's – Elisabeth Mary Manning.

Dad had told me that's where my name came from. He didn't want to talk about it but I guess I asked such a simple question he just had to answer. Before then I'd thought her name was just Lizzie.

'The first two letters of your mother's first name are EL and the first two of her second name were MA and that's it. Nothing more to say.'

Elma had lots of questions but could tell there would be no use asking him right then.

When Dad shuts me down, that's it – no point.

Elma left the boots and the hose out on the soggy lawn and headed across the deck, leaving a trail of watery footprints. Water drizzled from her t-shirt down the back of her legs and into the carpet, her seat squelched as she sat down in front of her desk and turned to face the mirror on the wall.

Yep that's the spitting image of me. I'm a mini-Mum.

She grabbed her towel and dabbed at her legs. She placed the towel on her chair and sat down again. In front of her was the tea towel with the mail wrapped inside. Elma took a deep breath and began unfolding the towel. A few insects scurried around, darting beneath the pile. She squished them with the tea towel.

Insect Relocation – Death Toll Rises

A musty smell rose and Elma wanted to scratch her nose, but couldn't as she'd touched the contaminated fabric. The itch gradually increased until it mounted to pre-sneeze level. She wiped her hands on her towel and then rubbed her nose with the back of her hand just in time.

Sneeze be gone.

The mail sat in the middle of the tea towel.

I'll start at the top, I suppose.

The first piece was an envelope addressed to her mother. She picked at the rubber where it stuck the envelope down and pulled out a grimy power bill, with bright red letters, FINAL NOTICE, slashed across the front of it. She gasped at the amount outstanding: $4000.

Elma placed the account back in the envelope and put it to one side. The second item was an A4 sheet of paper roughly folded into thirds.

Home of the silverfish.

She squashed one with a tissue as it tried to escape. The folds of paper were stuck to each other and, try as she might, Elma was unable to separate them without causing damage.

Whoops! I didn't mean to do that!

It was tatty and coffee-stained in one corner.

Coffee cup tyre print

The words were faint and written in pencil, making it hard for Elma to read. But it appeared to be a list of more debts.

Kinda looks like Dad's writing.

There were about twenty items on the list.

Elma couldn't read them all but she could tell they were all unpaid bills.

That's not like Dad. He always pays on time. Heck, we go without Nutella if the power bill needs paying.

She refolded the paper and put it aside. There were three more items and by the time Elma had worked her way through them she could tell it was probably her mum who had managed the business and home accounts and it was her mum who possibly hadn't paid them. In fact it looked like she'd overdrawn accounts creating a debt of nearly $500,000 dollars. She checked the date on the papers – it was just before her Mum had disappeared.

Had she taken the money? Taken the money and run away?

That's awful – why would anyone do that?

Elma sat bewildered.

What was she meant to think?

Had Liz not only abandoned her, but stolen her childhood home and forced them to rent a dodgy unit until Dad had worked his guts out to build this one?

Elma looked up from her desk. The sun was going down and she could hear the roller door bumping round as it wound closed.

What am I doing?

She stood up, sat down, stood again and then pulled open the desk drawer and stuffed the letters, tea towel and bugs inside. Shuddering at the thought of the bugs she shut the drawer quickly, snatching the licence from the desk and stuffing it into her pocket.

'Crickey, Elma where the heck are you? The shed door's open, the kitchen door's open and the slider's open as well! There's bloody insects everywhere!'

'I'm just getting changed,' Elma lied.

--

Elma stood on the bridge looking up at the waterfall. Her thoughts tumbling down with the spray. She watched as the water bubbled and frothed against the rocks and shivered for the second time that morning. It would only be a few more days and she would be away from this place – away from South Hobart, the café, Gran and her dad. She wanted to say something to him about what she'd discovered but she lacked the courage.

What am I scared of? Now I feel like a hypocrite. Like one of

115

them keeping secrets from me – from each other. I just hate it.

'One of them' included Aunt Livie, who'd previously escaped Elma's judgement.

But now – there were things she knew – surely. She must have known why Mum left and never told me.

Elma was thinking of her talk with Dr Gordon. Before that she hadn't considered who'd removed the wedding photos of her parents. There must have been photos.

The noise of the water falling onto the rocks, the solid cliff on one side clothed in ferns and mosses and the now familiar smell of the damp bush, captivated Elma as she stood in the centre of the wooden bridge.

Apart from the coolness I can't think of a prettier place to be. Two more shifts at work, one more 'Gran Day' and I'm gone.

Elma looked down at her boots and screamed. There, on her leg, just above her sock and below her leggings, was something black and wiggling. She stamped her foot and screamed again. Whatever it was wasn't going to release itself just because she screamed at it.

Noises came through the bush – voices and tramping feet.

'Hey! You okay? What's up?'

There were two of them, both male. One was dark, the other light.

Where did they come from? They certainly didn't come along the path.

She held in her third scream and pointed to the small black sausage on her leg. Her hands were shaking and the suppressed laughter from her two rescuers wasn't helpful.

'It's a leech. Hell, just a leech. It won't hurt you. Now hold still while I wiggle it off.'

'Get it off me! Get it off me!'

'Calm down, it's okay, it's okay. You never seen a leech before?'

'Of course I have! Just get it off me!'

Despite her ingratitude, the darker guy knelt down and held the thumb-sized creature between his fingers, gently wiggling it back and forwards for a few seconds before it released its grip on her leg and fell into his hand.

'It was about ready ay, to drop off anyway,' he said, cradling it in his palm.

'Look at this, Nige – it's a beaut.'

Elma was impressed

and revolted. How can he possibly touch that?

'Of course it's a baby compared to the big ones back home.'

They burst out laughing again.

Elma looked away. She was close to tears. Her rescuer sounded foreign. There were some words she hadn't understood at all.

They're laughing – making fun of me.

'Hey, sorry.'

The laughter stopped.

The odd voice behind her back sounded sincere.

'We're so rude. We forgot to introduce ourselves. I'm Fergus and this is Nigel.'

Elma still had her back to them.

I don't care who you are. Just go away.

She turned at a sound behind her. Fergus was down on his knees, his backpack open beside him.

'Here, take this,' he said, resting a small first aid kit on his leg and offering her a piece of gauze.

'Where is it now?' she said.

'I gave it to Nigel. Look, you'll need this to stop the bleeding.'

Elma looked down – a thick stream of blood was running down her leg. She couldn't feel any pain. She took the gauze and pressed it against her leg, looking warily at him.

'Are you okay?' Fergus asked again.

He's kind, even though I snapped at him.

'I think so.'

Embarrassed beyond belief, bleeding uncontrollably, but breathing – just!

'I'm Elma,' she said, finally.

'Cool, she does have a name. Are you not from 'round here?' Fergus continued, looking around to see if anyone else was with her.

Elma dabbed at the wound.

'It won't stop bleeding,' she said.

'Nup, that's the nature of a leech. They spit a bit of anticoagulant into the wound so you bleed easy.'

Elma looked around, up and down her other leg and over her arms.

I have to go! I couldn't bear another one. Ugh!

'I am a local –' she said, '– and I really need to go. Like right now.'

'Cool,' replied Fergus.

'We'll walk down with you.'

Elma looked at Fergus. He had a dark, bearded face and a mass of black woolly hair pulled back in a ponytail. Nigel was pale, clean-shaven and his ears stuck out from below his black and yellow striped beanie.

No, no just go away and leave me alone.

Fergus gave Elma another piece of gauze and a band-aid to stick it to her leg.

'We don't bite, if that's what's worrying ya,' Fergus added.

Nigel flicked the overfull leech off the bridge, towards the side of the stream. Its shiny body disappeared between the wet stones.

Elma shivered.

'Okay. Let's go,' she said, unable to think of what else to do.

By the time they'd trekked down to the top of Old Farm Road, Elma had learned that both Fergus and Nigel were studying bats at the UTAS.

'Of course it's too early in the season for bats to be out yet, but we're looking to see the best place to set up the equipment, come November.'

Elma was getting used to the way Fergus spoke,

I'd never laugh at him – but he does sound funny. Kind of cool.

'I've met New Zealanders before. They come into work sometimes. But I've never heard one that sounds the way you do.'

Nigel laughed, 'You haven't really been around long enough then – most Kiwis sound like him.'

Fergus rolled his eyes and mimed zipping his lips, 'Well, I'll keep my mouth shut from now on if that'll make youse happy.'

He laughed and kept on talking.

'Where do you work anyway?'

'Oh, just a little café on Sandy Bay Road, up past the casino. It used to be a service station. I'm just a dishwasher.'

Instantly Elma regretted her words.

Oh no. I didn't want them to know that. I hope they never come there.

Her face went red.

'Well,' said Fergus, 'here's the car. We can drop you somewhere on our way back to Uni.'

Sure they've been helpful. But there's no way I'm getting in a car with strangers.

'No thanks,' she said. 'I'll walk from here.'

Nigel proffered his hand.

'Thanks for your company. It sure made the walk more

enjoyable than just having Bat-Boy by my side.'

Reluctantly Elma accepted and shook Nigel's hand in return. *Please just go – I want to wash my wound. And wash my hands.* She turned to Fergus.

'Thanks for helping me out. Sorry I was so rude to you,' she said, still embarrassed by the situation but grateful they hadn't teased her more than their initial sniggering.

Fergus dropped his rucksack and learned against the car. Elma could see part of a tattoo on his forearm. Large bands of black s-shaped lines curved upwards under his sweatshirt. She wasn't sure she liked that. He, too, proffered his big hand and Elma was obliged to shake it.

'We'll catch you sometime. Check on that eel bite, ay.'

He smiled, a huge smile showing nearly all his teeth.

Elma dropped her hand; there was something wrong with him.

He's missing half a finger!

She looked away and then turned, walking off towards the track she'd climbed earlier that day.

'Okay, thanks again. I'm sure I'll see you 'round,' she said over her shoulder.

But she hoped she wouldn't.

Chapter 11

Fergus rocked up at the café Thursday afternoon, the day before Elma was due to fly out of Tasmania.

'Oh my goodness, Damien, what am I going to do?'

Elma ducked behind the counter and scuttled through to the kitchen.

'What?' said Damien, balancing a tray of plates ready to return to the front counter.

'That guy, the bat guy, the one I told you I met up the mountain – he's here – now! I saw him walking towards the door.'

Elma sank her hands straight into the full sink of water, vigorously moving pots and pans about.

'I'll stay here until he's gone. Oh, I hope he didn't see me.'

'You're a nut, Elma, seriously.'

Damien shook his head at her and headed out of the kitchen.

She stopped her frenzied activity and strained to hear the conversation. Other staff continued talking, the fridge clicked on, the radio played in the background.

This is useless. I can't hear anything.

She could hear Damien and Fergus talking. Damien was most likely taking his order and they were both laughing.

Elma was shaking – she could hear Fergus's thick New Zealand accent but not their conversation.

This is way too much for me.

She went back to swishing utensils about in the sink. The sweet smell of pumpkin soup and garlic mingled with the dish detergent. It was hard to think.

Elma pounced on Damien when he returned a few minutes later.

'Well, what happened? What did he say?'

'What? Elma! Stand down! It was just a guy after a takeaway coffee,' Damien said with a huge grin on his face.

'What did you tell him? You didn't tell him I was here, did you? Damien, I need to know.'

'Well, he seemed like a nice guy – sounded funny of course – but,' Damien stopped mid-sentence. There was someone else at the counter.

'Smashed avo and ham on focaccia times two,' he called to the kitchen hand on his return and placed the order on the clip above the service bench.

'What did he say?' Elma persisted each time Damien passed through the kitchen door.

'Sorry Elma we really didn't have time to talk, so I just gave him your number.'

They colour drained from Elma's face, she stared at Damien in disbelief, suds and water dripping from her gloves and apron.

'Oh, my goodness! You did what?'

'As if I'd do a thing like that!'

Damien's laugh was enough to set the entire kitchen staff into a fit of smirks and giggles.

Everyone is watching me; I don't know what to do.

'I'm never talking to you again.'

She dropped a load of plates from the dishwasher onto the bench the crashing noise signifying the end of the conversation.

'Take it easy Elma. It was just a joke, okay?'

I don't care if I don't come back to this stupid place, I should've stayed at school. I won't come back!

But she knew she would – there wasn't anything else to do and still another six weeks before the mid-year intake of her nursing course was due to start – that's if she decided to start it at all.

'Take PJ's coffee out to her, would you, please, Elma?' asked Damien.

She's here now? That's weird.

PJ looked up with her customary smile as she moved the newspaper off the table to make room for her coffee.

'How's tricks, Elma? Made any decisions about Uni yet?' she asked.

Elma shook off her annoyance with Damien and smiled back. PJ always had that effect on her.

'I was hoping ...' PJ began but was cut short by her phone ringing. She picked it up to take the call and Elma cleared the next table.

Yeah, everyone is hoping I'll go back to study – everyone but me ...

'Hey, Elma, sorry for teasing you earlier.'-

Damien spoke kindly to her as they closed up, after the rest of the staff had left.

'I hope you have a great trip to the Mainland – I mean that.

'There's another thing I need to talk to you about.'

He paused.

'There's money missing from the till. It hasn't balanced for a few weeks now.'

'And you are telling me this because …?'

He thinks I stole it! This could possibly be the worst day of my life!

'I'm telling you this because I have to, I just need you to be aware. You're a good staff member and we love having you here. If you think of anything or know anything that will help me out with this, please let me know. Okay, that's all. Just informing you of the situation. Now off you go.'

Damien placed his hand on her back and pushed her gently out of the kitchen.

Does he think I took the money?

She thought of her mother, wondering what she was like.

Was she a thief, a druggie, a gambler? What did she do with all Dad's money? I maybe need a new list in my notebook.

More Unanswered Questions!

She was surprised to see Fergus sitting at the bus stop across the road balancing the empty takeaway cup on his hand.

Oh, no, just what I don't need!

'Hi,' she said politely as she approached him.

'What are you doing here?'

'Just catching up on some sightseeing before I leave in a week or so. I'd wondered if that was where you worked.'

I can't believe I told him where I worked.

I don't need a stalker in my life, right now or ever.

Fergus interrupted her thoughts.

'I'm heading up to the Shot Tower, down the highway – in Taroona. Wanna join me?'

Oh, great, this is the bit where I say why not? And laugh, I think … That's what Chloe would do.

'Sorry. I can't. I've got a driving lesson shortly.'

'That's cool.'

'I don't think the Shot Tower would be open much longer.'

Elma looked at the time on her phone.

'4:30,' he said. 'I checked it out.'

He waved his phone back and forth in his hand.

Elma noticed the missing finger again and wondered what he'd done.

Not that I care and I'm not going to ask.

'What about tonight? Are you busy then?'

What about never?

She laughed, despite what she was thinking.

Fergus laughed too.

'You said about the mountain the other day – I just wanted to know more.'

Elma checked her memory. She couldn't remember everything she'd said.

It wasn't the most favourite day of my life, still today isn't much better. We didn't walk far; I remember enjoying his funny accent. That made me smile.

'Well, maybe we can catch up when I get back from Ballan. Tonight I have to pack.'

Well, at least that's true.

'Okay, you're on.' Fergus was nodding his head. 'Here's my number and here comes my bus.'

He showed his phone to Elma and she typed the number into her phone.

'Do you want to text me quickly now just to make sure it works?' he asked.

Elma ignored him and slid her phone in her pocket.

Chloe would have texted him right back – most likely with a flirty smile.

'Catch up later, Elma,' Fergus said, stepping aboard the bus, his dark curly hair out of control. He smiled and waved from the window as he flopped into a seat. The bus pulled away from the curb. She looked up to wave back.

I wonder what I said that intrigued him.

A strand of hair whipped into her face, she wiped it away and tucked the end of her scarf into her puffer jacket. White tips were forming on the river – spirit waves, her mother had called them.

'I'll race you,' she called to the water, suddenly in a light-hearted mood, and headed along the road towards the nursing home, Fergus still on her mind.

--

Elma stood at the front desk of the home. Her bag dropped down against the counter, her shoes moving up and down into the carpet as she transferred her weight from one foot to the other.

'But I've looked in her room – of course I have.'

Do you think I'm stupid?

'She's not there and she's not in the media lounge either, or the café,' Elma added.

The receptionist checked to see who was on the list for an outing, but Elma knew her gran never went out on a Thursday.

She's hardly been out at all, but that's most likely because of her pain and grump-ability.

'She'll be here, don't worry.'

The receptionist smiled, mauve lips matching her high collared shirt. Darker glass buttons lining up with an amethyst pendant swinging just above her cleavage. She seemed annoyed, as if Elma was taking her time away from real work that needed to be done.

'Look, I'll check which team is working with her and give the supervisor a call.'

She busied herself examining the roster and spoke briefly to the staff member sitting at a desk behind her. Elma continued to fidget, looking towards the café, then the entrance and back down the corridor. The corridor that usually led her over 99 roses to Gran's room.

The receptionist put the phone down and spoke in an unconcerned manner, 'She'll be here Love, just take a seat and I'll be back with you shortly.'

Elma glared at her.

'I'm not moving 'til you find her.'

'Honey, just take a seat. Maybe have a seat in the café.

I'll find you there, it won't be long. This happens all the time. She'll just be in the loo or visiting in another room.'

Elma continued to glare.

'Have you checked the physio or hairdresser's? She might just have changed her appointment time.'

Elma loosened her scarf and looked over towards the hairdressing salon.

Not likely, she thought.

'Jo's doing the ring-around now, see?'

Elma stared into the office. She could see the other clerk talking on a phone and scribbling something down on a piece of paper.

Should I ring Dad or just wait?

The two office workers were talking together and Elma heard the mention of CCTV files. She looked about the atrium and sure enough there were cameras pointing towards her at the desk and the outside entrance and the entrance to the hallways.

I never noticed them before. Oh Gran, where are you?

By the time Martin had been informed of the incident, Elma was long gone. She had thought that the security around the home was less than efficient. Some of the clients, or residents, or whatever you want to call them, were able to come and go by simply informing the staff and tapping the four digit code into the key lock beside the door. Elma had sometimes wondered what would happen if they just left without saying farewell.

Gran's watched them come and go and we all know how reliable she is. Some days totally clueless and some days she's thrashed me hands down at cards – mentally and physically. And yet, I swear there are days when she doesn't even know who she is. Oh Gran.

Elma left through the café door, typing in the code and walking out. She didn't bother to wave to the camera. She followed the path to the beach.

The wind had dropped. The white horses were resting somewhere beneath the surface.

Perhaps in underwater stables.

Where are you Gran?

The river had turned a melancholy grey.

She chose the path to the left without knowing why, but just feeling the need to do something.

It gets dark early now. Hope we find her soon.

She took a quick glance at her phone – no missed calls.

Elma followed the shore as far as she could before needing to hop along the rocks to avoid the incoming tide.-

Aw, Gran, I hope you're not out there, swallowed by the spirit of the timtumili minanya.

Water splashed at the hems of her rolled up jeans – her shoes were already soaked. The tide increased bit by bit until Elma was forced to climb the rocks and leave the beach via someone's back yard. The daylight was completely gone now and Elma crept along the side of the house close to the hedge hoping the front gate to the road was open.

128

If Gran had come this way it may have been early enough when the tide was out. She certainly wouldn't have been able to climb the rocks to get up here.

She checked her phone again.

Nothing – no missed calls or messages.

My feet are freezing.

Street lights were on and Elma made it to the road without incident. A jogger ran by. She opened her mouth to ask if he'd seen an old lady with a walking frame but by the time she got her words together he'd passed by. The café wasn't much further up the road. It was shut.

Well, of course, it is. It's never open at night

The fish shop next to it was brightly lit and full of people.

She scanned her eyes over the twenty or so customers.

No sign of Gran.

Pretty coloured lights swung gracefully from pole to pole along the footpath above the foreshore. Leafless trees spread their limbs, reaching out towards one another, beckoning Elma to follow the path towards the looming Casino.

The Casino!

She stared at it – tall and obvious.

If I was maybe oldish and out for a walk and maybe a little lost and maybe a little cold from wind from the beach. And I had left the nursing home while the tide was out and walked all the way along here with a walking frame –

she held her breath

– I reckon that's where I might be.

Elma had considered other options while she walked along beside the river.

She may have turned right – she may have gone out the front door – she may have been picked up hitchhiking for all I know.

Or she could be playing hide and seek somewhere in that stupid nursing home.

She rolled her jeans back down, untied and retied her hair, sanitised her hands and stood in front of the revolving door of the Casino's main entrance. She didn't feel clean enough to enter.

I might just have a look from the outside first.

She walked past the door and around towards the gymnasium, following the path down and around the river side of the building. Water splashed and foamed at the sea wall. The tide was almost in. Elma checked her phone again

Come on Dad! Tell me she's with you or at the home or something.

She peered through the huge uncurtained windows running the length of the building. There was no shortage of people but Elma was only looking for one. The casino was unfamiliar – she'd visited it, maybe three times in the last 17 years. People ate and drank, oblivious to being watched.

If Gran is in there she's not anywhere I can see.

She sighed.

I'm cold. Come on Gran, where are you?

She checked her phone once more.

Still nothing.

One more corner to go and still no Gran.

Elma walked through the car park bringing her full circle, back to the revolving doors. Only this time she went in – hoping no one would notice her wet jeans and dirty shoes.

I'm not dressed for this place. What do I do now?

She checked the toilets, the Bird Cage Bar and any other place that she thought she wouldn't have seen from the outside. The only place left to check was the gambling area. Cocktail dresses, suits and flashy jewellery swirled past her eyes.

Oh. I'm not allowed in there.

'Excuse me, Miss,' someone said.

What now? What now?

Elma let out a sigh

I didn't even make it to the doorway.

'Could I see your identification please?'

'My what?'

'Your ID. This is an adult only area. You need to be over eighteen to come in here and I need to see your proof of age.'

'I've lost my grandmother.'

Elma didn't expect him to understand what she was saying, but to her surprise his eyebrows went up and he nodded his head.

'Oh,' he said. 'Could her name be Scarlet by any chance?'

'Yes ... yes, no, maybe,' Elma stuttered.

'Well is it or isn't it?'

The smartly-dressed security guard looked Elma up and down with a confused look on his face.

'Yes, yes,' was all that came out.

Elma stood there in dirty jeans and wet shoes looking for roses in the carpet. Relieved, embarrassed, tired and hungry. She had no idea what to do.

'Please come this way. We're just waiting for the police to arrive.'

'The police?' repeated Elma as the security attendant led her along past the front entrance to a series of offices.

'What did she do?'

Elma followed obediently.

'Well, she hasn't done anything wrong but we found her wandering about outside and she doesn't have ID or any idea where she lives. Came from the water, I think she said.'

He stared at Elma's wet jeans.

'Maybe from the same place as you,' he said light-heartedly.

'We had to call the police. We just couldn't tell her to go home, now could we? We have a duty of care.'

'Well you can call them off now and I'll get Dad to pick us up.'

'Slow down, first things first: is Scarlet your grandmother?' he said, opening the office door.

'No, that's my gran. I don't know who Scarlet is.'

The man looked confused

'It's alright, Gran, I've found you now,' Elma said.

I can't ever remember being this happy to see her.

She burst into tears.

Gran and another female attendant sat on couches with a glass coffee table between them. The woman stood and placed a hand on Elma's shoulder.

'Come on sweetie, it's going to be all right.'

Elma looked at her smiling face and tried to stop her tears.

'Come on. Why don't you sit down next to your grandmother and join us for a mug of hot chocolate?'

She signalled to a staff member to fetch another cup and gently herded Elma past Miriam's walking frame and sat her on the couch next to the old lady.

'Are you all right, Gran?' Elma asked.

Miriam stared at her and dabbed at her top lip, removing traces of a chocolate moustache. She looked fine. Her hair was neat and pulled back like normal. Her clothes were clean and smart as usual. Even her shoes were immaculate.

How does she do it?

Elma looked down at her own clothes. Bits of pine bark stuck to her socks and sand jammed the eyelets of her sand-shoes. Tiny remnants tipped onto the floor. She pushed at them with her foot.

'Can you ring the police back?' the woman whispered to another attendant.

'She wouldn't tell us where she was from and she hasn't got any ID or even a handbag.'

The woman handed Elma a hot chocolate.

'The only thing we got out of her was her first name: Scarlet.'

Elma looked at Miriam, and Miriam looked back.

'I'm so glad we found you, Gran,' Elma said and began to cry again.

Chapter 12

Bag – check – jacket – check – phone – check – wallet in handbag and boarding pass – check.

'Hi Dad. I'm ready. Bags packed and dishes done.'

Elma left a message on her father's phone.

'It's only 10 am so I'm going to catch a bus to Gran's. You can pick me up from there on the way to the airport. Thanks Dad. Oh, and just in case you didn't know already – I need to be at the airport by 2 pm.'

With all the kerfuffle the night before Elma had forgotten to charge her phone.

30 percent charge remaining

She turned it off to conserve power

I'll need it later

Martin was working down the Channel on a kitchen renovation in a takeaway shop but had promised he'd be back in time to take her to the airport. They were both feeling a little bewildered over the previous night's events and, although the weather was foul, Elma felt the need to check in on Miriam before she left.

Her scarf whipped about her face as she entered the nursing home via the front door and stood for a few moments, letting her carry-on luggage drip onto the transition mat. Wheel marks in weather based shades formed two lines behind her, stopping at the threshold of the glass door. She wiped her face with her hands and slid them back over her head in a bid to wring the rain out of her hair. Raindrops fell from the end of her ponytail and silently dissolved into the doormat.

It was warmer inside, and the smell of a hot meal wafted past. *Curry?*

Elma looked about hoping not to see the same staff as last night.

Don't need any questions. I just want to say bye to Gran before I leave for the Mainland.

With her eyes down she headed for the passageway that led to her grandmother's room and didn't look up 'til the last corner, taking in a quick glance of Monet's garden – a huge print in a gilded frame. She expected to find Miriam sitting in her chair with a crocheted blanket on her knees. But she wasn't there. Her bed, her chair, and her bathroom were empty.

Oh no, if she's out in this rain it'll be the end of her.

Elma left her bag in the doorway and sprinted as fast as she could back to the office, not seeing anyone else on the way.

'She's gone, she's gone again!' she yelled breathlessly at the office window.

The bewildered office worker approached the counter and stared out at Elma, twirling her glasses back and forth between her fingers.

'I don't think so,' she said.

'Have you checked everywhere?'

'Of course I have,' Elma said.

'Honey, you've only been here two minutes.'

The woman's words were slow and deliberate. She looked directly at Elma with a bored look on her face.

'It is lunchtime, you know. They are usually all in the dining room about now ... unless they're poorly.'

Her eyes were looking somewhere behind Elma and her head was moving up and down in a condescending way.

Elma's face grew red.

Oh dear. I think I overreacted.

She stepped back from the counter.

'Sorry, I didn't think of that.'

She turned and headed in the direction of the nod.

I should have known it was lunch time. I could smell the dining room the minute I walked in.

She found Miram seated at a table by herself in the corner, sipping soup from a white china bowl. It was curried creamed cauliflower soup sprinkled with finely chopped parsley.

It smells great. It even looks all right.

The sourdough toast had been cut into skinny fingers and Miriam picked one up and dunked it in her soup before popping it into her mouth. Spoons and bowls chinked in a random beat beneath the constant murmur of eighty or so elderly eaters. The weather hurled wind and rain at the windows but was silenced by the double glazing.

It's gotten worse since I arrived. I hope it doesn't hold Dad up. No way do I want to miss my flight.

'Would you like a bowlful, Pet?' it was one of the kitchen staff bringing the trolley around for seconds.

'Mmmmm, no thanks,' Elma smiled at the offer.

Uh - uh, no way will I eat here ... smells good though. I am not your pet!

136

If there was one thing that bugged Elma it was being called Pet, Darling or Love by complete strangers.

If they weren't strangers then they'd know my name.

Miriam accepted a cheese and pickle sandwich and a jam roll from another staff member and Elma allowed a cup of tea to be placed on the table for her.

But only because she didn't call me Love or Darls and because I've had tea here before and didn't get sick.

She looked around the room wondering if Dr Gordon was eating with the locals. It was easy to tell the difference between the staff and residents because of their uniforms.

And age of course, well mostly, Dr Gordon could be a patient and by looks alone, Gran could be on staff, if it wasn't for her frame.

The nurses wore pale blue paisley uniforms and the kitchen staff wore the same pattern, only in a dark green. The cleaners also wore paisley but in autumn tones.

Must have been a sale on the paisleys – kind of cool I guess.

Residents were leaving the room now. Elma could see that the first ones to be seated had finished their meals entirely; whereas where she sat the staff were still delivering tea, coffee and second helpings of dessert.

Miriam looked quite content and sipped at her tea under Elma's watchful eye.

'So, are you okay today?' she asked, unable to see any signs of stress or tiredness.

'Today?'

Miriam placed her tea in front of her and patted her fingers lightly on the paper serviette beside her jam roll.

'Well, you know, after what happened last night. Did you sleep well? Find any bruises? Oh Gran, you know what I am talking about.'

'I'm sure I don't.'

Miriam seemed sincere.

'But if you can keep a secret I'll show you something.'

'Well, Gran, the way our family is with secrets, I'm sure one more isn't going to bust us.'

Miriam looked around. There were only a few people left now and the staff seemed happy to leave them alone in their corner while they cleared tables and cleaned up around them. The vacuum cleaner would prevent any eavesdroppers from hearing the secret that was to be divulged. Miriam appeared satisfied they were under no threat of being observed.

'I found this.'

Miriam began fishing under her chair.

Oh no, here we go again, she's looking for things that don't exist.

Unexpectedly the older woman straightened up,

'Oh dear, how silly of me, I thought I was sitting on my walker.'

She raised her hand and motioned towards the wall where her frame had been parked out of the way. Elma understood the non-verbal command and, like a well-trained puppy, fetched it, placed it next to the table and lifted the seat exposing the wire basket that hung beneath.

Miriam smacked Elma's hand out of the way.

'Don't touch that! That's not yours.'

'I'm only trying to help, Gran.'

'You're not – you're meddling.'

Miriam closed the lid and waited while Elma sat back down.

Come on then, what are you waiting for?

Elma rolled her eyes.

I totally know why we don't get on – you mean old control freak. I am this close to leaving!

She interlocked her fingers, leaving a small gap between her thumbs. But she didn't leave – there was nowhere to go.

Unless I want to stand outside in the rain while I wait for Dad.

Miriam glanced about, checking on the distance between the vacuum cleaner and herself. There was time – the only other person left was a kitchen hand who seemed in no hurry to clear or clean the tables as she worked her way slowly around the room with a trolley armed with a bucket of sudsy water.

'Well, do you want to see it or not?'

'What, Gran?'

Miriam lifted the seat and pulled out a postcard, passing it discreetly over the table towards Elma.

'Can I touch it, Gran?'

'Here take it – don't let them see it.'

Elma picked up the card, recognising the picture as one in a series that she'd seen the night before –there'd been twelve of them, one metre by one twenty, gold framed originals hung along the wall near the front foyer of the Casino. They had been very hard to miss. The postcard was a version of one of the pictures. Elma hadn't seen the postcards.

They must have been on sale at the gift shop or somewhere.

'Where did you get this from, Gran?'

'It's mine, from my photo album.'

Gran leaned over and pointed at the card.

'That's me on the lawn in the front.'

'Tis not!'

Elma laughed at the absurdity of it.

'Gran, that's not you at all, that's a young girl not an old lady.'

Miriam snatched the card back and stuffed it in between her cable knitted cardigan and the matching bodice of her olive green twin set.

She was adamant.

'Of courses it's me. I remember the day it was taken.'

She looked about again and pulled the postcard back out from beneath her cardigan.

'And that –,' she said, pointing, '– was his room.'

Elma, although sceptical, was intrigued and reached across the table with her hand held out.

'Please may I have another look, Gran?' she said in her most polite voice.

You don't remember what you did last night but you want to tell me that's you back in the sixties?

Miriam looked suspiciously at Elma.

She glanced around the room once more. Nothing had changed, well not much. The vacuum cleaner was a little closer and the table washer had disappeared. She let out an audible sigh and slowly gave the card to Elma again-

'You'll keep my secret, won't you Scarlet? Like Livie did,' she said.

Elma noted the look of confusion on her grandmother's face.

'It's okay, Gran.'

She tried to sound reassuring.

'I won't show it to them.'

Whoever they are.

A crack of lightning brightened the room and Elma jumped back a little. The card slipped through her fingers and onto the floor. Her mouth dropped open and she looked at her gran.

'I'm so sorry, that was an accident.'

As quickly as she could, she retrieved the card, holding her breath, waiting for the barrage of words that would come next from her grandmother's mouth. The words about her being stupid and foolish and dirty. She wiped both sides of the card with a serviette, waiting for the torrent to begin.

But she hasn't said anything and I'm still sitting here like a fool. Cripes, what's wrong with Gran?

Elma put the postcard on the table in front of her.

Maybe the lightning surprised her as much as it did me.

The card had a fancy gold edge similar to the large frames at the Casino. The print was in black and white. The photo was clearly labelled Springs Hotel, Summer, 1966. That was one year before it had burned down.

It appeared to Elma that the hotel had changed over the years as this photo showed the veranda had been built in.

I remember a photo of it with a round, rotunda thing at this corner.

I guess it could be Gran in the photo. She would have been about my age.

'Is this you, Gran?' she said aloud, pointing to a group of three young women wearing white aprons over their dresses.

'Yes that's me and that's,' she paused for a moment, 'Moira, I think. I don't remember the name of the other girl.'

She had a thoughtful look on her face.

'We were all seventeen when that was taken.'

'And –,' Elma added tentatively, smoothing the card flat with her finger, '– which room did you say was his?'

Elma thought of Charlie, Gran's ex. She'd never asked how he and Gran had met – well, why should she? It wasn't like they'd ever had any sort of a relationship where Elma felt at liberty to ask Gran anything. Truth be told, she'd never been interested in Gran's life. Her primary adolescent goal had been to steer clear of her.

The less I saw of her, the less chance I was in trouble.

She tried to convince herself now that she was only here as the result of a bargain struck between herself and her father for driving lessons.

There's more to you than meets the eye – isn't there, Gran?

'That one there.'

Gran pointed to the second floor of the wooden building.

'He always took the same room. Said he wouldn't stay if he didn't have that one.'

'So Charlie wasn't local then?' Elma asked.

She knew very little about her grandfather – just bits and pieces she'd picked up when she'd overheard Aunt Livie and her dad talking together.

Funny, but I though they all grew up in the same neighbourhood.

'Charlie?'

It was Gran's voice that sounded surprised now.

'Humph, Charlie stay up the mountain? Not likely.'

Miriam went quiet again and Elma wondered what she was remembering.

Was it a red card or a tricksy, sticky blue one?

'Oh, his name doesn't matter, does it?'

Elma didn't dare to answer but focussed her attention down-wards on the three happy girls with broad smiles.

Miriam, if it was her, had her arm in a friendly embrace around the joyful Moira.

'I can tell you it was a shock the first day we met, or rather,' Miriam laughed, 'the first day I laid eyes on him.'

Oh my goodness. Gran, do I really want to hear this?

Elma squirmed in her seat and looked about.

Oh, no, now I'm getting paranoid.

'I'd been working at the Springs Hotel for some time. I was quite good at it actually. Weekends and holidays mostly.'

Her smile is real – I think she liked her job.

'My father got me the position when I was fifteen. He was a saw doctor – sharpened knives at home or from the back of his truck. We lived directly below the hotel – well as the crow flies if you know the saying. I could get from home to work in half an hour, just straight up through the bush.'

Elma had never heard her grandmother speak so freely, or without criticising anyone.

'He chose that room because of the sunshine.'

Her face lit up, a dreamy glow in her eyes, her tone becoming softer with every word. Elma could hardly hear her.

'He loved the way it rose of a morning, stretching its arms across the hills to greet the day, "bringing life and colour into the world," he would say.'

She gave a little laugh.

Elma stared, dumbfounded, never expecting Gran to share such a romantic view of the world.

'Here I was,' Miriam's eyes became more animated, 'balancing a breakfast tray in one hand and a clean set of towels in the other, and I knocked on the door with my elbow.'

Miriam jabbed backwards, re-enacting the movement.

'I thought I heard him say come in, but I don't know, the door wasn't quite shut and it swung inwards all by itself. And that was it.'

And that was what, Gran?

Elma wanted to know what Gran had seen, but she knew better than to ask.

Just wait. She'll say if she wants to.

'He was standing there naked, well, nearly; he had a towel around him. We didn't have baths in the rooms but there was running water by the time I'd started working there.'

'The breakfast tray, Gran, you're getting side tracked, what happened to the breakfast tray?'

Miriam looked at Elma and stared straight into her blue eyes, as if trying to remember something important.

'I told you, Livinda. I told you that day when I got home, how could you forget that?'

Elma didn't dare to speak but she wanted to know what Gran was on about. The way she was talking was as if it was all real, like something that had truly happened. She wondered if they were both caught in some sort of time warp where the world goes on around you with people cleaning and building and doing everyday things that people do while you just sit still in one spot, eyes fixed on the eyes before you like a mirror, daring not to turn away in case the moment is destroyed and you get left stranded on your own, back in reality.

She thinks I'm her sister.

Elma sat so still she thought she might forget to breathe.

'The breakfast tray,' she repeated in a hushed tone, not wanting to break the spell.

'What happened to the breakfast tray?'

'Well, his towel dropped to the ground and my tray dropped only seconds after it.'

She let out a raucous laugh.

'Coffee and milk and sugar everywhere, I'd broken half the crockery.'

And she continued, 'I was so embarrassed I didn't have a clue what to do. I can only thank God that the sunshine was streaming in the window behind him so brightly that I couldn't see a thing.'

Elma looked away. She couldn't believe what she was hearing.

That is not the gran I know! What is going on?

'Gran!' was all she could say.

'It was Moira who came to my rescue; she'd heard the crash and helped me get things back to normal. We hid the broken cup and plates in my apron. Scott just laughed at us. Stood there naked, hushing us to be quiet, while he laughed his head off. Didn't care about the tray and said he wouldn't say anything about it to our boss, you know, he'd just keep it our little secret.'

She touched the side of her nose with her index finger.

'He didn't make us go and get more food or anything.'

Miriam smiled and gave a sigh.

'I'm sure I would have lost my job if he had'.

Well that wasn't right, Gran!

He shouldn't have said come in.

It was his fault, not yours.

What a creep!

Elma didn't like this "Scott" person, whoever he was. But that wasn't how Miriam was portraying him.

'I was very lucky I didn't lose my job.'

She looked as if there was more to say, but stopped as if her playback button had been paused.

Elma was working up to saying how rude she thought this bloke was, but just as she opened her mouth to speak, cold drips of water landed on her shoulder.

Where did that come from?

Dad! He was standing over her – water dripping from his hair and clothing.

'What the heck are you doing? I've been ringing your phone for the last ten minutes. Where the hell are your bags? Do you want a ride to the airport or not?'

Chapter 13

It was pelting down by the time they arrived at the airport roundabout. Martin hardly spoke during the 30 minute drive.

'I said I was sorry, Dad. I just didn't think to turn my phone back on. Gran had some interesting stuff to say today. I just didn't think about my phone.'

She tried smiling in his direction, but Martin wouldn't look her way.

'Elma, that's enough. I don't want to hear any of your excuses.'

The wipers were going flat chat, pushing water off one side of the windscreen and sprinting back to push more water off the other side. Elma hoped the plane would still be on time. She would add to **Gran's Ramblings** as soon as she was in the air.

'I'm wet through and I don't need any crap from you or her.' He stared straight ahead concentrating hard on driving in the rain.

He let her out at the curb and dumped her bag beside her.

If he regretted what he'd said, it didn't show. Elma hesitated in giving him a kiss goodbye.

'This time next week, hey Dad?'

She hurried to the shelter of the terminal and turned back to wave, but Martin was already gone from view.

It was still bucketing down when he slowed the ute and turned off onto the side road that led under the Tasman Bridge. There was sudden silence after the constant drumming of rain on the cab roof and its absence left the wipers at odds with themselves as they juddered back and forth on the drying windscreen. The bridge above carried five lanes of traffic but the sound was far enough away to be muted by the weather, with the occasional toot or rumble of a larger vehicle breaking the void in which Martin sat while gazing at the river.

The water swirled and churned angrily around the base of the great concrete pylons that held the bridge in place above him. A few seagulls fought over something caught between the rocks on the mid-tideline. The tide was maybe on its way out. Martin wasn't sure. He wasn't sure about a lot of things. He'd called in to see his mother on his way to work earlier that day. And who wouldn't, after what had happened the previous night?

He hadn't known what to say when he'd arrived to collect her and Elma from the Wrest Point Casino. The police were already there and, as a courtesy, they stayed for a few minutes to meet her family. His chest became tight as he thought about it.

'Bloody embarrassing,' he said aloud.

Water swished up from the rocks below, the wind pushed rain into his refuge.

'You'd think she'd have been happy to see me this morning, but she wasn't.'

She'd been in a foul mood, sitting up in bed with an empty breakfast tray on her bed table. The curtains had been open but it was early and the heavy rain prevented light from entering the room.

'Gee it's dark in here, Mum,' he'd said switching on the overhead light.

'Get out! And turn that off as you go,' Miriam said flailing her arm in the direction of the door.

Martin stood his ground.

'I'm only here for a minute, Mum – I'm on my way to work. Down the Channel,' he added.

'I wanted to make sure you were safe after last night.'

'Of course I'm safe! What? You think I can't look after myself?'

She glared at Martin who began tapping his finger up and down on the end of the bed.

'You won't look after me and you let Livinda run off to the Mainland. You can't look after anything – can't even look after yourself. Look at you, you're, you're, hopeless and ...'

'Woah, Mum,' Martin cut in, 'slow down a bit, what are you talking about?'

He often got a mouthful of unkindness from his mother, but somehow he just didn't always expect it and he certainly hadn't prepared himself for it this morning.

'Oh, you know, Martin. Letting that young girl of yours go off to the city. What do you think is going to happen? You don't know what she'll get up to. She's far too young to be out there all by herself. Don't be surprised if she gets herself in trouble. She's naive and clueless. What if she goes missing Martin? Gets raped or murdered or anything and here you are just standing there not giving a jolly damn.'

'Mum, what the hell are you on about?'

'Oh, just go, Martin. You were always such a disappointment.'

Miriam bowed her head and closed her eyes.

That was the end of that.

Martin, stood there, like he'd been hit on the head by a cricket bat.

'You all right?' came the voice of a nurse as she entered the room.

'Your mum sounds a bit upset.'

She looked at Miriam with her head bowed and eyes closed, her hair neatly pulled back and stacked in its usual high bun, the empty breakfast tray showing she wasn't off her food.

'Everything looks okay,' the nurse confirmed.

She looked at Martin and with a smile on her face gave him a wink, 'She's having her morning prayer, is she?'

Miriam's eye flashed open.

'Oh there we are, Miriam,' the nurse said cheerily. 'How are you today?'

'Go away, the pair of you. I want to be alone.'

Martin's virtual concussion receded. He took one quick glance at her as he turned and left the room, swearing to himself that he'd never go back.

Now he sat under the bridge to think the day through.

'It was crap leaving there and crap driving to work in the rain.'

'Why does she do it?'-

'I swore I wouldn't go back.'

'She's right. I can't help her and I'm not going to put myself through that every time I visit.'

Martin knew it wasn't every time – just sometimes – like once a week and, considering he popped in most mornings on his way past, once a week really wasn't every time.

'But I'm not doing it anymore!'

And that was what was really annoying him because he'd said that before and not stuck to it. And when he'd said it to himself, again, this morning he'd been more determined than ever not to break his vow.

'But she wouldn't answer her damned phone, so I had to

149

go in there again.'

'No, Mum's where she should be and that is where I'm leaving her. They're there to look after her. That's their job. They don't need me going in and upsetting her.'

Martin stared at the river wondering which way the tide was going. He didn't really know much about the Derwent, a bit of history about the Europeans building a settlement further upstream and then changing their minds and moving the township down to where Hobart is today. He remembered one of the pylons being hit by a boat and collapsing part of the bridge in the 70's, when he was about five years old. At the time he lived with his mother on the Eastern Shore. The closure hadn't seemed to affect them as they hardly ever crossed it, his mother going to local shops. And he remembered it being closed for a reconciliation march back in 2000, only because that was the year Elma was born. But most of that was about the bridge that went over the river and not about the river itself. Tides and weather patterns he knew nothing about.

He knew people jumped off the bridge. He knew the water had claimed many more lives than it had spared. He knew now the bridge was monitored with cameras – but it wasn't back then – back when his black dog day had dragged him up to the top – to the point of no return.

He'd walked from the city, across the Domain – drawn to the bridge for no apparent reason, maybe the arch of light twitching in the rain – or the symbolism of crossing from one side to the other and starting over. Or maybe to be away from here, from himself and from his failings.

The bottle of whisky he'd carried had slipped from his wet hand, making a dull clunk on the slushy gravel – one third of the liquid bleeding into miniature rivulets beneath his sodden boots. He stumbled forward, groping frantically in the dark, ignoring the cuts and grazes to his hands.

The bottle swayed back and forth chinking against his teeth each time he brought it to his lips.

He took a swig. And another. Closing his eyes as the quick flame licked the back of his throat. Each mouthful failed to quench the hopelessness rising in his gut.

He was drenched, angry and alone with only the wind and rain to witness his final 2am stagger to the brow of the bridge.

Martin slumped down, his back hard against the iron battens. The crazy shrill cry of the storm coursed through the bars. An empty bottle of Jack Daniels pushed against his legs, held there by the curtain of rain flowing along the path beneath his knees.

He cried aloud, over and over – 'you're useless, clueless, a stupid fool, you never listen …'

They were just words – they meant nothing – just cruel insults from his mother.

What hurt was Liz. He'd given her everything – everything he had – anything she wanted – whatever he could do to please his perfect, wonderful, beautiful, smart wife.

'Only she isn't any of those things,' he screamed at the wind.

'No! She's a liar. A cheat.' The words slurred from his mouth. She was not the woman he had fallen in love with.

She'd taken everything – everything he held dear, everything he valued, and she'd left him with what?

'Nothing – nothing at all!' he screamed at the wind – screamed at the water – screamed again and threw the bottle across the road. It glistened for an instant before smashing into pieces on the shiny bitumen and disappearing into the torrents of rain.

Martin pulled himself up from the ground gripping the rail

to steady himself before lunging towards the top of the barrier. He was shaking – unable to control his limbs. He tried repeatedly, slumping back to the ground again and again, each time a growing mess of depressive emotions – a puddle of nothing, a failure at even his own death.

For a moment he forgot his purpose – losing his will to succeed. He wiped his nose with the back of his hand smearing the mucous across his face.

One last time he rose, this time angry – determined to succeed. Neither his mother nor Liz were going to get the better of him – this was it! **This was it!** They didn't want him and he didn't want them. Not now – not ever. A little way to his left was a steel maintenance box, maybe a fire hydrant attached to the barrier. Did he have to jump from the top? What difference would a few metres make? He wedged his foot between the box and the railing, slipping twice before heaving himself upwards and flinging his leg over the top rail. He lay still, shaking – his chest flat against the cold steel –legs dangling one each side of the barrier. He'd made it. He gripped tightly, held flat by the rain. Was the wind trying to push him back to safety?

Of all the surprising things it was Elma who, without ever knowing it, saved the river from claiming Martin's life that night.

He'd tried to let go of the bridge and slide off into oblivion, but the wind had kept firm, demanding he not cross the line. And Elma – he saw her standing in a beam of light on the footpath only metres from his face, her little school bag with owls and rainbows scattered on the pink denim casing – so happy to be going off to school to play with her friends. She waved at him and blew him a kiss and suddenly he realised she had less than he had. She'd lost her mother only weeks earlier and now she would lose him as well. His heart broke for her. This was wrong. He slackened his grip, allowing the wind to push him back onto the footpath.

'I'm so sorry Elma, I'm so sorry, I'm here for you.'

His voice carried over the side of the bridge dropping into the churning waters below.

In his dark moments it was always timtumili minanya that appeared in his mind's eye. He was drawn to it. Sometimes it felt so real when anxiety seized him that he wondered if he'd really fallen that day. The pain felt so real.

'Strange though,' he thought. 'I always see myself pinned against the south side and the water doesn't flow that way. Or does it when the tide turns?'

Martin didn't have a clue. He knew the river was tidal but he didn't know if that changed the overall directive flow or whether the current could be going one way on the surface of the river and another way beneath his view.

He'd had a lot counselling in the beginning – even spent time in the hospital.

Back then he didn't understand why he could feel so much pain and the next minute talk about the bridge and the river like they didn't affect him.

The psychiatrist he'd seen back then had said it was normal for some people to disassociate themselves from something one moment and be caught in a tide of emotion the next.

'Trauma,' he'd said, 'can manifest in many ways. Sometimes the triggers are obvious and other times they sneak up on you and no one really knows why.'

That was the truth, Martin thought. Fine one minute – a complete mess the next.

He felt calmer now. The feeling of anxiety in his chest was easing along with the rain. He shivered and turned the engine on. It would be a few minutes before the warm air would seep in through the vents.

'Hmm,' he thought.

'I've made it through another day. Still, I wish I'd said a proper goodbye to Elma. Maybe I'll ring her tonight. After I give Paula a call.'

Chapter 14

'Well, I've been up the mountain a few times recently,' Elma babbled on, making friendly conversation with Cathy and Aunt Livie as they drove from Tullamarine Airport towards Ballan.

'It was raining cats and dogs when I left Hobart. Really rough in the air. I nearly threw up my lunch.'

This wasn't true, as Elma hadn't eaten lunch. But she couldn't stop smiling and chatting.

'I can't wait to see your new place, Aunt Livie.'

'Tomorrow, dear, that will be tomorrow. You're staying at Cathy's tonight.'

Cathy smiled at Elma in the rear view mirror.

'She's cooked us a lovely dinner. Joshua will drop me at my flat on his way back to Melton.'

'How's Martin going?' Cathy cut in.

'Good,' replied Elma.

Not talking to me – but good I suppose.

'And Aunt Miriam?'

'Yeah, she's good too.'

Apart from her escape last night and general bad attitude to the world.

155

Elma took Miriam's criticisms less personally these days and, after her talk with Dr Gordon, had come to realise Gran couldn't help herself and was probably doing her best.

Although I'm still not totally convinced that she doesn't know what she is doing … all the time.

'Oh, Aunt Livie, you look so good!'

She reached forward between the front car seats and patted her aunt's shoulder.

Livie raised her hand to her shoulder and held Elma's hand there for a few seconds. They both beamed.

Josh was bigger than Elma remembered.

Not the lanky teenager I used to play with.

He arrived shortly before they were ready to eat and was eager to leave as soon as he'd devoured his last mouthful.

'You're in a bit of a hurry, Josh?' Cathy queried.

'Gran doesn't need you rushing her out the door. Give her a minute to let her food settle at least.' Cathy picked up her fork and continued with what was left of her own meal.

Josh pulled a set of keys out of his pocket and plonked them on the table.

I think that means he's ready to go. What's the rush, I wonder?

Livie looked at Cathy and smiled, 'It's okay Cathy, really it is. I'm tired and need to go anyway.'

Cathy threw a terse glance at her son.

'See, Mum, Gran is ready. I told Nell I'd be back soon.'

Josh stood up, grabbed the keys and jangled them in his hand.

It was strange for Elma to hear Josh call Aunt Livie 'Gran'.

I guess we don't see each other often enough to make it sound normal.

And who was Nell? His new girlfriend?

The last few times she'd visited Cathy, Josh had been away on school trips and then sharing a flat in Ballarat while he was at Uni. And now he lived somewhere near Melton and worked at the airport.

I guess I haven't seen him for a couple of years now. Certainly I don't remember him looking so grown up.

'Hey Elma, I'll catch you tomorrow. Pick you up from Gran's about two-ish? I wanna get started on those driving lessons. I'm back on the work roster Wednesday arvo.

'All good, Josh. I'll be ready.'

Maybe – I don't know if I want to, there was so much traffic between here and the airport and I'm not sure if you'll be patient enough.

Elma stood up and gave Aunt Livie a hug.

'Oh, and Mum, don't forget to tell Dad I can't make it to the game this weekend.'

'Cathy,' Elma asked later, when Josh had left with Livie and she and Cathy were clearing up the dishes.

'Can I ask you a question?'

'Hmm, that sounds like it could be serious. Do you want me to make a cuppa?'

Cathy filled the kettle with water and switched it on without waiting for the reply. She and Steve usually had a cuppa after they'd cleaned up, but Steve was working late and she'd saved his dinner to reheat.

'You and Dad are pretty close – like I know you grew up together.'

Elma hesitated, wound the tea-towel around her hand a couple of times and fiddled with the corner seam.

'Well come on, spit it out, Girl.'

Cathy stopped making the tea and gave her full attention to the struggling Elma.

'Well, I just wanted to know what my mum was like. You must have met her?'

'Gee Elma, that's a biggie. What do you want to know? What do you know already?'

'Nothing. I don't know anything. No one ever mentions her. You know Dad. It's, well, it's a taboo subject. We don't talk about her.'

Elma had started with one question but now more and more questions were building up behind it. She just had to get them out. It didn't seem right for them to be hiding on the inside any longer, not now, not since she'd stumbled across the debt.

'I think I have a right to know. Don't I?'

She looked up at the wall behind the dining table. It was covered in frames of all shapes and sizes showing snippets of Cathy and Steve's lives through the years.

'Dad hasn't even shown me a photo. Like there aren't even any wedding photos in anyone's collection, even here,' she pointed at the wall.

'There are photos here of your life – you and Dad and your kids and Steve. Josh and Sarah and me as a baby. Look at that one, everyone at your wedding. But where is she? She's not in the photo. I've never seen a photo of Mum and Dad's wedding. I don't even really know if they were married.'

'Oh, Honey,' Cathy sighed and put her arms around Elma pulling her into a hug.

'I don't know what to say.'

She could feel the tension in Elma's body. Elma wasn't used to cuddles from anyone but Aunt Livie.

'Come on, let me make that tea.'

Cathy stepped back without moving her eyes from Elma's face, which was now looking down at the floor. Her arm holding the tea-towel hung by her side.

Cathy gently picked up Elma's hand and watched Elma's face rise up with it. She smiled a little smile at the sad-looking girl and waited a few moments for the tears to come, because she knew they would – and they did.

She pulled Elma close to her, breathing deeply as Elma sobbed into the soft fabric of her cotton scarf. Cathy stared out the window into the darkness. This was always going to happen, Cathy thought. You can't just make someone's mother disappear and expect the child not to notice. It was always wrong. Elma had the right to know what really happened.

By the time Steve arrived home Elma and Cathy were snuggled close together on the sofa, wrapped up in blankets and cradling mugs of hot chocolate.

'This looks cosy,' he said leaning over the back of the couch and kissing Cathy on the head.

'Hiya, Elma. I see you made it here okay.'

Elma looked up, giving Steve a smile. She sniffed and wiped her eyes with a tissue. She wasn't sure what to say.

'Thanks,' was all she managed.

Cathy turned her head around to catch her husband's eye and placed her finger on her lips.

'Your dinner's on the bench and the heater's still on in the dining room, Darling.'

She flicked her fingers at him in a motion to go away. He looked at the two of them bundled up close on the couch and took the hint to leave, bowing low as he stepped back quietly.

'Yes, sure Cath. I'll pop it in the microwave and eat by the heater.'

Cathy blew him a kiss.

'You didn't have to do that,' Elma said.

'Thanks, though.'

'It's okay, Elma, we all need a bit of cry time without the men about.'

Cathy smiled.

'It must be a bit hard at your place now, with just you and Martin.'

Elma studied Cathy's face. She was calm. She looked like her mother, with the same fly-away hair and, like most of the family, had blue eyes, *soft blue,* thought Elma reaching for a fresh tissue to dab at her nose.

Elma had never had so many questions answered at one time in her life.

She'd been surprised to learn that, even though Martin and Cathy had grown up so close in age and proximity, they weren't the best friends they had once been.

'After your Dad made the decision to just let Lizzie get away with everything she'd done – I felt so let down I had trouble supporting him anymore. I know he was hurting but we were hurting too and I guess I was disappointed that there was never any justice. Well, as far as I was concerned, anyway.'

Cathy looked away.

Elma could tell she was crying again.

I didn't know. I just thought no one cared enough to tell me.

'Mum was just as bad as Martin.'

'Cathy!' Cathy used her mother's voice, and Elma nearly giggled.

'If it's Martin's wishes not to talk about it, then I suggest we respect his wishes.'

'In the end that's why I left Tassie. I just couldn't play their games anymore.'

She smiled a weak smile at Elma and sipped at her warm drink.

'What about Gran? What did she think of Dad keeping it all a secret?' Elma asked.

'Well, I know it was over twelve years ago but Aunt Miriam's mind was already playing up by then and no one really told her anything.'

Cathy gave an awkward laugh.

'She, I think, ended up with the same impression as you, that Lizzie had run off with some rich dude from overseas. And forgive me if you don't hear me calling that woman your mum, because as far as I'm concerned she never mothered you.'

Elma felt somewhat empowered by the conversation.

As surreal as it is, I'm not freaking out at all. I just want to know. I'm sorry I haven't always made it easy for Dad.

'What happened after she took all Dad's money? I mean why didn't he do something about that?'

'Elma, I can only give you my opinion and, it may not be the truth, but I think it was pride. Firstly, he'd been set up and ripped off, and secondly, I think he refused to declare himself bankrupt and thought that if he worked hard enough he'd regain the money without losing face. He probably thought that he was protecting you.'

'So she never went to prison or anything?'

'Well, yeah, but that's another story.'

'Another story?'

Elma raised her eyebrows.

'She went to prison about six years later because she tried the same thing again with someone else, only this time there were no children involved and the new husband didn't let her get away with it.'

'Wow, my mother was a criminal!'

What did that mean? Stealing from Martin was one thing but going to prison was another.

Or does it matter? Are you only a criminal if you get caught?

'Your mother was a whiz at maths and accounting but I'm sorry to say she did way more than just manipulate numbers in a book. And I still can't believe Martin just stood by and let it happen.'

It was complicated and confusing.

'But if that was years ago and Dad worked hard, why is the money so tight now?'

It was hard for Elma to put it all together; some of the dots were still not connected.

Maybe Cathy doesn't know everything, maybe, I don't ... I don't know what to think.

'Oh, he's got money all right,' Cathy blurted the words out before she had a chance to check them.

'He just doesn't like to spend it. He lives in poverty to punish himself. Whoops, sorry Elma. That probably isn't true. I just get so angry at him.'

He does have money! He's just afraid to spend it.

Is he scared I'll rip him off like she did?

Elma turned away and Cathy knew she'd said too much. She was supposed to be the adult in this conversation and only after the words had escaped did she realise how angry she still was about the whole thing.

'Hey Elma, it was very hard for your dad to get back on his feet and he did an amazing job given the circumstances. The global financial crisis was a huge blow, but regardless he did carry on. You have been the light of his life. I don't like to think how he would have gotten by without you.'

'Did Gran help him out?'

'No, your gran –' she gave a laugh, '– she never had money. In fact, it's your Dad who's paying for her to be in one of the best nursing homes in Tassie.'

Elma hadn't considered how expensive Gran's care might be.

I guess I was wrapped up in how Aunt Livie leaving was going to affect me. Didn't think about anything but myself.

'Well, I guess he had to do that really, didn't he?' said Elma, trying to sound logical.

'She is his mum, after all.'

'No, not at all. Martin is a saint for doing it. If my mum treated me the way Aunt Miriam treated Martin, I wouldn't have given her the time of day.'

'I don't understand. She is his mum, right?'

'Yeah, but she mothered him as much as yours mothered you. And that was zero.'

She continued, 'That woman used to upset me so much.'

'Like how?' Elma ventured to say, not really sure if Cathy was remembering everything correctly.

'Your gran liked me and didn't like Martin. Simple as that. Mum always said it might have been different for Martin if he'd been a girl. But she was a bit of a cow.'

Elma put her mug down on the table and wiped her hands on a tissue. She was quiet, hoping Cathy would continue without her asking. She yawned and stretched a little.

Who would have known the last forty-eight hours would be so eventful.

'A cow?' she said when Cathy didn't respond in the given time. *I don't know how much more I can cope with tonight or anytime. It's all so mucked up.*

'Oh, she was so mean to him. We'd both be there, I could do no wrong and he could do no right.' She put on her best Miriam voice and Elma thought she should, maybe, go into acting.

"Get your shoes off the couch Martin! Can't you think for yourself just once in your life? Look at Cathy – you're both the same age but you don't see her with feet on the couch, do you?"

'She'd go on and on and we were only like eight years old.'

Cathy put her cup down and looked up at the clock.

'You know, when Dad passed away I felt sure Mum would come over here and live but instead she let Aunt Miriam move in with her.'

Cathy shook her head.

'I'm sorry, Elma. I really thought you should have known all this earlier but families are just such a strange lot. You okay?'

--

The sun shone in through the window, briefly disorientating Elma who had intended sleeping in Cathy's spare room but found herself still on the lounge room couch.

Must have fallen asleep.

She had a pillow under her head and despite being in the middle of a room, felt warm and cosy. She lay there soaking in the warmth as the sleep melted away from her mind. Last night's memories and dreams began sorting themselves into order; she wondered which ones were there before she'd fallen asleep and which ones had been created overnight.

The sweet smell of blueberry pancakes swirled over the top of the couch and landed on the coffee table as Steve placed a steamy hot plate of food in front of her nose.

'Orders from the boss,' he said, 'she wants to know if Madame prefers tea or coffee at this hour?'

Maybe –

– maybe today things will fall into place.

Maybe today it will work out okay.

164

Chapter 15

Saturday was warmer in Ballan than it had been since the beginning of May.

A top of 14 – it's warmer in Tas, maybe showers later this afternoon. She unplugged her phone from the charger; intending to take it with her to Aunt Livie's but knowing there was no free WIFI at her aunt's place and she'd used up all her own data a week ago. Aunt Livie didn't have a computer of any sort unless you included her solar powered calculator or Fisher & Paykel washing machine.

Elma stuffed her phone into the side pocket of her suitcase. 'Done,' she said.

Cathy and Steve watched her wheel her case towards the front door. Against their strongest persuasions Elma had convinced them that she would walk the one and a half kilometres to Aunt Livie's place.

'I know exactly where it is. I've studied the map,' she gave a cheery smile

'And if I don't ring in half an hour you have my full permission to come find me.'

'Hmm. What if it rains, Elma? We don't want you coming all this way just to catch your death from a cold.'

What does that even mean?

'Oh, Steve. Stop fussing. I'll be all right.'

'I'm coming too.'

Cathy grabbed her boots from the rack beside the front door and started pulling them on.

'It's okay. I can do this,' said Elma swinging her bag over her shoulder and gripping the handle of her "must be less than 7kg" suitcase.

'It's not going to rain 'til late this afternoon.'

'Come on, let's go.'

Cathy ignored Elma's plea and stepped forward down the path.

'Come get me in an hour and bring Elma's bag with you,' she said and began prising Elma's fingers from the handle of her suitcase.

Elma gave a laugh but no resistance,

'Okay all right. You can take the bag.'

'I'll get it,' Steve called as he waved farewell.

The wind cooled the air temperature by a few degrees. Winter was truly on its way.

Elma pulled the hood of her jacket up over her head.

Cathy shivered despite the pace at which they were walking.

'I can ring Steve now, if you like.'

'No, we're nearly there.'

Elma was glad she'd left her suitcase behind.

I kinda like Ballan, picket fences, arty gardens and leafless trees.

A few of the large ashes and oaks weren't completely bare, but harboured one or two stubborn leaves on their twiggy branches. Occasionally, in a sheltered spot, piles of raked leaves could be seen mulching beneath the naked trees, leaves gone – taken by the wind or council depending on where they'd fallen.

I bet Aunt Livie has raked up a pile for her garden.

'That's it there,' Cathy pointed to the other end of the road as they rounded the final corner completing their walk from the south to the north side of town. They had crossed the main street of Ballan a couple of blocks back but Elma avoided the shops and chose to walk on the side streets.

I want Aunt Livie to take me there tomorrow.

She remembered a couple of cafés, a gift shop and a supermarket.

If they're open on a Sunday.

The wind gave a sudden gust and the lightweight hood of her jacket blew back from her head. She left it down, allowing the wind to blow the cobwebs out of her brain. I needed that walk, she thought, piling all her questions into the right compartments, stacking them in cubicles in her mind. There was a lot to sort through, and none of them behaved as they should, some bits of information wanting to be in two or three imaginary slots at once. Slivers of the answers here, missing bits over there – questions needing to be peeled apart leaving gaps, like the sticky dockets and papers in her drawer back home. She'd never considered her father going through her desk while she was away.

But what if he did?

More questions.

What if he found the pile of papers still wrapped in the tea towel, bits of failing red rubber unable to keep them together? What would he think? He'd go off his rocker! That was for sure.

It was confusing and she knew "what if" questions were dangerous. She knew that from her old school psychologist, who labelled them "over thinking" – they could take you places you never needed to go – the more questions answered, the more questions created.

I'll clean out that drawer as soon as I get home

Dad lost his money, no it was stolen – he lost everything – he didn't lose me – he lied to me – Lizzie, she lied to him – she took his money – no, she took their money – why didn't she like me? – She never wanted me? – Maybe Dad doesn't either?

No, don't go there, don't even think it – why did she do it? – Gran doesn't like me – Did Gran like Lizzie? – Why did Dad let Gran treat him like that? Or Lizzie – is that weak or strong? They all lied to me – Did I save Fergus' number? And how did he even get into this mess of questions? I totally don't need him in my head right now. I think my head is going to explode.

Elma took a lead from Cathy and decided that she'd refer to her mother as Lizzie. Somehow it kept her at an emotional distance. She looked at Cathy who was walking beside her.

Why didn't she say anything to me earlier?

That question was probably the easiest to sort as Cathy had explained last night,

she hadn't said anything "by orders from her mother" and the need to respect Martin's wishes.

But why? If something is wrong, it is wrong ... Shouldn't we speak out when something is wrong?

It seemed like even sweet Aunt Livie wasn't without fault. And there she was standing in front of them on her new porch already surrounded by plants in terracotta pots.

'Not much colour at this time of the year,' she told Elma.

'I could pot some begonias but I'm afraid the frosts might get them.'

'Wow,' said Elma peering into the small courtyard outside Livie's new flat.

Auntie Livie showed her the guest room.

Sunshine in the morning. I like that.

The lounge looked out towards the road and across to parkland covered in birds and bushes. A noisy bunch of sulphur-crested cockatoos rose in unison, heading for another site.

Perhaps they're heading for the hills.

'This is nice, Aunt Livie I can see why you would want this unit.'

It was one of three – unit – car shed – unit – car shed – unit – car shed. "The triplets" thought Elma, she considered Aunt Livie's unit well positioned.

The corner unit had more views than the other two.

The Formica table with its hazy green and blue speckles, direct from her Tasmanian kitchen, was laid with two familiar plates, two cups and a tea pot.

Same, same but different.

Uncle Dave's cabinet settled against the wall, contents arranged as expected. The kitchen floor mat was still planted in floral patterns just as Elma remembered it. So familiar and comforting and yet so different.

No front porch for long talks, no river of conversation flowing beneath a bridge. Just a kitchen table with a sandwich lunch and peppermint tea. Steve had long since picked up Cathy and dropped off Elma's bag.

'Oh, and by the way,' Cathy said on her way out, 'I just got a text from Josh to say he won't make it in time for the lesson today but he'll be here tomorrow by midday and will take you for lunch and a driving lesson. Sorry Elma.'

Cathy gave a big sigh.

I wonder why he didn't just text me himself.

And then she realised he probably had, but as usual her phone was turned off.

169

'Aunt Livie,' Elma jumped into the deep end before she had time to talk herself out of it.

This was her other set of questions, the ones about Gran and her ramblings.

'Who was Scott?'

'Sorry, Elma, Scott who?'

It was obvious Livie had no idea who Elma was referring to.

'Gran's Scott, the one from the Springs Hotel up the mountain.'

The colour, if Elma was to use a cliché, simply drained from Livie's face. A new type of grey, one that she had never thought she'd see, deathly grey. Her aunt's lip quivered as if forming words that weren't adequate to pass out into the open. Aunt Livie's china tea cup had been poised at her lips but now as Elma watched Aunt Livie lowered it in increments like the second hand on the carved wooden clock that had once sat on the mantelpiece in a faraway place in Aunt Livie's mind.

Elma's own hand began to shake –

What have I done?

She raced around to the other side of the table. She wanted to shake Aunt Livie, bring her back to herself.

What have I done? What have I done!

She placed her arm around her aunt hoping with all her might the old lady wouldn't collapse completely.

'No Elma, sit. It's okay. I'm okay.'

Livie's voice was soft, her colour returning, her words concise and clear. Livie knew there were very few people in the world who would have known anything about Miriam and Scott. Elma could only know one of them.

'What did she tell you Elma? You know she doesn't always tell the truth, she gets confused.'

170

Elma pulled a chair up next to Aunt Livie and sat on the edge facing her aunt.

I wonder who she is covering for, her sister or herself,

'Oh, Aunt, I didn't want to upset you. I just need to know.'

'I don't know that you do need to know,' Livie turned her face from the table to look directly at Elma,

'That was Miriam's past, why don't we just leave it there?'

'Please, Aunt,'

Elma was certain there was more to the story than just that first towel dropping incident.

'You used to tell me how Gran loved working up there.'

'Well she did, that was the truth.'

'Then what's the problem?'

I wish I'd taken a photo of the postcard. Maybe when I'm back at Cathy's I'll find it online.

'What did she tell you?'

Livie moved her cup around on the saucer and glanced off through the glass door into the backyard. A blackbird was flitting about in the mulch, kicking leaves this way and that, determined to find and extract every insect it could from beneath the litter.

'Let's get the dishes done and have a game of Scrabble.'

'No, I don't want to play Scrabble.'

Elma's heart pounded in her chest.

'I want to know about you and Gran growing up and I want to know about this Scott person.'

There, she'd done it. Finally said what she wanted to, although she was still worried about Aunt Livie turning grey again.

'Scott. Hmm. Scott Hamilton is the man you are referring to and what my sister ever saw in him I'll never know. He was bad news from the start to the finish. Me telling you about him isn't going to change things one little bit.'

But to Elma's surprise Aunt Livie continued to talk.

'He was a lot older than her, of course, and she'd been warned to keep away from him.'

Elma dared not ask why, but sat biting her lip and waiting.

'He worked for a pharmaceutical company on the Mainland – somewhere that only serviced Tassie every three months or so. He'd do his visits and then spend his last weekend up at the Springs before flying back to wherever it was he came from,' she circled her hand in the air indicating a city or town somewhere in the distance.

'I believe two other girls had already been dismissed the previous year because of his shenanigans. What the thrill was in giving young people alcohol, I'll never know.'

Aunt Livie shook her head and gave a sigh.

'Miriam loved her job so she didn't talk to anyone up there about him but she'd confide in me.'

She's on a roll – don't stop now.

Elma was confused when Aunt Livie gave a warm smile as if remembering something with fondness.

'We had our codes, Miriam and I. You know if we were on the watch out for Dad we'd blow imaginary smoke rings into the air and if we needed to talk about Scott Hamilton we'd use his initials like this.'

Aunt Livie held her pointer finger up to her lips and made a shh sound as if telling Elma to be quiet.

'Did Gran drink, Aunt Livie?'

Is that the secret?

'What? No, I don't think so, why would she do that?'

'Because you just said –'

Livie cut her off before she finished her question.

'I never said such a thing.'

Elma took a deep breath, sat back in her chair and waited.

'I never met him.'

She looked out the window – the bird had a huge earthworm wiggling in its beak.

'Apparently he loved the bush. Knew a lot about plants and trees. They had that in common.'

She hmmphed.

'When Miriam was offered a permanent job up there she didn't even ask Dad, she just said yes and that was that. I was left to get down town and catch the bus out to Ogilvie all by myself.'

Elma knew this wasn't exactly true as Aunt Livie and half of South Hobart caught the same bus to Ogilvie Girls' High School, the only state-run school for girls in Tasmania.

'Anyway, we didn't see much of each other through the daytime then. The following year I left school and started at Garrets.'

Elma wanted to interrupt her aunt and get her back on the Scott track –

but what if she stops talking altogether.

'Yeah, I know Garrets. You told me it was a sewing factory where you worked as a machine operator. You sewed school uniforms and stuff.'

The factory was upstairs in a building on the corner of Liverpool and Harrington where Spotlight is now. You can still see the concrete writing 'Garrets' on the second storey of the building.

'You were saying about Miriam and Scott?'

'Oh yes, he was much older, nearly thirty I think. She was completely head over heels about him. I didn't understand all the implications of their meetings at the time. I was good at keeping secrets. I still am. She always praised me for that you know.'

Elma was quite certain now that not all secrets should be kept. *I really don't like this Scott guy at all.*

'6 am Miriam had to be up there in time to help cook breakfast, serve the patrons and clean the rooms if people were leaving and service them if they were staying. They had some lovely gardens, such a lovely place, over one hundred rhododendrons and azalea bushes. It's different now ... since the fire.'

Elma wanted to know about the gardens –

but not right now – please stay on track, Livie.

'Mum and Dad were too busy to notice what time she got home from work. Well, Dad never got home 'til dark half the time and I got back from school about 4:30 so no one seemed to care that she finished work between one and two but was never home 'til after 4pm.'

Where did she go, Aunt Livie?'

'Oh, everywhere,' her face lit up with a smile.

'She knew all the tracks, all the huts, every bend and turn on the damned mountain.'

She stopped and took a sip of the now-cold tea.

'Maybe that was the attraction? She knew the mountain and he needed a guide.'

Aunt Livie began gathering the things from the table and placing them in the sink.

Elma followed closely.

'So what happened?'

'Elma, I don't think it's your business to know.'

'Oh, come on Aunt Livie, why not? It was years ago. Why does it have to be a secret now? What did they do so wrong? Did they murder someone and bury them up there?'

Aunt Livie looked aghast.

Oh no!

Elma closed her eyes.

I've done it again – said too much – so stupid!

She wanted to kick herself.

They finished the dishes in silence.

Chapter 16

Cars revved and accelerated past in the outer lane. Elma focussed on the road, two wide lanes of traffic streaming in the same direction. It felt good. She wore her black skinny jeans and flannel shirt.

'Fashion is a fickle thing,' Cathy had said when she saw the red and black checked shirt the day Elma had arrived.

'It's exactly the same as the one Steve wore 30 years ago when we first met.'

'But,' she added with a wink, 'it looks much better on you.'

'A bit faster, Elma.'

'What? No I'm already at 90,' Elma said, checking the speedometer.

'Speed limit's 110,' Josh retorted.

'Josh I'm on my L's, remember? This is a driving lesson. 90 is the limit.'

Don't push me. I'm doing my best.

'What are you on about? You're in Victoria now. The speed limit is 110.'

Elma wasn't satisfied.

'I'm not going faster,' she said in disbelief.

'Look,' Josh said, doing a quick check on Google, 'I am totally right. Here is the Victorian law for learner drivers.'

He read it from his phone.

'Wow, sorry, I should have known.'

She gripped the steering wheel a little tighter and pushed down on the accelerator, feeling the car surge forward as she did so.

'It's the fastest I've ever driven in my life.'

'We ain't in Tassie now, are we Toto?'

The words were not wasted on her, but she didn't respond. Ararat was an hour away, a lot of concentration was still needed between now and then; she'd save her energy for that.

Josh had the whole afternoon free, 'May as well make the most of it.'

Road signs, speed limits and exits whipped past.

'Might come back to that,' Josh said as they passed the sign saying Buangor cemetery.

'Why?'

There seemed to be less traffic now and Josh had increased the volume on the radio.

I'm doing all right; it's easier than I thought.

'So I can show you the grave with your name on it,' he said over the top of the music.

'What? What are you talking about?'

Is he joking?

She kept her eyes on the road.

'There isn't really a grave with my name on it, is there?'

'Yeah, of course there is. I wouldn't say it if it wasn't true, would I?'

He had a grin on his face.

Elma wasn't sure.

I don't really know you well enough to know. You're kind and then you're not. You snap at your mum and avoid your dad. I want to ask you stuff, but I'm scared.

'I don't know,' was all she could come up with,

I don't know your sense of humour.

She remembered back when they were younger – Sarah and Josh would come over for holidays at Aunt Livie's, or Gran as they called her. It was such a long time ago. They were always patient with her when they played board games and cards and she remembered laughing a lot but couldn't remember exactly what it was they laughed about.

It just felt nice being part of a bigger family. I always looked forward to it. It seems like we're all grown-ups now.

'Went there for a history trip with school once and I saw your name. Always thought I'd show you someday.'

'My name?'

'Well not quite your name, but very similar,' Josh said, laughing a little louder.

It wasn't Josh's idea to take Elma driving. It was Cathy who'd volunteered him.

'Not quite?' she asked waiting for a punchline or an explanation.

'We'll go back after lunch and I'll show you. Here now, slow down – that's our exit coming up in half a k.'

The car was automatic, slow downs were easy, not a lot of thinking needed – just put your foot on the brake and the gearbox did the rest. Still, she had to check the mirrors and indicate her intention to turn.

The smell of garlic rose from sourdough rolls and pumpkin soup as Josh and Elma headed into a café on the main street of Ararat. It had been easy to park, *different than Hobart and way bigger than Ballan.*

'Are we eating in or taking away?'

Elma shrugged her shoulders; she wasn't paying and didn't want to make the call.

'Come on, what do you want?' Josh flicked his wallet from one hand to the other. There were people in line behind them. Elma tried to say she didn't mind but the words wouldn't come out.

'Well?'

She looked up at Josh; he was at least 30cm taller than her. She looked at the people behind her but was still unable to say what she wanted.

'Okay we're eating in. Can we have a table for two?' he said to the waitress without using his manners.

--

'You're a bit of a mouse,' Josh said, hoeing into his burger. Sauce escaped from his mouth and rested on his chin.

Elma sat quietly sipping tomato soup from a white enamel bowl. She had more questions now. Aunt Livie had volunteered additional information earlier that morning. It was unexpected and there'd been no time to write it down. She was still processing the conversation.

Livie's lightweight gardening gloves were covered in a pink floral pattern.

'I've been thinking about yesterday and the talk we had at the lunch table.'

They were outside the unit, pulling weeds from between the pavers while they waited for Josh to arrive.

Elma held her breath,

Go on. What?

179

Aunt Livie sat herself down on the low brick wall that separated the garden from the driveway, a piece of grass twirled between her thumb and forefinger. The wind wisped her hair about her face but she didn't seem to mind.

'There really isn't any reason not to tell you about Miriam and her escapades. I mean what problems could it possibly cause now, 50 something years later? It's not like he's even alive to trouble her.'

Oh, so many questions.

'Who, Aunt Livie, who's not alive?'

and why and when and what trouble?

Although she did have some ideas she didn't want to overwhelm Aunt Livie by blurting it all out at once.

And dead or alive, Gran still seems troubled by something.

'Well, I think it was more than head over heels for Miriam. Oh, initially she was wary. They had told her to stay away from him. But the problem was nobody had told him he had to stay away from her. Well, you wouldn't, would you? He was a paying customer, a regular with money and no business is going to want that to leave, are they?'

It wasn't a question that Elma thought needed answering – it was more like a statement of fact or Aunt Livie's opinion anyway.

'He was somehow always on the same track as her. How he did it I'll never know. Seemed like whatever time she finished work and headed for home there he'd be, on the track ready to walk with her. Never all the way home mind you. Like I said, I never met him. And how he knew which way she was going to be coming home was always a mystery to me.'

Elma pulled off her gardening gloves.

'Go on,' she said, hoping to sound encouraging. 'What happened?'

She knew from previous conversations there were a number of tracks leading from the upper slopes of kunanyi down to the fire trail and Inglewood Road where Aunt Livie had lived as a child.

'I thought they spent too much time together. We'd lie in bed at night. We could hear Mum and Dad out in the lounge or kitchen so when it was safe to talk she'd tell me her secrets. Only to me of course, she could trust me.'

Aunt Livie turned and looked Elma straight in the eye.

'I suppose that's why I never said anything to anyone.'

Elma wondered what the time was and checked her pocket for her phone.

I've left it inside, I hope Josh doesn't arrive too soon I really want to know about Gran and SH.

She'd decided she didn't like the name Scott Hamilton and would refer to him only by his initials. It somehow made him less important, distant, maybe for the same reasons she'd decided to call her mum 'Lizzie'.

Maybe it's what you do to people you don't want to be close to.

'In the beginning it was Mr Hamilton this and Mr Hamilton that,' Aunt Livie paused and frowned. 'We couldn't have a conversation without his name coming up. He may have only stayed up at the Springs four or five weekends a year but it was enough to keep Miriam besotted.'

Aunt Livie lowered her voice; Elma could hardly hear her over the wind whooshing through the blue gums in the parkland across the road.

'If you asked me I wish they'd been found out sooner. Hindsight is a funny thing,' she'd smiled a sad smile.

'Do you mean their relationship, Aunt Livie, or did they do something wrong?'

'Well he was older than her and rather sneaky. She never knew when he'd be there and every meeting was a secret and then they started going to the hut.'

'The hut, Aunt Livie? Which hut?'

Immediately Elma thought of Scout Hut, the one her dad had talked about,

but that can't be because it wasn't built until the eighties … I think …

'There were a number of huts along our side of the mountain, so lovely they were too. People spent a lot of time building and decorating them from the bush. We had the key to one on the ridge, above the gully. It was a shame they had to lock it but that's how it was, vandals you know, nothing more to do than destroy someone else's hard work.'

She laughed wistfully.

'They're all gone now only the odd bits of ruins visible, here and there. '

'You had the key?'

'Yes, it wasn't a fancy hut like some of them, no extravagantly carved decorations or pergola or tennis court.'

'Tennis court?' Elma interrupted.

'Yes, there was one in a clearing not too far from us. It was all good fun. A bit of a competition at times – but always a friendly one.'

'Well some things have changed; you certainly wouldn't chop a tree down now and no way would anyone build a tennis court.'

I've seen the bush up there – where on earth would you put a tennis court?

'It's different now, Elma, people didn't mean harm by it and we didn't have the same transport back then,' Aunt Livie spoke, reflecting on her life as a teenager.

'You couldn't just jump in a car and drive down the Peninsula or up the coast like you do today. No, we made do with what we had and built what we needed from the space around us. I know you wouldn't eat a rabbit or a wallaby but I wouldn't be here now if we hadn't. I'm not saying it's better or worse now, it's just different for you than it was for me.'

'The hut, Aunt Livie. You were saying about the hut on the ridge above the gully?'

'Josh is late,' Aunt Livie said, looking down at her watch and staring along the road as if he would appear sooner if she was watching for him. Elma let her eyes follow her aunt's gaze all the while thinking of questions to keep her on track.

I don't want to talk about the late Josh Jacobson right now – I want the answers before he arrives.

'You were saying your hut wasn't as fancy as some.'

'Oh, that didn't matter, it still did the job. We were allowed to stay there if it was vacant, which it usually was. Only had one room and one window, but it did have a beaut fire place to cook the wallaby on.'

Livie looked sideways at Elma, her lips forming a bit of a smile.

'One table, built into the wall beneath the window and one bed, which was neither a single nor a double but somewhere in between. That was also built into the wall, and padded with a lumpy, handmade kapok mattress. I always thought I could have made a better one. Oh, and there was also a canvas camp bed stored beneath it.'

'And Gran stayed there without you?'

'Without me? If you mean with Scott? The short answer is yes. Yes she did. It was –' Aunt Livie looked awkward, '– it was their love nest.'

183

She put her nose in the air.

Elma raised her eyebrows. Her eyes and ears were wide open – *uncomfortable to say the least, but keep going pleeease ...*

'She was daft about it. Even when he wasn't around she'd go there after work and potter around making it "homely".'

Aunt Livie raised her hands and used two fingers from each hand to emphasize the word homely. 'She strutted around like she was so grown up.'

'She must have really liked him,' Elma said lamely.

'She sure did. She went to great lengths to "beautify" it. Even stole plants from the gardens at the Springs.'

'Really!? Gran stole stuff?'

'Only plants and cuttings. She wasn't a real thief.'

I wonder what a real thief steals?

Straight away Elma thought about the money missing from the till at the café back home.

'What sort of plants?' Elma asked wanting the conversation to continue.

'Well a bright red rhododendron for a start.'

'A what!?'

'Oh, Elma you know what a rhododendron looks likes, surely.'

Elma cut her off.

'Yes of course I do, I'm just surprised you said that.'

Aunt Livie looked at Elma curiously.

'I don't know why you'd be surprised about that at all. Both Miriam and I have always loved gardening.'

I know you have, but it seems I don't know much about Gran at all.

'Was Gran's hut up above the Myrtle Gully Track?'

'Why, yes, the ridge ran parallel to the creek down in the gully. It wasn't far from the creek at all, which was convenient as the tin roof didn't always catch much rain. I remember one time when an old possum managed to get trapped in the water tank and drowned. It was pretty foul and even after they cleaned it out I wasn't keen to drink from it.'

Elma wasn't listening now, her mind was on the rhododendron tree growing near the ruined chimney on the ridge above the Myrtle Gully Track.

I've been there. Hard to believe, but I really think they're the ruins that Sarah and Josh took me to all those years ago. I wonder. It's in the right place. I am going to find it as soon as I get back home.

'Elma,' it was Josh.

'Elma, Earth to Elma. Come in, Elma.'

Pieces of parsley floated on the top of her creamy soup. She pushed them beneath the surface with the back of the spoon.

'Josh do you remember one time about eight years ago, you and Sarah took me for a bushwalk up kunanyi and we …'

'Coon what nee?' Josh cut in.

'Kunanyi, Mt Wellington.'

'Well why didn't you say so. We went up there a few times if I remember.'

'Yes, but this was a specific walk, no adults and you had a friend with you and he showed us some ruins of an old chimney from a burnt-out shack.'

'Oh, I remember. It was hot and you whinged all the way there.'

'Eek, sorry. I hope you got over that. I was pretty small.'

'Well, Mouse, what about it?'

'I'd like to go there but I don't know where to go.'

and please don't call me Mouse.

By the time the coffee and pecan pie had been consumed, Josh had Google searched the area in question and explained to Elma the best he could where she could expect to find the ruins.

'Sounds a bit mysterious,' Josh commented when Elma explained what she could about Gran's hut and the rhododendron bush.

I don't want to give him all the details until I know the full story, but it's not a lie to let him think that that is where his gran and my gran were allowed to go camping in their spare time.

Elma's phone may have been back at Aunt Livie's place but her hand sanitiser was not. She pulled it from her bag while Josh finished the last of his coffee.

'Keep me posted. Let me know if you find it. Didn't have a camera on my phone back then.'

He laughed.

'Those were the days.'

He pushed back on his chair and headed for the counter.

'Okay then, let's go find that cemetery and get you home before dark.'

Chapter 17

'Take the next corner on your right, down Princes Street. We'll stick to the back roads through Langi Logan, maybe cut across Mount Challicum Rd. And then,' he paused, 'the cemetery, mwah, ha ha.'

It all sounded strange to Elma but the drive in had been easy.

I can't see why the drive home should be any different. I'm intrigued about my name on a grave. Plus I've got a good lead on Gran's hut.

'Confidence, confidence, that's all you need,' Josh called out over the noise of the radio.

'It's certainly more fun than driving with Dad,' Elma yelled back.

'He never lets me have music on even if it's quiet background stuff.'

The countryside raced past – cattle grazed behind wire fences, chewing on winter hay and the odd tuft of grass. Two alpacas loped playfully across an open field heading towards a larger mob on the far side. A few spits of rain – not enough to turn the wipers on.

Josh is right though, she thought, I do need more confidence *in everything – not just driving* wooden fences, hedges, side road, dirty sheep, a bit more rain, the odd oncoming car. Countryside whizzed by like a nature movie on Netflix. Driving was almost relaxing, she thought

and that's my favourite song

she wiggled her fingers and sang along to George Ezra's "Shotgun" in her mind.

'I just love this song,' she ventured, enthused by the sound of the deep voice crooning from the audio system. Josh reached forward and turned the volume up even higher.

Elma sang aloud, taking a quick glance across at Josh. His elbow rested on the open window. His long-sleeved smart Adidas top fitted closely to his body. He was singing too. The noise level increased with every chorus.

'There's a bit of a bend coming up and round the corner is a railway crossing,' Josh shouted.

'A what?'

Elma tapped out the tune on the steering wheel – it really was going well.

Dad would never be this chill about driving. And the roads are better too. I'm loving it.

'A railway crossing.'

'I've never done a crossing – should I slow down.'

'Not unless there's a train coming' he laughed.

'Shit!' he caught a glimpse of something moving fast behind the trees and shrubs.

His face dropped, his voice suddenly urgent, 'Elma, there's a train coming!'

Her foot jammed hard down on the brake. Was there any way to stop the car in time? Train crash movies flashed through her mind. Bits of bloodied bodies painted across the engines like graffiti. Pieces of jagged car parts strewn either side of the track – run through by a can opener operating at half the speed of lightning.

Pressure marks formed creases in the fabric where Elma's fingers coiled tight around the steering wheel. Her eyes clamped shut – her screams morphing with the screech of brakes and the thundering sound of the train. An acrid smell of skidding, brake fumes and burning rubber rushed in through Josh's open window. Louder and louder. Closer and closer. Tyres squealed. Elma's body moved forward, tight against the seat belt, the black strap cutting into the side of her neck. She braced herself for impact. But something changed. Had they slowed or even stopped? She couldn't tell. Her hands were someone else's – her body not responding to her brain. What was happening? She opened her eyes – the noise was so intense it was somehow muted – as surreal as if the events were taking place underwater.

Help me, Josh

She turned to search for his familiar face. Rabbit scared eyes stared back at her. His mouth was wide open, screaming something at her that she couldn't make out. His face contorted, arms flailing as if he too were drowning.

But I know we're not.

Flickers of light appeared in the top of her vision – she took a breath in, still the flickers increased, her eyes closed again and in slow motion she leant back and fainted.

'Elma, answer me. Can you hear me?'

There was panic in Josh's voice.

'Hey! Come on, wake up!'

Elma opened her eyes not understanding where she was.

The train should be in front of me.

She could hear it. It was close. She could feel it, a constant buffering against the car, she could see where her hands had been clamped upon the shaking steering wheel, but she couldn't see the train.

'Where is it?' she mouthed at Josh, her voice struggling up through her shaking body.

'Behind us,' Josh shouted.

'You drove straight over the track.'

Elma turned to look over her shoulder just as the last carriage flashed past. She watched in disbelief as the noise decreased and the train moved out of sight around the next bend. Josh slammed his fist against the knob on the dash and George's voice disappeared in an instant.

'Bloody hell that was close.'

He ran his hands through his hair. Visible beads of sweat dripped down his forehead.

'I'll drive! We have to get out of here!'

Elma looked confused.

'In case they call the cops.'

His voice held a mixture of demand and fear.

'I can't lose my job. I don't need this right now.'

Elma felt her stomach relax and contract, a nauseous feeling swished about her mouth.

'I feel sick'

'Please don't – not in the car.'

Josh pushed his door open.

Elma felt along the door panel for the lever on her side, her head spun. The car wasn't where she expected it to be, but had skidded to a halt on the other side of the railroad crossing with the back bumper so close to the track it was hard to believe a train had passed without touching it ... It was also on the gravelly verge on the wrong side of the road. Her head was still spinning. Her cheeks felt thin like paper and her spit tasted salty. She released the clip on her seat belt and pushed weakly on the door.

Open, come on open.

Josh had climbed out.

'I'll come and help you. Just hold on.' He moved as fast as he could around to the front of the car. An open drain made it difficult to approach.

'Bloody hell we could have ended up in that ditch,' he said, the full impact of the near accident dawning on him. Elma leant her head against the door

Hurry.

Josh squeezed between the car and the ditch, a rock moved under his foot.

Can't hold it.

The door swung open. Elma leaned out, her stomach contents rising to her mouth as she did so. Her hand slipped from the bottom of the door and she toppled forward, instinctively extending her forearm to protect her head from smacking into the rocks at the bottom of the embankment. There was a snap that sounded like twisting a plastic picnic fork, only it came from inside a sleeve of flesh and blood.

Elma fainted again.

When she came to, Josh was squatting beside her with an anxious expression on his face. At first it was hard for Elma to understand what he was saying. Beneath her head was a beach towel. She wiped her hand against the side of her face. Warm blood appeared on her fingers.

'It's nothing Elma, just a scratch on your cheek. Maybe a bit of a bruise. Elma, can you hear me?'

Using only one arm she pushed herself into a sitting position.

Josh encouraged her as much as he could.

'I know this is going to hurt but I need you to raise your arm up here and place it across your chest.' He mimicked the position with his own arm.

Elma did as she was told. Weirdly, it wasn't as painful as she expected.

Doesn't feel like my arm.

She gave a weak laugh.

'Now I'm going to pull your shirt up over your arm to keep it from moving.'

He undid most of the buttons, leaving the top two and lifted the shirt front up and pulled the fabric up over her elbow and forearm and kept it in place by bringing the other shirt front behind her back and tying the two pieces together at her shoulder.

Elma screamed as he fastened it into place.

'It's okay, we'll go to the hospital – we'll be there soon. It's all right. Most likely just a sprain.'

But probably not, he thought.

The taste of vomit lingered on her breath. Splats of red tomato with flecks of parsley decorated the rocks.

Elma tried not to think.

'Come on, I have to get you to the hospital.'

--

The triage nurse had checked her over. No blood, minimal pain, fingers dirty, but all the right colour. It was going to be a long wait.

There were things she needed to remember.

Don't mention the train, don't mention where.

'Just tell them you got car sick and you fell down a bank getting out of the car. Okay, got it?'

It was true about being sick and true about falling down the bank but what about the train, the screams were still there, the panic and –

'What the hell is Dad going to say?'

He didn't want me coming here by myself – nor did Gran.

The phone felt warm in her hand.

Do I ring now or after I've seen a doctor?

It wasn't her phone but Josh had placed it in her good hand while he'd gone to park the car.

'Won't be long. It's just down that way a bit,' he pointed at the sliding door near where she was sitting. Vomit still burned in her nose. Dust stuck to the tears smeared across her cheeks.

Germ Free Hospital

Please Wash Hands

On Arrival

– a giant container of automatically dispensed hand sanitiser taunted her.

Dirt and germs began multiplying on her skin, under her shirt, between her fingers and through her hair. A clean blue hospital issue sling hung neatly around her neck, incongruent with the rest of her clothing. The triage nurse had kindly put her arm in it.

'Your boyfriend's done a good job on immobilising your arm, but this one will take the pressure off your neck, give you a little more comfort while you wait.'

An ambulance siren whoop-whooped in the background.

Elma didn't say anything, didn't feel the need to correct the nurse – to tell her they were cousins.

We could probably pass as siblings.

She'd always wanted a brother or a sister but wasn't so sure anymore. Wasn't sure of anything.

Don't even know if it's broken. I might have just imagined the snap.

'You still here then?' Josh asked, sitting down next to Elma.

'I'm sorry Josh, I'm so sorry, I really am. I could have killed us.'

The tears began afresh.

Josh looked this way and that, put his finger to his mouth and shushed Elma.

'Well, you didn't. We're still here and I'm supposed to be the responsible driver, so you can't take all the blame. Can you leave it 'til later? I'd rather talk in private than in here. Just chat, keep calm.'

'I don't feel calm. I'm worried Dad's going to jump on a plane and drag me home.'

'Then don't tell him.'

What did Josh mean don't tell him?

'What? I can't do that.'

'I mean don't tell 'til you are all nice and cosied back at Gran's place.'

Elma took a deep breath and tried to make calm chit-chat: 'You're good at first aid, Josh.'

'It's just part of the job. We all get trained in first aid.'

'What is it that you do?'

Elma felt foolish for not knowing, but Josh used the opportunity to talk, focussing on keeping Elma calm.

'I am a mechatronic engineer. It's a hybrid between electronic and mechanical engineering, and I've heard all the jokes, so don't even try.'

He gave a laugh, 'Spell check doesn't even recognise me.'

'Sorry,' Elma said again.

'What are you sorry for this time?'

She was glad he hadn't added "Mouse".

'I don't know – you just don't seem to get along with yourself.'

Josh didn't respond but rubbed at his chin as if in thought. Elma wanted to apologise again

for opening my stupid mouth

but managed to keep it shut.

It was still daylight when they left. 5:15 to be precise, thought Elma peeking at the clock behind the counter.

She felt relieved after she phoned Martin.

'I know, Dad,' she said speaking to him on Josh's phone, 'but I'm all right, I really am. It was just an accident. I ate too much soup. I know, but I'm okay, really. It's just if I get a washable cast it costs money. No, not upfront I just need your permission; yes they will send you the bill. No. Of course I don't want to come home early. No, I'll let you know when I get back to Aunt Livie's.'

That was it, it was easy: it was a broken bone in the forearm. *I think she said radius, or ulna, I forget.*

There was very little swelling and until the x-ray came back the doctor wasn't sure that it was broken at all. She'd had gas while they mucked around with it and then some pain-killers and an orange fiberglass cast over a plaster one simply because she couldn't imagine going without a "proper" bath or shower for four weeks. Now she sat in Josh's car staring at her fluoro coloured arm wondering why she'd chosen work-vest orange over hot pink or kryptonite green.

'Will I see you again before I leave?' Elma asked Josh as they pulled into the driveway at Aunt Livie's.

'Maybe,' said Josh, closing his eyes while he thought.

'Maybe family dinner on Thursday night, Sarah usually comes. I'm not sure if I'm working. I can't remember what was on the roster.'

Elma suddenly felt overwhelmed and tired. Josh opened the door and helped her out of the car.

'I'll take you to the door but I have to go. I haven't texted Nell yet to say I'm running late.'

Nell? Who's Nell? His girlfriend? Flatmate? I forgot to ask?

But Elma was too fatigued to talk and only nodded. She'd hoped he might have stayed to help explain the situation to his gran. There was a huge battle taking place inside her as to whether she should have a shower or just fall into bed and close her eyes.

--

'Thanks, Aunt Livie but I'm not hungry, I just want to sleep.'

Her dad had phoned twice, Aunt Livie hadn't ceased to fuss and Cathy had come straight round. She'd helped Elma in the shower and tucked her in as best she could. She seemed quite angry and asked question after question that Elma couldn't answer.

'Sorry Cathy, I really am. I didn't mean to cause you any trouble.'

'Oh it's not you Elma, it's Josh,' she said placing a cup of water on the bedside table.

'He should have known better. What was he thinking taking you so far away and then doing all the higgledy piggledy farm roads on the way back. Sometimes I wonder where that boy's brains are.'

'It wasn't his fault Cathy, he didn't know I would get car sick.'

'Where did you say you were again?'

'I don't recall the name of the road we were on. It was somewhere between Ararat and Ballarat, maybe near a cemetery.'

Elma lied, trying to be vague.

We were sort of more on a train track than on the road when I threw up.

196

'There was an accident out that way today, or nearly. Another car playing silly buggers on the railway line. Shot straight out in front of a train. The stupid kids do it for a joke. Somehow they think it's funny. People get killed and the train drivers never recover from the guilt. Just shocking. They put cameras on the front of trains now. Hope they catch them. It's just becoming too common.'

Elma slid further down in her bed. Her arm was propped up on a cushion covered in a cotton fabric, bright red, with strawberries the colour of tomatoes, and leaves of parsley green. She felt sick again.

Chapter 18

All week the secrets gathered, building up power in her notebook. Gran's affair with SH had been recorded in **Gran's Ramblings**. Her mother being a criminal had been noted.

She was pleased she could talk to Cathy about that, but understood it was still a secret.

'Don't tell your dad I told you,' Cathy said.

She doesn't want the fallout from Dad or Aunt Livie, I guess.

She was thankful that she could write with her left hand, even if it was uncomfortable and awkward to get the pages to stay open.

Was Lizzie smart or stupid? She was a criminal, so definitely not smart ... I think.

Elma had, for most of her life, kept her mother out of her thoughts, but now things were different –

She left me but I replaced her with Aunt Livie – Dad had no one.

She gave a sigh and shut her book.

'I found some photos for you, Elma, of –' Cathy hesitated, '– of your mother.'

Elma grimaced, 'Please call her Liz or Lizzie; you know she didn't mother me.'

Cathy smiled, 'I just wanted you to know it should be your choice what to call her, not mine.'

Elma shivered. It was cold in Cathy's kitchen despite the heater being on. She sat on a wooden chair with her fluoro arm on the table and her back to the sliding door.

Hope I'm not catching something.

A haze of memories rose from the top of the shoe box as Cathy placed it on the table.

'I'm pretty sure we'll find something in here,' she said, lifting off the lid leaving her thumb prints in the deep layer of dust.

Elma sneezed. What would she find? She hadn't always wanted to know about her mum but the discovery of the licence had stirred her curiosity.

'Excuse the housework.'

Cathy pulled a face.

'This one's been sitting on top of the bedroom cupboard since the day we moved in.'

'Hey, here's Gran and Dad. And here's you and Aunt Livie and Dad and –' Elma stopped talking and stared at the photo in her hand.

'– is that her?' she asked, expecting to have recognised her straight away.

'Yes, it is,' Cathy replied.

'Not a great shot, that one. Didn't know what you were going to get 'til you got them developed way back then.'

She laughed.

'Times have changed so quick I'd forgotten how much money we wasted on taking bad photos.'

She leaned over, her chair tipping onto two legs.

'Mum was the worst – there was always someone with their head chopped off or blurred beyond recognition.'

She laughed again, 'Those were the days. I swear she moved the camera up to the button rather than pushing the button down.'

The whole photo was out of focus but Elma could easily recognise her dad and Cathy and Aunt Livie. It was just Liz who didn't fit Elma's expectation. For one thing she was taller than Martin and for two her skin was dark.

'Are you sure this is Liz?' Elma asked, confused between the photo of "herself" in the licence and the woman in front of her now.

She handed the photo to Cathy for a closer look.

'Yep that's her all right. We were up the East Coast for a day trip but I think we can find a better shot than this one. Here we are. Are you ready for this? It's their wedding day.'

She passed the Kodak 10x15 cm print to Elma.

Here goes – I can't un-see what I am about to see

'Wow, she looks just like me,'

only taller and browner.

Elma stared at the photo. Her dad looked so happy in a blue suit and a head full of hair, spikey on the top and long down the back. Liz wore a traditionally-styled wedding gown but not in a traditional colour. No, the dress was light blue. And her skin was light brown. What Elma had remembered as tanned skin was now obviously more than that.

'Yes, of course your mother was a Maori – but maybe you didn't know that, did you?' she continued slowly, becoming aware that the situation may be confronting for Elma. She'd known Liz for a long time – Liz was Maori – Liz had brown skin – so what? She hadn't thought any more of it.

'She came from New Zealand?' Elma asked, thinking of Fergus with his lovely brown skin and pulled up the sleeve of her good arm to examine it.

'But I'm white.'

'Well, you look white.'

'I'm a Maori?'

'I guess you are.'

'But she's white in my photo.'

'What photo, Elma? I thought you'd never seen one.'

'Well, I hadn't really until recently when I found her licence in a bag of stuff that Dad had forgotten to throw out.'

She wiped invisible traces of dust and grime from her fingers on a table napkin and reached over to the other seat to get her wallet from her bag. Two nearly identical licences sat on the placemat in front of her – one of herself and one of her mother. She could see now that the older one was faded and had a washed out look. It wasn't a true representation of skin colour at all.

'Wow,' said Cathy, 'who would have known?'

It was a lot to take in.

I'm a New Zealander, a Maori or part one on my mother's side. Wow, what do I know about that? Nothing.

Fergus came to mind again – his broad, confident smile, his funny way of saying goodbye at the bus stop.

There were so many questions she'd never considered.

What did she want to know now?

I don't want to know anything – or at least I didn't – no, I still don't.

Her self-talk sounded less than convincing. She picked out three photos to take back with her to Tasmania.

Later that night she sent a text message to Fergus, knowing full well there was no way to go back once she pressed Send. He'd have her number forever – unless she bought a new SIM card. It was just a simple message asking what day he was expecting to leave Tasmania. And then she waited. Would he reply straight away – or make her wait – or was he busy – his phone flat – or turned off for his flight back home?

I kinda wish I'd asked Cathy which part of New Zealand Liz was from – but I didn't want to talk about it. And does it really matter? I don't know anything about the place anyway.

There was an inconceivable idea forming in her mind that Fergus could be a relation of hers –

distant cousin twice removed or something.

She wouldn't mention it but considered starting a heading in her notebook – **Family Secrets**

--

Elma was grateful to spend time with Aunt Livie, but by the end of the week she was more than ready to return to Tasmania. So much had happened – she'd nearly lost her life and *could've killed Josh in the process.* She'd broken the law – although she wasn't sure which one – she'd broken her arm, and she felt as though she'd broken her father's trust by not only lying to him but to the whole family.

I wish Josh hadn't said don't tell – it feels wrong to deceive Cathy when she's been so kind to me.

Although it'd been good to catch up with Cathy, Elma was disappointed to discover they weren't the Happy Family she'd imagined them to be. There had been a few awkward moments and a couple of occasions where she'd felt downright uncomfortable – by far Thursday's family dinner had been the worst.

'Oh you made it, did you?' Steve spoke accusingly to Josh.

'Stand down, Dad.' Sarah stepped in on her brother's behalf. 'We've got company.'

She looked at Elma, smiling awkwardly in the kitchen doorway carrying a jug of water to the table.

'Don't drop it.' Aunt Livie was fussing. 'Let me do that for you.'

Elma had liked Sarah from the minute she'd swung into the room with her head of purple hair and a bold tattoo of a lyrebird on her forearm, its tail feathers stretching right up and over her shoulder. She'd worn a green corduroy smock, flared out over darker green leggings and black dress boots that must've taken ages to lace correctly.

She doesn't need correct, everything looks correct on her.

'Geez, Dad, I'm here, okay. Nice to see you too,' Josh retorted, pushing the side door shut a little too hard, startling Elma who was now sloshing the water jug down on a placemat.

The food was laid out in dishes along the centre of the table.

Way posher than home – smells amazing.

Elma served herself some peas

'How's the arm now, Mouse?'

Sarah glared at her brother.

Elma gave a weak smile, 'Fine.'

'No pain?'

'No, no pain.'

and only one more day 'til I leave.

Was she looking forward to seeing her father?

Of course I am. And definitely not.

'Can I drop you at the airport?'

This time the whole table turned to stare at him.

Elma hesitated.

What do I say?

There was no need to say anything – they were all speaking on her behalf.

'It's all organised,' said Cathy as the noise died down.

'Mum and I have it planned; we'll stop in at the Factory Outlet on the way. Do you want to join us there for coffee?'

She looked at Josh, knowing what the answer would be.

It was better than her dad flying over and escorting her home, but so far removed from her plans of catching a train into Melbourne, spending the day browsing the shops alone and jumping on a SkyBus for the evening flight home.

It was the reason I only brought carry-on luggage so I could store it easily at the train station and spend the day in Melbourne on my own.

'You didn't make the game last week.'

Was Steve attacking Josh again or was he just changing the subject?

'Can you pass me the sweet potato, please?'

Sarah put out her hand to receive it from the other end of the table.

--

'I took Elma out for a drive. You know that.' Josh put his hand in his pocket. He's looking for his car keys, thought Elma.

She knew what the problem was now. Steve didn't like Nell.

'Dad wouldn't even give Nell the time of day,' Josh had said to Elma at Aunt Livie's place when he'd visited her earlier that week.

'Does your mum?'

'She's okay and so is Sarah,' he'd said, gazing out the window to where Livie was hanging out a few items of hand washing.

Elma's eyes followed to where Josh was staring.

'And your gran?' she wondered what could possibly be so wrong with Nell that Steve had to show his feelings every time he saw his son.

'They like each other fine,' he continued.

'We've had dinner here a few times. Nell is always more than happy to eat one of Gran's famous potato pies.'

He smiled.

Elma could tell there was affection for both of them.

'But –' he added, his voice dropping, '– Gran thinks that we're just flatmates, okay. And Mum says to just leave it that way. All right?'

Elma nodded. It seemed the right thing to do at the time and she would have stuck to her nod except the words "just leave it that way" got stuck on reply in her mind. Try as she might she was only able to "leave it that way," 'til Wednesday when it came up in conversation over a game of Scrabble in Aunt Livie's lounge room. The weather was still gloomy – an all-over grey day – a good day to be inside.

Across the road a raucous bunch of cockatoos were full swing into a game of "destroy the pine tree". Screeches and white and yellow feathers filled the air. Elma switched her focus between the birds and the scrabble board.

'Why doesn't Josh get on with his dad?' Elma asked turning an upside down tile, the letter Q, up the right way.

'Is it because he doesn't like Nell?'

'Who said that, dear? Are you minding your own business?'

'It's just a feeling I get when they're both in the same room.'

'It's not Nell he doesn't like and not Josh either, he just needs more time.'

'Oh?' Elma pulled a 'U' out of the bag and placed it on her stand between the 'Q' and the 'R'. She looked down at the board for another vowel to use on her next turn.

'It's more than that.'

Aunt Livie gave a sigh.

'Elma, they won't tell me, so I suspect they won't tell you.'

She switched a couple of letters around and looked across to Elma.

'I've already spilled enough secrets this week so I guess one more isn't going to kill me. Nelson isn't Josh's flatmate – Josh is gay and that's that. Steve hasn't come to terms with having a gay son and no one ever talks to me about it.'

Elma's mouth fell open,

Oh my goodness, how stupid of me – why didn't I realise that – it's not Nell, it's Nel, Nelson. It all makes sense now.

'I'm sorry Aunt Livie, I just didn't think about it, I thought Nel was Nelly, you know a girl.'

She laughed.

That's why I didn't catch on.

'So, they think you don't know?' Elma asked her aunt.

'Well really, Elma, it makes it easier for me not to be involved with it all. Still, I'd like to be able to support Josh more, but if he can't talk to me about it that's not my fault and, like I said, that is that.'

So, that was that.

Aunt Livie had shut her mouth and no one else mentioned it, but at least when the tension rose at the Thursday family dinner Elma was aware what the friction was about.

The other awkward conversation that night at the dinner table was the broken arm.

'So you were driving, right?' Cathy asked Josh, who nodded his head.

'And Elma was in the passenger's seat, wasn't she?'

Josh nodded again.

What's this leading to?

Elma moved a pea around in her mouth.

Hope no one asks me anything.

She kept her head down, staring at the carrots on her plate.

A sort of carrot orange, only not so dark.

'Oh nothing. I was just thinking that if I was in the passenger's seat and leant out the door to throw up and fell on my arm and broke it, I think it would most likely be my left arm not my right one.'

'She rolled a bit, Mum, like flipped right over – you saw the mess she was in.'

Elma continued to scrutinise her vegetables.

Are they looking at me? Poor Josh. This is all my fault.

'And I'm still unsure why you would bring her home that way.'

'Aw, come on Mum it was an opportunity to show her a bit of the countryside. Is this pick on Josh night?'

Elma held her breath; there were hardly any veggies left to stare at,

should I just say something? Or will that make it worse.

She made a small cave at the base of her mashed potato and sheltered her last pea inside.

I still don't know what he wanted to show me in the cemetery – I forgot to ask.

A Week's Worth Of Secrets

How many is that as a quantifiable measure?

Her father had kept a heap from her and charged others not to share them. Cathy had shared with her opinion that "you have the right to know". Gran's secrets were seeping out through a fractured memory and Aunt Livie's had reached a time-out limit. Josh kept some of his from selective people and they both shared one that was never to be told. Or was there a time-out limit on that too? Elma wasn't sure.

Am I the only one who feels uncomfortable keeping secrets? Maybe it will get easier.

Chapter 19

No cheese, no eggs, not even a tub of yoghurt. Nothing – the fridge may as well have been empty. Elma turned her nose up at a half-eaten bowl of beans and a limp piece of celery; there was nothing she felt like eating.

I've been back less than a week and I swear he's only been home twice. Once for clothing and once to do his bookwork.

Bring me food! Elma tapped out a text on her phone. When are you getting groceries?

She read and re-read it. It sounded rude, maybe a little angry with a side dish of hunger.

Hopefully.

Should she be pleased for her father finding love again? She wasn't.

He's not home when he should be – he didn't pick me up when I missed the bus.

'There'll be no driving lessons 'til your arm has healed completely,' he'd said.

Completely – I don't even know what that means.

Still it's not his fault he fell in love, she thought, and not his fault I lost my job either –

or as good as.

'Sorry Elma,' Damien shook his head, 'waterproof cast or not, I can't let you work here until it's been removed.'

'But that could be another three weeks,' Elma pleaded. 'I can do everything with it on, I promise.'

'Not the point Elma, it's a hygiene thing. Do you know how many germs are hiding inside your cast right now?'

Elma didn't answer – she couldn't – what could she say?

She'd lain awake at night thinking about bacterial and staphylococcal infections breeding under the light weight, fluoro, non-biodegradable piece of plastic clamped around her arm – a constant reminder of the secret, festering beneath her tongue – the secret that sent her too close to breaking every time "Shotgun" came on over the airways.

The song had taken on a whole new meaning – it was no longer her favourite

not for driving, or for ever

Fibreglass cast or not she still had to cover it – prevent dirty water getting beneath it by wearing a rubber glove.

'I should have worn a glove today,' she thought, standing at the base of the falls, Fergus only an arm's-length away.

He'd picked her up from the Lost Sock Laundry on Macquarie Street. She wasn't ready for him to know exactly where she lived.

He'd returned her text from Ballan and they'd exchanged messages daily. It was the whole point of swapping numbers wasn't it, he'd said, like it was such an everyday thing.

It might be for someone like you – not shy and vomity like me.

She was beginning to appreciate people who could keep their calm in emergencies – of course there was quite a difference between a train crash and the removal of a leech.

Still, I panicked at both events.

They'd driven to the top of Old Farm Road and parked the car. Rain and wind whipped round Elma's legs as they trudged their way up through the bush, her leggings tucked into her socks – Leech Protection 101. She was learning the ways of the wild. This was it – there were only three days left before Fergus flew back to NZ. Although they'd messaged each other, this was the first chance they'd had to catch up in person since Elma had returned from Ballan.

'So why this hut, Elma?'

Fergus was well-equipped with thermals, wet weather gear and a high end Macpac day bag.

'Oh, it's not a whole hut I'm looking for, just the ruins of a chimney from a hut I believe my gran and great aunt used to camp in when they were teenagers.'

Not the whole truth but not a lie. He doesn't need the details.

'Nigel said there were a few about before '67, so how'll you know if you've got the right one.'

'I don't know for sure but I think I've been there before and I just think I'll know when I see it.'

She looked down at her boots, clumps of mud and leaves clung to the wet leather but nothing wiggling that she could see.

'Oh, psychic,' he said with a laugh, removing his woollen hat as he spoke. Wild hair escaped flicking this way and that about his face, tangling in his beard. He took the hair tie Elma offered and pulled it back. Elma laughed too, watching long strands of hair blow in the wind like a movie. If he was a movie star, who would he be?

Captain Jack Sparrow or Russell Brand maybe …

'I think the weather's getting worse, I'll need to get all this gear washed and dried before I leave for home.'

Elma licked her lips, her face moist with the spray from the falls. This was where they'd first met. She'd been desperate to escape his and Nigel's gaze back then but so fearful of the leech and being alone on the mountain she'd been forced to accept their help.

So embarrassing.

'I promised I'd have Nigel's car back by four.'

'I reckon we should stop for lunch shortly and turn back if we haven't found our destination by 2pm.'

'Good with me.'

I feel safer having you here than doing this alone.

She gazed at him, his dark wayward curls pulled back against his head.

Who'd have thought we'd have anything in common? Will I pluck up the courage to ask questions about our history?

Josh had given her a fairly clear idea where she should leave the regular track and enter the unmapped paths concealed from the general public. Myrtle Gully with its rich fernery, rushing waters and mossy tracks drew Elma deeper and deeper into a peaceful place somewhere inside herself.

Gran would have done this path a million times. No bridge then, I imagine.

She breathed in deeply, sucking the earthy smell into her lungs, almost enjoying the sensation.

Follow the path above the falls until you come to a rock "about as tall as you".

Elma looked up at the slippery trail criss-crossed with fallen branches from recent strong winds.

'Turn left, turn right, go up, and up and up like forever,' she repeated Josh's instructions to Fergus.

'I've lived in South Hobart most of my life and I don't think I've ever seen a bat,' she continued.

She slipped a little on the track, sliding back into Fergus. Moss and bark gunge stuck to her hand where she grabbed at a skinny branch. Mud changed the colour of her knees from light blue to kunanyi brown.

'You should get out more,' he said, stopping abruptly, allowing her to regain her footing and move forward.

'Ha, ha. Maybe you're not really a bat catcher?' she said shaking the debris from her hand.

But I know you are.

She'd looked up the programme at UTAS and Massey University.

There was no way she'd be here if anything he'd said didn't add up.

Still, I've never seen a bat in Tasmania.

'Well, they're not that big.'

'Sorry?' she said, losing the thread of the conversation.

'Tassie bats are only about the size of a large leech.'

Was he smiling? Was he teasing her? Maybe yes and maybe no.

I think he's always smiling. Beard or no beard, you can't hide that smile.

She turned to look at him

No, maybe not.

'Okay, so where are all the bat caves? No one has ever told me about them.'

'Most of Tassie's bats don't live in caves. Seriously, the maximum size of a Tassie bat is only 5cm long.'

He held up his thumb, 'Smaller than this.'

'No way. Where do they live then?'

'Under the bark of trees, mostly. They don't come out 'til

their predators have all gone to bed.'

'Who'd eat a bat?'

Elma veered left and right as they wove their way between the trees. The wind whipped away their voices and increased the intensity of rustling in the canopy of leaves above them. There was less shelter here along the top of the ridge. Lots of trees, mostly gums, skinny and swaying this way and that, their pom-pom heads like cheerleaders calling them forward. Elma could almost hear them as she struggled up the steep incline: "Come on, Elma, you can do it!"

She repeated their call to herself and began playing mind games. 10 steps then rest. 9 steps then rest. 8 steps to the next tree on the bend.

'We have to stop soon.'

This is killing me. He'll think I'm a real weakling.

'Yep, water break I reckon. Maybe a bite to eat?'

He can still talk – he's not even puffing.

'So what did you do to your arm again? Car accident?'

It had come up in their texting but Elma had been vague.

Embarrassed and worried about betraying Josh.

'No. Well, yes, no, sort of – but no.'

'The thing is where I come from if you ask a sensible question you get a sensible answer.'

'Well, um, the car's all right. I just fell out of it. That's all.'

She could feel her face going red. The arm with the cast was throbbing from the extra effort of hiking up hill. She held it across her chest like she'd been told to if it started to ache and picked at the broken pieces of leaves embedded between her flesh and her cast, nausea swelling in her stomach.

'I was car sick, okay.'

The words came out in a rush.

'Okay, no drama.'

Fergus took a step back away from Elma.

'I'm sorry,' she said 'I didn't mean to sound rude.'

'Nup, it's alright, no offence taken.'

But Elma felt sure there was.

I'd be upset if someone spoke to me like that.

The wind roared above them.

Too loud to talk.

They sheltered as best they could, crouching down at the base of a tree trunk to eat their food in silence.

Fergus looked across at Elma. Her hair was dark – not curly. Her blue eyes had captured him from the beginning – they were clear like frozen snow caught in a pure light. Not that he'd seen too much of them, she was often looking at the ground – shy – unlike most of the girls he knew. There was something different about her, he thought. She lived close by but didn't often walk the mountain. It felt good helping her to achieve a goal – however small it was, he thought.

'It can't be far now,' Elma said as she packed away the remains of her muesli bar.

'Come on, I'm getting cold.'

She was right, it wasn't far before they made their discovery – but it wasn't the discovery Elma was hoping for.

'A path? We've walked all this way, not gone left or right but stuck straight to the track, the only track.'

She shook her head.

No, something's wrong – we didn't pass it. I'd know if we'd passed it.

She turned to Fergus, 'I'm really sorry,' she said pulling her hair away from her mouth with her good hand. The ridge had flattened out – the bush had thickened up but the wind was still strong and cold.

We've climbed for over an hour up a stupid hill and nothing!

'It's okay, it was a nice walk.'

It was a nice walk?

There was a mocking voice in Elma's head.

It was a nice walk? What kind of statement is that? I'm covered in muck and leaves, I can't feel my toes, my hair is a mess, my life's a mess and he says, "It was a nice walk!"

She looked at him.

I'm so cold.

What do I really know about him?

Apart from bat catching?

Why would he be happy to follow her all this way off track in the middle of a storm? Water ran down the back of her neck, dripping in from her beanie.

Don't be paranoid.

You're just disappointed because you didn't find the ruins. And a bit of rain doesn't make it a storm.

Her sodden tights clung uncomfortably to her legs. They were more camouflage brown now than powder blue, and her rain jacket wasn't as waterproof as she'd thought.

'Come on, it's raining again. We should keep moving. There's a public shelter north of here – Junction Cabin – shouldn't take us long.'

'Come on,' he said again. 'You look cold. I'm sure it's not far.'

Fergus stepped up past her onto the wider track and held out his hand to help Elma up over the lip that separated the two paths.

'How do you know where we are?

'Elma,' he laughed, his cheery voice lifting the gloom. 'I'm a bat catcher. I'm studying bats on kunanyi.'

Elma looked at him, 'So?'

'So Nige and me come up here all the time.'

'That's I.'

'Sorry?'

It was hard to know who looked more confused.

'Nige and I come up here all the time, not Nige and –'
Elma didn't finish her sentence.

'You and Nige come up here, Elma?'

'No, not me – '

She could hear him laughing and looked up at him.

'Okay, okay, I get it. Let's just keep walking, aye,' she said, mocking his kiwi accent and putting her good arm forward for him to take.

Junction Cabin was right where Fergus had said. Elma hoped to have a decent look at her map and work out where things had gone wrong. She stared at the folded paper, safe and dry inside its zip-lock bag. Her eyes adjusted to the dim light of the concrete shelter. The grimy window as good as useless.

Just open it, Elma! What's your problem?

The problem was that the fingers on her left hand were cold and they fumbled back and forth over the tab, unable to grip the flimsy plastic strip.

'It stinks in here,' she said without thinking. She shivered and shook the rain from her beanie.

'Oi, that's me you're showering,' said Fergus stamping the wetness from his boots.

He pulled at the ill-fitting door, obscuring the remaining light. Gusts of wind and rain whooshed through the cracks, chilling the uninsulated hut.

Rain had seeped in through Elma's coat. Her clothes were heavy and cold against her skin. She began to shake.

Blasts of wind plummeted down the chimney, stirring the ashes, pushing powdery flakes onto the hard concrete floor of the public shelter. Elma's eyes were adjusting to the dark. She could just make out a pile of firewood stacked against the wall.

'We-we could fight a lire and dr- dr -dry off,' she stuttered, the words tripping from her lips.

'Don't get comfy.'

Fergus spoke with authority.

'We're not lighting the fire. Take your coat off now and it still won't be dry by the time we have to leave. Come on, let's just get back to the car and warm you up on the way.'

Elma looked at Fergus. She felt miserable.

I just want to get warm. I'm shaking all over.

'Can't we just light it for a bit?'

'No, you'll warm up while we walk. Here –' he said removing his own coat and handing it to her.

'Give me your jacket and put this on.'

Elma looked at the grubby, well-worn coat proffered in front of her.

'I'm not wearing that,' she said, trying to shake her head.

The room was spinning slightly; it was hard to stay focussed. Fergus gave her no choice.

'Come on Elma you're cold and wet. This is dry on the inside, and warm. We'll get you to the car and sort things out from there.'

Fergus helped her to pull her saturated coat down off her shoulders and stuffed it in his own bag, along with the un-opened map. He turned her around gently to dress her in his huge jacket. Elma fumbled with the zip. Her arm with the cast was heavy and uncoordinated, her good arm just as useless. She couldn't work out what she was doing wrong.

Don't cry.

'It's okay,' Fergus said. 'That zipper is tricky – let me help.'

Elma tried to say thanks but it didn't make it out through her chattering teeth.

She didn't want to go anywhere,

especially not with him.

She wanted to light the fire and stay warm in the dark, smoky, smelly hut and go to sleep.

'I'm not wearing your jacket,' she said and then realised he was leading her out of the gloom of the shelter and back into the wind and rain.

Step by step they continued the journey downhill. Fergus was right beside her as she stumbled on loose rocks, encouraging her to walk as fast as she could to get the blood flowing through her and hopefully generate some warmth inside his hi-tech jacket. He'd tweaked the jacket a few times, closing all the vents and pulling the cords as tight as he could, trying to create a warm envelope around her.

He calculated that it was only 45 minutes maximum to the car; it certainly seemed like a better choice to push through than be hours late, hungry and probably still cold. There were a number of tracks leading from Junction Cabin to various other mountain paths and suburban destinations. Fergus chose the fire trail. It ran almost parallel to the Myrtle Gully Track, only it wasn't next to the river, there were no bridges to cross and it was on a road wide enough for council workers and fire trucks to access Wellington Park.

Keeping a worried eye on her, he factored in that this track would allow an ambulance to get to them if she collapsed. But they were so close to the car now that he'd be able to carry her if necessary.

Her speech had returned to normal half way down the fire

218

trail. Her fingers no longer felt like clumsy numb icy-poles attached to the ends of her arms.

'I'm so sorry I got so cold. I really didn't mean to,' she said. 'That's never happened to me before.'

Fergus' coat smelled like citrus. She breathed his smell – a mixture of sweat and sweet lime. Her senses were returning to normal.

She looked at Fergus walking beside her without any protection at all to the weather.

'Aren't you cold?' she exclaimed, 'I'm wearing your coat.'

'It's alright, Elma. I've still got me sheep. I'll be alright.'

He pointed to the merino tag on the outside of his thermal top, grinning at her.

The rain was almost non-existent now – small grooves of brown water trickled through the dirt and gravel beneath their boots.

'Is there someone home at your place?' he asked Elma as they drove the short distance back to South Hobart.

'No,' she said, 'but I promise I'll be all right now.'

'I don't know if I can just drop and leave you. You got pretty cold up there. I want to make sure you're okay.'

Elma was pleased he cared but also a bit put out that it took so much to convince him she really was okay.

'I'll text every ten minutes if it'll make you happy,' she said.

'Let's compromise,' he said with a smile. 'You accept a hot chocolate and I'll drop you at the corner of your street.'

By the time she finally collapsed into bed, Elma was smiling, warm and grateful for his kindness. She pulled the doona up close to her chin and breathed in through her nose. *I'm going to miss that lime scent,* she thought as she drifted off to sleep.

Chapter 20

Could the weather change so fast?

'Yes, this is Tasmania, 35 degrees one day and snowing the next. That's just the way it is,' Elma tried to explain to Fergus when he rang the following day.

'Well, it's neither 35 degrees nor snowing. 20 degrees, no rain in sight and not a puff of wind.'

Probably just the right sort of day for a bush walk on a mountain.

But after yesterday's embarrassing battle with potential hypothermia, Elma was not about to suggest it.

'I've still got your map and,' Fergus added, 'Nige has lent me the car for one last day. Would you like to try again?'

Elma hesitated,

Of course I would but I don't think I'm quite up to another uphill marathon just yet.

'Umm, yes but –' she stammered.

'No buts. I've thought about it and if we start from the Springs we can work our way down. Save a heap of time and energy, hey. How about it? I'll pick you up in an hour.'

An hour! How much could Elma get done in an hour? She rang her dad.

'No,' Martin insisted, 'after yesterday you are not going anywhere.'

'Dad please! It's not like it's cold or windy or anything.'

Elma tried to convince him; she could tell he was driving. She'd rung him from the landline.

No credit for calls on my mobile.

'Are you still working down the Channel?' she asked, changing the subject.

'Yes, but I'll be back tonight. Paula is off to Launceston for a few days. Gotta go. I'm in traffic.'

'Can you get food on the way? There's nothing here to eat.'

She hadn't yet warmed to Paula; in fact, she still hadn't met her yet and was prepared to go to great lengths to keep it that way.

She's messed up so much already, Dad's never home, there's no food, no takeaways.

She let out a sigh. On the upside, she'd been able to do whatever she wanted, whenever she wanted.

Not that there's much I can do with no money and an arm in a stupid cast. And I'm really sure he would have picked me up from Gran's the other night if it hadn't been for her.

Elma remembered her visit to Gran just after returning from Victoria.

She had stood in the doorway, the dim light of the corridor creating a faint silhouette about her. Across the room she could see a lump of crumpled blankets on the bed. Gran was in there somewhere, she could hear a gentle snoring. The lump moved slightly. Things seemed different somehow. She wasn't sure what it was, but knew it involved the secrets Aunt Livie had

221

shared in Ballan. She had her own secrets now, and although they weren't great, they were still playing on her mind. Should she tell her dad?

No, he'd ring Cathy straight away and then Josh would cop it even more from her and Steve.

And Gran? Should she tell her what she's knows about her relationship with SH? She stared at the lump. Why was Gran in bed at this hour? It was 10:30 am.

'She hasn't been well lately.'

The staff member walked in beside her and spoke as if reading her mind.

'She's not usually still in bed when morning cuppa's being served in the day room.'

'Will she be okay?' asked Elma watching the bedclothes move about in response to the conversation. The last time she'd seen Gran was the morning after the 'Great Escape'.

Did she overdo it? Get too wet and cold? Oh Gran, I didn't think to ask Dad how you were.

'Oh, I'm not the doctor or anything but the notes just say a bit of a cold. She's on a few extra supplements. I reckon she's a bit run down.'

Elma felt tears welling in her eyes and turned her face from the nurse.

'It's okay, Love, I'm sure she'll be all right in a day or two.'

She took Miriam's temperature and wrote some notes in her book.

'All pretty normal,' she reassured Elma and left the room.

'Can't leave me in peace for a minute, can they?'

Miriam accused no one in particular and turned over to view her visitor.

'It's you, is it? Come back for more money, have you? Well, I haven't got any so you may as well bugger off now!'

Elma's eyes were wide with surprise.

Insults and nastiness were normal from Gran – swearing was saved for special occasions.

'What are you gawking at? You silly girl. Get back to your cleaning and leave me be!'

'Gran, it's me! Elma! I just got back from Ballan.'

I'm not the cleaner or a thief.

Miriam lay still for bit, her dark eyes peeking out over the white sheets and floral doona.

'Oh look at you – you're all grown up. I remember when you were just a wee sweet girl swinging around in a full circle dress.'

'Gran?'

Elma looked at Miriam, her head pressing into the pillow, relaxed curls of brown falling about her face. A patch of hairless scalp was visible near the top of her head.

The skin's all puckered – it looks like a burn. Her bun usually covers that bit.

'You only saw me last week.'

She clamped her hand across her mouth remembering Dr Gordon and her promise to herself not to contradict her grandmother anymore; knowing that she possibly believed what she said was reality. She couldn't think if she'd even seen her gran with her hair out or not. Photos maybe. This was the first time in person.

She doesn't look well at all, kinda yellow. Maybe it's just the dim light.

'It was a red dress, your favourite colour. I bought it for you at the markets.'

You've never bought me a dress. I've never owned a red dress in my life.

'This one, Gran? Do you mean this one?'

Elma picked a photo down from off the shelf above Miriam's head. The black and white print showed a small girl of about five years old, mid twirl, a blur of fabric fanning out like an open umbrella.

'Is this you, Gran?' she handed Miriam the silver framed photo.

Miriam squeezed her hands out from beneath the blanket and wiggled about in the bed.

'Here you are.' Elma said, sliding an extra pillow behind the head of the fragile figure and pressing the head up button on the control panel at the top of the bed.

'That's enough! That's enough!' Miriam said. 'You'll tip me out of this confounded thing.'

'It's okay Gran, it's okay,'

Fickle as!

Miriam's bony fingers clasped the shaking frame, unable to keep it from moving.

'Can I help? Elma suggested, trying to take the photo from Miriam.

But Miriam clasped it to her chest.

'Is that you, Gran?' Elma repeated.

'No,' a half smile creased the older woman's face. 'It's my Scarlet.' She looked directly at Elma.

'Where did you get this? Did you take my album?'

'No Gran. Of course not. It's from your shelf.'

Maybe a photo of Cathy? I'll check when I put it back. That reminds me …

Elma looked about the room for Gran's walker; it stood against the wall on the other side of the bed. Without permission she walked across the room and lifted the lid on the basket seat of the walking frame.

'What are you doing?' Miriam demanded. Her breath was short and raspy.

'Nothing, Gran. Just looking for that postcard you took from the Casino.'

She rummaged through the stack of hidden papers piled inside. There it was – the postcard that Gran had taken the night she'd run away *or escaped* from the nursing home. Elma picked it up and brought it over to the window. She didn't dare to turn on the light.

'What have you got? Show me, come on, show me.'

Elma passed the card over to Miriam and put her hand out for the framed photo.

'No, no, not yet. This is Scarlet. This is my little Scarlet.'

'Scarlet, Gran?' Elma said, cautiously manoeuvring herself 'til she sat on the side of the bed.

'She was such a good girl. Just the sort of girl you'd imagine in your dreams. Well behaved, polite and always clean.'

Miriam polished the frame with the sheet.

I'll bet, thought Elma not wanting to interrupt her.

Just like you'd imagine in your dreams.

'Where is she now, Gran?'

'Scarlet? Oh I don't know where she is. She grew up and went away.'

Miriam spoke matter of factly, as if it was the most normal thing for a little girl to do. Just grow up and go away.

'Oh,' said Elma, 'I wonder why.'

'She was happy, you know, a very happy girl.'

Miriam took a slow breath in and breathed out a sigh.

'Is she in the postcard, Gran?'

'No, no that's me and my friend. We worked up at the hotel. "The Pub With No Beer" that's what everybody called it.'

She stopped talking, took a few quick breaths, smoothed her hair back behind her ears and began again.

'That photo was the year I got married.'

'To Charlie?'

That doesn't seem right – you weren't working up there when you got married.

'Charlie, who's Charlie?'

Miriam looked confused and turned the postcard over and over in her hand. Elma grabbed for the picture frame as it slid off the bed covers and caught it just as it reached the floor.

Good save, Elma!

'Take it easy, Gran. You sound a little wheezy.'

A white sticker stuck to the back of the frame.

Cathy – aged 5 – written in Aunt Livie's handwriting.

'Scott! He's the man I married. We were so happy up there on our mountain. Young love.'

The older woman gave a little giggle.

'Just the two of us, candle-lit dinners, outside under the trees. A carpet of wild-scented grass. Birds singing, flitting here and there.'

'At the Springs Hotel, Gran?' Elma interrupted.

'Of course not, why would we want to live there? We had a better place than that. The most beautiful place in the world. Cosy, private, our piece of the mountain. Didn't need to share that with them, now did we?'

She gave a sigh.

'Those were the days. Open fire, slow cooked wallaby, pumpkin soup or a piece of lamb.'

'Just wait, love might come to you some day.'

Elma couldn't believe what she was hearing.

It's not true — none of this is true! Someone's swapped cranky Gran for a sweet old lady who lives in the woods. What the heck is going on?

She fumbled in her pocket for her hand sanitiser, dropping it to the floor as she tried to pass it from her good arm to her plastered hand.

'Blast it.'

'Beg yours? Who do you think you are coming in here and talking like a piece of trash?'

What just happened?

'Scott and I were always happy. He thought the world of me and I thought the world of him.'

She laid the card on her raised knees in front of her and stared into the past, a pleasant smile on her face.

'We lived on the mountain for a year in that wooden hut with its tin roof at the top of Myrtle Gully Ridge. Sometimes I'd walk down the track to where the twin creeks met and go and visit my mother and my father. My father was a saw doctor and very good at it too. Can you keep a secret?'

She looked past Elma towards the window.

'Livinda could.'

'Yes, I know that. You already told me.'

She regretted the words as soon as they'd left her tongue and was surprised that Miriam continued with her story.

'I stole one once.'

'One what?'

'A knife. It wasn't one of the customers'. It was just one of the ones he'd made himself. He was very good at making knives.'

'Yes, you told me that already.'

Elma rolled her eyes, she'd done it again, backchatted her gran.

Elma, keep your mouth shut and just listen – this is important.
'What did you do with the knife, Gran?'
That's something I've never heard about.

'I took it up to our little house. Scott wasn't always around, he had to work away a lot, but when he was there it was just the best of times. I remember sitting on the little wooden steps while he carved our names on the handle, Scott and Miriam Hamilton. Beautiful cursive writing – took him such a long time. He took some charcoal from the fire, mixed it with a bit of oil, I think, and then smudged it into the carved grooves. I was so proud of him.'

True – not true – true – not true.

Some of it seemed obvious but some of it confused Elma as she later sat up on the mezzanine floor, trying her best to write the information onto the appropriate page.

We know she didn't marry SH. We know they didn't have a baby – or do we? Hmm. My great grandfather was a saw doctor – true. My grandfather ... Charlie was a drinker – I don't know any more about him than that – Dad's not one for talking. Maybe another trip to Ballan? Nah on that one – maybe I'll ring Aunt Livie.

Elma left shortly after that. It just seemed like far too much information or misinformation to take in for one day. From what she'd understood from Aunt Livie this was not the gentleman Miriam had formed the clandestine relationship with at all.

But why does she lie about it? Why not just say he was a creep who kept her waiting and only turned up if no one else knew he was with her.

It hadn't made it easy when she managed to miss two busses; one from the nursing home to Hobart and the other from Hobart to South Hobart.

Gran's a nut. Dad's being held hostage by Paula Pug Face. I'm wet through.

I don't get it – I still need more info from Aunt Livie or Dad maybe.

--

'Dad, please,' Elma begged, 'My friend leaves tomorrow, it's the last chance we have,' but it was too late, the call had ended.

She replaced the phone on the wall and turned to gaze out the window. Should she stay home like Dad had said to? What could be the harm in a little walk in the sunshine?

What the heck?

She pressed Send at the bottom of the text message on her phone.

'Meet you on Macquarie St outside St John's Hospital'

She figured the sign was big enough for even a foreigner to notice and besides, Fergus would be looking for her anyway.

What can Dad do? Get angry, not buy food. I'll be back before he gets home from work.

She stuffed a beanie into the pocket of her jacket and stuffed her jacket in her backpack.

I hope my boots have dried.

Elma found them by the back door caked in mud. She slipped her feet inside.

A bit damp but dry enough to wear.

--

In less than an hour she was sitting at The Springs with her back to the sun.

'So this is where I think the hut should be.'

Elma rested her plastered arm on the wooden picnic table and pointed to a ridge on the map with her other hand.

'But you see this track here?'

Fergus learned in to get a closer look.

'It wasn't there ten years ago!'

'Ahh,' he nodded as she continued. Their heads were less than a metre apart, his dark curly hair pulled back and tied with a hair tie.

Maybe the one I gave him yesterday.

Elma caught a whiff of shampoo, the familiar smell of his coat from the previous day. She gave a little shiver – a warm one this time.

'Now, this is the new, or not-so-new North/South Bike Track.'

She faltered, looking up from the map. His eyes were at the same level as hers. She stared briefly into his brown eyes. She could feel his breath on her bare arm.

'And this is the path I thought we were on.'

She pointed to a track running parallel to the first one.

Can he hear my heart beat?

'Then this is where those ruins of yours should be,' said Fergus, pointing to an area between the two tracks. Elma looked back down at the map to where he was pointing, his hand almost touching hers. She drew back a little. Fergus used his middle finger rather than his missing pointer.

Well, of course you can't point with something you haven't got.

'One flat white and a cappuccino,' called a voice from the servery window of the café.

'I'll get it,' Fergus said, jumping up from the table and bounding effortlessly up the steps to the converted shipping container.

'Do you want to hear a funny sad story?' he asked, handing the hot drink to Elma and slipping back down onto the wooden bench. Elma lifted her shoulders and sat up a little straighter. It felt all right sitting up at The Springs, coffee in hand, with good company and the sun shining warmly on her face.

Way different than yesterday. I bet he's going to tell me about how he lost his finger.

'Yeah, okay, I'm ready for it.'

'Well, a few years back, when the Uni used to come up here to kunanyi to study the bats they would capture them, weigh them, you know take all their measurements and that, pretty much the way we do now, except before they released them a small band would be clamped around one of their little legs.'

He wiggled his pinkie and Elma laughed.

'Problem was the poor little bats were really light and the bands were a wee bit heavy, well,' he paused, 'actually they were all way too heavy and the bats that were banded weren't able to fly very well and a lot of them died.'

He screwed his face into a funny shape and Elma burst out laughing.

'That is so not true.'

'Unfortunately, it is. I told you it was a funny sad story'

'No,' she laughed again. 'That was only sad. I'm sure.'

--

The sun may have been out but the path was still in shadow. When they reached a part on the path where the sun didn't reach Elma pulled her jacket from her bag and put it on.

'We can't stop here today, or maybe we can on our way back,' Elma said, indicating the turnoff towards Sphinx Rock.

'It's okay,' Fergus replied. 'I've been out there a dozen times. Last time there was a school group abseiling over the side.'

Glad that didn't happen at any school I went to.

I'd have been too scared going over the side of a cliff with the ground a million miles below.

'It's a great view of Hobart, but I have trouble going near the edge. Don't think I could do that,' she said.

231

'Fair enough,' Fergus replied easily.

She liked him. He wasn't scared of anything.

But doesn't care that I am.

She thought of Chloe – always ready to tease her for being timid.

Josh was just the same.

It seemed like hours before they arrived at the place where perhaps the ridge met the path.

'It's pretty hard to tell, hey.'

Fergus checked his phone.

Elma was getting used to the way he said things a little differently than she did. She didn't laugh or cringe anymore when he added extra words like, hey or yeah or aye at the end of his sentences.

'The ruins have to be below us – usually there's some kind of marking to say where the unmarked path is.'

'Hardly unmarked then, if they're marked.'

Unmarked on the map but marked on the path – if you know what you're looking for.

'Maybe a cairn or a piece of coloured ribbon or sometimes a mark on a tree or a rock.'

'I looked up online about that tattoo on your arm,' Elma said, offering him some nuts from a bag she'd stashed in her pocket.

Fergus extended his arm to take the food.

'I know that it might tell where you are from and I know that those curly bits there are koru and represent new life or loved ones or people or something.'

She suddenly felt her face burning.

'Sounds like you've done your homework,' Fergus said. Then he pulled up his sleeve and told her the meaning of some of the other symbols embedded in black on his arm.

By 1pm the hidden track was still hidden. Elma and Fergus had walked three kilometres to Junction Cabin and three kilometres back.

'Sorry, Elma. I guess it's one of those tricky tracks that don't appear until someone shows you and then you go "Oh yeah, that's so obvious I don't know how I missed it."'

He tilted his head back and forth in time to his words and they both burst out laughing.

When they became serious again Elma mentioned the hut up near Big Bend.

'Chloe and I spent all day looking for that one and never found it.'

Fergus dumped his backpack in the boot of the car and removed his boots, replacing them with his running shoes.

'There are two huts up there. Which one were you looking for?'

'You know them?'

'Of course. I told you Nige and I come up here all the time.'

He emphasised the word I and swung his foot up to the bumper to tie his laces.

'Which one were you after?'

'Scout Hut, I think Dad called it.'

She fumbled in her bag for her phone and flicked through, finding a picture of Chloe and herself on top of the rock where they had eaten their lunch.

'Here it is. This is where it is – I mean this is where we ate lunch. No hut, see.'

She showed him the two photos – one facing the summit and the other facing away from it with the beautiful hazy hills and valleys in the background.

'Yep, I know exactly where Scout Hut is. You were pretty close. It's a wonder you didn't trip over it.'

Elma looked at him suspiciously,

How can he know that just by looking at two photos?

'Really?' she said wanting to believe him.

'Well, look there, just behind your arm. See that thin pipe looking thing?'

Elma took a closer look, 'Yeah – there's something sticking out of the rock in the background.'

'Well that's most likely the chimney.'

'Really?' she repeated.

Yes really. I can take you there if you like but it won't be until I get back from NZ in November.'

Elma didn't know what to say,

he wants to see me again when he gets back ...

'Really?'

Fergus laughed, a broad smile spreading across his face.

He liked the way her eyes lit up with excitement.

He was going to miss her.

I'm going to miss him.

'Well,' she said, suddenly sounding serious, 'I can't make any promises that I'll be available when you get back, I've got my course starting soon and that will take up a lot of time.'

He's different than I first thought.

Elma smiled for no reason at all.

'How about a late lunch at the Ferntree Tavern? My shout.'

He added 'Since it's my last day here – for a while.'

'Okay, yes.'

Elma surprised herself.

I might even let you drop me home.

Chapter 21

By the middle of August Elma had settled into a routine of study, study and more study. The fast-track nursing course was full-on but she had Chloe's support and a stack of encouraging letters and cards from Aunt Livie.

And a few distracting texts from NZ.

She spent at least half a day on the weekend with her gran and was comfortable to sit in the lounge or café or wherever she found Miriam and play cards or study. The things she was learning in her course made her look at Gran's condition from a different perspective.

'Chloe, I had no idea what dementia meant. I just thought it was a disease that old people got to make them forget what hopeless people they were.'

Chloe laughed,

'Can't say I'd even thought about it 'til your gran got it. And even then I just thought she was being cantankerous. Like, I didn't know she couldn't help it.'

Elma thought about some of the 'oldies' who passed by while she sat with Miriam in the lounge or café.

Mr Black – who repeated himself continually to anyone and everyone who had the time to listen.

Leonard Lip Smacker –

I shouldn't call him that – he doesn't call me Elma Washalot.

Miss Kitty who doesn't speak at all but just wanders around most days looking for something she can't find.

A bit like Gran's invisible photo album.

Catherine, who prefers to be called Kate. She can hold a wonderful conversation on nearly every subject under the sun – except on the days she can't and no one knows which days those will be.

So many people, all with dementia but all with a different type.

George was usually positioned in a sunny spot, his day chair reclined completely back to keep him from falling out. A slim line of dribble escaped from the corner of his mouth on the side he was facing.

His whole body just forgot how to function, like overnight. And Mrs Curtis, who I used to think was so strange because she took a really big step to get over the strip of black tiles before entering the bathroom, like there was a giant ditch she had to jump. And then I found out the black tiles truly appear as a bottomless pit to her – it's not so funny now.

There were some with sensory processing issues who freaked out at loud noises

or even music

and others who had no sense of time or space.

Mrs Cornhill often tried to fit herself between chairs and into places that seemed obviously too small for her.

Anthony spoke with a very English accent and often had bruises on his face and hands, because sometimes his balance just disappeared without warning.

Gran, it seems has the superpower of believing an alternate reality,

Which, in Elma's opinion, caused so much anxiety for Martin he hardly ever came to visit her. It was strange for Elma to see Gran from another point of view.

'Growing up', Chloe's mum called it.

She wasn't sure her dad felt the same way

About me growing up – thinking for myself.

Martin was hardly home.

He'd often drive directly to Paula's house after work to shower and change. Driving lessons had gone by the wayside.

Not that I really want to drive at the moment. I feel like vomiting every time driving lessons are mentioned.

Paula kept asking Martin to arrange to catch up with Elma but Elma declined every time. Paula took up most of Martin's spare time.

Elma was okay with that.

The less I see of him the better.

Tonight was one of those rare nights where she and Martin were home at the same time.

'Well, if you can't be trusted, I'll get Paula to move in here rather than me spend time at her place.' Martin pushed his coffee to the side of the table and flicked through his work diary. Elma stopped midway mashing the potatoes. The electric beater dropped onto the bench, bits of spud flicking up the wall like mud from the back tyre of a trail bike.

'You can't mean that, Dad. Of course I can be trusted.'

Elma remembered their previous "squabble" back in June.

It was the last time she'd seen Fergus.

She knew what Martin was referring to – she hoped he'd forget about it.

I know I'm trying to.

'Geez, Dad, I said sorry, didn't I? Can't we just get over it?' She dabbed the dishcloth at the wall, smearing the potato across the tiles.

'Elma, you only said sorry because you got caught. You asked me if you could go back up the mountain and I said no, and you went anyway.'

'Dad, that was months ago,'

At least two – definitely two – exactly two.

Elma had been counting the days since Fergus had left for New Zealand

Didn't know I'd miss him this much.

--

It had been 3pm when she waved goodbye to Fergus that last day.

Happy – sad.

She watched the little red car drive off down the road and disappear around the corner. His beanie slid from the car roof where he'd placed it while saying goodbye. She'd picked it up and held it to her face, enjoying the comfort of his now-familiar smell.

They hadn't found Gran's ruins but Elma had discovered other things – quite by accident. She opened the kitchen door with a smile on her face and a skip in her heart.

I may have a broken arm, no job and zero funds but I don't care – I feel great! I haven't felt like this forever.

She swung the door inwards and dropped her backpack on the floor before flopping herself down backwards onto the sofa, her boots hanging over the edge. A deep sigh escaped her lungs and she stared blissfully at the skylight above her.

A shadow fell across her face.

'What the hell do you think you're doing?'

Martin stood staring down at her – silhouetted in the frame of the skylight. She couldn't see the frown on his face but had no trouble hearing the anger in his voice. What could she say? Nothing, there weren't words quick enough or strong enough to appease him. She jerked herself up and around into a sitting position, pulling her legs up to her chest and wrapped her arms awkwardly about her knees. The fiberglass cast offered no protection to the onslaught of words.

'Who was that in the car?' Martin said, standing sideways to the sofa, half focussed on Elma, half focussed on the phone on the wall as if waiting for a call. His arms were folded – his hands were clenched.

'You know who, Dad – I told you this morning.'

'Who? Who was it?'

She watched as Martin unclenched his fists and clenched them again.

'Umm, Fergus,' Elma offered,

'Remember – the bat catcher I told you about – the one from New Zealand?' she muttered the last few words almost under her breath. Any euphoric feeling had fled with the first blast of Martin's interrogation.

'A New Zealander!' Martin's full attention was on Elma now.

'Yes, Dad, a Kiwi – you know, a Maori.'

Like Liz…

'What the hell do you mean you're dating a Maori?' Martin lashed out.

His face changed from hardworking brown to an angry shade of red. Elma stared at the veins bulging from the side of his neck. His greying hair was dishevelled. She'd never seen him like this. He turned away from her and faced the sliding door, hesitating before storming out to the deck.

What do I do now?

Hot tears stung her cheeks,

I really didn't think that one through.

Where's the ute? Why is he home now? He's supposed to be working.

She sat there waiting for answers to pop into her head, but nothing came. She closed her eyes.

Best day – worst day. Why does he have to spoil it for me?

She could feel the vibrations across the floor as Martin stomped back into the studio, his heavy boots still on his feet.

That's not usual.

She opened her eyes and looked up.

'What the hell do you think you are doing?'

Martin glared at her, 'I pay for your food, your schooling, your trips, and your clothes – everything. I pay for everything and you run off with some bloody Maori!'

The volume increased with every word, the crescendo ending with Martin spitting the words down at the trembling Elma.

Elma cowered.

'We're just friends, Dad. What's your problem?'

Oh no! Don't say that, Elma. Don't say anything! Let him calm down.

Martin raised his hand.

Elma's eyes opened wide. She squealed involuntarily, closing her eyes and raising her plastered arm in front of her face.

She heard the sound of her own scream. For an instant she thought it came from someone. By the time she opened her eyes he was gone. The room was empty, a patch of sunshine spreading in the shape of a shield across the carpet in the middle of the room.

No car, no Dad, no noise.

Her legs wobbled as she pulled herself up off the sofa and into a standing position. Her stomach felt heavy.

I really thought he was going to hit me.

The room was strangely quiet. The outside door stood open. A dog barked somewhere in the street. The faint sound of school kids could be heard in the distance.

Martin's ute and house keys were on the table with a piece of folded paper. Elma unfolded it – $1100 a quote from the garage for two new tyres, a replacement headlight and repairs to a front panel.

I wonder what happened to the ute?

She didn't ask when he returned later but new headlines appeared in her notebook.

Father Threatens Child

There wasn't anything punny or funny about the headline at all, but Elma wrote it down and stared at it for a long time that night before shutting her notebook. She made a promise to herself to better conceal the stolen traces of dockets and notes still wrapped in the tea-towel that she'd stuffed in the drawer of her desk. And the photos she'd taken from Cathy's.

God knows how angry he might get if he finds out what I know about him and Liz.

They didn't see much of each other after that. Martin's belongings drizzled out of the flat.

He must be filling up Paula's place.

--

Elma said, carefully, 'I can be trusted Dad. You know I can,'

She looked at the potato still smeared across the olive green tiles.

I hate potatoes.

She knew she'd need to clean the tiles off properly after dinner.

'Course going well?' Martin asked, changing the subject from Paula moving in.

Like that will ever happen.

'Great,' Elma replied, pressing her fork slowly down on a chickpea at the side of her curry.

'And work?'

'Fine.'

Elma repeated and watched the chickpea crush beneath her fork.

What's the point? Nothing I say will make a difference – no point trying – just eat and breathe.

She let out a sigh and stirred at the curry looking for another chickpea to attack.

She'd had tried – *for a second* – to think kindly of Paula, after all, as Chloe had pointed out, he was a lot happier.

--

'Who would have thought things would turn out like this?' mused Chloe as they sat in the Mall contemplating what they might do to celebrate the first day of spring only two "more sleeps" away.

'Not sure if spring is my favourite season or not. It certainly is Aunt Livie's,' Elma said, watching a council worker replacing potted plants in a floral display.

'Seasons! My mum says, "Life is a series of seasons"'

Chloe put on her best mother voice.

"As sure as sunlight after rain, your true life is born from pain."

'What the heck does that mean?' Elma laughed.

'Don't know, the whole poem is about accepting life and its changes. I still haven't worked out what "it" is.' Chloe joined in the laughter.

'Yeah I know, but just when you think you've got it, whatever "it" is, changes.'

Elma stopped laughing and stared at the budding flowers in the pots – each one secreting a compressed flower.

Of unknown colour.

'Well at least I'm your flatmate now – not everything is as bad as it seems.'

She put her mother's voice back on, 'It's just a season.'

'Yeah, I suppose,' said Elma, 'But I miss my old dad and I really hate how awkward it is between us. I didn't think family was like that.'

She looked down at the little gutter beneath her feet. A ripped piece of rubbish from a chocolate wrapper floated by.

Chapter 22

'Hey Gran, I'm taking one last walk up the mountain to-morrow – a do or die attempt to find your hut.'

Sand slipped through Elma's fingers, fine particles glistening as she poured them from one hand to the other, something she wouldn't have done a year ago

or even six months for that matter.

Still she wasn't completely at ease with the grains sticking to her fingers and used her longest nail to evict reluctant fragments from beneath her unpainted nails. Gran's walking frame was parked at an angle beside the wooden seat, a collection of papers and memorabilia sticking through the sides of the under seat basket. Miriam swung her feet in time to 'Brown Eyed Girl' crooning out from a speaker remotely attached to an iPhone metres away. It belonged to the family playing in the pre-spring day.

'Definitely feels like spring, hey Gran?' Elma smiled, surprised to see Miriam singing along to the song.

Who would have thought – guess it is an old people's radio station.

She laughed quietly to herself.

'Did you hear me, Gran? I'm going up the mountain to-morrow – do you want to come?'

She made Bambi eyes at the happy woman on the seat expecting a tongue-lash at least.

'I know you're making fun of me,' Miriam stated without releasing her smile.

Elma closed her eyes – it was true.

'Sorry Gran. That was wrong of me.'

She wiped the remaining grains of sand from her hands and clothes, watching the fragments fall and hide themselves in the sandy universe below her sneakers.

Miriam's feet were clad as usual in her sensible Hush Puppy shoes and socks, her legs covered by her smart blue gabardine slacks but, as Elma stared beneath the seat she caught a glimpse of the scar on her grandmother's leg. The stain of purple discolouration failed to conceal itself between the hem of the trousers and the scrunched-down sock.

Elma braved up, 'Can I ask you something, Gran?'

Last time I asked she bit my head off.

Would today be any different?

'She didn't know.'

Miriam stared out over the river, her eyes fixed on some spot on the Eastern Shore. The tall lights of the Cricket Grounds, maybe, or the top of Mt Canopus – it didn't matter.

'Who Gran? Who didn't know?

'She didn't know he was married. She didn't know he had a wife and child. She thought she was the only one. The only one in the world that he had eyes for. She felt like a princess. So important, so vain. Stupid girl. Stupid, stupid girl.'

Miriam shook her head. Her feet were still happily swinging, it was just her face that marked the change.

'He was so handsome, wise and sophisticated,' she added.

'He told her how mature she was, not like the other scatty girls her age. No, she was someone special, someone worth spending his time with. And he told her how responsible she was, able to make grown-up decisions on her own. A person who didn't need parents controlling her every move.'

For an instant Miriam looked down and up again.

'He said her knowledge of the area was second to none. She should be proud of herself for being so independent and capable. Just the kind of person he'd been waiting for. A rare find indeed.'

Her feet stopped swinging and Elma wondered how Miriam had been able to keep it all to herself for so long. Or had she? Did Livie know all this?

She must have – although she was still at school then, so maybe not. I don't know.

I wish I had my notebook.

Elma cursed herself for leaving it in her grandmother's room, never expecting the third person account of Gran's early years. They were only going for a short walk to the beach and back. It was a good day for Gran. Elma hadn't needed to drag her from her room or convince Miriam they were only going as far as the café. No, today Miriam had been happy to be led wherever Elma chose to go.

She certainly seemed to have climbed out of the right side of the bed. Or maybe she's just not in any pain.

That always makes a difference – turns cranky Gran into 'The Incredible Crank'. Cranky I've gotten used to. The other one is unpredictable and violent.

'He seemed like such a good thing. Always complimented her on her hair or clothes or even the way she laughed.'

Elma waited for Gran to continue.

'She should have listened to them. They warned her – more than once. But would she listen to them?'

'He told her not to talk to them – said they were jealous – didn't know what he was really like. Best just to keep it all a secret. Meet after work, down the path. She'd take one path, he'd take another. Never at the same time though. That would have been too obvious. No, she'd leave work as she usually did and wait for him to catch up or meet on another track. There were plenty of tracks to choose from. That girl knew them all.'

A change came over Miriam's face, lines and crevices began forming on her forehead increasing until her whole face scowled.

'He was a piece of work.'

She glared across the river and shook her head.

'I'd have killed him myself if she hadn't.'

The words were more spat than spoken, hurtling out of the old woman's mouth in much the same way Martin's had the day Elma had disobeyed him.

'What! Gran, what are you on about?'

Elma glared at Gran.

'Did you kill him, Gran? Did you kill Scott?'

She stood up so suddenly the oxygen drained from her head and for a few seconds everything went dark as tiny flicks of light danced about in front of her eyes. She wobbled forward, and just managed to steady herself by holding onto the back of the park bench.

I don't get it.

'I don't get it, Gran! What are you talking about?'

Whatever it was Elma had hoped to discover it was lost with her outburst. Gran got up, pulled the walking frame to herself and started the trip back to the nursing home leaving

247

Elma totally flabbergasted with the thought that Gran might be a murderer.

Well of course she isn't. How could she be?

Elma raced to catch up to Miriam.

Damn – I left my phone in her room.

She pulled alongside the walking frame, bursting with questions.

'Gran, can you stop! Please. Can you tell me what happened?'

Miriam ignored her pleas and continued her shuffle-thud back up the ramp and into the café area, her breath laboured – her destination fixed. The security door opened – the gritty sound of sand in the slider made an uncomfortable noise as it grated shut behind them. Elma stood and watched Miriam slog across the room towards the fountain. She wanted to scream and shout at the old lady,

shake her even.

You're just impossible Gran. I don't care what anyone says – you know exactly what you're doing.

'You all right there, young Elma?'

It was Dr Gordon.

No, no. Please, not now.

'It's just that you're standing in the door way and there's someone behind you … trying to get in.' He took her by the elbow and stepped her to the side, out of the way of the opening door.

'Oh, my goodness. Sorry, I um –'

'Are you all right?' the kindly gentleman asked again, 'you look a little confused.'

A little confused …

'I left my bag in Gran's room.'

She spoke without looking at the bearded doctor.

'Do you need a cup of tea, Elma? You seem quite distract-ed.'

'All good,' she said gaining her composure, 'I've just got a few things on my mind today but nothing's wrong.'

Gran was well out of sight now

like the white rabbit down a rabbit hole – she knows exactly how to get to her room. Never gets lost. She knows, she knows.

True or not true?

True: Elma was confused. True: she was angry. True: her gran had killed someone? Most likely not.

But totally frustrating trying to make sense of it all.

She sat in the mezzanine area, staring down at the table. All the contents of her bag were laid out in front of her. Study folder furthest to her left, her notebook next and beside that, her wallet. All items decreasing down in size, ending on her right with her hand sanitiser and lastly her house keys. Order. There needed to be some sort of order. Colour? No – too messy. Size? Yes. That worked. She picked her phone out of the line-up and scrolled down to Aunt Livie's number.

Please be home.

The drinks lady was serving afternoon tea and she'd left Miriam in her room with a cup of weak coffee and a biscuit from the trolley. There'd be no way of extracting information from Miriam by force or coercion. Miriam ran her own agenda.

No wonder Dad doesn't visit anymore – she's such hard work to be around. She's such a …

Elma held the phone to her ear.

'Oh, what a nice surprise! I wasn't expecting a call from my favourite niece today. I hope everything is okay?'

'Well, Aunt Livie, it's not.'

'Oh, what's the trouble Darling? You sound upset.'

'Did Gran kill someone?'

There it was – out before she had time to think about it, or the impact it might have on Livie.

'Sorry? I think you just asked me if Miriam killed someone. How strange. Are you okay?'

'You didn't answer my question,' Elma persisted.

'I didn't think you were being serious. Surely I'd know if my sister had killed anyone. What a silly question. Elma, what are you up to?'

'Sorry, I wasn't thinking straight.'

Elma could hear some resistance rising in her aunt's voice.

'What I meant to say was, is Scott Hamilton still alive and where does he live?'

There was silence.

Oh no what have I done?

She remembered the shade of grey Aunt Livie had turned when confronted last time over the blue laminated table top in Ballan.

'Are you there Aunt Livie? Speak to me please? Are you there?'

'Slow down Elma. Have you gone mad?'

Phew.

'You're okay, Aunt Livie?'

'Yes, I am but I'm not sure about you. Now start again. What do you want to know?'

Elma took a deep breath and closed her eyes, struggling to calm herself.

'Well, I just wondered if –' she paused.

Was it worth pursuing?

Not sure, but I can't just drop it – can I?

'– if –,' she stuttered, '– if Scott Hamilton was still alive and whether Gran kept in contact with him?'

'Did you ask her that? Oh Elma, whatever were you thinking?'

There was a brief pause and Livie added, 'Is she okay? Is Miriam okay?'

'Of course she is.'

She's the same as always.

It was Elma's turn to be offended. A bit of regret began to sprout – slowly at first but the more they talked the more it grew.

It seemed like such a simple question but now it looks like I've upset everyone from Aunt Livie to Dr Gordon. Oh Gran you are so, so, so... annoying.

'Aunt Livie, I don't mean to be a pain but you still haven't answered my question.'

'He died the day of the fire Elma. But believe me Miriam had no hand in killing him. He was trapped up there the same as anyone who didn't leave when they should've. It only took a few minutes for the fire to get from the Springs Hotel down to our place that day. He didn't stand a chance. They found him days later on a track up near the hotel. No one knew he was still on the mountain – they thought he'd caught his plane home earlier that day. No one missed him. Why would they? The hotel had been evacuated much earlier.'

Elma was watching Dr Gordon chuckling with a resident on the ground floor not far from where she'd encountered him earlier. The day staff had handed over to the evening staff, who were now herding the oldies to their rooms for their evening meals. The world was working as normal, but Elma wasn't part of it. She was somewhere off with the gods – watching life pass by from the mezzanine floor.

'I didn't know, Aunt Livie,' was all she could respond. 'I didn't know.'

'Of course you didn't. How could you? No one did – well, not until his wife called the police to say he hadn't arrived home. The police interviewed all the staff. God knows what they thought. Miriam was still in hospital – would be for months, but that didn't stop them, did it? No, they bowled in there with their note pads and pens and a never-ending list of silly questions. My goodness, they had a nerve. Upset Mum that's for sure. She was livid – here was Miriam burnt to pieces, blisters and scars all over, half her hair missing and them wanting to know where she was at the time of the fire! '

Elma waited for Aunt Livie to catch her breath. 'Was he at the hut, Aunt Livie? Is that where they found him?'

She was still fishing for a connection between Miriam and her desire to kill the man. Should she feel sympathy for some-one she thought was such a jerk? A creep who preyed upon a girl half his age. Or should she be upset that his was one of the lives taken that day?

Who am I to judge who should live or die?

Why should I feel bad about disliking him?

'No, no.' Aunt Livie was emphatic, 'I told you, Elma, they found Scott on a track near the hotel – he wasn't at the hut. Miriam never saw him that day. She told me so herself.'

'But she was there, wasn't she? She was caught in the fire too.'

Elma pinched the bridge of her nose squeezing the skin back and forth in a bid to clear her mind.

I need to know.

'Didn't you tell me she swore an oath never to set foot on the mountain again? Wasn't she so traumatised by it all she forced all of you to move to the Eastern Shore to live? Away from the mountain?'

What is missing? It doesn't make sense.

'Yes, she was on the mountain but not up at The Springs or at the hut.'

Elma tapped the table, her fingers running up and down on the spot.

'Then where was she?'

'Calm down, Elma. What's wrong with you today? I am certainly not used to you being so demanding. Do you need to know everything? Can't you just leave it be?'

Oh no, I've crossed the line again.

'Sorry. I mean, thanks for being so patient with me. Aunt Livie, I always feel safe when I talk to you.'

That sounded so hollow.

'It's okay, Love, I understand.'

I bet you don't.

One more try and then I leave it.

'Did Gran get evacuated with the other hotel staff?' she asked as calmly as she could.

'They closed the hotel early, Elma. Miriam never went to work that day.'

Then why was she on the mountain?

Livie answered, as if reading her mind.

'I don't think she understood how serious the fires were. I was at school, Mum was out and Dad was at work. She told me the power had gone out, the radio wouldn't run on batteries and she was worried about me. She couldn't work out where all the smoke was coming from. And,' her voice became certain, 'she decided to cut through the bush to Lenah Valley – to meet me at school.'

'But you weren't there, were you?'

'No, we'd been dismissed. She would never have found me. She misjudged it, got caught in that blasted fire and is lucky to be alive. Lots of people died, Elma, it wasn't easy for anyone.'

'Okay, Aunt Livie, I'm sorry I brought it all up again. Sorry that you had to go through all that.'

'It's okay, Love. Just try not to stress poor Miriam; she's been through enough you know. She doesn't need any more trouble. Just let her rest.'

'Okay. Love you plenty, Aunt Livie. I miss you so much.'

She's hiding something, I just know it. Or maybe she doesn't know the full story?

Ideas collected like dry leaves in Elma's mind, sweeping themselves into piles of kindling waiting, waiting for whatever they needed to ignite them.

She wrote everything she could remember in her notebook and left for the 6:40 bus.

Chapter 23

'Elma! You're addicted to that phone!' Chloe wagged her finger at Elma who sat across from her at the kitchen table. 'You used to talk to me before you started texting Lover Boy.'

'That's so not true and you know it,' Elma retorted, not taking her eyes off the screen.

'Well, when will I get to meet this Fergus guy? Will you bring him home for food sometime?' Chloe made a leering smile and leaned in close to Elma.

'I don't really want to bring him here. Not after the way Dad reacted when I mentioned he was a Kiwi.'

'Yeah that was wild,' Chloe said.

'He never struck me as the racist type.'

Elma snapped her face away from the screen.

'Oh I don't think he's racist, Chloe.'

Chloe raised her eyes with a look of disbelief.

'I mean, if you got pushed over by a short person you might be wary of the next short person you met.'

'That is so not sensible and you know it – you're defending him because he's your dad.'

'No, I'm not.' Elma cut in.

'I'm sure when he meets him it'll all be all right.'

'Hmm, have you met Paula yet?'

'You know I haven't. Why would I want to meet her?'

Chloe laughed loudly, 'Ha, ha I bet you'll like her when you do.'

She pulled a face at Elma.

'Actually I think your dad's been much nicer since he's been hanging around with Paula, you know? I haven't heard him go off at you for ages.'

'So?'

'So, she's a counsellor, isn't she?'

Elma pushed her phone around in a circle on the table.

'How the heck would I know?' she said hoping Chloe would just quit it with the questions.

'And look how chilled he was about me moving in here, "to keep you company".'

'"As long as you pay the rent on time it's all fine with me",' Chloe said trying to mimic Martin's voice.

Elma still didn't want to think good thoughts about Martin, but it was true. He was a lot more relaxed these days, about everything.

He even put money on my phone without me asking.

Chloe changed the subject.

'Well, come on then – when do I get to meet the famous Fergus?'

'He might need a ride to town from the airport at the beginning of November,' Elma said.

I hope I'm doing the right thing, telling her this …

'Oh yay, so when's the happy event? I'll need all the details,' Chloe jumped up clapping her hand together in delight.

'So you'll do it?'

'Of course – if it's at a reasonable hour … and I'm not work-ing … or at the hospital, blah, blah, blah,' she made sweeping hand gestures with every blah.

'Okay, I don't know the date or the times yet but Nigel is happy to do it if you can't or anything crops up. Blah, blah, blah.'

She pulled a face at her friend.

'Only eight weeks then and you can get a Fergus fix.'

'Stop it, Chloe.'

Elma looked back down at her phone.

'You know it's not like that.'

'You're just too sensitive for your own good. How are you ever going to get along in life if you can't laugh a little at yourself?'

'Sorry, Chloe, I'm just not like you.'

And she didn't want to be either – Chloe was happy to be the centre of attention whereas Elma couldn't think of anything worse.

'Now about the first day of spring – have we decided yet how to celebrate it?

--

Elma checked her map for the fiftieth time.

This is it. No going back. Today's the day I will find Gran's chimney if it **ruins** *me.*

She was happy with the pun she'd made.

I'll have to remember it for later.

She wondered if Fergus would get it.

I'll text him tonight.

And what if I don't find the chimney?

No question, Elma – you will find it.

Water dribbled from the top of her raincoat and over the back of her neck.

'Ha, ha, you can't get in,' she yelled at the rain, the hood of her jacket fastened tightly around her face. Mud squished beneath her feet.

Good boots, dry boots.

She wiggled her toes inside of the dark brown leather, *warm and safe,* unlike her map which had gathered condensation inside its plastic sleeve. Elma stared at the dark shadows seeping across the contours of the folded paper.

Blast it – I'm wrecking it.

She knew where she was though; she'd done this part with Fergus back in June.

He'll be back soon.

Her heart raced at the thought.

He's hardly thought about you since he left

– not true, Elma – he messages with you nearly every day.

He's probably just bored.

– not true, Elma, bored people don't message

Yes, they do

– no they don't.

It was one of those days. It didn't matter how much self-talk *or squabble*

went through Elma's head she couldn't seem to arrive at a conclusion.

On and on, up and up. Where to start?

She knew what Chloe would say – she'd quote "Do Re Me" from The Sound of Music.

The beginning, of course, the very beginning.

The words from the musical sloshed with the rain through her mind. Today was the first day of spring.

Not very springy I must say. Yesterday with Gran was warm and dry and then the change came in the evening and the rain just fell out of the sky. Maybe I should have picked movie time with Chloe.

Both girls had decided that whatever they chose to do, it wasn't allowed to be study.

Elma licked the rain from her lips and remembered this morning's conversation.

'I'm helping you make the lunch but it's raining and I am not going up there,' Chloe pointed towards the wall in the direction of the mountain.

Elma cocked her head to one side.

'I'm not asking you to climb the wall, Chloe, just a little walk up kunanyi, you know, to keep me company.'

'No, it's raining, and I know for a fact it will be all day. I'm staying here with my mate, Julie Andrews and the Sound of Music, and if you reconsider, we can share the sandwiches here on the floor. I'll let you bring out a floral blanket and pretend it's an Austrian picnic.'

'I don't think it'll rain forever. It was fine all day yesterday.'

Elma looked out at the gloomy yard. A layer of pattering water moved across the deck. Drenched man fern fronds hung down, dragging their greenery on the ground, absorbing brown paint with their muddy tips.

'They don't always get the forecast right, you know.'

'Elma, even if the rain stops now it's going to be slush up there.'

She looked towards the wall again and Elma burst out laughing. A vision of mashed potato and mud raced down the paintwork like raindrops on the windows of Aunt Livie's old front room.

'I'll cope. What's the worst that can happen?'

'Are you seriously asking me that question after the last time when you jolly near killed yourself with hyperthermia!'

'It wasn't last time and it's hy-po-ther-mia, not hy-per-ther-mia – you should know the difference – studying nursing are we?'

'Oh well, please yourself,' Chloe continued to pack the lunch. 'But I'm not going with you, and that's that.'

She wanted to add, "What would your dad say?" but thought it better not to bring his name up. After all, Elma surely must be aware of his feelings – the last time wasn't that long ago.

Elma sat huddled beside a rock close to a skinny gum tree on the ridge, not far from where she and Fergus had sheltered on that cold, wet day back in June.

And that's that – Chloe had sounded just like Aunt Livie. *I bet she was worried about what dad would say.*

She thought of "that day" and the one after, when she'd gone against her father's wishes and discovered a side of him she'd not seen before, and definitely something she wasn't expecting.

The wind this time wasn't as wicked back then, when she'd worn her light blue cotton leggings, thinking they looked good and that was what she thought mattered at the time. She'd since bought herself a pair of merino thermals, not cheap.

--

Damien had stuck to his word and the day the "worm ridden" cast was removed, Elma had fronted up at work looking for a space on the roster.

'You're lucky there's one shift going,' Damien said admiring her skinny pale arm.

'Good and blotchy, but no more greeblies I suspect,' he said.

'It was always clean,' Elma feigned offence.

She liked Damien and really wanted to be back there with the dirty dishes and a washcloth, or out the front serving customers. Even that didn't scare her as much as it used to. It was only once a week but it was all day from opening time until closing time. Things were a bit different at the café since she'd been on her "break".

'We've had security cameras installed above the till,' Damien said, with a forced smile.

'Hope it doesn't make you feel too self-conscious, but it's a modern necessity and the problem of the missing money has disappeared.'

Elma wasn't sure where to look. Should she follow Damien's lead and smile at the camera?

'Oh, you silly billy. No one thinks it was you. We caught the culprit weeks back. This is just to deter future wannabe thieves and protect our honest staff.'

He placed his hand on her shoulder, encouraging her to lift her head and look his way.

'Thanks, Damien. I didn't think for one minute you would consider me a thief.'

She smiled.

She was thankful for the job, thankful for the regular customers who called her by name and gave good tips. She was especially thankful for the merino leggings, and pleased with herself for buying them with her own savings.

--

Water dripped forward from her hood into her thermos cup. It was wet. Really wet.

Forecast was right.

Steam rose from her cup, fighting against the splats of rain. She fastened the thermos lid back in place, fumbling a little – there was still a slight weakness in the muscles of her forearm.

I can't imagine how lucky we were that day. We really should be dead.

261

She thought of Josh struggling with his parents about his being gay.

I didn't get to meet Nelson – maybe next time.

Although she doubted next time would be very soon as she still had study for another year and seven months and there was no way she could find time to work more than one shift at the café – even if there was a shift to be had. She refused to drive and still cringed at the sound of George Ezra's voice or even the mention of his name. But if part of her life had stayed still or even gone backwards, like the conflict between herself and her father, other things were moving forward, or at least Elma felt so. She'd made headway on events regarding Miriam's squizzled memories.

Aunt Livie shared more than I expected on that front.

And a lot of her own memories were now being recategorised because of the new photos and information provided by Cathy. What had previously seemed black and white was merging into 'shades of grey'.

I've learnt more about myself this year than I've known my entire life. I'm not close to Dad at the moment and I miss him.

Elma shivered. There was no snow on the Mountain today but there had been a massive fall only the week before and it was always cooler up here than down in Hobart.

Especially if the wind was blowing.

And it was.

Just need to get to the North-South Track and look out for markings on either side of the trail. That's what we didn't do the first time. Because I didn't really understand why the ruins hadn't already shown themselves. And the next time we came from The Springs Track and didn't find any markings as we had no reference to how far along the path we needed to be.

Everything was back in its place in her backpack. Her hands were washed – a pointless task as they would be wet and grubby as soon as she needed to grab a tree for balance.

So, I know that the ruins are somewhere between the North-South Bike Track and The Springs Track.

It didn't seem like such a big area to cover but Elma already knew how elusive Gran's hut was.

If I just stick to the track and cross the new/old path I'll find it.

Determined? Yes. Hopeful? Yes. Confident? Yes. Dirty? Not really, but that would happen soon enough. She marched forward.

Today is the day.

The tree root caught her unaware. She lost her footing and slipped forward, mud dashing up to meet her.

'Crap!' she yelled, trying hard to catch her balance and throwing her weight sideways in an attempt to prevent a full frontal smack in the mud. In hindsight, the face plant would have been preferable,

and less painful,

than being captured by untamed pampas grass. She grabbed at it in a bid to prevent herself falling further. Its sword-like serrated claws ripped into the palms of her hands. Instinctively she released her grip and screamed insults out to the wind.

Kunanyi had captured her, rolled her in mud and left her to bleed. She had a cry, trapped in a gully of man-eating plants, her clothing a living camouflage, her esteem below zero.

'I can't believe I did that,' she cried, looking at her bloodied hands.

'I am just too stupid.'

There was no one here to rescue her this time, and for all she knew she was covered in leeches. A rock stuck into her back, just below her pack.

I guess it could be worse,

but she wasn't sure how. Clamping her hand shut to stop it bleeding she wiggled around onto all fours before regaining enough balance to stand. Above her the track was just out of view.

She reasoned to herself that if she moved downwards a bit, she could find the trail she'd fallen from. It wasn't far – it was just impossible to climb back over the pampas grass.

Best I just go down and around.

--

She recalled her adventure while Chloe dressed her wounds and gave her a mock-fatherly 'I told you so' lecture about bush-walking alone on a dangerous mountain.

'But I found the hut, Chloe! The ruins – you know what I mean. Not then, but when I did get back to the trail I continued on to the North-South Track and the markings were so obvious I can't believe we ever missed them in the first place.'

'Well,' said Chloe, 'I know why.'

Elma looked at her and furrowed her brow, 'why?'

'Fergus, you daft, idiot. You followed Fergus up that path and wherever his cute bum went your eyes followed.'

'Chloe! You never give up, do you?'

Elma looked down at her hands suddenly aware she might have offended the indomitable Chloe. Her cuts weren't bad – just scratches really – although they'd caned no end when Elma had washed the dried blood off in the shower.

It was kind of Chloe to dress them for her.

'Sorry,' she said unable to make eye contact.

'You are such a chook,' Chloe retorted. 'Just admit you like the guy and we'll leave it at that.'

She pressed the tape in place over the bandage and Elma winced.

I do like him. I just don't want you to tease me about it.

'Sorry, Chloe – he's just a friend. Like you and me – like any friend.'

Chloe laughed her familiar laugh and shook her head.

'Oh Elma, you'll be 18 very soon, and I don't think you've even been kissed.'

Elma was deflated – there wasn't anything she could think of to say.

It's not a have-to-do thing – not everyone is like you.

I kinda like being me.

Well, that was a new thought – Elma quite often wanted to be anyone but herself.

It was another of those 'good day-bad day' days.

Elma sat at her desk in her room. Rain on the window reminded her that Aunt Livie was no longer living in Tasmania. The notebook pressed open, the new heading at the top. The skinny bandage didn't prevent her from holding her biro. It ached a bit and smarted when she opened her palms fully

but it'll be fine by tomorrow.

"Study as usual"

She put that under the heading **Good Day**.

"Wounds may get infected"

That went under the heading **Bad Day**.

Although it was only a thought and not an actual happening so technically it shouldn't have made it to the list at all.

Upset Chloe – **Bad Day**

Did I really or have I overthought it?

Wrecked her clothes – **Bad Day**

Seriously Elma, they can be washed and mended if they need it.

Walked alone – **Good Day**

This is an accomplishment, despite what Dad or Chloe think.

Been attacked by the bush – **Bad Day**

Survived – **Good day**

Found Gran's chimney –– **Good Day, Good Day, Good Day**.

It's been a long time coming – after two failed attempts.

One near-death experience and one success – just.

The marker ribbon had hung from a branch and fluttered a dull/fluoro pink just above eye height. How had they missed it the first time?

Easy – we weren't looking for it because I had no idea about the North-South Bike Track and because I was wet and cold and because it wasn't right on the path sticking out like a sign post saying, 'This is the Way to Gran's Hut'.

The ribbons were not close to the main track, but were set back from it by about four or five metres.

You would really have to know what you were looking for, I guess.

She felt it was comparable to finding 'Where's Wally' on a double page. Once you knew where he was it was as obvious as the Wrest Point Casino on a clear day.

Chapter 24

'Check again this afternoon.' Livie repeated, 'It would be a shame if it was lost.'

'The mail only comes once a day,' Elma assured her.

'But Darling he may not have been yet – he may be running late.'

Seven days? Her aunt's letters usually only took three or four days to arrive. It was possible it was lost in the post, but she hoped not.

It was Murphy's Law: the more you want something the more likely it will arrive late … or not at all.

She wanted this letter. But when it did arrive on day ten, Elma didn't have time to read it straight away.

'Thanks, thanks,' she yelled at the back of the fluoro-clad postie, his motor bike revving off, his sights set on the next delivery, her gratitude lost in the noise of the engine.

She gripped the lumpy oversized envelope and flung her bag over her shoulder.

Out of breath and nearly out of time. The bus slowed to the

curb just as she made it to the main road.

Throughout the morning the envelope beckoned to be opened.

I can't. I'm in class,

She rummaged in her bag, pushing it to the bottom as if the action would free her mind. She could feel the lecturer's eyes upon her,

'You seem to be having trouble focussing this morning Elma, is everything all right?

'Yes, of course,' she replied too quickly

all eyes on me and a letter burning its way through my bag. Oh Aunt Livie.

She'd hoped her nagging for her aunt to read the letter over the phone may have worked but when Aunt Livie was in her 'and that is that' mood you may as well nag a brick wall.

'You might find it interesting,' was all she said. 'I'm not sure I need to re-read it myself – the past is, after all, the past.'

Elma found the comment a narrow perspective and wanted to tell her aunt how, in her opinion, we are all shaped by our past and we can only learn from it if we revisit it

not all the time – no one wants that but if we don't revisit it, surely we will make the same mistakes over and over again?

The water in her drink bottle swished back and forth, making a voosh voosh sound in her backpack.

I hope the lid's on tight

Elma hurried to the bus mall after leaving her course early so she could head down to the nursing home in Nutgrove. She was tempted to open the envelope on the bus but refrained.

What if I miss the stop or get too... I don't know ... emotional to get off. You are such a sook Elma – you don't even know what's in it.

She rubbed a second dose of Evening Jasmine super-scented

sanitiser into the palm of her hands and worked it vigorously between each finger. She'd been just as nervous the day Fergus had arrived from New Zealand, with his grin bigger than the sides of his face.

--

Elma had watched Fergus walking past the sniffer dog, his day pack slung across his shoulder and the usual broad grin on his face.

'Hi,' he'd said and she said nothing, just stood there like a zombie, until Chloe pushed past her.

'Oh, my goodness, you are like a love sick sloth,' she said to Elma.

Then, to Fergus, 'How are you, Fergus? I'm Chloe, Elma's flatmate. But you may not know that because she doesn't always communicate like normal people.'

Fergus held out his hand, 'Hi,' he said 'Pleased to meet you. Elma's told me so much about you.'

--

The envelope sat on Elma's lap in the familiar shade of the parlour palm. Elma tried slipping her finger under the end of the padded envelope; the gum stretched a little but refused to open; the plastic bubble liner prevented it from ripping easily. She resorted to puncturing it with a pen from her bag. It ended up being a mess of thin plastic stretched into misshapen shards – uneven and ugly as far as Elma was concerned. Ripping. Like a wound.

Plastic bubble wrapping – squeeze or not? 'Stress relief'. Chloe's terminology not Elma's. She hated the stuff. The feeling of squeezing the pressurised bubbles together waiting for the instant of pop caused more anxiety than relief.

There were three items inside the parcel. Some fine chocolate from a Ballan chocolatier – she smoothed her fingers over the packet wondering if she'd ever eaten un-fine chocolate. Livie had wrapped the 200g block with a page from an old calendar. Vincent Van Gough's Starry Night. Immediately Elma was taken back to Aunt Livie's kitchen. That was the month of May.

I remember it being on the wall beside the cabinet.

She turned it over and smoothed the creases out to take a closer look at the date.

Oh, you silly billy – it won't have your doings on it – they'll be on the back of April's picture.

She was right of course. But disappointed.

Never mind.. I'm sure there were days I don't want to remember.

Item number two was a postcard from Ballarat Botanical gardens featuring cineraria flowers in every possible colour of purple and lastly

and most interestingly,

an envelope with a note attached to it.

"Dear Elma, I was going through a box of bits and pieces recently and thought this letter might be of some interest to you. I wrote it to a friend a long time ago describing the things we talked about on the phone. My friend's house had burned down in the fires and she lost her mother and a brother and was shipped off to live with an aunty on the Mainland. Unfortunately the letter was returned to me unopened and I can only presume her family moved without leaving a forwarding address. I was heartbroken at the time and tried other ways to find her but her there were no relatives down our way and that was that."

And "that was that",
I think I could write a heading of epitaphs and put that on

Aunt Livie's gravestone.

Elma turned the envelope over a few times before lifting the unsealed flap. Red, white and blue diagonal stripes bordered the edges and a par avion airmail sticker in blue stood out at the top next to a 5 cent stamp of a small native bird. She stared at the black outline of a stamped fist with its index finger sticking straight out pointing to Livie's Tasmania address. Return to sender, unknown at this address.

Wow, a letter written by Aunt Livie 50 years ago.

It somehow seemed important to hold it carefully in her hands like a thin piece of chocolate that could melt and change shape unexpectedly.

"Dear Barbara,

How are you? I am well. It has been nearly a year since you left and I am very sorry that I have not kept in touch like I promised to.

Thank you for your letter. I am glad you are enjoying country life in Victoria but I do miss you so. Miriam is near impossible to be with and hardly speaks to anyone. I imagine she is lying in her room right now just staring at the ceiling. If ever there was an award for sulking I believe she would win it hands down. Nothing's the same since the fires. I do like the new house though, it's brick and two storeys high with a fabulous river view, but it's not the same as living in South Hobart. I miss all the mountain walks I used to do with Miriam and you of course. I miss the church and even "Mr Groucho" our old bus driver.

Miriam made a vow never to set foot on the mountain again for as long as she lives and I fear she will stick to it. She wrote it up on some parchment paper and made me sign it as a witness. Yelled at me when I said I didn't know if it was the best thing to do. I said I'd tell mum about Scott Hamilton, she said she'd kill me. Don't tell, but I really was scared. She is just not the same.

On a happier note, I'm working 4 days a week now at Garrets and I love it. My sewing has improved and I am saving for an electric machine. I might get good enough to start my own business in mending and dress-making. I still go to youth group on Friday nights – Mum makes me take Miriam but she doesn't enjoy it. Charles has a soft spot for her and often tries to get her to join in with the activities. We all caught the bus out to Moonah last week, to The Windjammer. Do you remember when we were too young to do this sort of thing? I just love it there. Rock and Roll must be the best music of all time and my favourite song would have to be Rock around the Clock. Do you have a favourite band or song?

Marge had a makeup party at her house and I splashed out and bought the best lipstick from the Holiday Magic range. I put my name down to have a party too. Only hope Mum says yes. You get a prize just for being the hostess and cheaper makeup depending on your sales and how many other Holiday Magic parties are booked from yours. I hope to invite everyone from youth group and also the ladies from my work … Oh, I do hope Mum says yes. Dad never cares too much about that sort of thing – says there are far more important things to spend money on. I am sure he thinks I should just save the lot and have no fun at all.

I bus across the Tasman Bridge to get to town and then it's only a five minute walk to work. The best thing about living on the Eastern Shore is the shopping centre. It still has a new feel about it and is as modern as the Mainland, some people say. It only takes 15 minutes to walk there from our new place. We certainly didn't have one like it in South Hobart. Mum is hoping Miriam might try and get a job there. But because of the burns on her legs Miriam says she is too ugly to get a job anywhere. Oh, I wish she'd just get better.

Myself, I am in love. Yes, it is true! Do you remember David? Of course you do! A perfect match don't you think? He is in the third year of his apprenticeship as a joiner and cabinet maker but I think, (now don't tell anyone) when he is finished at the end of this year he will propose to me! Oh I do so hope you will be able to make it over for our wedding. I wanted to ask if you would be a bridesmaid but as I don't have a date yet it may be too early to speak of these things.

Well I know I was tardy in writing to you but I do hope you will write back soon.

Yours Sincerely,

Lavinda

P.S. hugs and kisses to everyone xxxxx

Well – it's interesting in a historical kind of way, yes, but not really much I didn't already know except maybe Gran being scared and bitter.

Elma refolded the letter taking care to crease it in exactly the way it had arrived and placed it carefully back into the bag of protective bubble-wrap with the intent of secreting it away with her growing collection of puzzle pieces – a wooden box hidden beneath her shoes and her old school bag in the bottom of her wardrobe. This is where the letter would be stored along with the licence and photos of Liz and Dad and the "bundle of discrepancies" still wrapped in the kitchen tea towel.

'Here you are, Gran.'

Elma peered into the day room.

'Of course I'm here,' Miriam said. 'Where else would I be? It's not like they let anyone just walk out of this damned prison, do they?'

'Ummm,'

Elma looked about the room, everywhere except at her gran and the physiotherapist who was bending Miriam's fingers back and forth in a bid to keep them flexible and maybe ease the joint pain.

Elma pulled a chair out from a nearby table. A crocheted blanket slipped to the floor, circles and squares looped together to create a bold pattern in orange and black. Elma tried to ignore it.

leave it there – just pretend you didn't see it.

Tentatively she picked it up by the corner and placed it back on the same chair with the intent of using the next one.

'It won't bite you.'

The physio seemed amused.

'Here, have my chair. I'm off now anyway. I hope that helps a bit, Miriam,' she said as she packed away her creams and proceeded to clean her own fingers with a hand wipe.

'Gran do you remember the makeup, Holiday Magic?'

Elma skipped the pleasantries; she was fishing for ways to get into her gran's mind. She doubted she'd get a response from such a random question.

'Aunt Livie said she was going to have a Holiday Magic party, did she have one? Did you go?'

Miriam took a slow breath in and moved her index finger in a gentle motion across her top lip, perhaps, thought Elma, breathing in the scent of the hand lotion. It was maybe more than a minute before she spoke and when she began Elma wondered who she was talking to. Miriam seemed not to see her but rather someone or something in the distance behind her. Elma was sure there was no one there but turned her head *just in case.*

'Oh, Mother thought it might be a good idea – give the sullen girl a bit of fun – get her out of her mood.'

Miriam pulled her gaze away from the far wall and looked down at her freshly oiled fingers.

'Father didn't think so. Said it was a silly idea, pyramid selling, he called it. Said someone else was making the money sitting on their backside while you did all the work.'

She worked her fingers together systematically in much the same way Elma did when she sanitised her own hands.

Wow, is this me in 50 years?

She looked down at her knuckles locked together in her lap.

'It didn't work though, did it?'

The question seemed rhetorical.

'You can't just tell someone to be happy and magically they are.'

'Do you mean the sullen girl, Gran? Can you tell me what happened?'

'They made her do a lot of things she didn't want to do,'

'Who, Gran? Who were they?'

Elma leaned forward, her voice so soft she wondered if Miriam would hear her.

'Her parents for one, the doctors for the other and all the silly "do gooders" in between. Yes, they all thought they knew what was best for her.'

'Why, Gran? What happened to make them want to tell

her what to do?'

'You know what,' Gran said adamantly, looking straight at Elma rather than through her.

Elma stared blankly back at Miriam, wondering what to say. But she needn't have worried.

The older woman began her story and spoke continuously for the next thirty minutes.

--

That evening, for the first time Elma took the long way home, if that was such a thing. She left through the sliding door in the café, turned left and walked as far as she could. She never noticed the colour of the water or the colour of the sky, nor the change from light to dark as the sun took all the colours with it, nor the tears that flowed freely down her cheeks.

Once upon a time, after she'd given up trying to please her grandmother, she'd gone through a phase where she couldn't have cared less what "The Old Crab" thought or said or did. She remembered trying to avoid her as much as possible, only visiting the nursing home under duress

because I wanted something,

because she was desperate for driving lessons. She needed to drive and she needed a car – now she couldn't remember why it had been so important. It seemed like such a long time ago and yet she knew it wasn't. Today Gran had shared secrets that she'd never divulged with anyone.

As far as Elma could tell, not even Aunt Livie knew all of this.

Elma recalled a snippet of what Aunt Livie had said about Miriam being unwell but avoiding their mother and swearing her to secrecy – said she was scared that if her mum and dad knew she'd caught the stomach virus from the hotel they might make her finish working there.

Virus my foot – the first thing I thought of was that she was either hiding a pregnancy or a hangover or maybe both. She was so close to 18, just like me.

That troubled Elma.

What would I have done in the same position? 50 years ago ...

What would she have done? What would she do now if she was pregnant?

Which I'm not.

Lists were forming in her mind

Same Same but Different.

Same age, same mountain, same suburb, same family – but that was about it. No siblings, only one parent,

One parent who was present, anyway.

Gran was seemingly not shy, and then there was a blend of possibilities that seemed to define them both.

Gran loved the mountain.

I think I'm starting to.

Gran worked in hospitality.

I do, one day a week.

They both had Livie in their lives supporting and nurturing – precious Aunt Livie with the irony of her name – meaning 'the older sister' – which of course she wasn't, but she certainly had fulfilled that role for Miriam as long as Elma could remember.

It was after seven when she finally arrived home, having walked along Sandy Bay Road into the city, then up Collins Street before reaching the Rivulet Track.

Chloe was already eating.

'Yours is on the bench, and you're later than usual, what's up?'

'Nothing,' Elma responded vaguely, retrieving the food from

the bench and joining Chloe at the table.

Green leafy vegetables adorned her plate surrounding a creamy white mash. Potatoes again.

Cheap, I guess. If I grow up and have a family I doubt whether I'll make them eat their spuds.

This time they were undercooked and mashed with lumps.

Popular somewhere in the world – but not here in Tasmania.

She tried to squash a hard bit with the back of her fork but it just slipped sideways.

'Gran's arthritis is playing up,' she said flatly, 'and I think she may have more than dementia,' she ventured.

'You don't say,' Chloe returned flippantly, observing Elma separate the potato on her plate into piles of lumped and un-lumped.

'Well, Cathy said when Dad was born Gran should have been diagnosed with postnatal depression but they didn't really understand it back then. She reckons if they had, Charlie might have hung around a bit longer, but he couldn't cope with her bouts of anger and depression and instead he took to alcohol and slept out in the shed to cope with it all. And apparently, the day Dad started school, Charlie kissed Gran goodbye and walked out the driveway leaving her with the house, the car and the bank account – like, everything, and was never seen or heard from again.'

'Cathy's a good story teller, is she?' Chloe asked.

'No, it's just that at the moment our class is studying Post-natal Depression and stuff and –'

Chloe interrupted '– and you think you know more than the doctor?'

'No, but you know Gran and you did this part of the course last year – I was just wondering what you think, because,' she continued quickly hoping Chloe wouldn't interrupt again before she'd had her say, 'I read a letter from Aunt Livie earlier today and I think Gran may have more than postnatal depression.'

Chloe laughed, 'I should imagine after 45 years or so it couldn't be postnatal any longer and –' she added, '– and the bastard up and left her.'

'Chloe! How could you say such a thing?'

'Sorry Elma, it's just my opinion that he didn't do a great thing by walking out like that.'

She looked dolefully at Elma still squirming in her seat.

'Okay, so she probably did have PND – what of it?'

'Well, I think she may have more than that. Like she may have PTSD. And –' she added, thinking about the conversation she'd had with her gran down on the beach where she referred to herself in the third person, '– Dissociative Identity Disorder.'

'Yeah, I still have all my notes on that. I reckon you'll probably have a unit on LTDD coming up soon,' Chloe said before standing to clear the table. 'You finished with this?'

Elma looked down at the piles of mash and un-mash and nodded her head.

'I guess so.'

DID – OCD – PND – PTSD – I know those acronyms from my course. What's LTDD? Do I ask or just wait 'til I learn it at school? I can look online later.

'I'm waiting,' Chloe announced, wiping the table with a wet dishcloth.

'For what?' Elma asked.

'For you to ask me what LTDD stands for.'

Chloe stopped wiping and tapped her fingers on the top of a wooden chair.

'Well, what then? What does it stand for?'

'Let The Doctor Diagnose.'

There was a grin on Chloe's face.

'You're training to be a nurse, not a doctor, so just leave it alone – it's not your problem.'

She may as well have slashed a knife into an over-inflated inner tube.

'I'm going for a walk,' Elma said excusing herself,

That was unfair, Chloe, totally unfair.

For an instant Elma wished Chloe would find somewhere else to live.

But really that's not what I want.

She sighed and went outside, walking a little way up the road – regretting having left her phone on the table.

I could have messaged Fergus.

Gravel and dirt scuffed under her shoes as she headed back towards the rivulet, crossing over one of the parkland bridges. She desperately felt the need to talk about Gran, but who with?

Not Chloe. She just laughed at me.

Not Dad – we haven't talked properly in a long time.

Not Fergus – he doesn't need to know all this stuff about my family and I can't believe he'd be interested either.

Aunt Livie? No, she doesn't seem like the right choice either.

But maybe Cathy? Maybe. But when will I see her again?

The evening bird song ended and the only sounds were the crunch of her shoes on the gravel and the continuous prattle of the river. Willow and wattle – a blend of European and indigenous trees lined the bank. Moss grew on the planks of wood on the second bridge and Elma, forgetting her frustration with Chloe, wondered if she should look for trolls before crossing. She stopped here and watched the flow of the river trickling over rock and concrete as it made its way down the valley before disappearing under the city and escaping into the Derwent River somewhere on the other side of the Regatta Grounds.

Funny, I really don't know where it comes out. It can't be too far from the hospital because I can see it there when I walk past that way.

Elma turned and her eyes traced the path that ran beside the rivulet.

This was Gran's creek.

The Guy Fawkes Rivulet ran not far from Gran's hut and down over the Myrtle Gully Track falls, turikina truwala, before becoming part of twin creeks which in turn joined with other tributaries and fused together to become the Hobart Rivulet.

'Gran's creek', she repeated to herself.

The waters were giving up their secrets. Kunanyi had the power to claim or set lives free – to banish or capture. She herself was becoming more and more enthralled and horrified. She could see now why Gran had vowed never to return.

Chapter 25

'No, Chloe. I don't want a party, 18th or any other.'

The girls sat on rustic chairs outside a South Hobart café, the aroma of coffee wafting through the air, an extravagance they enjoyed on rare occasions. They both loved the smell of coffee but Elma still preferred to drink tea – it was a family thing,

a cup of tea ... Aunt Livie ... and me ...

'But I'm not asking you, I'm telling you this is what is happening. And –' Chloe continued quickly, speaking over the top of the protesting Elma, '– it's not really a party, it's just going out for dinner – your choice of restaurant.'

'Then I choose nowhere.'

'Not an option – it's already planned. Your birthday is on a Friday. I've spoken to your dad and Fergus, and that is that.'

She lifted up the serviette, deliberately placing a pocket calendar, page open, in front of Elma.

'Fergus never said anything,' Elma protested,

he knows I don't like going out with lots of people,

'Elma, it's done, he's arranged the car and all.'

It's not done, I haven't said yes.

She brought her tea cup to her lips while she considered the best approach. Aunt Livie's reflection appeared on the surface of the hot liquid. If it was a trick of her imagination it was a convincing one, she turned her head to check.

looking over my shoulder a lot lately – paranoid?

Probably not – more likely a blend of light from the window and the movement of the passing bus.

'I can't do it, it's just too dangerous. What if Dad punches Fergus or I spit at Paula.' She shook her head.

Chloe was laughing.

'I've invited your Aunt Livie.'

'You have not!'

'Well, yes I have and, wait for it …'

She raised her eyebrows and put on a posh voice, 'Her daughter is happy to bring her.'

Elma glared at Chloe, strong emotions surging up through her body. She breathed in, hoping the moment would pass quickly. Scared of what Chloe would look like with a hot cup of tea splashed across her face, or how the newspapers would react to the body swung under a moving vehicle.

Teenager Resists Adulthood – Throws Childhood Friend Under Bus

It didn't look good; every ending had too many options – too many unknowns, so much chance of failure. But there was still the growing need to talk in person to someone about what happened to Gran that day on the mountain.

The day her whole life changed.

The statement was not entirely true as there were many events with many choices for Miriam to have made leading up to the events of that day, but still it seemed to Elma **that** was the day her gran had exchanged her "ten thousand joys for ten thousand sorrows".

Aunt Livie herself had often said how happy and fun and full of life her sister had been "back in the day".

A positive attitude can overcome the biggest of problems. Maybe …

but maybe we aren't all able to think far enough ahead to even consider the outcomes of today's choices.

'I bet you want to see Aunt Livie. Imagine how rejected she'll feel if you have to ring up and say don't come?'

'What have you done? I can't do that! How could you, Chloe?'

I do want to see them but … but not like this.

The proverbial "Rock and a Hard Place" or "Catch 22".

How could she get out of it and not disappoint Aunt Livie? How could she see Aunt Livie and Cathy and not have a party?

I can't say yes – I can't say no.

'I'll think about it Chloe, but don't ever –' Elma put great emphasis on the ever, '– make plans for me again without talking to me first. And sit down! Everyone is staring at us.'

But it was too late – Chloe was swinging around the lamp post whistling the tune from the musical Singing in the Rain. Elma stood and went inside to pay, letting the wooden screen door bang shut behind her.

--

It was decided, unanimously, that Miriam wouldn't be coming to the restaurant – for the benefit of herself, of course. They were all concerned about "overstimulating" or "overwhelming" the frail old lady. What if she didn't cope with seeing all of them at once? Or made a scene to spoil Elma's special day? And besides, she refused most outings anyway – clearly she preferred her own company. Earlier she'd told Elma how much she was looking forward to seeing Livinda , "after all it's been well over a decade since we last met – I'll be surprised if we even recognise each other" she'd said. And Elma had smiled, quite proud of herself for not correcting her knowing it had really only been six months since her Aunt Livie had moved to the Mainland.

'We've got cheap tickets and it's all arranged.'

Aunt Livie had spoken excitedly over the phone to Elma, 'Martin will pick Cathy and me up from the airport and your lovely friend Chloe said she'd move back to her mum's for the weekend and I'll have her room.'

More likely she'll move into my room …

Elma already knew the arrangements and she was still angry at Chloe, still upset at the lack of choice she'd been given and still fearful of meeting Paula or, even worse, Martin confronting Fergus.

'Just take a chill pill Elma, I'm sure your dad's not a monster out to get every foreigner he meets.'

It was easy for Fergus to say such things.

'I don't know. You haven't met him, what if –'

Fergus cut her off,

'– what if the sun moves too close to the Earth and we all burn up two minutes before eleven am the day before the dinner and we haven't even ironed our undies?'

'Do I really sound that ridiculous?' Elma asked, feeling brave for voicing her question and wanting at the same time, to evaporate into thin air.

'Yeah, nah, yeah,'

Fergus' smile stretched across his face and Elma's fears lessened.

If he did have concerns about meeting Elma's family he hadn't shared them with Elma.

Right now they were on a bus headed for Nutgrove Nursing Home and a quick visit to meet the "Infamous Gran," and maybe, afterwards, some "Elma and Fergus" time at the beach.

It sounded good. The jam tart they'd bought looked good, and, thought Elma, he's right, there really is no point worrying about a million things that will probably never happen.

'Your gran,' the receptionist said, when they arrived, 'is in the café playing cards. There's a tournament on today and I wouldn't be surprised if the whole home is in there.'

Not very private – still it'll make her easy to find.

It didn't though – the room was crowded, full of residents and staff having their annual "Fun for All" competition. Two bulky electric wheelchairs and a reclining day bed filled the area between the fountain and the café, making it hard to approach the entrance.

'Hello, Miss Elma.'

Dr Gordon stood and greeted them as they entered the crowded room.

'It's very hard to get everyone into the same spot, but I think they've managed it nicely this year.'

Fergus stared at the fountain.

'That one is a hybridized miniature Dicksonia, I believe,' the doctor said as he touched the frond of one of the man ferns.

'Ponga tree where I come from,' said Fergus, putting his hand out to greet the doctor.

He does that so easily – not afraid at all – gets on with everyone –

'There she is.'

She grabbed Fergus' hand and pulled him, zigzagging between noisy card games and happy people, over to the far side where Gran was shuffling cards for a new game of Patience.

Oh my goodness what am I doing?

She quickly released her grip on Fergus and stuffed her hand into her pocket.

Sensory alert!

Germ attack.

And a secret feel-good sensation.

What have I done?

She stared down at her feet, desperate for her sanitiser but in no position to get it from her bag. She stood in front of Gran's table biting her bottom lip, unable to think of anything sensible to say. Fergus pulled up beside her.

'Wow, this place is packed.'

Miriam stared up from her game of cards,

'What is this all about, Elma? Bursting in here and then not even having the decency to speak?'

'I didn't burst in.'

Elma defended herself before realising it wouldn't matter what she'd said.

Gran was in a "There'll be no pleasing me today,' mood.

'Hello Gran.'

Fergus ventured confidently thrusting his hand out towards the smartly dressed lady with a bun on top of her head. She didn't look old enough to be there, Fergus said later to Elma.

'Who the hell are you?' Miriam's eyes darted from Elma to Fergus, an ace of spades clenched between her fingers.

He'd worn his best shirt, clean runners and smoothed his hair back into a tight ponytail. Elma stole a quick glance.

He's even trimmed his beard.

'This is the friend I told you about – the one from New Zealand.'

Fergus re-offered his hand, a little wary that Miriam might snap again.

'Oh, I don't think you did tell me or I'd have been expecting you.'

She placed her card on the table and looked him up and down while Elma cringed.

Gran politely took the outstretched hand then suddenly pulled her hand back, screaming hysterically, her elbow ramming into the chair next to her.

'What the heck is going on, Gran?' Elma yelled over the commotion, staring from Fergus to Miriam and back again.

'Get him away from me,' she yelled.

'Don't let him touch me! Help, help!' she screamed, 'He's dead.'

She stood, flinging her chair back.

A loud smack reverberated through the room as the metal chair hit the glass window.

Elma was beside herself, 'Gran! Gran!' she yelled.

'Come on Elma, let's go!'

Fergus grabbed her shoulder in a bid to turn her around as Miriam put both her hands under the table and flicked it up with all her might, all the time screaming for someone to get rid of Fergus.

Elma couldn't move.

'Now! Come now!'

She could hear Fergus but didn't know what to do. It was like the near train crash all over again. She closed her eyes.

Confusion spread as quickly as butter on a frying pan. One minute the residents were contentedly winning and losing and now cards flew through the air. Tables moved and scuffed in every direction. Walking frames, chairs and crockery toppled. Everyone looked for shelter from the torrential barrage gushing from Miriam's mouth.

Staff hopelessly negotiated the crowded entrance as panicked residents tried to leave the room.

Miriam's voice was lost in the commotion. A lay-back electric chair blocked the way of people trying to get out. The day-bed trapped staff between the fountain and the doorway.

Elma opened her eyes and gasped for breath

'Calm down. You're safe now.'

It was Fergus' voice.

She sat up.

'Where am I?

A staff member handed her a drink of water.

'We're here at Nutgrove. You fainted, Darling, that's all.'

'I fainted?'

Elma looked around in disbelief.

She could see a stream of paisley uniforms passing to and fro beyond the open door of the treatment room.

The clipped voices of authority commanded staff this way and that.

'Those ones up the back –no, no – that's it. Wipe the tables. Yes, that's good.

Dr G? Yes – Nurse Cooper took him earlier. No – no - over there with the other frames. He's in his room – asleep. Yes, start the tea round earlier if possible.

The chaos was passing – order was being restored.

The nurse wore paisley.

Fergus has brown eyes

This is water

I'm safe.

'Where's Gran? Is she okay? What happened?'

'She's okay, Darling,' the nurse responded, 'She's resting in her room. Perhaps a bit of psychosis. She really packed a tanty.

Tore the place apart.'

'She did not,' Fergus said, not wanting to upset Elma more than necessary.

'Well, if I ever feel the need to start a revolution, your gran will be the one to get the ball rolling.' The nurse took the empty glass and placed it on the sink.

'There's going to be a bit of kickback from this one.'

Both Elma and Fergus looked confused.

'Think about it. What are the residents going to tell their families? Apart from the sheer mayhem, Mr Debone is off in the ambulance with a suspected broken hip and sweet little Sophie May is lucky to get away with just four stiches to the side of her face. We are bloody lucky, excuse my French, that no one had a heart attack.'

The colour drained from Elma's face. The nurse handed her a cardboard bowl to vomit in.

Fergus sat quietly in the treatment room wondering if meeting Elma's dad was such a good idea after all.

Nigel was off somewhere up north and wouldn't be able to pick them up anytime soon and Elma was too embarrassed to ring her father.

I'm sure he's already on his way.

'Why don't we just go hang at the beach, you know, stick to the original plan?' Fergus suggested. 'We can catch a bus back to the city later if we choose.'

'Wow, you're still prepared to hang out with me after that display of family affection?'

'I think a walk along the beach would be good. If you're up to it?' he added.

Fresh air sounded wonderful.

Elma looked at the nurse.

'Am I allowed to leave?'

'Well, no one's called the police, so I can't stop you. This is a nursing home and I don't think you're a resident on my list.'

She gave a laugh and held the door open.

'Just take it a bit easy and drink some more water if you can.'

'What about Gran?'

Elma's concern was real. She knew what Miriam had been through but couldn't work out why Fergus had triggered such a strong reaction in her.

Was SH a Maori too?

I don't think so – something's just not adding up and I can't figure it out.

'Your dad's been contacted and your gran's snoring off the medication the doctor gave her. It's best to bypass her, I think. I'm sure she'll be alright.'

'Come on.'

Fergus was up and standing at the door ready to exit as soon as Elma gave the nod. They walked out through the café. Chairs and tables were back in place, gingham table clothes adjusted correctly with posies of flowers on each. Not a card in sight – everything appeared normal.

Crazy – I must have been out of it for longer than I thought.

She gazed around the room for a minute before pressing the numbers on the keypad.

He must think I'm such an idiot for fainting like that. Maybe I should just catch a bus home. Poor Gran – what if they have to keep her in her room forever or worse kick her out? Is that such a thing?

'I'm so sorry,' she said as they walked down the ramp to the beach. 'I had no idea that was going to happen.'

'It's okay, I won't take it personally.'

They wandered along the shoreline towards Long Beach, before stopping on a grassy knoll in the play park while Elma emptied the sand from her shoes. Anxious? Relaxed? Fearful? Elma wasn't sure what she felt.

Exhausted and hungry – definitely hungry

The happy noises of small children whizzing down slides and digging for treasure in the sand surrounding the play equipment distracted her for a while.

'I think –' she said,

... maybe it was Fergus's missing finger ...

'– I'm hungry.'

'So am I,' said Fergus, and they both laughed, knowing the best pizza on the beach was only just out of sight around the corner – maybe only 200 metres further along the esplanade. Fergus looked at his phone, 'I reckon they'll be opening just about now?'

Chapter 26

'I think I know what triggered it.'

Elma pulled at a piece of crust, the golden mozzarella unwilling to be parted from the other slices of pizza.

'Are you teasing me, Elma?'

'No, sorry.'

Fergus had a look on his face that Elma couldn't read.

'It was this,' he said holding up his hand, his half-missing pointer finger as obvious as an All Black player in an Aussie cricket game.

'I have an effect on some people that is totally out of my control, ay.'

Elma put her pizza down and wiped her hands on the black serviette.

'Sorry,' she said again.

'Would you stop apologising? What good is that going to do? It's not your fault, is it?'

Somehow she felt it was. Somehow, at this present moment, all the wrongs in the world were her fault, even though she knew it wasn't possible.

Sorry.

She wanted to say it again, but contained herself and said nothing. A small yacht cruised past down river, its sail catching the wind and the sun striking lux white against the darkening blue of the timtumili minanya.

'Do you want to know how I lost it?' he said with a huge outbreath, maybe the prelude to a well-rehearsed story.

Elma came quickly back to the real moment.

Yes – yes I do – I've wanted to know that since the first day we met – or maybe it was the second day – I didn't even want to see you again after the first day,

'I guess so,' she said in a noncommittal voice.

'Well, I have this cousin back home, we're good mates, ay, and we were staying at our Uncle Jack's place as we did back then and, unlike here in Tassie, New Zealanders don't care about protecting possums. They're a pest and have been overrunning the country since the day they arrived there from Tasmania – back in the day.'

Already Elma had her doubts about the authenticity of the story but held her opinion to herself – this was Fergus' story after all.

And how would I know where their possums came from.

'I was ten – I know this because I spent my eleventh birthday in hospital. Anyway, Pasta dared me,'

'Pasta?' Elma cut in.

'Not his real name, his nickname but that's another story,'

Elma stared at a smudge on the window and locked her hands together holding her serviette captive beneath her little fingers. People talked and laughed, strolling along the esplanade between the water and the pizza shop. Their voices muted by the glass.

Gran lost it big time and I'm sitting here eating pizza with ...
Mr Ninefinger ...

She added quietly to herself, mesmerised by the sound of his voice, almost ready to forgive him for having facial hair.

'Are you listening?'

Fergus stopped talking and looked to where Elma's gaze appeared on the window.

'Of course I am.'

'I was just thinking of Gran and wondering what they're doing to keep her calm.'

'We can ring or nip back in if you like.'

'No, no. Please tell me the story.'

'Well, Uncle Jack was pretty old and didn't care too much what us boys got up to and we were happy about that, although looking back I'm surprised we were even allowed to stay up at the old place.'

He chuckled as he described the run-down homestead with its tall ceilings; every room full of junk or 'treasure', cast-offs from decades of living. Three microwave ovens were stacked precariously upon a wobbly table which sloped towards the wall where the floorboards had breathed in enough damp air to make them soggy.

'It always seemed to rain when we stayed up there, or maybe we just noticed it more because the roof leaked.'

'I guess we nagged a fair bit and wore the aunties down, you know, Pasta's mum and my mum are sisters and Jack is their brother ... but he never married or had kids. They used to tell us all the fun stuff they got up to as kids at that place, hiding in the roof and dropping coins through the ceiling boards and fishing for eels and that. I guess they didn't want us missing out on country life altogether, ay. Anyway he didn't have too many mod-cons but what he did have were possum traps in his shed, old style ones that you can't use anymore 'cause they are too cruel and outdated. Illegal now – their springs were too strong and their teeth too sharp. Maimed a lot of animals not just possums.'

A wistful look came over his face, kind of sad, Elma thought – *and sincere.*

She nodded again, pretty sure now where this story was going.

'We picked one out. They were all pretty rusty and the one we chose wouldn't even open – we used a hell of a lot of CRC to get it working again. It had these great big teeth on it that interlocked when they snapped together.'

He pressed his fingernails into the webbing of his opposite hands and pulled them back flat to show the function of the possum trap. Elma cringed and moved her own fingers off the table resting them out of harm's way on her lap.

'Pasta got a bundle of sticks and we took turns in pushing the trigger in the centre. Thought it was hilarious, jumped sky high every time the bloody thing snapped shut, never quite knowing where the pieces of stick would land,' he laughed.

'Nearly poked me eye out a couple of times. Sometimes they broke and sometimes they just got jammed. We must have gone through Uncle Jack's entire pile of kindling before he found us in the shed.'

Fergus turned his head momentarily as the pizza shop door swung open.

Elma looked up, almost expecting Fergus' Uncle Jack to walk through the door.

'Don't know how long he'd been standing in there before he spoke but I nearly crapped myself when he did. Lost all concentration on what I was doing and the stick slipped into the trap along with my finger.'

Elma didn't say anything, she could feel the usual tightening in her stomach, and taste the usual salty sensation in her mouth.

I'm never going to make a nurse – I can't even listen to a story about an accident that happened almost forever ago.

Fergus wriggled the stump around observing what fate had left of his finger.

'Never been much of a problem for me as long as my nose doesn't need picking.'

He laughed.

Elma winced.

'What did your parents say?'

Lame question, Elma.

'It was hard to know who got in more trouble. We'd been told to stay out of that shed so many times we never took any notice in the end; it was just like a mandatory safety announcement on an aeroplane.

"If you boys are going up to Jack's place make sure you keep out of his sheds – God know what poisons he's keeping in there."

Elma laughed at the imitation of Fergus' mum or aunt.

'Well, funny thing, Mum hasn't talked to her brother since then. Said they'd told him time and time again to get rid of those traps. They weren't illegal at the time but we all knew how fierce they were.

'Me and Pasta didn't see each other again for a long time either.'

He laughed again,

'I think everyone got a bit of the blame except me. Well, I did get blame, just no punishment. I guess they felt sorry for me 'cause of the pain I went through.'

She raised her eyebrows to signify she was still engaged in the story.

'I guess you didn't know any better.'

'But I did know better, Elma. It was my own fault, what happened, and I don't blame anyone but myself. It was my choice,' he continued.

'I knew what we were doing was wrong and I continued to do it.'

That was a huge thing, Elma thought – to accept responsibility for one's owns actions rather than blame someone else for your situation.

She considered it for some time.

Maybe a little too long.

Fergus asked concerned, 'Are you okay?'

'I'm fine, and I'm sorry about your finger.'

Fergus laughed and rolled his eyes, 'We'll have to work harder on that apologetic nature of yours. Come on, let's go check on Gran and I'll see what Nige is up to.'

He stood and turned to pay the bill.

'I'll wait outside her room though – if you don't mind.'

Chapter 27

'I saw Gran today,' she said to Chloe while they prepared their makeup and clothes for the evening out.

'And?' Chloe responded, stretching her lips at the mirror as she applied a second layer of mink purple lipstick, meticulously sticking inside the darker outline of midnight purple.

'She's not the same.'

'Oh?'

'She hasn't yelled at me for weeks now, not even snapped at me if I've turned up late or early or whatever.'

Elma let out a sigh,

Are you really listening Chloe? Or am I talking to myself – again?

'It's the medication I think,' she ventured to say, despite her self-promise not to talk "shop" about Gran.

'Well, I'm not surprised,' Chloe responded, her eyes still focussed on the mirror. Her makeup and gear were spread about Elma's desk and room like a tossed salad. The spare mattress was on the floor – like it had been so often when they were younger.

'Sorry – why would you say that?'

Chloe put down the lipstick and turned towards Elma, a look of disbelief on her face.

'Think about it Elma. The nursing home just can't let your gran loose now can they?'

Elma didn't respond. 'If she had another psychotic episode, you know, like what happened when she was playing cards, they'd have to kick her out. Where would she be then? Think about it, they can't take the risk.'

'But she didn't mean to do that, she was ...'

'Doesn't matter,' Chloe cut in. 'It doesn't matter what her intentions were – she's a danger.'

'She was frightened, scared, she didn't understand,' Elma defended Miriam, tears welling in her eyes. 'She didn't do anything wrong, she was upset.'

'Upset all right, you're lucky it didn't make the papers. There were some fairly "upset" rellies from what I heard.'

You weren't there – you don't really know. Gran had her reasons.

'Sorry, Elma,' Chloe stood and hugged her friend.

'Please don't take it personally. It's your gran with the problem, not you.'

She continued in a bright voice, 'Hey, girlfriend, it's your birthday, you can cry if you want to ... But I'd rather you didn't!'

Elma gave a weak smile and continued to organise the mess mounting in her room,

and head.

'Do I look all right?'

Elma stepped back from the full-length mirror so Chloe would get a better view.

'Conservative, predictable but none the less absolutely gorgeous,' Chloe said, pulling her own dress on over her head.

'How do I look?'

'I think we are the opposites-attract kind,' said Elma, collecting her hair back into a ponytail that now *thankfully* included the growing-out undercut that Chloe, in a moment of Summer Silliness, had convinced her to get.

The kitchen door was open to the garage area. Aunt Livie and Cathy were already waiting at the table when they heard the ute arrive.

'Oh Darling, you look lovely,' Livie and Cathy said almost simultaneously as Elma entered the room.

I don't feel it – I'd like to crawl back into bed.

'I think your dad's here,' Aunt Livie said stating the obvious. *And Paula.*

Martin's plan was to leave his ute in the driveway and take Livie and Cathy in Paula's sedan up to the Ferntree Tavern for the evening celebrations.

Elma, Fergus and Chloe would follow in Nigel's car and, since Chloe was "in between" relationships, she was insisting Nigel came too.

Elma fiddled with a button on the bodice of her dress, attempting to seem busy as her dad and Paula stepped in through the doorway. Cathy and Aunt Livie stood for the greeting – hugging Martin as if they hadn't already seen him earlier and politely shaking hands with Paula.

'Pleased to meet you at long last – we've heard so much about you.'

'Only good stuff I hope,' replied Paula.

I know that voice. I'm sure I do!

Elma looked up in surprise.

'PJ?' she said, puzzled why she would be standing here *in my house and not at her usual seat at the café.*

'Hi Elma,' Paula continued, aware that all eyes were on them.

'Happy birthday!'

'Thank you.'

Elma replied not sure how to respond but relieved to see a familiar face.

She liked PJ. It was only the name Paula that attracted her animosity.

Paula, who took away all her "Father Daughter" time – Paula who gave Martin advice that didn't always make her life easy – Paula who she'd been determined to dislike. Paula who was really Paula Jean Allen, someone she liked. Betrayed didn't seem like the right word – PJ was her friend.

Everyone appeared confused except the confident PJ.

'I hope this is all right, Elma. I know I met you way before I met your dad, but I never quite found the space to tell you. I tried.'

That's true,

I just thought she wanted to tell me to take up studying – like the rest of them.

Paula looked at Martin and smiled.

Elma could see genuine affection between them.

Turning to the rest of the family, PJ explained, 'I've been a customer at the café where Elma works for the past year.'

Then, turning back to Elma, she said, 'I hope we can still be friends.'

'Hi, Um, Yes – I like you,' Elma blurted out.

'Why didn't you tell me you knew Elma …' Martin began, but his question was lost in the eruption of laughter.

And relief.

Martin stepped forward and hugged Elma.

'Thanks for that. Paula means a lot to me,' he said into her ear.

Wow – who would have thought of this scenario?

Still, Dad hasn't met Fergus yet. I hope they leave before he gets here.

Public spaces and good company – that was Elma's plan.

Keep everyone accountable for controlling their emotions.

And she knew Chloe would sit them at opposite ends of the table.

What a day this has been already

Chloe making me breakfast, racing off to the café for work, Damien insisting I eat my lunch with Cathy and Aunt Livie when they dropped in. A quick visit with Gran and back home in time to get ready.

Thankfully meeting Paula was a non-event

now it's 6:30pm

and I'm ready to call it a day.

She sat with Chloe on the front fence waiting for Fergus and Nigel to turn up.

Why didn't PJ tell Dad she knew me?

--

Martin had driven Aunt Livie and Cathy straight to the nursing home from the airport and then dropped them at home in South Hobart before racing off to the renovation job he was working on in Sandy Bay.

Elma and Chloe had cleared and cleaned the "guest room", used the best linen and set a vase of bought flowers on the bedside table.

'It looks so cheerful,' Chloe had commented but, despite this, the mood of the house was sombre.

Aunt Livie clearly felt the pain of her sister's deterioration more than all of them.

'I just didn't expect there'd be such a change in her in only six months.'

'Mum, you did your best,' Cathy said encouragingly.

'No, I should've stayed. I've let her down. We should never have let her go into that dreadful nursing home.'

'Mum!' Cathy raised her voice and then calmed it a little.

'Mum, you did your best. You couldn't have done any more than you have. Aunt Miriam is unwell and it's not your fault. Or the nursing home's.'

Elma felt for Aunt Livie.

--

Some birthday this is.

Fergus and Nigel are running late.

'I've seen photos of the tavern before it burnt down,' Elma said to Chloe as they sat waiting.

'Sorry, what do you mean? The tavern was still there this morning!'

'No, I mean the one before the fires.'

'Oh yeah, the "Fires of '67",' Chloe added in her "Why are you always so fixated about those fires?" voice.

'I see you and Paula are good friends already,' she added, changing the subject.

'Oh look, here they are.'

It was squashy in Nigel's car. Elma's body was pressed against Fergus's thigh.

She tried to make small talk while easing slightly away.

'Gran's sedated.'

Fergus turned sideways to acknowledge her statement, pressing them closer again.

'Is that a good thing?'

His teeth showed white against his beard and moustache.

'Hell, yeah!' Chloe said from the front seat.

'No, no, it's not. It means she's medicated, subdued – living in a dream world for all I know.'

'Oh Elma,' Chloe turned in her seat stretching the seat belt with her as she did so. 'They don't have a choice. I told you that.'

Elma wished Chloe would shut up. It was her fault Aunt Livie was even here, distressed about her sister. If Chloe hadn't organised this stupid dinner party ...

Fergus ventured another 'Oh' and sat with his back pressed against the passenger-side door. It didn't sound like any conversation was going to be safe tonight and he still had to meet Elma's dad and other rellies.

The Tavern carpark was too small for the number of vehicles in it.

'Oops,' Nigel said as he opened the driver's side door onto a grey sedan, creating a minor dent as he squeezed himself out of the car.

Fergus looked at the distance between the cars and slid over to Elma's side to get out.

'Thanks for the lift,' he called in Nigel's direction.

'Yes, thanks,' both girls said in unison.

--

'That's so beautiful,' Elma said to Aunt Livie as she sat herself down near the end of the table. 'Yes,' Aunt Livie agreed, looking out the low window directly into a grove of rhododendron bushes.

'The scarlet coloured ones were always Miriam's favourite.'

Gobsmacked, Elma finally put the remaining puzzle pieces into place.

That's it! The red rhododendrons she planted at the hut! That's why she called her Scarlet. I get it now.

Elma desperately wanted to share her discovery
but who with?
She looked around the table – who could she trust?
Cathy had been her first thought –
she might be safe.
Fergus? No, why would he want to hear all Gran's troubles after what she did to him?
Aunt Livie, Martin and Chloe were out of the question and it was no concern for PJ or Nigel.
But would there be time? Cathy leaves Sunday.
And I know there are other people she wants to catch up with. Maybe tonight?
She looked about the table, her father at the far end and Fergus who had sat himself at her end.
No, it's too complicated.
'So, you work with bats?'
It was Paula who asked the question from the other end of the table and everyone turned to look at Fergus. Martin had shaken his hand when they'd first walked in and then they'd parted to sit at opposite ends of the party.
He was kind because it's my birthday and because I was cool with Paula.
'Work with – or study – I guess it's all the same.' Fergus spoke with his usual relaxed accent.
'Didn't know they had bats in Tassie,' said Cathy 'I didn't think bats liked cold weather.'
'Some do, some don't.' said Fergus in a non-committal tone.
Guess he's trying to avoid being centre of attention.
'Is there enough fruit for them to eat down here?' asked Cathy, sounding intrigued.

'They're not fruit bats here. No, Tassie bats are very small and eat insects, you know mozzies and such.'

'Oh.'

'But if you want to hear a funny story—'

Elma though Fergus was about to repeat the one he'd told her, but it seemed there was more than one funny story about bats in Tasmania.

'— a few years ago there was a pretty severe drought up Queensland way and as the fruit bats ran low on food they foraged further and further south for the season 'til a bunch of them ended up in Victoria where they were hit by a fierce storm that blew them right across Bass Strait.'

Fergus had never openly lied to Elma that she could tell, but she was often unsure whether all his "funny stories" were entirely true.

Still, they're all listening. Perhaps Chloe's right – I have a problem with trust.

'And what then?' Cathy asked.

'One of them turned up on a lemon tree in Sandy Bay.'

'Really?'

'Yeah, I never saw it but both Nige and I have seen the newspaper article.'

All eyes turned to Nigel who was stuffing his face with a piece of roast pumpkin.

'Yep,' he said as a bit of onion fell from his lip.

'As true as I'm sitting here,' he confirmed without any sign of authority.

Elma shook her head. How could she challenge it? Yet it didn't sound right. Fruit bats in Tasmania? Tasmanian possums in New Zealand? What would she find if she ever got round to checking it out?

Beer and wine was poured – birthday toasts were made.

I hope it's all over soon.

'And the pressie? Give her the pressie.'

Chloe snatched an envelope from Cathy and presented it to Elma.

'A gift from the whole family,' she said spreading her arms wide to include the entire table and nearly toppling an empty wine bottle with the back of her hand.

Elma kept her groan to herself. She didn't want the attention – especially from a pub full of people staring at a tipsy teenager.

She placed it beside her empty cake plate. Her glass the only one still full of wine which she refused to drink.

I might be 18 but I'm not turning to alcohol because of it.

She'd tried to refuse it but no one seemed to listen and they filled her glass anyway.

'No, Elma. Open it now –' Chloe insisted, '– so you can thank us while we're all here.'

She looked at Fergus. He hunched his shoulders and pushed out his lips. Clearly he had no idea.

'Come on –' Chloe continued, '– we're waiting.'

Was the whole room watching her or just the table of eight?

It feels like the whole world. What if I don't like it?

She prepared her face for a smile – genuine or forced. She'd smile, say thank you and hope that would stop any more attention.

Later I'll kill Chloe for this and the cake and the singing!
It's only good manners keeping me from walking out
and the fact that I have nowhere to go and no way to get there.

The present was a voucher for driving lessons – a set of five.

'Thank you,' she said with as much energy as she could muster and leaned over to hug Aunt Livie.

'Now you'll be right, Love. That will get you back on the road. We all know how important it is for you to get your licence.'

Memories of trains, noise and pain came crashing in.

Elma burst into tears and turned to Aunt Livie, hugging her close, not sure if the night could get any worse.

'Thanks,' she repeated, the words sounding as hollow as she felt.

'I hope I get a happier reaction when you open my pressie,' said Fergus.

They all laughed, except Elma.

I doubt whether anyone could give me a present worse than that.

She wiped her face, mascara smearing her arm, the same arm she'd broken the last time she'd driven.

I'm falling apart.

Fergus handed her a small box the size you might put a ring in. Elma stared at it and hoped beyond hope there wasn't a ring in it.

'Well,' said Fergus, 'Come on then.'

'He's waiting for that big juicy hug,' said Chloe, then turned bright red when she received glares from Martin, Aunt Livie and Elma.

Cathy laughed and looked across to Nigel who was choking on his beer.

'Now? You want me to open it now?' Elma said.

She stood abruptly and said, 'I'll be back in a second,' as she headed for the ladies' toilets.

The toilet lid opened just in time to collect the evening meal.

'Are you okay?' Chloe burst through the door several minutes later.

'I'm fine,' Elma replied, dabbing at her make up with a tissue.

--

'It's green stone,' Fergus said when she finally returned and opened his present.

She stared at the dark green spiral.

'Koru,' Fergus said, 'and I made the cord myself out of New Zealand bat fur.'

'Really?'

The whole table burst into laughter.

'Nup, me auntie did though, out of flax.'

'Really?'

'Yeah, she's a traditional carver. She made it 'specially for me to give to you.'

Wow

'It's beautiful,' she said, touching the glassy surface of the stone. It felt comfortable in her hand.

Oohs and aahs filled the table as the necklace was passed around and Nigel gave Fergus a hug saying, 'Because it looks like Elma's not going to give you one.'

'Thanks, mate,' said Fergus returning the affection, 'I'm cool with waiting.'

'It's after ten. I think it's best I get Mum home,' Cathy suggested.

'I'm all right,' Livie snapped, suppressing a yawn. 'It's not every day I get to see Elma turn 18.'

Paula, who sat beside Cathy, looked at her watch.

'Oh yes, it's well after ten. I'll need to be running along myself.'

She looked at Martin who was in the process of swigging down another premium lager.

'Yes, yes, of course,' he affirmed, glad he wasn't going to be driving.

'And it's so nice to meet you properly, Elma,' Paula said, smiling. Everyone laughed.

Chapter 28

'I don't think it'll take her long to fall asleep.' Cathy said to Martin later, a smile on her face. 'She drank more wine than Elma and I put together.'

She was pleased that Martin had accepted her offer of coffee.

'I don't think Elma had any,' Martin replied.

Paula had dropped him off in South Hobart to pick up the ute and the young people had headed directly to the city to check out the night clubs.

'I'm going to tell her,' he said, his words a little slurred.

'Don't you dare, Martin. That's the most stupid idea I've ever heard from you,' Cathy retorted, tightening her grip on the hot coffee mug.

Martin huffed, 'That's rich. You were the one who always said she should know the truth.'

'Yeah, but not that – and you know it.'

Neither of them knew Elma hadn't gone all the way to town with her friends but had insisted on being dropped off at the corner.

I just need to be alone.

The screen door was shut when she arrived but the door itself was open.

Tell me what?

She slipped her bottom down to the doorstep and sat wondering what the conversation was about.

'She a big girl now, she can take the truth.'

'Martin don't be a fool, what would anyone gain from you saying anything now? And on her birthday!'

Elma sat, stock still, in the dark, listening,

'What's this all about?'

'I'm not her real father – you know it and it's probably about time she knew too!'

'Martin you're drunk,' Cathy pushed her coffee mug to the middle of the table.

Elma stood up impulsively, pulling open the door.

It was hard to know whose face looked most surprised.

'I don't get it, how can you not be my dad?' she said staring at Martin in disbelief.

Martin opened his mouth to say something but Elma turned and ran out through the carport, her stupid "dress-up" shoes slipping on the polished concrete.

'Elma wait, wait for me,' Cathy called, out of breath, catching up to her near the road.

'What did he mean? What did Dad mean?' Elma demanded.

'It was your mum, Elma. It was Liz. She, she didn't always come home at night. Martin did his best to look after you, provide for you, but it wasn't easy.'

'He's not my dad? That's not true!'

'Come on, come back inside and talk about it, Love.'

'Get away from me. You knew! You knew all this time and never said anything!'

Cathy placed her arm around Elma's shoulder.

'No that's it!' Elma said, pulling away. 'I'm done with the lot of you.'

She wiggled out of Cathy's hold and headed back to the house, storming through the kitchen, ignoring her father and Cathy calling in the background. The bedroom door shuddered and banged shut behind her – probably loud enough to wake Aunt Livie.

What do I need?

She swiped along the desktop pushing Chloe's makeup to the floor.

'I don't need your mess,' she said and stuffed her wallet, sanitiser and a few essentials into her backpack.

She pulled at her dress – buttons flew off at random angles.

stupid dress – stupid shoes!

'Where are you?' she said, pushing Chloe's clothing off the bed in a bid to find a pair of jeans.

By the time Cathy knocked and ventured into the room Elma had donned her jacket and was lacing her boots.

'Calm down, Elma, your dad and I want to talk to you.'

Elma glared at Cathy, flung her bag across her back and brushed past her through the doorway. Martin was still sitting at the table.

She glanced up the hallway where Aunt Livie slept. Light shone through the gap at the bottom of the door.

I don't care if I woke you – you knew too.

'You all knew,' she said before walking out into the dark November night.

'And I'm never coming back!' she shouted over her shoulder as she strode up the road.

Elma walked up the Rivulet Track. She'd done this before but usually with intent. Tonight there was no intent, there was only numbness. Up and up she climbed, unaware of the sights or the sounds of the night, finally stopping, almost an hour later with the freshness of the Myrtle Gully Falls pushing a breeze towards her face. She shivered and looked around. She was alone both physically and spiritually. The whole world had deserted her.

'Oh Gran,' she began, bursting into tears – suddenly feeling the pain ripping through the thin veil of numbness.

'How did you do it? How did you stay together with so much crap happening around you?'

She laughed out loud, her voice sounding macabre in the dark of the night.

'You didn't cope. You didn't cope. You got angry and bitter. You destroyed yourself and tried to destroy everyone around you.'

She was talking to the mountain. No answer was expected. No answer was required. Kunanyi knew her place in the world. Kunanyi knew how to nurture, how to grow, how to heal. But it was up to the people if they wanted kunanyi's help or not. Elma knew Miriam had refused the healing, chosen to stay bitter – to hold onto every frame of pain like a video playing over and over, until she believed there was no other way.

'I'm not choosing that path, Gran.'

But I can't stand here hoping the world will disappear.
I can't face Dad. I'm too angry at him.

She wasn't concerned that they'd be worried about her.

I'm a big girl now.

She rummaged through her bag for her phone. Dampness seeped into her backside from where she sat at the side of the stream.

I don't even remember climbing the barrier.
Ring or text?

The gravel crunched under her feet as she shifted her weight from one foot to the other. Her phone felt cold against her ear. Somewhere not far away a possum screeched.

'Hi Fergus, yep it's me – oh, I didn't know Cathy knew your number,' she pulled her phone away from her ear.

Sure enough she'd missed calls from Cathy, Chloe and Fergus.

'No, I'm all right. Are you able to drive? – without them?' She was kind of okay that he'd dropped them in town and gone home himself.

'Can you pick me up?

– Where we first met, I'm doing a night walk.

– Yep, I know, crazy right?

'Okay, top of Old Farm Road. Oh, and bring a bottle of wine? Please.' she added.

Elma pressed her finger against the keypad to end the call before he could ask questions.

Would he do it? Would he get the wine? Would he even turn up? What if he rang Martin or Cathy? It was getting complicated – again.

Why is it so hard? One day Martin's my dad and the next day he's not. And Cathy – I trusted her. I thought she could be trusted but she knew all along. I bet Aunt Livie knew too.

She tried to think back to conversations that would make sense of this. But nothing. Nothing came to mind. Martin though, maybe that was clearer, maybe that's why he sometimes seemed distant or too fixated on the money aspect of the relationship,

Nah, that doesn't make sense, why would he do it? He doesn't care about me at all. None of them do. I hate him, I hate them all.

She walked back down the track.

Car lights rounded the corner. Elma stayed out of view. If Fergus wasn't alone she wasn't going to greet him. She wasn't even sure if she really wanted to see him. But who else could she ring? Who else could she trust? No one.

Everyone I know has let me down.

Even Josh had made her promise not to tell about the car accident.

To protect himself.

Fergus was alone in the car.

'Hi Fergus, I am so sorry about this,' she burst into tears as he got out of the car and, without thinking, allowed him to wrap his arms around her, enveloping her in a protective hug.

'Hey, hey, it's alright,' he soothed. 'Cathy said you argued with your dad and ran away. Can I take you home? They're all worried about you.'

'No,' Elma squeezed out between sobs, and wiped her face with the sleeve of her sweatshirt. Her nose cleared long enough to take in Fergus's comforting smell.

'I'm so sorry,' she repeated over and over.

Fergus released his embrace and pulled her head away from his chest.

'Hey, talk to the face.' he said, 'Whatever it is you've done, it's not the end of the world.'

Elma burst out crying again,

'You don't understand, I haven't done anything. It's them, not me, and I don't ever want to go back there.'

'Okay, I was only trying to help.'

'It's okay,' he repeated. 'I'm glad you rang me.'

'You promised to take me up to Scout Hut, you know the one Chloe and I couldn't find up near Big Bend.'

'Yeah, I remember. But you don't mean now, do you?'

'Yeah, now. Let's just go up together.'

Elma sat in the momentary silence of the car, moving to accommodate the three bottles of wine at her feet. She saw a packet of salt and vinegar chips and some other supplies Fergus had bought from the bottle shop.

'Well –' he said as they drove the few kilometres of winding roads up the mountain. '– I didn't know what you wanted, red, white or bubbles.'

She looked at him sideways, suddenly wondering why he'd come

he didn't have to – I'm not his responsibility – he could leave ... if he wanted to.

Elma picked up the bottle of white wine and stashed it in her bag while Fergus locked the car.

'Hey, Elma. Why don't we just hang at The Springs for a bit? Then go home again?' he said.

But Elma was already crossing the road heading west.

Yep, this is the way Chloe and I came.

'Hold on, I'm thirsty,' she said, sitting on a rock and swinging her bag from her shoulder to grab the wine from the bag.

'Don't you want to wait 'til we get there?' Fergus said. 'Or we can just hang out here. You don't really want to go walking in the middle of the night, do you?'

'Geez, your dad is going to really hate me now,' he said, almost to himself.

Elma didn't answer.

She handed him the bottle and he twisted the top. It made a snapping sound as it came away from the neck of the bottle. He handed it back and Elma took her first swig.

'Yuck, that's disgusting.'

She spat most of it out.

She brought the bottle back up to her lips, this time taking a sip.

'It's very sweet.'

'It's wine,' he said.

'Do you want some?' she handed the bottle to him and he returned the lid to its place without drinking any, putting it into his own backpack.

'Nope, I'm getting cold, come on.'

Elma followed. It was a different path than she'd taken with Chloe. They seemed to be moving around the base of a cliff rather than over the top. The wine swished in her empty stomach.

What if he murders me? No one knows where we are.

She laughed,

That's not funny

– yes it is

– you wouldn't have called him if you didn't trust him.

It was true. He'd never crossed the line or let her down.

'It's just up there.' Fergus pointed skyward.

'I'm scratched to pieces, are you sure this is the right path?'

'Come on, you go first, but be careful, sometimes these rocks are slippery.'

The moon tried to hide behind a cloud allowing only slivers of light to escape here and there.

How does he know where we are?

'Can you see in the dark?' she asked.

'It's easy if you know where to go.'

I'll see tomorrow on the way back.

I'm glad I'm not alone.

I'm glad I won't be spending the night on my own in the secret hut on the side of a mountain.

Anything could happen.

And that was okay with her.

'I've twisted my ankle, I think,' she said, nearing the top of the sloping rocks. 'Is it much further to go? I'm stuffed.'

'Come on, I promise it's just over that next boulder.'

Elma rubbed at her ankle, hesitant to place weight on it. Fergus was close behind her. She could hear his breathing and just make out the outline of his body.

'You're black,' she laughed.

'And you've only had a sniff of grog and you're drunk.'

'I am not!' she snapped. 'I'm happy.'

Am I? Did I say that?

'I want another drink.'

'Just get there, Elma.'

He stepped past her and onto the flat path only a metre above her head.

'Wait here if you like and I'll go find some light.'

There was no way Elma was going to let Fergus leave her alone in the dark however much she trusted him,

which is zero – trust no one never, ever, ever.

Her foot recovered quickly.

She stood in front of Scout Hut, a tenuous thread to her past. Where it had come from was a mystery but there it was pressed into the side of the cliff with its corrugated tin porch and moonlight reflecting off a solitary window.

There's glass and a door…

Moonlight. How romantic.

She thought of Martin and Liz, and burped loudly.

'Ex-cuuuse me,' she said and stumbled in behind Fergus, a musty smell stirring up from the ragged carpet under his feet.

'This is amazing,' she stared at drawings on the wall. The pictures blended one into another.

There was a wizard smoking something, a scrawny cat cut into pieces, the tree of life drawn with charcoal and smudged across its lower branches where someone had leaned against it. Some art works were signed and dated, some were done in colours, others in black ink or paint – it was hard to tell in the dim light.

'Take a seat.' Fergus offered, lighting tea light candles and placing them along the narrow shelf above the window. Two low benches ran in an L-shape along the wall and under the sill, each padded with thin mattresses and a pile of crocheted and scratchy woollen blankets.

'It's small,' she said, sitting down by the window, avoiding all things crocheted and knocking her head on a ladder that seemed to grow out of the middle of the room.

'There's upstairs as well. Sleeps about 4 to 8 depending on size,' he said.

Elma looked at her hands. They felt scratched and bruised from the climb but she didn't care.

Without asking she reclaimed the bottle of wine from Fergus' backpack.

'Hey, easy girl. It's not a race.'

'I'm hungry, I think,' she said.

To Elma's surprise, Fergus lifted the corner of the carpet revealing a trap door in the floor and dragged out a bag of wood. A "secret stash".

'I'll replace it, don't worry.'

Elma wasn't worried. She was counting peanuts in her hand – 'One for me – one for you,' – and putting them either in her mouth or on the edge of the blanket.

The fireplace was an upturned 44 gallon drum cut in various places to let the draught and wood in and the chimney pipe and smoke out. The wall behind it was part of the cliff and the hearth was solid rock.

She imagined the smoke was going out the chimney he had shown her in the photo.

Fergus stoked the fire, continuously glancing at Elma and the bottle of wine.

'I'm still hungry.' Elma stated, reaching again for Fergus's bag, peanuts spilling to the floor.

'Wow, what happened?' she said overreaching her target and toppling forward.

'Why did you move the bag?'

Elma sat back up with Fergus's help and pulled his pack close to her.

'What would you like, Doritos or Clix?'

She looked around for the bottle that had been in her hand before she'd fallen. Miraculously it was in an upright position beside her foot. She reached down, putting it to her lips as she sat back up. A sour taste mingled with the sickly-sweet flavour in her mouth. Fergus took the bottle from her.

'My face has gone funny.'

She patted the side of her cheek. 'I can't feel it. It's nub.'

'You mean numb,' Fergus corrected.

'That's what I said. I like you Fergus. I do. I really, reeeally do,' she slurred.

She tried to breathe in the smell of his body, but instead inhaled wood smoke and the taste of salty peanuts.

'I've never had alc- alc-carhole before.'

'I know,' Fergus responded without correcting her. He checked his phone – no internet, no reception.

'Just one more little drink … Pleeease?' she added making a small sign with her thumb and first finger.

He handed her back the bottle. Only a third of its contents remained.

Elma looked at it and changed her mind.

'I need some fresh air,' she stood and tottered sideways. The room swayed. The door was further away than she remembered. Fergus grabbed her, preventing her from using the top of the fire drum to steady herself.

'Don't touch me!' she bellowed and fell through the door, before tripping on the stoop and face-planting down three steps.

'I'm sorwee, I'm sorwee,' she repeated. 'I didn't mean that.'

She squirmed around into a sitting position with her legs crossed, her back leaning against a boulder, and then threw herself forward as she vomited the curdled wine from her body.

'I don't feel so good.'

She didn't look so good either but Fergus kept his mouth shut and helped her back into the hut, hoping she would sleep it off on the narrow makeshift bed. The room swung back and forth. The floor rose and lowered with each step. She wanted to say thanks but it didn't happen.

The room swirled even more as she tilted her head sideways in a bid to lie down. Not that blanket – not that one – but Fergus didn't hear her and tucked the crocheted blanket over her shoulder and up to her chin. She screwed up her face and tried to stay as still as she could but the room kept moving, kept spinning – slowly – around and around and she wondered how she might get back to the door to throw up again. But instead she vomited directly onto the carpet and fell asleep.

Chapter 29

It was mid-morning when Elma woke. No sunshine, but a small amount of light filtered in through a blanket hung over the window.

She rubbed her eyes but the dusty feeling remained.

Where's my water bottle?

Hand sanitiser? Hair brush? Oh my goodness, my head hurts.

It was quiet, maybe a bird now and then, but no traffic or people noises.

Fergus, I wonder where he is?

She covered her mouth – that feeling again – the room began moving slowly up and down.

'Oh no, what have I done?' she said aloud. But no answer came.

Where's Fergus?

There were no sounds from upstairs. No snoring, no sleepy breathing. Did he even stay the night?

Did he just leave me here and go? I don't remember.

A yawn built up and she let it out, her ears popping as she did.

There was a bit of vomit still on the floor beside her.

How could she ever face him again?

I'm glad he's not here.

She rose from the bed, her head pounding as she moved about the room.

Where was Fergus? His bag was gone. The fire was out. Perhaps he'd left her abandoned on the mountain.

It was less gloomy outside and Elma sat down on a rock to think. But it didn't happen – the headache took up too much room.

Am I hungry?

She scratched at her head, messily retying her hair. There was dirt under her nails and dried bits of blood on her legs – scratches from the climb up last night.

My stuff's in my bag, my bag's in there and –

Elma sat there lacking the will to move.

'Oh, you're up.'

Fergus looked fresh and clean, a backdrop of the Derwent Valley behind him as he scrambled up over the cliff, balancing two takeaway cups in a cardboard tray, which he placed down in front of Elma.

'But wait, there's more.'

He opened his backpack to produce a plastic container holding two hot English muffins dripping with maple syrup and butter.

'You'll feel better if you eat a bit.'

He tossed his head sideways, hair flowing wild and free.

Elma looked up at him. She'd only seen his hair loose once before and had given him her own hair tie to tame it. Today it didn't seem to matter. Nothing seemed to matter. Well, maybe being hungry and abandoned. That mattered.

How will I face Martin and Cathy?
What about Aunt Livie? She must have known too!
If I could hide up here maybe the world would disappear.
Hell no – I need a shower!
'Thanks Fergus. Sorry.'

She bit into the muffin. The carbs mopped up the acid in her stomach.

'This tastes good. You amaze me.'

'Didn't have to go far. The café down at The Springs is open.'

Elma nodded

My head feels so heavy.

'Get you back home?'

'No I can't face them – just yet.'

Maybe never.

'I want to walk down to the ruins of Gran's hut. I know exactly how to get there – will you come with me?'

'Well, I haven't got anything better to do. I guess I could. It might be best if I do 'cause if you get lost up here I'll get the blame. Last one to see you alive and all.'

'They don't care.'

'Who?'

'My family – none of them really care about me.'

'I wasn't thinking of your family. I was referring to the police.'

He smiled his broad smile and Elma smiled back.

'Thanks Fergus. And thanks for cleaning up the mess.'

He looked about to where Elma had thrown up the night before.

'That wasn't me – that was most likely possums,' he laughed

'And the ones what cleaned up inside? That was rats. Definitely rats. Little beggars kept me awake half the night.'

Elma shivered despite the warming air temperature. She'd vomited, that was true.

He must have cleaned it up, he must have.

They took a diversion to The Springs, where Elma splashed water on herself in an attempt to be clean, but the restroom was small and there was a queue of impatient bushwalkers outside the door. She consoled herself with another drink from the cafe. Hot chocolate this time, her shout and a thank you to Fergus for being there with her.

What will I do with my family?

There was a feeling in her heart she couldn't describe.

I don't care if I never see them again,

'I still think you should call your aunty, Elma – people will be worrying about you,' Fergus tried for the fourth time to get her to call home.

The sun was high in the sky by the time they reached the tree marker at the track to the ruins.

'I still feel yuck,' she said, stepping down onto the unmapped path, flicking a wayward branch from her face as the bush thickened about her. She knew the path now – knew where the gradient changed and the pampas grass grew. Knew this was the ridge where Gran's track had most likely been.

A currawong swooped low overhead – its satiny black feathers catching the sun – calling out its song, 'now-you-see-me – now-you-don't.'

Elma swiped at the thin thread of a cobweb clinging to her face.

Spider trip wire – we're the first through here today.

'Well,' she said stepping into the clearing, 'What do you think?'

'I think we made it.'

Fergus dropped his pack to the ground.

'1967, ay? She still looks pretty strong for a burnt-out chimney.'

Elma breathed in, filling her lungs to capacity.

'It was built before the fires – could be 60 or 70 years old – I don't know exactly.'

She reached out, picking at a piece of moss from one of the stones.

'I could ask Aunt Livie when I see her.'

No I can't – I'm not talking to her – not any of them.

The moss fell with her thoughts, losing shape in the litter at the base of the structure.

'Hello, hellooooo ….'

Elma smiled at the back of Fergus' shoulders, his head was missing,

eaten by the shaft of the chimney.

'Hey there's a spade in here, too. Cool that people leave things where they find them.'

She smiled again,

he seems so honest.

All his stories have checked out - not believable – but true.

'It's peaceful up here,' she said, wiggling her bum to fit between the roots of a tree and leaning back with her eyes half closed while Fergus looked around. A small fly buzzed past her ear.

Fergus reached his hand up above the shoulder of the chimney and Elma worried for a moment he might want to climb the remaining metre or so to the top. She sighed, glad when he didn't. The chimney sheltered beneath a fifty-year-old canopy of trees – shrubs and grasses grew where a table or bed may have been.

Weathered and grey, what she thought of as Gran's Monument stood painted in moss greens and lichen blues embroidered together by alpine weavers, their webs forming elaborate art works in and around the structure, matted together in grooves and cracks where time had taken the mortar.

Nurseries and aged-care for spiders.

Fergus tested the strength of a turkey tail fungus with the toe of his boot.

'Nigel said he's been here.'

The decayed wood collapsed beneath his foot.

'He said he could have shown us earlier – if we'd asked.'

He laughed.

'Drink?'

'Yes, please.'

He passed her his water bottle.

'Red or white?'

Elma groaned.

I deserve that, but I don't need it right now.

'Can I tell you something – ?'

She wasn't sure how to start.

'Sure, I'm all ears.'

Fergus noted her seriousness and refrained from making a joke.

'I know why Gran freaked out about your finger.'

'Oh, why?'

'Gran was here on the day of the fires – back in '67.'

Fergus listened intently. He was trying to work out Elma's crazy family – maybe this was a clue.

'She told Aunt Livie she was on her way to fetch her from Ogilvie High School, but that wasn't true. She'd already planned to meet her lover, Scott Hamilton, here and spend the day with him. He was leaving for Melbourne – his bags were at the bus depot in the city.

'Miriam was my age – well, 17 not 18, but you know what I mean.'

Fergus nodded, taking the water bottle back.

She noticed that he didn't wipe the top off before drinking from it.

'She thought he loved her. But she didn't know about his wife and child. She was pregnant with his baby. She thought he'd be excited to hear the news – thought he'd move to Tasmania and marry her. She was so in love.'

Elma looked wistfully at the scarlet red flowers on the straggly tree not far from where she sat. It would have been large, healthy and covered in flowers if planted in the right location, instead it had grown vine-like, unable to compete for space and light with the native flora.

'She planted that tree there to "brighten" the place up, make it homely – she loved being up here.'

Elma closed her eyes remembering back to the day Miriam shared her story. She had held onto it, waiting for the right member of the family to tell, but that had never happened. Not that they deserved her to trust them.

There were so many secrets in her family – as it turned out, even more than she'd imagined.

At least Martin stuck around and looked after me when Mum left.

And Aunt Livie picked up the pieces and supported both of us the best she could while looking after her own sister. That can't have been easy.

And Cathy – her mum spent all her time looking after Miriam and Martin.

It was all so complicated. Yet there was a time before all this when Miriam and Livie were young like herself – facing the beginnings of their adult futures just as she was now.

The chimney was dappled in a camouflage of greens and greys as the mid-spring sun rose higher in the sky. Elma imagined a square frame with corrugated iron covering it – one low window with a built-in table, a hearth stacked with pots and pans and a cupboard, perhaps like the one at Scout Hut.

Only cleaner.

It was easier to see and smell it now that she'd slept on the mountain, breathed the air inside and out of a small shelter with musty carpets and a smoke-stained ceiling.

I think Gran's hut would have been airier and pretty. Yes, young Gran would have been fussy with that sort of thing – just like me.

She considered the nurture/nature component of her upbringing.

If Dad and I aren't blood relatives then neither are Gran and I.
Oh, Gran …

'It was different,' Gran had said, 'when I told him about the baby. I knew he'd be surprised. He always told me how much I meant to him – how I was the jewel of his life – how it broke his heart not to be near me – how hard it was that he had to live on the Mainland. When I told him that I was pregnant he told me to meet him back at the hut the next day. You can't begin to imagine how excited I was.

'"A surprise," he'd said.

'I thought of a ring.

'An extravagant one at that. The skies were full of smoke – had been for days, on and off. Everyone I knew was sick of the sticky heat – I could never get used to it. Scott said the fires were a long way off – that he'd be back by twelve tomorrow, with a surprise for me.'

'I met him there about midday. I hadn't slept a wink. It was so hot – none of us could sleep. I spent the night thinking up baby names. Scott, of course, for a boy and Scarlet for a girl. I tossed and turned so much that night – just couldn't wait for morning. I'd hoped it would cool down but it didn't. I thought he was off browsing the jewellery shops – buying my engagement ring. Livinda – she worked out that I was pregnant. She'd caught me throwing up a couple of times and threatened to tell Mother. I told her she was wrong and to mind her own business. She went off to her first day back at school in a foul mood with me. Stupid girl. I felt sure it would all turn out okay.

'I thought that the handsome Scott Hamilton would declare his love and bring that engagement ring up to the hut and then I'd invite Livinda to be bridesmaid and it would all be so wonderful.'

That next day Miriam had put on her prettiest border-print dress. It was deliciously modern, she told Elma – she'd helped her mother make it as part of her Christmas present. No one would ever have known what was hiding under that bright floral print. She brushed her hair until it shone. Hardly able to wait.

It was a surprise all right.

Scott had offered her something to drink as soon as he'd arrived at the hut. He'd poured it from a bottle in his pharmacy bag. She should have noticed then that he was different – the stubble on his usually clean face and the smell of whisky and stale coffee on his breath.

'Here take this,' Scott handed her a bottle. 'It's vitamins.'

'Vitamins,' she said, happy but disappointed at the same time. She picked the bottle up from the table. There was no label – it was a brown medicine bottle. It smelled like alcohol and car oil.

She screwed her nose up and placed it back on the table.

'No thanks,' she said and laughed, 'It smells like poison.'

'Drink it,' Scott commanded raising his voice.

His face changed. His smile was gone. He towered over her, his rough face angry now.

Where was the handsome Scott – the love of her life?

'Drink it!' he repeated.

She pulled away, confused by his angry tone.

'Drink it or I'll make you.'

No way was she going to drink it now.

She stood and backed away further and further from the table.

Scott took a step closer and grabbed Miriam by her ponytail, scooping up the glass bottle as he did so.

'Stop, you're hurting me,' she yelled, but he didn't stop.

He tipped her head backwards, forcing her mouth open by tilting her neck. The nasty brown liquid poured from the bottle to her mouth and smeared across her face, a rash of dark liquid splashing down onto her dress. She twisted away from him – legs bending at the knees, losing her balance and falling onto the floor, spitting out the liquid as she fell.

She pulled herself into a crawling position.

He'd drawn back his foot and slammed a kick into her stomach.

Miriam slumped to the floor, her belly blazing from the sudden blow, her stomach contents reaching the rustic floorboards only moments before her face. Bile and blood smeared into the graze on her cheekbone. An acrid taste burned at the back of her throat, increasing her urge to gag again.

She wiped her bare arm across her face.

The crack of an exploding gum tree punctuated the shouts from the man in front of her. It sounded close. When had the wind picked up? Her thoughts swirled and crashed like diminishing waves. Sweat dripped from her forehead. Miriam held her stomach with one arm and raised herself up far enough to turn her head toward the door. He was there – she could feel him standing over her. Could see his dusty boots close to her face; so close she could smell the possum scat on the soles of his Blundstones.

She shuddered.

Past him, on the steps through the doorway, rough splinters of wood stood out silhouetted by the half-light. It was darker now than it should have been. It felt like night. Miriam could taste the smoke on the mountain, sticking to her tongue like the raked floor of the chook house. She screwed up her nose and held her breath to control the reflex action of her body. Thin strips of blood oozed from the cracks on her lips. The taste of vomit and the potion were still strong in her mouth. Nothing felt the way it should.

She knew she wasn't far from home – 20 minutes if she ran. If she could get out.

But could she? The kick to her stomach was keeping her down – she called for mercy but her throat was too parched. Her words failed her, prevented her from rising. Again her body slumped forward – a growing pain twisted inside her gut.

Scott paced back and forth between her and the door, pausing for a moment each time he turned, an invisible pathway forming in the hazy room. An ash flake swirled past him, landing on Miriam's forearm – dissolving in a bead of sweat.

The smoke and wind stole their shadows and left them in a strange twilight. More ash flakes swirled around Scott's legs. The wind forced itself into unseen cavities, whistling and coughing up dusty leaves. Floorboards rattled – sticks twanged against the roof as they ripped past with fury.

'Just stay where you are!' Scott ordered, shoving the door so hard it swung back at him as he strode out.

Miriam sat up.

The shutters banged against their frames and grunted their protest as the metal pegs grated into place.

He'd shut her in! He was going to leave her there to burn.

She struggled to her feet, groaning, a hand pressed to her belly. She looked frantically around the room for something she could use to get out. Struggling to her feet she stumbled forward towards the door, the air heavy and hard to breathe.

The door swung open.

'What are you doing?'

Scott's eyes met hers, his familiar face now streaked with ashen war paint, his body blocking her way to freedom.

'I told you to stay!'

He rushed at her and pushed her hard, the palm of his hand against her chest. Miriam stepped back, moving sideways as she did, catching his lower leg with hers and accidently tripping him as he followed through with his shove.

Without looking back she scrambled for the door, falling again just short of getting through it. Scott grabbed her leg and pulled her down. Miriam screamed again and again.

He'd wanted to kill the baby inside her and now he was trying to kill her as well.

She twisted over onto her back as he turned her leg sideways. It was then she saw it – the knife she'd stolen from her father – slotted between two iron pots on the hearth. She inched her way towards it.

Scott heaved his body on top of hers just as a gust of smoke pushed through the door, causing him to cough. Miriam's own eyes smarted – she squinted them shut as far as she could, her screams gone – dried up in her throat – but a new determination growing fiercely with each struggling breath.

She let her body go limp. It worked. Scott released his hold and sat up, his head in the thick layer of smoke that filled the room. He continued to cough, moving sideways, crab-like toward to the door.

Miriam waited. He'd have to get past her to get to the door. She shut her eyes and counted – one ... two... three... go ...

She sprang into a crouched position and grabbed the knife as she did so.

With all her might she lunged at the coughing Scott. He reacted as she thrust at him. The point of the knife came down with force between the first and second knuckle of his right hand. He sat upright, his fist pulled instinctively to his chest, spraying a fine mist of blood up the front of Miriam's best dress and across her face.

Half of his index finger rested in fine ash on the floor between them.

Scott sat gasping while Miriam pulled herself up and fled for the door, slamming it shut behind her. She thrust at the bolt, catching the fleshy part of her hand as it slid into the locking position. Blood dripped from the rip, congealing between her fingers. Bruises erupted on her knuckles.

She ran.

The fire was on them.

Hot air caught in her throat, evaporating her saliva. Embers burned on the wooden steps. She lunged forward. Her feet were sweating – her nylon socks sticking to her toes – her shoes still inside the hut as she rushed into the bush. Vines and debris lashed at her as she half-fell, half-crawled down the eastern side of the mountain.

Rocks moved under her feet. Her ankle rolled and twisted.

Where was the fire now? There were swathes of bright flames ahead and behind her. Trees moved in and out of focus – vague shapes appeared and disappeared – smoke thickened and thinned. Her eyes smarted, but she dared not raise her hands to her face or slow down.

Branches grabbed and ripped her clothes, scratching her face, stealing hunks of hair. Swelling appeared on her knees as she smashed into rocks on the uneven path in front of her.

Could she hear his screaming like the wind or was the wind screaming like a man?

Is he screaming? Is he screaming?

Miriam didn't know, couldn't know.

The track – where had it gone? Down, still down, slaloming through the trees and finally, finally falling onto a path, a wider path and the creek.

She lunged forward into the creek, grabbing at her stomach. The creek flowed with only a small trickle of water. An uneven rock caught her off balance and she collapsed, falling sideways onto her hip. The smoke was thick – so thick. She kept her face low to the ground.

She now knew where she was – she couldn't see – could hardly breathe – but she'd made it to the creeks. Just in front of her was a drain that tunnelled from one side of the path to the other. Twin creeks – she'd made it to the base of the hill, but what now?

The fire was only metres away – so hot her hair singed and stuck into her blistered skin. She dragged herself over the path above the drain and dropped down the bank where the two creeks joined and pushed herself as far up under the earthen bank as she could. Water trickled over her ankles and thighs, across her blistered skin.

The roaring noise, heat, smoke and pain increased.

Miriam passed out, overwhelmed and exhausted.

It was later in the dark of night that she woke again from the pain.

Not the pain of the burns or scalds on her legs, nor the pain of blisters and cuts on her face. No this pain was different – this pain was from her abdomen.

Cramps came unrelentingly.

She cried, broken, alone – a fragile stick of humanity in the ashes of a Tasmanian bushfire.

Elma paused in telling the story.

She could imagine Miriam losing her child in the smoke and darkness – terrified.

Lying in the dirt, she'd have been unable to see the trickle of red running down across the top of her leg and turning pink to grey as it seeped into the ash-filled waters of kunanyi.

She'd have felt the flesh of the placenta being pulled away in a strong convulsion as the mountain drew the lifeless babe from her body. Her Scarlet, lost to the mountain.

Kunanyi stayed strong – cradled all Miriam's hopes and dreams in folds of black ash and silt, but left Miriam smeared in blood. A naïve prisoner of time and circumstances, trapped in pain and unforgiveness.

Chapter 30

Although the events were 50 years apart, life changed that day on the mountain for Miriam and Elma, the latter putting her nursing course aside 'for the moment'.

She walked most days down the rivulet and along Sandy Bay Road either to the café for work or to 'sit and stare at the walls' with Gran in the nursing home.

'It's not the same is it?' Elma said to Gran, her notebook open in her lap, pages flicking to and fro as she absently moved her knee up and down. 'Game of cards?' she asked, without conviction.

Gran turned her head to face Elma and shook it with a look of 'Why do you bother?'

Yeah, I know it would take too much energy – you're always tired – so tired – you never look well,

The nursing home couldn't afford another psychotic episode from Miriam and the best way to keep her safe was with medication. Tears welled in Elma's eyes. Gran was constantly calm, no psychosis, no fight, no nothing. Never happy or sad – just there – day after day – sitting in her lounge chair or slipping sideways on one in the media room.

Sometimes, if Elma felt up to it, she would wheel Gran to the games-room café to drink lukewarm tea from a sipper cup and stare out the window the same as she did wherever they went.

Today they were still in Gran's room – neither of them motivated enough for a change of scenery,

or bothered to be asked the same questions over and over.

Elma placed her hand on her notebook and looked down to see what was recorded where she'd stopped – **Pointless Questions**.

That's what she'd get if they left the room. The residents meant well, but it drove her nuts.

'How are you?'

Fine, thanks.

'Are you visiting your gran today?'

No, I just like standing here being asked pointless questions.

'Studying hard?'

No.

'If you need to talk just get someone to find me, okay?'

Not likely.

'How is your dad?'

What dad?

'I bet you're looking forward to Christmas?'

The list went on.

Elma shut the book and stared past the impassive woman to the window behind her.

Christmas had come and gone. She hadn't looked forward to it, hadn't enjoyed it and didn't care if there would be another one. Apart from the secret surprise outing Fergus sprung on her one warm evening, her entire summer social list of events consisted of Netflix and hot chocolate.

'It's great,' Fergus said 'I love couch and screen time. It's just that I leave soon and I'd like to take you somewhere special,' he made doe eyes and continued, 'no crowds, no noise, no dress code – I promise.' He placed three fingers against his head Scout style.

Most of Elma said no but her mouth said, 'Okay.'

'Yes!' Fergus jumped up from the couch and grabbed both Elma's hands and pulled her to her feet.

'No.' Elma protested.

Fergus' smile disappeared. He released Elma's hands and let her fall back onto the couch. 'What?'

'Well yes but not if you're going to act like an overexcited puppy – that's Chloe's job.' She looked around and smiled, glad Chloe was out of earshot.

'Come on then let's go.' He pressed a few keys on his phone, 'Uber is waiting.'

Elma looked confused, 'I thought you had Nigel's car.'

'Yeah I do. I'm just letting him know he'll have to get a cab home if we're not back in time.'

'Oh,' Elma knew Fergus and Nigel had a deal which meant if either one of them were drinking, the other would be driving. Usually that meant Fergus picked Nigel up from the city on his way home from Elma's place.

'Oh,' she said again when Fergus parked the car in a spot between the highway and the river.

'Come on,' he said opening the door for her and beckoning her across the road.

Elma was full of questions, 'Where are we going? What are you doing? Is this legal?'

Fergus gripped her hand and tugged her across the road to the Botanical Gardens ignoring all her questions. 'Shh or I'll have to gag and carry you.'

Elma laughed. She knew him well enough now to know he would never do such a thing. Bat catchers, she'd decided, were not the violent type. They crept along the fence line until they were hidden completely from the road by the thickening trees. 'Come on, not much further. There's a little something I prepared earlier.' He climbed the fence and helped Elma over, laughing as he slipped, falling backwards landing with a thump on the ground.

'Are you alright?' Elma laughed letting him pull her closer until they were wrapped in a bear hug, the sweet smell of warm grass close to her nose – his whiskers tickling her cheek. It felt good to be held tightly by Fergus.

Fergus released her and moved further up the incline before rummaging through a stack of branches piled beneath a bush. 'Here we go,' he declared as he pulled out a cardboard box.

'You really did prepare earlier.' Elma watched as he opened the box and pulled out a package wrapped in a travel blanket. He spread the blanket on the ground and loosely arranged the contents in the centre.

Dried fruit, nuts, chocolate and a bottle of grape juice,

'Wow. I'm impressed. How long has all this been here?' She thought of all the other times he'd suggested going out on a quiet date.

Fergus laughed, 'A while. I was a bit worried the possums may have had a party before we got round to it.'

Elma smiled. He was always so patient.

She looked across to Miriam and back down at the note book on her lap,

well at least I managed one happy day.
I don't deserve the effort he goes too – I wish he wasn't leaving …

She had felt bad for declining the New Year's Eve party and was still ignoring Chloe – the annoying, frustrating, happy, stupid Chloe who'd gone in her place.

They avoided each other these days, mostly by Elma staying in her own room with her headphones on, listening to whatever was on her play list and not remembering two seconds after, what it was.

She didn't eat much either – unless she had to.

Damien made her eat at the café.

'Hey sunshine, sit here. I've got food for you and you're not leaving 'til you've eaten it.'

She ate it – but never all of it. It made her stomach hurt. She preferred to stay empty.

Paula insisted on catching up,

'You might not be talking to Martin but that's got nothing to do with you and me having a walk or talk together on my way to work.'

Paula sometimes met her in the small green park at the bottom of the Rivulet Track.

'I've made breakfast muffins – they're hot and yummy.'

'Thanks,' Elma said taking the proffered muffin reluctantly and picking the pieces of corn out – she placed them one at a time in her mouth.

It was Paula who'd helped Elma to defer her studies. She gave neither advice nor opinions but usually just sat or walked with Elma until it was time for her to race off to work.

Letters sat unopened on Gran's bedside table. The cheery stickers decorating the colourful envelopes showed they were from Aunt Livie. Elma thought of her own unopened stack at the studio and her phone full of missed calls. The last one Martin had left said how rude it was of her not to reply to Aunt Livie. Elma deleted it. Then blocked his number.

'It's going to rain.'

She looked up surprised, 'Sorry Gran, what did you say?'

'It's going to rain,' Miriam repeated, turning her head back towards the window.

For an instant Elma wanted to correct her and tell her it was 38 degrees out there. That what she was really looking at was smoke haze and not an overcast morning. She wanted to tell her there were dozens of fires burning out of control down south and on the Central Highlands and that some of them threatened homes and livelihoods.

'Mmm,' she said, 'maybe.'

I guess you can't smell the smoke here inside with air conditioning.

This was the third day this week that Elma had been unable to see from one side of the river to the other – the smoke was so thick in the air. Places down the Huon Valley were being evacuated, schools shut and everyone was a little nervous, talking constantly of the previous big fires of Dunalley. Elma caught snippets of conversations at the café – people were scared it might be like the fires of '67 all over again – they compared the sameness and the differences – each person having an opinion on how things should be handled – vocal on whether the government should care more or less about the national parks and iconic trees.

There were thunderstorms without rain – total fire bans – smoke warnings encouraging people with breathing problems to take it easy, stay inside and keep medications close – predictions of high winds and unfavourable weather. Bushfire plans in place or ready to act on — and the possibility of flight delays.

At work on Friday the 3pm weather forecast announced the temperature as 29 degrees, visibility: poor. Air quality: well she didn't need some guy on the radio to tell her that, she could taste it.

Headache all day. I just want to get out of here.

She'd been tempted to shut the café early, but rules were rules. Damien had raced off to sort out accommodation for his parents who were evacuating from Franklin.

'The fire's getting closer and it's unpredictable,' he'd said.

'I can't leave them down there any longer, especially without air con.'

He hadn't needed to make excuses – it was certainly the right thing to do. It was better to think about these things early than to race out the front door while the fire lashed at the back. Damien's problem was that his parents had time to choose what to stack in the car. Everything seemed important to his mother, while his father was insistent all they needed was a change of clothes and a few documents.

'I can handle this place on my own,' Elma had said. 'It's not like we're busy.'

She placed black coffees on the table between two customers. No thanks, no smiles – they just continued their conversation, deeply concerned for animals, native or otherwise. Neither of them had heard birdcalls all week.

Gran didn't make comments about the news reports – maybe she hadn't seen any. Elma wondered what she knew, but didn't dare to ask.

For Elma it was all a bit surreal – the skies a variety of Armageddon scenes – hot and oppressive – moving like the underside of oceans in pink and grey. Of all the colours in her notebooks, she'd thought green was the most prominent in the world. But now she wasn't so sure. She'd seen the greens become blues and then greys where the smoke covered them like a filter on the lens of a camera.

She had so many new kinds of grey for her notebook, but

didn't want to describe any of them.

It had been a crazy weather year for Tassie – severe rain – floods – winds – snow and now fire.

Gran's been inside here, oblivious to all of it – just existing day after day in the same boring air-conditioned comfort.

I guess I'm doing pretty much the same.

Elma was filling in time there, day after day – sometimes thinking about what young Gran had gone through, sometimes going over her notes and comparing what Miriam had said with what Aunt Livie had told her earlier. She thought about Dad and her mum and all the secrets.

She remembered bits of conversations with Livie when she'd talked to her a little about Miriam's story. Livie had told her about not seeing her sister for the first week of her hospitalisation.

Her father had been frantic and had gone looking for Miriam as soon as he could set foot on the hot ground after the fire passed. She'd been missing for over 24 hours. When they found her she was half dead, half naked and half the hair on her head was missing – burnt off, blisters on her scalp and feet. There were people who did not expect her to live. Aunt Livie had been sent to stay at a friend's place on the Eastern Shore and although their house on Inglewood Road wasn't caught in the fire, there was no power or water. Their animals suffered badly and the chickens that hadn't already died were just limp piles of feathers in the dust. Aunt Livie had cried when her dad dug a hole and finished them off.

'Better to put them out of their misery,' he'd said.

Their dad, like so many others, became busy helping survivors relocate – there was so much to rebuild. So many people displaced, fearful and homeless. Everyone helped each other. Everyone was affected.

After the wounds healed and her hair had regrown a bit, her mother had thought Miriam would come round, but she didn't.

'She said she wished she could be finished off too. Mum took her to all sorts of doctors – even expensive ones in Melbourne, but it was all a waste of time and money.'

I want to tell Livie what Miriam told me, but Livie lied to me. They all did. I can't trust them.

She looked over at Miriam propped up in her bed waiting for the rain to start.

'It wasn't your fault he died – it really wasn't.'

Gran gave a weak smile and Elma wondered if she was aware of what she was referring to.

--

At the end of January, less than a week later, Elma got a message.

She sat at the kitchen table and turned her phone on, surprised to see three missed calls from Paula. She was at home contemplating how she'd explain to Fergus why she wasn't up to going out for a meal. Yes, she knew he was leaving soon – in only two and a half weeks.

Maybe they could catch up tomorrow instead.

She still felt that certain thrill when they were close and was grateful for his support the night her world imploded, but just now she needed to look after Gran.

I'm sure Fergus would rather not deal with that.

It wasn't usual for Paula to be so persistent or for Elma to listen to voice messages, but she pressed play.

'Hey, Elma, Honey, ring me as soon as you get this message. Please.'

It was her dad's voice, not Paula's.

Elma tried to think what he'd be wanting.

Is he sick?

About to announce his marriage proposal?

Well, that's weird – I *can't remember the last time he called me Honey*

'Meet me at the nursing home, will you? Mum's not well.'

What? Why did they tell you and not me? I'm the one who visits her. You never go anywhere near there, Dad!

--

Elma scrambled out of the taxi and straightened her skirt while she waited for Martin to cross the road.

'Sorry Dad, I didn't have enough to pay for the taxi.'

Martin gave a nod in her direction and handed a fifty dollar note to the driver.

Native birds squawked from the pine trees, waves hushed somewhere in the background. Martin slid his change carefully into his wallet as the taxi turned and sped off around the corner, tyres squealing. The evening sky was a smear of pinks and purples.

They walked across the road, an awkward silence between them.

Since her birthday their communication had been a one-sided affair where Elma let her dad do all the talking and she just added a Yes or No as required.

Paula had tried to start up the driving lessons again: 'You spend half an hour each week with your dad and I'll take you out for an hour on the road.'

But Elma didn't feel up to driving just yet. It has slipped into the void of unimportant things. And spending time with Martin seemed less appealing than eating burnt potatoes.

I just can't find the motivation – and he still doesn't know what to say.

'Is she that sick, Dad? Why didn't they ring me?'

Elma's voice was shaky. 'She was fine yesterday – a little cough but she was talking and moving around.'

'Calm down, Elma, of course they called me. She's my mother, for God's sake.'

'Will she go to hospital?' Elma asked as they headed towards Miriam's room.

'You know as much as I do,' Martin replied, his eyes fixed on the gilded frame at the end of the first passage. The lily pond in Monet's garden. They turned left; staff were coming and going from the open door of Miriam's room.

A strange grey – almost yellow, but not – what would the right word be …?

Elma stared at her grandmother – propped up by pillows in a bed of floral pinks and blues of wild cornflowers as she coughed spasmodically over **The Land of Counterpane**.

I can't believe I just thought that.

It was another one of her mother's sayings. She tried hard to remember the poem by Robert Louis Stevenson but failed. The first two lines were about being sick in bed and having two pillows at her head, but the rest of the words wouldn't be found, although she knew the Land of Counterpane was an agreeable place to be.

Her nursing studies should have given her some idea of what was happening but they didn't. This wasn't a patient or a client or a scenario to be learned about – this was Gran, and besides she hadn't studied for months now.

Gran, the immovable force of will, with a tongue that could lash dragons to the ground, teeth that could chew through souls and eyes as fierce as daggers. She sometimes wondered how Martin had managed to keep her in here against her will.

She looks so helpless now.

'Will she be all right?'

She looked at her father and shrank away as he smiled and held his arm out for a hug.

Not likely, Elma thought. You weren't here for either of us – don't try to be Mr Nice Guy now. She turned her back on him, unaware of the slump in his shoulders and the look of hopelessness on his face.

The young doctor beckoned them both out of the room while a nurse adjusted Miriam's oxygen and tended her needs.

Hi, Dr Meerding,' she said, and held out her hand for Martin to shake. 'I presume she's your mother and grandmother.' They both nodded and Martin shook the doctor's hand.

'What's wrong with Mum?' Martin asked clearing his throat for a second time before the words came out.

Elma was surprised to see him choked up.

I hadn't thought he cared.

She shuffled forward towards him and placed her hand on his shoulder, guilty for rejecting him only minutes earlier.

'Sorry, Dad,' she said, looking down at the floor, completely covering a golden rose with her not-so-new sandshoes. Last year's 'bright and shineys' – this year's 'let's make do with'.

'Your mother has a chest infection and decreasing kidney function. We're running tests at the moment.'

She looked too young to make such important announcements.

'Our main concern for someone in your mother's condition is pneumonia.'

Oh! Old people die from that.

--

349

She sat on the café deck of the nursing home staring at the sky, a cup of tea resting in the palms of her hands.

'Hey, a penny for your thoughts.'

It was Fergus.

'Your dad told me where to find you. Paula sent a text to say that your gran isn't too good,' he added.

'Oh Fergus, I've been such a cow. I haven't spoken to Dad since November,' Elma said, looking into her cup,

'And even worse I've been ignoring Aunt Livie and you and everyone.'

She burst into sobs.

'Hey, hey girl, it's cool.'

'It's not cool, I'm an idiot.'

Fergus said nothing but pulled his chair around to sit beside Elma – not comfortable to touch her. 'Hey, you love your gran. She means a lot to you.'

'But I hated her – didn't want anything to do with her – I really thought she deserved all the pain she got because she was so ... so –' Elma choked up.

'I treated her like she treated me and that was wrong.'

'Elma, you were just a kid. You didn't know ... you were protecting yourself.'

The fact was, Miriam had mistreated her – had given her a standard she could never live up to, insulted her at every opportunity, made her think she was lazy, dirty, unworthy of love. But somehow now Elma could see it wasn't really about herself, it was about Miriam. Miriam treated everyone badly –

'She changed as the dementia got worse; weirdly, she got softer, nicer. I felt sorry for her.'

Elma looked sideways into Fergus' lap – his hands were clasped together, his missing fingertip a reminder that there was now a secret that only they knew. Elma doubted she would share it with anyone else.

'I'm sorry – I've been mean to you as well.'

Fergus shrugged his shoulders.

Elma leaned in towards him, his familiar fragrance mixing with memories of the mountain – happy and sad. She reached out for his hand and he took it, squeezing her small fingers between his strong palms.

How would I have coped with the trauma Miriam had survived? The abuse of a lover, the terror fire, the pain of miscarriage and dreams crushed into the ground? And always that nagging thought in the back of my mind that I'd murdered someone?

Post-traumatic stress, depression and everything, I'm surprised Martin coped as well as he did. He had all her problems – and he was abandoned by his father, not to mention the Lizzie stuff and pretending I was his kid.

Poor Dad.

Chapter 31

'Thanks Fergus, but I have to do this by myself.'

Elma pulled the drawstring closed at the top of her bag and walked a little way up the Myrtle Gully Track with Fergus by her side.

'Okay,' he said, 'but I'll be here waiting in the car when you're ready.'

He stopped walking and held his hand out to Elma.

She took it and smiled.

'Thanks, I won't be too long.'

'Won't be long? Elma, it'll take you at least an hour just to get up there. But don't worry – I'll be busy writing up my final notes on bats,' he laughed. 'I won't even miss you.'

But I'll miss you when you leave next week.

She touched the greenstone necklace tied around her neck.

'Okay, thanks again,' she said and was gone, boots sure on the gravelly steps.

I can feel you here on the mountain, Gran.

She breathed in the scent of rich warm soil laced with the smell of gum and acacia trees.

When she arrived at the ruins of the hut, she knelt down, still breathless from the steep hike.

'For you, Gran,' Elma said aloud, rummaging through her bag, pulling out the contents, holding them carefully. She placed them on the hearth in front of the chimney – examining them.

Thirty-something pages of writing – almost an entire note-book – pulled out one page at a time from its cover, a shoe box containing Liz's list of wrongdoings, still wrapped in the tea-towel, now bug-less but still smelling of hessian.

Regardless of the fire ban, Elma lit paper in the old chimney and fed it leaves and twigs until it was ready to consume all the memories of her year. She re-read bits and pieces about Charlie and forgave him for not understanding, for letting Miriam and Martin down. She read about Aunt Livie, and the grey colours they'd created.

'Thank you, Aunt Livie,' she said and forgave her for hiding the truth.

And Cathy who'd kept secrets from her and told her the truth – perhaps for her own good, she supposed … and Josh – selfish Josh.

I would have done the same, she thought, and placed another page in the flames.

Could she forgive Liz and Martin?

Liz, yes. She meant nothing to her – she didn't know Liz. She was almost excused through her absence.

The bills and receipts darkened before catching alight in the flames. She tore the shoe box into smaller pieces, watching them burn one at a time.

And Martin – she still wasn't sure about Martin.

Today was about Gran. Today she'd weep for the life that Miriam never had.

353

She breathed in, drawing the mountain air into her lungs – smelling the warm grass and native flowers. A little blue wren flitted about, catching insects in the haze of the summer day.

'Hey Gran, I like your home. You did well to keep it so lovely. Look at all the beautiful things up here. Your tree … your Scarlet tree. You made this part of the world a better place.'

Elma let the tears fall.

'Hey, if I ever have a baby girl,' she whispered, 'I'm going to name her after you and tell her how special and loved she is every day of her life. I love you Gran. Goodbye.'

--

She spoke to Martin later that day.

He was sitting out on the deck crying.

'I just wanted to do the right thing,' he said between sobs.

'Just wanted to please her, make her happy – she was right. I was never good enough. Never able to get it right. Thought if I just tried harder ... But there was no pleasing her, no pleasing Liz. I couldn't even get it right with you. Hell, I couldn't get it right with anyone.'

He looked up, tears running down his cheeks, seeping into the crevices on his weathered skin.

Elma went to hug him, tears welling in her own eyes.

Why had she been mean to him? He was her dad.

Then she stopped and remembered.

'You lied to me Dad. You lied to me from the minute I was born.'

'I thought I could make a good life for you – treat you better than she did – show you love and commitment. Love you better than my mum ever loved me.'

'But that was wrong.'

She looked up at the mountain and down again to the man ferns along the back fence.

That was unfair, he didn't know at the time, did he?
He was doing it for me.
He lied, Elma – kept the truth from you.
He was trying to make me happy,
He really did love me – does love me.
She was torn between empathy and anger.

In the end it was Martin who made the first move. He stood up and pulled her into his arms. She let him give her a hug, but only for a brief time.

This doesn't fix things – doesn't make it better.
'I'll see you tomorrow. Cornelian Bay at ten,' she said.

--

Miriam lay there, her smooth face brushed with foundation to hide her translucent skin. Her hair was loose but combed, carefully framing the sides of her face – a contrast of dark brown against the white silk lining of the coffin. Excess spit gathered inside Elma's mouth – she swallowed.

I'm not going to cry – I'm not going to cry.
Focus on the mantra she told herself, but other thoughts kept barging in. She glared at the still body.

Gran would never have worn her hair down like that. She never wore it out – always kept it tight – up off her face – always hid her scars.
Other things were wrong too.

The lipstick is too bright and …
And that was it – the tears came – flooding down her face

Aunt Livie was on her left – her father on the right. She stared down into the coffin, avoiding eye contact with her family.

Fergus had stayed outside, 'It's okay,' he'd said. 'I'll make sure no one steals the cars.'

His face was serious, but only a twitch away from smiling.

Livie had picked out the floral dress Miriam was wearing – the only floral dress in her sister's wardrobe.

Gran never wore florals – she was plaid or plain.

The dress had been a present from Livie to Miriam – a sister thing.

I guess Aunt Livie always wanted her to wear it … and now she has no choice.

Dirty streams of ash-black mascara coursed unchecked down Elma's cheeks.

The fragrance of flowers and artificial deodoriser lingered in the room with the family.

'Just pass by and give your respects,' Chloe had said,

'That's what we all did when Auntie Kate died.'

Chloe knows everything. Still, she's right. We've been in here too long – I need fresh air.

She stepped back, excusing herself, taking one last glance at the woman in the coffin with the Tas Oak lid leaning against the wall behind it. The date of Gran's birth and death were printed on a brass plaque attached to its centre. The text stood out prominently under the white beam of light shining directly over it.

Elma stared at the lid, unable to drag her eyes away.

That lid will go on top of her.

She'll be trapped inside

she's dead, you fool

of course they'll put the lid on

they can't bury her without it.

Her brain formed a vision of the shiny wooden box buried beneath a ton of earth with Gran trapped, clean and surreal, inside it.

Elma turned and ran outside.

This was real.

This was really happening.

Gran is not sick in a hospital bed – Gran is dead. Dead, dead, dead.

As helpless as the wooden box they'll bury her in.

No choice – no change – no chance – she's dead.

She tried to calm herself – tried to think of the pleasant sad things from the day before, but she failed. Where had they gone?

Water dripped from the veranda of the chapel as the mourning party walked towards the grave for the committal.

Aunt Livie swished her brolly before closing it – droplets flicked against Elma's face.

The weather was clearing. She could hear the sound of children playing in the park down by the bay. Elma stood with her back to kunanyi and looked out through the trees, watching a yacht pass under the bridge.

February 7th 2019 was wet.

She looked back over her shoulder to check on kunanyi; the mountain was shrouded in grey.

That seemed exactly right on a day like today.

Boots crunched on the gravel beside her and she looked down, knowing whose they were. Fergus slipped his big hand into hers.

A black cockatoo screeched onto a pine branch, unsettling the mob. They lifted inharmoniously into the sky and Elma let her eyes follow the black stream as they careened overhead.

She and Fergus both looked back at the mountain.

Kunanyi was clearing – lifting the veil.

Aunt Livie sobbed as Miriam's coffin was lowered into the ground. Elma looked up through the trees to see the Tasman Bridge caught in a stream of sunlight.

She squeezed Fergus's hand.

Look, Gran. There's the bridge to guide you, the river to soothe you, and the mountain to protect your soul.

Rest in peace Gran – your time has come.

She bowed her head and her prayers fell gently into the grave.

THE END

The author of this book wishes to acknowledge the ancient land of the Muwinina people and pay her respects to the Elders, past, present and emerging. She acknowledges their custodian-ship of, and deep connection to the land.

Acknowledgements

It is hard to know where to begin or end when the time comes to acknowledge all the support I have needed or wanted to write this novel.

Firstly my family – for allowing me to steal time away from my wifely and motherly duties. I owe them a lifetime's worth of laundry, dishes and food. I am grateful for all the opportu-nities of carpark and waiting room writing they gave me, while attending their medical and sporting events.

I am forever indebted to my A-Team of editors, Evelyn, Moira and Peter. Their "anal-ability" to check the details of spelling, misuse of homonyms and grammatical errors keeps them as the best team ever.

Thank you also to my 'other' editors, Suzi and Ruth who went above and beyond to enable the production of this story.

Special thanks to Maria Grist who so generously shared her research about the huts on kunanyi.

And lastly a special mention to spell check, my pre-readers, and the people who inspired me – without any or all of them, this story would not exist.